# GOLDEN MOMENTS

SPHERE

First published in Great Britain by Sphere Books Ltd 1979
Reissued by Sphere in 2008

9 11 13 15 17 18 16 14 12 10

Copyright © 1976 by Danielle Steel

Originally published in the U.S.A. as Passion Promise
Published by arrangement with Dell Publishing Co. Inc

A CIP catalogue record for this book
is available from the British Library.

Acknowledgement
Lines from 'Getting There' by Sylvia Plath are reprinted from Ariel (1965) by
Sylvia Plath. Copyright © 1963 Ted Hughes. Reprinted by permission of Harp-
er & Row, Publishers, Inc., Faber & Faber, London and Olwyn Hughes.

ISBN 978-0-7515-4139-7

Printed and bound in Great Britain by Clays Ltd, Elcograf S.p.A.

Papers used by Sphere are from well-managed forests
and other responsible sources.

Sphere
An imprint of
Little, Brown Book Group
Carmelite House
50 Victoria Embankment
London EC4Y 0DZ

An Hachette UK Company
www.hachette.co.uk

www.littlebrown.co.uk

Danielle Steel is one of the world's most popular and highly acclaimed authors, with over ninety international bestselling novels in print and more than 600 million copies of her novels sold. She is also the author of *His Bright Light*, the story of her son Nick Traina's life and death; *A Gift of Hope*, a memoir of her work with the homeless; and *Pure Joy*, about the dogs she and her family have loved.

To discover more about Danielle Steel and her books visit her website at www.daniellesteel.com

You can also connect with Danielle on Facebook at www.facebook.com/DanielleSteelOfficial or on Twitter: @daniellesteel

## By Danielle Steel

'I shall bury the wounded like pupas,
I shall count and bury the dead.
Let their souls writhe in a dew,
Incense in my track.
The carriages rock, they are cradles.
And I, stepping from this skin
Of old bandages, boredoms, old faces

Step to you from the black car of Lethe,
Pure as a baby.'

From 'Getting There'
by Sylvia Plath, *Ariel*.

# CHAPTER I

Edward Hascomb Rawlings sat in his office and smiled at the morning paper on his desk. Page five showed a large photograph of a smiling young woman coming down the ramp of a plane. The Honourable Kezia Saint Martin. Another smaller photograph showed her on the arm of a tall, attractive man, leaving the terminal for the seclusion of a waiting limousine. The man, as Edward knew, was Whitney Hayworth III, the youngest partner of the legal firm of Benton, Thatcher, Powers, and Frye. Edward had known Whit since the boy got out of law school. And that had been ten years ago. But he wasn't interested in Whit. He was interested in the diminutive woman on his arm. Edward knew her almost jet black hair, deep blue eyes, and creamy English complexion so well.

And she looked well now, even in newsprint. She was smiling. She seemed tanned. And she was finally back. Her absences always seemed interminable to Edward. The paper said that she had just come from Marbella, where she had been seen over the weekend, staying at the Spanish summer home of her aunt, the Contessa di San Ricamini, née Hilary Saint Martin. Before that Kezia had summered in the South of France, in 'almost total seclusion'. Edward laughed at the thought. He had seen her column regularly all summer, with reports from London, Paris, Barcelona, Nice, and Rome. She had had a busy summer, in 'seclusion'.

A paragraph further down the same page mentioned three others who had arrived on the same flight as Kezia. The so suddenly powerful daughter of the Greek shipping magnate, who had left her, his only heir, the bulk of his fortune. And there was mention as well of the Belgian princess, fresh from the Paris collections for a little junket to New York. Kezia had been in good company on the flight, and Edward wondered how much money she had taken from them at backgammon. Kezia was a most effective player. It struck him too that it was once again Kezia who got most of the press coverage. It was that way for her. Always the centre of attention, the sparkle, the thunder, the flash of cameras as she walked into restaurants and out of theatres. It had been at its cruellest peak when she was in her teens; the photographers and reporters were always hungry, curious, prying, then. For years it had seemed that she was followed everywhere by a fleet of piranhas, but that was when she had first inherited her father's fortune. Now they were used to her, and their attention seemed kinder.

At first Edward had tried hard to shield her from the press. That first year. That first, godawful, intolerable, excruciating year, when she was nine. But the scavengers had only been waiting. And they hadn't waited long. It came as a shock to Kezia when she was thirteen, to be followed by a red-hot young woman reporter into Elizabeth Arden's. Kezia hadn't understood. But the reporter had. She had understood plenty. Edward's face grew hard at the memory. Bitch. How could she do that to a child? She had asked her about Liane, right there in front of everyone. 'How did you feel when your mother . . .' The reporter was four years late with her story. And out of a job by noon the next day. Edward was disappointed: he had hoped to have her job by the same night. And that was Kezia's first taste of it. Notoriety. Power. A fortune. A name. Parents with histories. And grandparents with histories and power and money. Nine generations of it on her mother's side. Only three worth mentioning on her father's. History. Power. Money. Things you can't conjure up, or lie about, or steal. You have to be born with them running thick in your veins. All three. And beauty. And style. And then some other magical ingredient dancing in you at lightning speed, then . . . and only then, are you Kezia Saint Martin. And there was only one.

Edward stirred the coffee in the white-and-gold Limoges cup on his desk, and settled back to look at the view. The East River, dotted with small boats and barges, was a narrow grey ribbon far below on his right. He faced north from where he sat, and gazed peacefully over the congestion of midtown Manhattan, past its skyscrapers, to look down on the sturdy residential fortresses of Park Avenue and Fifth, huddled near the clump of browning green that was Central Park, and in the distance, a blur that was Harlem. It was merely a part of his view, and not a part that interested him a great deal. Edward was a busy man.

He sipped the coffee, and turned to 'Martin Hallam's' column to see who among his acquaintances was allegedly in love with whom, who was giving a dinner party where, who would attend, and who would presumably not show up because of the latest social feud. He knew only too well that there would be an item or two from Marbella. He knew Kezia's style well enough to know that she would mention herself. She was thorough and prudent. And he was right. 'On the list of returning refugees after a summer abroad: Scooter Hollingsworth, Bibi Adams-Jones, Melissa Sentry, Jean-Claude Reims, Kezia Saint Martin, and Julian Bodley. Hail, hail, the gang's all here! Everyone is coming home!'

It was September, and he could still hear Kezia's voice of a September seven years before . . .

'. . . All right, Edward, I've done it. I did Vassar, and the Sorbonne, and I just did another summer at Aunt Hil's. I'm twenty-one years old and now I'm going to do what I want for a change. No more guilt trips about what my father would have wanted, or my mother would have preferred and what you feel is "sensible". I've done it all, for them and for you. And now I'm going to do it for me . . .'

She had marched up and down his office with a stormy look on her face, while he worried about the 'it' she was referring to.

'And what exactly are you planning to do?' He was dying inside. But she was awfully young and very beautiful.

'I don't know exactly. But I have some ideas.'

'Share them with me.'

'I plan to, but don't be disagreeable, Edward.' She had turned towards him with fiery amethyst lights in her rich blue eyes. She was a striking girl, even more so when she was angry. Then the eyes would become almost purple, the cameo skin would blush faintly under the cheekbones, and the contrast made her dark hair shine like onyx. It almost made you forget how tiny she was. She was barely more than five feet tall, but well proportioned, with a face that in anger drew one like a magnet, riveting her victim's eyes to her own. And the entire package was Edward's responsibility, had been since her parents' deaths. Ever since then, the burden of those fierce blue eyes had belonged to him, and her governess, Mrs. Townsend, and her Aunt Hilary, the Contessa di San Ricamini.

Hilary, of course, didn't want to be bothered. She was perfectly willing, in fact nowadays frankly delighted, to have the girl stay with her in London at Christmas, or come to the house in Marbella for the summer. But she did not want to be bothered with what she referred to as 'trivia'. Kezia's fascination with the Peace Corps had been 'trivia', as had her much-publicized romance with the Argentinian ambassador's son three years before. Her depression when the boy had married his cousin had also been 'trivia', as had Kezia's other passing fascinations with people, places, and causes. Maybe Hilary had a point; it all fell by the wayside eventually anyway. But until it did, it was inevitably Edward's problem. At twenty-one, she had already been a burden on his shoulders for twelve long years. But it was a burden he had cherished.

'Well, Kezia, you've been wearing out the rug in my office, but you still haven't told me what these mysterious plans of yours are. What about that course in journalism at Columbia? Have you lost interest in trying that?'

'As a matter of fact, I have. Edward, I want to go to work.'

'Oh?' He had shuddered almost visibly. God, let it be for some charity organization. Please. 'For whom?'

'I want to work for a newspaper, and study journalism at night.' There was a look of fierce defiance in her eyes. She knew what he would say. And why.

'I think you'd be a good deal wiser to take the course at Columbia, get your master's, and then think about working. Do it sensibly.'

'And after I get my master's, what sort of newspaper would you suggest, Edward? *Women's Wear Daily* maybe?' He thought he saw tears of anger and frustration in her eyes. Lord, she was going to be difficult again. She grew more stubborn each year. She was just like her father.

'What sort of paper were you considering, Kezia? *The Village Voice* or the *Berkeley Barb*?'

'No. *The New York Times*.' At least the girl had style. She had never lacked that.

'I heartily agree, my dear. I think it's a marvellous idea. But if that's what you have in mind, I think you'd be far wiser to attend Columbia, get your master's, and . . .' She cut him off, rising from the arm of the chair where she'd been perched, and glared at him angrily across his desk.

'And marry some terribly "nice" boy in the business school. Right?'

'Not unless that's what you want to do.' Tedious, tedious, tedious. And dangerous. She was that too. Like her mother.

'Well, that's not what I want to do.' She had stalked out of his office then, and he found out later that she already had the job at the *Times*. She kept it for exactly three and a half weeks.

It all happened precisely as he had feared it would. As one of the fifty wealthiest women in the world, she became the puppy of the paparazzi again. Every day in some newspaper, there was a mention or a photograph or a blurb or a quote or a joke. Other papers sent their society

11

reporters over to catch glimpses of her. *Women's Wear* had a field day. It was a continuation of the nightmare that had shadowed her: the fourteenth-birthday party broken into by photographers. The evening at the opera with Edward, over the Christmas holidays when she was only fifteen, which they had turned into such a horror. A pigsty of suggestion about Edward and Kezia. After that he had not taken her out publicly for years ... and for years after that, there were the photographs of her that were repressed, and those that were not. The dates she was afraid to have, and then had and regretted, until at seventeen she had feared notoriety more than anything. At eighteen she had hated it. Hated the seclusion it forced on her, the caution she had to exercise, the constant secretiveness and discretion. It was absurd and unhealthy for a girl her age, but there was nothing Edward could do to lighten the burden for her. She had a tradition to live up to, and a difficult one. It was impossible for the daughter of Lady Liane Holmes-Aubrey Saint Martin and Keenan Saint Martin to go ignored. Kezia was 'worth a tidy sum', in common parlance, and she was beautiful. She was young, she was interesting. And she made news. There was no way to avoid that, however much Kezia wanted to pretend she could change that. She couldn't. She never would. At least that was what Edward had thought. But he was surprised at her skill at avoiding photographers when she wanted to (now he even took her to the opera again) and the marvellous way she had of putting down reporters, with a wide dazzling smile and a word or two that made them wonder if she was laughing at them or with them, or about to call the police. She had that about her. Something threatening, the raw edge of power. But she had something gentle too. It was that that baffled everyone. She was a peculiar combination of her parents.

Kezia had the satiny delicacy of her mother and the sheer strength of her father. The two had always been an unusual couple. A surprising couple. And Kezia was like both of them, although more like her father. Edward saw it constantly. But what frightened him was the resemblance to Liane. Hundreds of years of British tradition, a maternal great-grandfather who was a duke – although her paternal grandfather had only been an earl – but Liane had such breeding, such style, such elegance of spirit. Such stature. Edward had fallen head over heels in love with her right from the first. And she had never known. Never. Edward knew that he couldn't . . . couldn't . . . but she had done something so much worse. Madness . . . blackmail . . . nightmare. At least they had averted a public scandal. No one had known. Except her husband, and Edward . . . and . . . him. Edward had never understood it. What had she seen in the boy? He was so much less a man than Keenan. And so . . . so coarse. Crude almost. She had made a poor choice. A very poor choice. Liane had taken Kezia's French tutor as her lover. It was almost grotesque, except that it was so costly. In the end, it had cost Liane her life. And it had cost Keenan thousands to keep it quiet.

Keenan had had the young man 'removed' from the household, and deported to France. After that it took Liane less than a year to drown herself in cognac and champagne, and, secretly, pills. She had paid a high price for her betrayal. Keenan died ten months later in an accident. There had been no doubt it was an accident, but such a waste. More waste. Keenan hadn't given a damn about anything after Liane died, and Edward had always suspected that he had just let it happen, just let the Mercedes slide along the barrier, let it career into the oncoming highway traffic. He had probably been drunk, or maybe only very tired. Not really a suicide, just the end.

No, Keenan hadn't cared about anything in those last months, not even, really, about his daughter. He had said as much to Edward, but only to Edward. Everyone's confidant, Edward. Liane had even told him her ugly stories, over tea one day, and he had nodded sagely and prayed not to get sick in her drawing room. She had looked at him so mournfully, it had made him want to cry.

Edward always cared. He cared too much – for Liane, who had been too perfect to be touched (or so he had thought) and for her child. Edward had always wondered if it excited her to have someone so far from her own class, or maybe it was just that the man was young, or maybe because he was French.

At least he could protect Kezia from that kind of madness, and he had long ago promised himself that he would. She was his duty now, his responsibility, and he was going to see to it that she lived up to every ounce of her breeding. He had sworn to himself that there would be no disasters in Kezia's life, no blackmailing, boy-faced French tutors. With Kezia it would be different. She would live up to her noble ancestry on her mother's side and to the powerful people on her father's side. Edward felt he owed that much to Keenan and Liane. And to Kezia, as well. And he knew what it would take. How he would have to inculcate her with a sense of duty, a sense of the mantle of tradition she wore. As she grew up, Kezia had jokingly referred to it as her hair shirt. but she understood. Edward always saw to it that she did. That was the one thing he could give her objectively, he thought: a sense of who and what she was. She was Kezia Saint Martin. The Honourable Kezia Holmes-Aubrey Saint Martin, offspring of British nobility and American aristocracy, with a father who had used millions to make millions, in steel, copper, rubber, petroleum, and oil. When there was big money to be made on unthinkable scales, Keenan Saint Martin was there. It had made him an international legend, and a kind of American prince. His was the legend Kezia had inherited with the fortune. Of course, by some standards Keenan had had to get his hands a little bit dirty, but not very. He was always so spectacular, and such a gentleman, the kind of man whom people forgave anything, even the fact that he made much of his own money.

Liane, on the other hand, was Kezia's threat, her terror . . . her reminder that if she crossed the invisible boundaries into forbidden lands, she, like her mother, would die.

14

Edward wanted her to be more like her father. It was so much less painful for him that way. But so often ... too often ... she was the image of Liane, only stronger, and better, smarter, and so much more beautiful even than Liane.

Kezia was born of extraordinary people. She was the last surviving link in a long chain of almost mythical beauty and grace. And it was up to Edward now to see that the chain was not broken. Liane had threatened it. But the chain was still safe, and Edward, like all lonely people who never quite dare, who are never quite beautiful, who are never quite strong – was impressed by it. His own modestly elegant family in Philadelphia was so much less impressive than these magical people to whom he had given his soul. He was their guardian now. The keeper of the Holy Grail: Kezia. The treasure. His treasure. Which was why he had been so glad when her plan to work at the *Times* had failed so dismally. Everything would be peaceful again. For a while. She was his to protect, and he was hers to command. She did not yet command him, but he feared that one day she would. Just as her parents had. He had been trusted and commanded, never loved.

In the case of the *Times*, he had not had to command. She had quit. She had gone back to school for a while, fled to Europe for the summer, but in the fall, everything had changed again. Mostly Kezia. For Edward it had been almost terrifying.

She had returned to New York with something crisper about her manner, something more womanly. This time she didn't consult Edward, even after the fact, and she didn't make claims to being grown-up. At twenty-two she had sold the co-op on Park Avenue where she had lived with Mrs. Townsend – Totie – for thirteen very comfortable years, and rented two smaller apartments, one for herself, and the other for Totie, who was gently but firmly put out to pasture, despite Edward's protests and Totie's tears. Then she had gone about solving the problem of a job as resolutely as she had the matter of the

15

apartment. The solution she chose was astonishingly ingenious.

She had announced the news to Edward over dinner in her new apartment, while serving him a very pleasant Pouilly Fumé '54 to soften the blow.

Kezia had acquired a literary agent, and stunned Edward by announcing that she had already published three articles that summer, which she had sent in from Europe. And the amazing thing was that he had read them all, and rather liked them. He remembered them – a political piece she had written in Italy, a haunting article about a nomadic tribe she had come across in the Middle East, and a very funny spoof on the Polo Club in Paris. All three had appeared in national publications under the name of K. S. Miller. It was the last article that had set off the next chain of events.

They had opened another bottle of wine, and Kezia had suddenly begun to look mischievous, as she tried to extort a promise from him. Suddenly, he had that sinking sensation in his stomach again. There was more, he could tell. He got that feeling every time she got *that* look in her eyes. The look that reminded him so acutely of her father. The look that said the plans had been made, the decisions taken, and there wasn't a hell of a lot you could do about it. Now what?

She had pulled out a copy of the morning's paper, and folded it to a page in the second section. He couldn't imagine what he might have missed. He read the paper thoroughly every morning. But she was pointing to the society column by Martin Hallam, and that morning he hadn't bothered to read it.

It was a strange column, actually, and had begun appearing only a month before. It was a well-informed, slightly cynical, and highly astute account of Jet Set doings in their private haunts. No one had any idea who Martin Hallam was, and everyone was still trying to guess who the traitor might be. Whoever he was, he wrote without malice – but certainly with a great deal of inside

16

information. And now Kezia was pointing to something at the top of the column.

He read it through, but found no mention of Kezia.

'So?'

'So, I'd like you to meet a friend of mine. Martin Hallam.' She was laughing openly, and Edward felt faintly foolish. And then she stuck out a hand to shake his, with a gurgle of laughter and those familiar amethyst lights in her eyes. 'Hello, Edward. I'm Martin. How do you do?'

'What? Kezia, you're joking!'

'I'm not. And no one will ever know. Even the editor doesn't know who writes it. Everything goes through my literary agent, and he's extremely discreet. I had to give them a month of sample columns to show that I knew what I was talking about, but word came back to us today. The column will now run as a regular feature three times a week. Isn't it divine?'

'Divine? It's ungodly. Kezia, how could you?'

'Why not? I don't say anything I could get sued for, and I don't let out any secrets that will destroy anyone's life. I just keep everyone ... well, "informed", shall we say ... and amused.'

And that was Kezia. The Honourable Kezia Saint Martin, K. S. Miller, and Martin Hallam. And now she was home after another summer away. Seven summers had passed since her career began. She was successful now, and it only added to her charm. To Edward, it gave her a mysterious sparkle, an almost unbearable allure. Who but Kezia could pull it off? And for such a long time. Edward and her agent were the only two people she had entrusted with the secret that the Honourable Kezia Saint Martin had another life, other than the one so lavishly depicted in *WWD*, *Town and Country*, and occasionally in the 'People' column of *Time*.

Edward looked at his watch again. He could call her now. It was just past ten o'clock. He reached for the phone. This was one number he always dialled himself. It rang twice, and she answered. The voice was husky, the way she always sounded in the morning. The way he liked best. There was something very private about that voice. He often wondered what she wore to bed, and then reprimanded himself for the thought.

'Welcome home, Kezia.' He smiled at the newspaper photograph still lying on his desk.

'Edward!' He felt warm at the delight in her voice. 'How I've missed you!'

'But not enough to send me so much as a postcard, you little minx! I had lunch with Totie last Saturday, and she at least gets an occasional letter from you.'

'That's different. She'd go into a decline if I didn't let her know I'm alive.' She laughed, and he heard the clink of a cup against the phone. Tea. No sugar. A dash of cream.

'And you don't think I'd go into a decline?'

'Of course not. You're far too stoic. It would be bad form. *Noblesse oblige*, et cetera, et cetera.'

'All right, all right.' Her directness often embarrassed him. She was right, too. He had a distinct sense of 'form'. It was why he had never told her that he loved her. Why he had never told her mother that he had loved her.

'And how was Marbella?'

'Dreadful. I must be getting old. Aunt Hil's house was absolutely crawling with all sorts of eighteen-year-old children. Good God, Edward, they were born eleven years after I was! Why aren't they at home with their nannies?' He laughed at the sound of her voice. She still looked twenty. But a very sophisticated twenty. 'Thank God I was only there for the weekend.'

'And before that?'

'Didn't you read the column this morning? It said I was in seclusion in the South of France for most of the summer.' She laughed again, and he smiled. It was so good to hear her voice.

'Actually, I was there for a while. On a boat I rented, and it was very pleasant. And peaceful. I got a lot of writing done.'

'I saw the article you did on the three Americans imprisoned in Turkey. Depressing, but excellent. Were you there?'

'Of course I was. And yes, it was depressing as hell.'

'Where else did you go?' He wanted to get her off the subject. Disagreeable issues were unnecessary.

'Oh, I went to a party in Rome, to the collections in Paris, to London to see the Queen . . . Pussycat, pussycat, where have you been? I've been to London to see the . . .'

'Kezia, you're impossible.' But delightfully so.

'Yeah.' She took a long swallow of tea and hiccuped in his ear. 'But I missed you. It's a pain in the ass not being able to tell anyone what I'm really doing.'

'Well, come and tell me what you really did. Lunch at La Grenouille today?'

'Perfect. I have to see Simpson, but I can meet you after that. Is one all right with you?'

'Fine. And Kezia . . .'

'Yes?' Her voice was low and gentle, suddenly not quite so brisk. In her own way, she loved him too. For almost twenty years now, he had softened the blow of the absence of her father.

'It really is good to know you're back.'

'And it really is good to know that someone gives a damn.'

'Silly child, you make it sound as though no one else cares.'

'It's called the Poor Little Rich Girl Syndrome, Edward. Occupational hazard for an heiress.' She laughed, but there was an edge to her voice that troubled him. 'See you at one.'

She hung up, and Edward stared out at the view.

Twenty-two blocks from where he sat, Kezia was lying in bed, finishing her tea. There was a stack of newspapers on her bed, a pile of mail on the table next to her. The curtains were drawn back, and she had a peaceful view of the garden behind the townhouse next door. A bird was cooing on the air conditioner. And the doorbell was ringing.

'Damn.' She pulled a white satin robe off the foot of the bed, wondering who it might be, then suspecting quickly. She was right. When she opened the door, a slim, nervous Puerto Rican boy held out a long white box.

She knew what was in the box even before she traded the boy a dollar for his burden. She knew who the box was from. She even knew the florist. And knew also that she would recognize his secretary's writing on the card. After four years, you let your secretary write the cards: 'Oh, you know, Effy, something like "You can't imagine how I've missed you", et cetera.' Effy did a fine job of it. She said just what any romantic fifty-four-year-old virgin would say on a card to accompany a dozen red roses. And Kezia didn't really care if the card was from Effy or Whit. It didn't make much difference anymore. None at all, in fact.

This time Effy had added 'Dinner tonight?' to the usual flowery message, and Kezia paused with the card in her hand. She sat down in a prim blue velvet chair that had been her mother's, and played with the card. She hadn't seen Whit in a month. Not since he had flown to London on business, and they had partied at Annabel's before he left again the next day. Of course he had met her at the airport the night before, but they hadn't really talked. They never really did.

She leaned pensively towards the phone on the small fruitwood desk, the card still in her hand. She glanced across the neat stacks of invitations her twice-weekly secretary had arranged for her – those she had missed, and those that were for the near and reasonably near future. Dinners, cocktails, gallery openings, fashion shows, benefits. Two wedding announcements, and a birth announcement.

She dialled Whit's office and waited.

'Up already, Kezia darling? You must be exhausted.'

'A bit, but I'll live. And the roses are splendid.' She

allowed a small smile to escape her and hoped that it wouldn't show in her voice.

'Are they nice? I'm glad. Kezia, you looked marvellous last night.' She laughed at him and looked at the tree growing in the neighbouring garden. The tree had grown more in four years than Whit had.

'You were sweet to pick me up at the airport. And the roses started my day off just right. I was beginning to gloom over unpacking my bags.'

She had had the bad judgment to arrive on one of the cleaning woman's days off. But the bags could wait.

'And what about my dinner invitation? The Orniers are having a dinner, and if you're not too tired, Xavier suggested we all go to Raffles afterwards.' The Orniers had an endless suite in the tower at the Hotel Pierre, which they kept for their annual trips to New York. Even for a few weeks it was 'worth it': 'Yo7 know how ghastly it is to be in a different room each time, a strange place.' They paid a high price for familiarity, but that was not new to Kezia. And their dinner party was just the sort of thing she ought to cover for the column. She had to get back into the swing of things, and lunch at La Grenouille with Edward would be a good start, but ... damn. She wanted to go downtown instead. There were delights downtown that Whit would never dream she knew. She smiled to herself and suddenly remembered Whit in the silence.

'Sorry, darling. I'd love to, but I'm so awfully tired. Jet lag, and probably all that wild life at Hilary's this weekend. Can you possibly tell the Orniers I died, and I'll try to catch a glimpse of them before they leave. For you, I will resurrect tomorrow. But today, I'm simply gone.' She yawned slightly, and then giggled. 'Good Lord, I didn't mean to yawn in your ear. Sorry.'

'Quite all right. And I think you're right about tonight. They probably won't serve dinner till nine. You know how they are, and it'll be two before you get home after Raffles ...' Dancing in that over-decorated basement, Kezia thought, just what I don't need ...

'I'm glad you understand, love. Actually, I think I'll put my phone on the service, and just trot off to bed at seven or eight. And tomorrow I'll be blazing.'

'Good. Dinner tomorrow then?' Obviously, darling. Obviously.

'Yes. I have a thing on my desk for some sort of gala at the St. Regis. Want to try that? I think the Marshes are taking over the Maisonette for their ninety-eighth wedding anniversary or something.'

'Nasty sarcastic girl. It's only their twenty-fifth. I'll take a table at La Côte Basque, and we can go next door late.'

'Perfect, darling. Till tomorrow, then.'

'Pick you up at seven?'

'Make it eight.' Make it never.

'Fine, darling. See you then.'

She sat swinging one leg over the other after she hung up. She really was going to have to be nicer to Whit. What was the point of being disagreeable to him? Everyone thought of them as a couple, and he was nice to her, and useful in a way. Her constant escort. Darling Whitney . . . poor Whit. So predictable and so perfect, so beautiful and so impeccably tailored. It was unbearable really. Precisely six feet and one inch, ice-blue eyes, short thick blond hair, thirty-five years old, Gucci shoes, Dior ties, Givenchy cologne, Piaget watch, apartment on Park and Sixty-third, fine reputation as a lawyer, and loved by all his friends. The obvious mate for Kezia, and that in itself was enough to make her hate him, not that she really hated him. She only resented him, and her need of him. Despite the lover on Sutton Place that he didn't know she knew about.

The Whit and Kezia game was a farce, but a discreet one. And a useful one. He was the ideal and eternal escort, and so totally safe. It was appalling to remember that a year or two before she had even considered marrying him. There didn't seem any reason not to. They would go on doing the same things they were doing, and Kezia would tell him about the column. They would go to the same parties, see the same people, and lead their own lives. He'd

22

bring her roses instead of send them. They would have separate bedrooms, and when Kezia gave someone a tour of the house Whit's would be shown as 'the guest room'. And she would go downtown, and he to Sutton Place, and no one would have to be the wiser. They would never mention it to each other, of course; she would 'play bridge' and he would 'see a client' and they would meet at breakfast the next day, pacified, mollified, appeased, and loved, each by their respective lovers. What an insane fantasy. She laughed thinking back on it now. She still had more hope than that. She regarded Whit now as an old friend. She was fond of him in an odd way. And she was used to him, which in some ways was worse.

Kezia wandered slowly back to her bedroom and smiled to herself. It was good to be home. Nice to be back in the comfort of her own apartment, in the huge white bed with the silver fox bedspread that had been such an appalling extravagance, but still pleased her so much. The small, delicate furniture had been her mother's. The painting she had bought in Lisbon the year before hung over the bed, a watermelon sun over a rich countryside and a man working the fields. There was something warm and friendly about her bedroom that she found nowhere else in the world. Not in Hilary's palazzo in Marbella, or in the lovely home in Kensington where she had her own room – Hilary had so many rooms in the London house that she could afford to give them away to absent friends and family like so many lace handkerchiefs. But nowhere did Kezia feel like this, except at home. There was a fireplace in the bedroom too, and she had found the brass bed in London years before; there was one soft brown velvet chair near the fireplace, and a white fur rug that made you want to dance barefoot across the floor. Plants stood in corners and hung near the windows, and candles on the mantel gave the room a soft glow late at night. It was very good to be home.

She laughed softly to herself, a sound of pure pleasure as she put Mahler on the stereo and started her bath. And tonight ... downtown. To Mark. First, her agent, then

23

lunch with Edward. And finally, Mark. Saving the best till last . . . as long as nothing had changed.

'Kezia,' she spoke aloud to herself, looking in the bathroom mirror as she stood naked before it, humming to the music that echoed through the house, 'You are a very naughty girl!' She wagged a finger at her reflection, and tossed back her head and laughed, her long black hair sweeping back to her waist. She stood very still then and looked deep into her own eyes. 'Yeah, I know. I'm a rat. But what else can I do? A girl's got to live, and there are a lot of different ways to do it.' She sank into the bathtub, wondering about it all. The dichotomies, the contrasts, the secrets . . . but at least no lies. She said nothing to anyone. But she did not lie. Almost never anyway. Lies were too hard to live with. Secrets were better.

As she sank into the warmth of the water, she thought about Mark. Delicious Marcus. The wild crazy hair, the incredible smile, the smell of his loft, the chess games, the laughter, the music, his body, his fire. Mark Wooly. She closed her eyes and drew an imaginary line down his back with the tip of one finger and then traced it gently across his lips. Something small squirmed low in the pit of her stomach, and she turned slowly in the tub, sending ripples gently away from her.

Twenty minutes later she stepped out of the bath, brushed her hair into a sleek knot, and slipped a plain white wool Dior dress over the new champagne lace underwear she had bought in Florence.

'Do you suppose I'm a schizophrenic?' she asked the mirror as she carefully fitted a hat into place and tilted it slowly over one eye. But she didn't look like a schizophrenic. She looked like 'the' Kezia Saint Martin, on her way to lunch at La Grenouille in New York, or Fouquet's in Paris.

'Taxi!' Kezia held up an arm and dashed past the doorman as a cab stopped a few feet away at the kerb. She smiled at the doorman and slid into the cab. Her New York season had just begun. And what did this one have in store?

A book? A man? Mark Wooly? A dozen juicy articles for major magazines? A host of tiny cherished moments? Solitude and secrecy and splendour. She had it all. And another 'season' in the palm of her hand.

In his office, Edward was strutting in front of the view. He looked at his watch for the eleventh time in an hour. In just a few minutes he would watch her walk in, she would see him and laugh, and then reach up and touch his face with her hand . . . 'Oh Edward, it's so good to see you!' She would hug him and giggle, and settle in at his side – while 'Martin Hallam' took mental notes about who was at what table with whom, and K. S. Miller mulled over the possibility of a book.

## CHAPTER II

Kezia fought her way past the tight knot of men hovering between the cloak room and the bar of La Grenouille. The luncheon crowd was thick, the bar was jammed, the tables were full, the waiters were bustling, and the decor was unchanged. Red leather seats, pink tablecloths, bright oil paintings on the walls, and flowers on every table. The room was full of red anemones and smiling faces, with silver buckets of white wine chilling at almost every table while champagne corks popped demurely here and there.

The women were beautiful, or had worked hard at appearing so. Cartier's wares were displayed in wild profusion. And the murmur of conversation throughout the room was distinctly French. The men wore dark suits and white shirts, and had grey at their temples, and shared their wealth of Romanoff cigars from Cuba via Switzerland in unmarked brown packages.

La Grenouille was the watering hole of the very rich and the very chic. Merely having an ample expense account to pay the tab was not adequate entree. You had to belong. It had to be part of you, a style you exuded from the pores of your Pucci.

'Kezia?' A hand touched her elbow, and she looked into the tanned face of Amory Strongwell.

'No darling. It's my ghost.' He won a teasing smile.

'You look marvellous.'

'And you look so pale. Poor Amory.' She gazed in mock sympathy at the deep bronze he had acquired in Greece, as he squeezed her shoulder carefully and kissed her cheek.

'Where's Whit?'

Probably at Sutton Place, darling. 'Working like mad, presumably. Will we see you at the Marsh party tomorrow night?' The question was rhetorical, and he nodded absently in answer. 'I'm meeting Edward just now.'

'Lucky bastard.' She gave him a last smile and edged through the crowd to the front, where the head waiter would be waiting to shepherd her to Edward. As it happened, she found Edward without assistance; he was at his favourite table, a bottle of champagne chilling nearby. Louis Roederer 1959, as always.

He saw her too and stood up to meet her as she walked easily past the other tables and across the room. She felt eyes on her, acknowledged discreet greetings as she passed tables of people she knew, and the waiters smiled. She had grown into it all years ago. Recognition. At sixteen it had agonized her, at eighteen it was a custom, at twenty-two she had fought against it, and now at twenty-nine she enjoyed it. It amused her. It was her private joke. The women would say 'marvellous dress', the men would muse about Whit; the women would decide that with the same fortune they could get away with the same sort of hat, and the waiters would nudge each other and murmur in French, 'Saint Martin'. By the time she left, there might, or there might not, be a photographer from *Women's Wear* waiting to snap her photograph paparazzi-style as she came through the door. It amused her. She played the game well.

'Edward, you look wonderful!' She gave him a searching look, an enormous squeeze, and sank onto the banquette at his side.

'Lord, child, you look well.' She kissed his cheek gently, and then smoothed her hand over it tenderly with a smile.

'So do you.'

'And how was this morning with Simpson?'

'Pleasant and productive. We've been discussing some ideas I have for a book. He gives me good advice, but let's not . . . here . . .' They both knew that there was too much noise to allow anyone to piece much together. But they rarely spoke of her career in public. 'Discretion is the better part of valour,' as Edward often said.

'Right. Champagne?'

'Have I ever said no?' He signalled the waiter, and the ritual of the Louis Roederer was begun. 'God, I love that stuff.' She smiled at him again and gazed slowly around the room as he began to laugh.

'I know what you're doing, Kezia, and you're impossible.' She was checking out the scene for her column. He raised his glass to her, and smiled. 'To you, mademoiselle, welcome home.' They clinked glasses and sipped slowly at the champagne. It was precisely the way they liked it, a good year and icy cold.

'How's Whit, by the way? Seeing him for dinner tonight?'

'Fine. And no, I'm going to bed to recover from the trip.'

'I don't think I believe that, but I'll accept it if you say so.'

'What a wise man you are, Edward. That's probably why I love you.'

He looked at her for a moment then, and took her hand. 'Kezia, be careful. Please.'

'Yes, Edward. I know. I am.'

The lunch was pleasant, as all their lunches were. She inquired about all his most important clients, remembered all their names, and wanted to know what he had done about the couch in his apartment that so desperately

27

needed re-upholstering. They said hello to everyone they knew, and were joined for brief moments by two of his partners in the firm. She told him a little about her trip, and she kept an eye on the comings and goings and pairings of the natives.

She left him outside at three. The 'surprise' photographer from *Women's Wear* dutifully took their photograph, and Edward hailed her a cab before he walked back to his office. He always felt better when he knew she was back in town. He could be there if she needed him, and he felt closer to her life. He never really knew, but he had an idea that there was more to her life than Raffles and parties given by the Marshes. And much more to her life than Whit. But she didn't tell Edward, and he didn't ask. He didn't really want to know as long as she was all right – 'careful', as he put it. But there was too much of her father in her to be satisfied with a man like Whit. Edward knew that only too well. It had taken more than two years to settle her father's will discreetly, and execute the arrangements for the two women no one had known about.

The cab took Kezia home and deposited her at her door with a flourish of brakes and scattered kerbside litter, and Kezia went upstairs and hung the white Dior dress neatly in the closet. Half an hour later she was in jeans, her hair hanging free, the answering service instructed to pick up her calls. She was 'resting' and didn't want to be disturbed until the following noon. A few moments later, she was gone.

She walked away from her house and slipped quietly into the subway at Seventy-seventh Street and Lexington Avenue. No make-up, no handbag, just a coin purse in her pocket and a smile in her eyes.

The subway was like a concentrated potion of New York, each sound and smell magnified, each character more extreme. Funny old ladies with faces made up like masks, gay boys in pants so tight one could almost see the hair on their legs, magnificent girls carrying portfolios on their way to modelling engagements, and men who smelled of sweat and cigars, whom one wanted not to be near, and the occasional passenger for Wall Street in striped suit, short hair, and hornrims. It was a symphony of sights and odours and sounds conducted to the shrieking background beat of the trains, brakes screaming, wheels rattling. Kezia stood holding her breath and closing her eyes against the hot breeze and flying litter swept up by the oncoming train, then moved inside quickly, sidestepping the doors as they closed.

She found a seat next to an old woman carrying a shopping bag. A young couple sat down next to her at the next stop, and furtively shared a joint, unobserved by the transit patrolman who moved through the car, eyes fixed ahead of him. Kezia found herself smiling, wondering if the old woman on her other side would get high from the smell. Then the train screeched to a halt at Canal Street and it was time to get off. Kezia danced quickly up the steps and looked around.

She was home again. Another home. Warehouses and tired tenements, fire escapes and delicatessens, and a few blocks away the art galleries and coffee houses and lofts crowded with artists and writers, sculptors and poets, beards and bandannas. A place where Camus and Sartre were still revered, and de Kooning and Pollock were gods. She walked along with a quick step and a little throb in her heart. It shouldn't matter so much . . . not at her age . . . not the way things were between them . . . it shouldn't feel so good to be back . . . it might all be different now. . . . But it did feel good to be back, and she wanted everything to be the same.

'Hey girl. Where've you been?' A tall, lithe black man wallpapered into white jeans greeted her with surprise delight.

'George!' He swept her off her feet in a vast embrace and whirled her around. He was in the ballet corps of the Metropolitan Opera. 'Oh, it's good to see you!' He deposited her, breathless and smiling, on the pavement beside him, and put an arm around her shoulders.

'You've been gone for a mighty long time, lady.' His eyes

29

danced and his grin was a long row of ivory in the bearded midnight face.

'It feels like it. I almost wondered if the neighbourhood would be gone.'

'Never! SoHo is sacred.' They laughed and he fell into step beside her. 'Where're you going?'

'How about The Partridge for coffee?' She was suddenly afraid to see Mark. Afraid that everything was different. George would know, but she didn't want to ask him.

'Make it wine, and I'm yours for an hour. We have rehearsal at six.'

They shared a carafe of wine at The Partridge. George drank most of it while Kezia played with her glass.

'Know something, baby?'

'What, George?'

'You make me laugh.'

'Terrific. How come?'

'Because I know what you're so nervous about, and you're so damn scared you won't even ask me. You gonna ask or do I have to volunteer the answer?' He was laughing at her.

'Is there something that maybe I don't want to know?'

'Shit, Kezia. Why don't you just go on up to his studio and find out? It's better that way.' He stood up, put a hand in his pocket, and pulled out three dollars. 'My treat. You just go on home.' Home? To Mark? Yes, in a way . . . even she knew it.

He shooed her out the door with another ripple of laughter, and she found herself in the familiar doorway across the street. She hadn't even looked up at the window, but instead nervously searched strangers' faces.

Her heart hammered as she ran up the five flights. She reached the landing, breathless and dizzy, and raised a hand to knock at the door. It flew open almost before she touched it, and she was suddenly wrapped in the arms of an endlessly tall, hopelessly thin, fuzzy-haired man. He kissed her and lifted her into his arms, pulling her inside with a shout and a grin.

30

'Hey, you guys! It's Kezia! How the hell are you, baby?'

'Happy.' He set her down and she looked around. The same faces, the same loft, the same Mark. Nothing had changed. It was a victorious return. 'Christ, it feels like I've been gone for a year!' She laughed again, and someone handed her a glass of red wine.

'You're telling me. And now, ladies and gentlemen . . .' The endlessly tall young man bowed low, and swept an arm from his friends to the door. 'My lady has returned. In other words, you guys, beat it!' They laughed good-naturedly and murmured hellos and goodbyes as they left. The door had barely closed when Mark pulled her into his arms again.

'Oh baby, I'm glad you're home.'

'Me too.' She slid a hand under his ragged, paint-splattered shirt and smiled into his eyes.

'Let me look at you.' He slowly pulled her shirt over her head, and she stood straight and still, her hair falling across one shoulder, a warm light in her rich blue eyes, a living reflection of the sketch of a nude that hung on the wall behind her. He had done it the previous winter, soon after they had met. She reached out to him slowly then, and he came into her arms smiling at the same moment that there was a knock at the door.

'Go away!'

'No, I won't.' It was George.

'Shit, motherfucker, what do you want?' He pulled open the door as Kezia darted bare-chested into the bedroom. George loomed large and smiling in the doorway with a small split of champagne in one hand.

'For your wedding night, Marcus.'

'George, you're beautiful.' George danced down the stairs with a wave, and Mark closed the door with a burst of laughter. 'Hey, Kezia! Could you dig a glass of cham-pagne?' She returned to the room smiling and naked, her hair swinging loose down her back, the vision of cham-pagne at La Grenouille in the Dior dress bringing laughter to her eyes now. The comparison was absurd.

She lounged in the doorway, her head to one side, watching him open the champagne. And suddenly she felt as though she loved him, and that was absurd too. They both knew she didn't. It wasn't that kind of thing. They both understood ... but it would have been nice not to understand, just for a moment. Not to be rational, or make sense. It would have been lovely to love him, to love someone – anyone – and why not Mark?

'I missed you, Kezia.'

'So did I, darling. So did I. And I also wondered if you had another lady by now.' She smiled and took a sip of the too-sweet, bubbly wine. 'I was queasy as hell about coming up. I even stopped and had some wine at The Partridge with George.'

'Asshole. You could have come here first.'

'I was afraid to.' She walked towards him and traced a finger across his chest as he looked down at her.

'You know something weird, Kezia?'

'What?' Her eyes filled with dreams.

'I've got syphilis.'

'WHAT!' She stared at him, horrified, and he chuckled.

'I just wondered what you'd say. I don't really have it.' But he looked amused at his joke.

'Jesus.' She settled back into his arms with a shake of the head and a grin. 'I'm not so sure about your sense of humour, kiddo.' But it was the same Mark.

He followed her into the bedroom and his voice sounded husky as he spoke from behind her. 'I saw a picture of some girl in the paper the other day. She looked sort of like you, only older, and very uptight.' There was a question in his voice. One she was not planning to answer.

'So?'

'Her last name was French. Not "Miller", but her first name was blurred. I couldn't read it. You related to anyone like that? She looked pretty fancy.'

'No, I'm not related to anyone like that. Why?' And now the lies had even begun with Mark. Not just sins of omission; now they were sins of commission too. Damn.

32

'I don't know. I was just curious. She was interesting looking, in a fierce, unhappy sort of way.'

'And you fell in love with her, and decided that you had to find her and rescue her, so you could both live happily ever after. Right?' Her voice was light, but not as light as she wanted it to be. His answer was lost as he kissed her and eased her gently onto the bed. There was at least an hour of truth amid the lifetime of lies. Bodies are generally honest.

## CHAPTER III

'Ready?'

'Ready.' Whit smiled at her across the last of their coffee and mousse au chocolat. They were two hours late for the Marshes' party at the St. Regis, but no one would notice. The Marshes had invited more than five hundred guests.

Kezia was resplendent in a blue-grey satin dress that circled her neck in a halter and left her back bare to show her deep summer tan. Small diamond earrings glistened at her ears, and her hair was swept into a neat knot high on her head. Whit's impeccable evening clothes set off his classic good looks. They made a very spectacular couple. By now, they took it for granted.

The crowd at the entrance to the Maisonette at the St. Regis was enormous. Elegantly dinner-jacketed men whose names appeared regularly in *Fortune*; women in diamonds and Balenciagas and Givenchys and Diors whose faces and living rooms appeared constantly in *Vogue*. European titles, American scions of society, friends from Palm Beach and Grosse Pointe and Scottsdale and Beverly Hills. The Marshes had outdone themselves. Waiters circulated through the ever-thickening crowd, offering Moët et Chandon champagne and little platters boasting caviar and pâté.

There was cold lobster on a buffet at the back of the room, and later on there would appear the pièce de résistance, an enormous wedding cake, a replica of the original served a quarter of a century before. Each guest would be given a tiny box of dream cake, the wrapping carefully inscribed with the couple's name and the date. 'More than a little tacky,' as Martin Hallam would note in his column the next day. Whit handed Kezia a glass of champagne from a passing tray and gently took her arm.

'Do you want to dance, or circulate for a while?'

'Circulate, I think, if it's humanly possible.' She smiled quietly at him, and he squeezed her arm.

A photographer hired by their hosts snapped a picture of them looking lovingly at each other, and Whit slipped an arm about her waist. She was comfortable with him. After her night with Mark, she felt benign and benevolent, even with Whit. It was odd to think that at dawn that morning she had wandered the streets of SoHo with Mark, then left him reluctantly at three that afternoon to phone in her column to her agent, clear her desk, and rest before the onslaught of the evening. Edward had called to see how she was, and they had chuckled for a few moments about her mention of their lunch in the morning's column.

'How in God's name can you call me "dashing," Kezia? I'm over sixty years old.'

'You're a mere sixty-one. And you *are* dashing, Edward. Look at you.'

'I try very hard not to.'

'Silly man.' They had moved on to other topics, both of them careful not to mention what she had done the night before. . . .

'More champagne, Kezia?'

'Mm?' She had drifted through the first glass without even noticing it. She had been thinking of other things: Edward; the new article she'd just been commissioned to write, a piece on the outstanding women candidates in the upcoming national elections. She had forgotten all about Whit, and the Marshes' party. 'Good Heavens, did I finish

34

that already?' She smiled at Whit again, and he looked at her quizzically.

'Still tired from the trip?'

'No, just a little dreamy. Drifting, I suppose.'

'That's quite a knack in a furore like this.' She exchanged her empty glass for a full one, and they found a secluded corner where they could watch the dance floor. Her eyes took in all the couples and she made rapid mental notes as to who was with whom, and who was wearing what. Opera divas, bankers, famous beauties, celebrated playboys, and an extravagance of rubies and sapphires and diamonds and emeralds.

'You look more beautiful than ever, Kezia.'

'You flatter me, Whit.'

'No. I love you.'

It was foolish of him to say it. They both knew otherwise. But she inclined her head demurely with a slender smile. Perhaps he did love her, after a fashion. Perhaps she even loved him, like a favourite brother or a childhood friend. He was a sweet man; it wasn't really difficult to like him. But love him? That was different.

'It looks as though the summer did you good.'

'Europe always does. Oh, no!'

'What?' He turned in the direction that had brought a look of dismay to her face, but it was too late. The Baron von Schnellingen was bearing down on them, with perspiration pouring from his temples, and a look of ecstasy at having spotted the pair.

'Oh Christ, tell him you've got the curse, and you can't dance,' Whit whispered.

Kezia burst into laughter, which the chubby little German Baron misinterpreted as delight.

'I am zo happy to zee you too, my dear. Good evening, Vitney. Kee-zee-ah, you are exquisite tonight.'

'Thank you, Manfred. You're looking well.' And hot and sweaty. And obese, and disgusting. And lecherous, as usual.

'It is a valtz. Chust for us. *Ja*?' *Nein*, but why the hell not? She couldn't say no. He was always sure to remind her

35

of how much he had loved her dear departed father. It was simpler to concede one waltz with him, for her 'father's sake.' At least he was a proficient dancer. At the waltz in any case. She bowed her head gently and extended a hand to be led to the floor. The Baron patted her hand ecstatically and led her away, just as Whit whispered in her ear, 'I'll rescue you right after the waltz.'

'You'd better, darling.' She said it through clenched teeth and a well-practised smile.

How could she ever explain something like this to Mark? She began to laugh to herself at the thought of explaining Mark and her anonymous forays into SoHo to anyone at the Maisonette that night. Surely the Baron would understand. He probably crept off to far more unusual places than SoHo, but he didn't expect Kezia to. No one did. Not Kezia, a woman, *the* Kezia Saint Martin . . . and that was different anyway. Like the other men she knew, the Baron conducted his adventures differently, and for different reasons . . . or was it different? Was she simply being a poor little rich girl running away to get laid and play with her Bohemian friends? Were any of them real to her? Sometimes she wondered. The Maisonette was real. Whit was real. The Baron was real. So real it made her feel hopeless at times. A gilded cage from which one never escapes. One never escapes one's name and one's face and one's ancestors and one's father or one's mother, no matter how many years they've been dead. One never escapes all the bullshit about *Noblesse oblige*. Or does one? Does one simply get on the subway with a token and a smile, never to return? The mysterious disappearance of the Honourable Kezia Saint Martin. No, if one leaves, one leaves elegantly and openly. With style. Not fleeing on a subway in total silence. If she really wanted SoHo, she had to say so, if only for her own sake. She knew that much. But was that what she wanted? How much better was SoHo than this? It was zabaglione instead of soufflé Grand Marnier. But neither was very nourishing. What she needed was good, wholesome steak. Counting on Mark's world for sustenance was like hiding with a six-month supply of Oreo cookies and nothing else. She simply had one world to offset the other, one man to complement another, and the worst of it was that she knew it. Nothing was whole. . . . 'Am I?' She didn't realize that she had said it aloud.

'Are you vat?' the Baron cooed in her ear.

'Oh. Sorry. Am I stepping on your foot?'

'No, my beauty. Only my heart. And you dance like an angel.'

Nauseating. She smiled pleasantly and swirled in his arms. 'Thank you, Manfred.'

They swept gracefully about once more, and at last her eye met Whit's, as the waltz drew to a merciful close. She stood slightly apart from the Baron and thanked him again.

'But perhaps they play another?' His disappointment was almost childlike.

'You dance a very handsome waltz, sir.' Whitney was at their side, bowing slightly to the perspiring German.

'And you are a very lucky man, Vitney.' Kezia and Whit exchanged a beatific glance and Kezia bestowed a last smile on the Baron as they glided away.

'Still alive?'

'Very much so. And I've really been hopelessly lazy. I haven't talked to a soul tonight.' She had work to do and the evening was young.

'Want to stop and talk to some of your cronies now?'

'Why not? I haven't seen any of them since I got back.'

'Then onwards, milady. Let us throw ourselves to the lions, and see who's here.'

Everyone was, as Kezia had observed upon entering. And after a round of a dozen tables, and six or seven small groups standing near the dance floor, she was grateful to spot two of her friends. Whitney left her to them, and went to share a cigar with his senior partner. A little congenial talk over a good Monte Cristo never hurt. He waved her on her way, and vanished in a cluster of black and white emitting the pungent fumes of Havana's finest.

'Hi, you two.' Kezia joined two tall thin young women who seemed surprised to see her arrive.

'I didn't know you were back!' Cheeks almost met as kisses flew into midair, and the three looked at each other with pleasure. Tiffany Benjamin was more than a little drunk, but Marina Walters looked bright and alive. Tiffany was married to William Patterson Benjamin IV, the number two man in the biggest brokerage house on Wall Street. And Marina was divorced. And loved it that way, or so she said. Kezia knew otherwise.

'When did you get back from Europe?' Marina smiled at her, and appraised the dress. 'Hell of a neat dress, by the way. Saint Laurent?'

Kezia nodded.

'I thought so.'

'And so's yours, Madame Hawkeye.' Marina nodded pleased assent, but Kezia knew it for a copy. 'Christ, I got back two days ago, and I'm beginning to wonder if I was ever away.' Kezia spoke while keeping a casual eye on the room.

'I know the feeling. I got back last week, in time to get the kids back to school. By the time we'd done orthodontists, shoes, school uniforms, and three birthday parties, I forgot I'd ever been away. I'm ready for another summer. Where'd you go this year, Kezia?'

'The South of France, and I spent the last few days at Hilary's in Marbella. You, Marina?'

'The Hamptons all summer. Boring as hell. This was not my most glowing summer.'

Kezia raised an eyebrow. 'How come?'

'No men, or something like that.' She was creeping towards thirty-six and was thinking about having something done about the bags under her eyes. The summer before, she had had her breasts firmed up by 'the most marvellous doctor' in Zurich. Kezia had hinted at it in the column, and Marina had been livid.

Tiffany had been to Greece for the summer, and she had also spent a few days with distant cousins in Rome. Bill

38

had had to come home early. Bullock and Benjamin seemed to require the presence of its director almost constantly. But he thrived on it. He ate it and slept it and loved it. The Dow Jones ticked somewhere in his heart, and his pulse rate went up and down with the market. That was what Martin Hallam said in his column. But Tiffany understood; her father had been the same way. He had been the president of the Stock Exchange when he finally retired to a month of golf before the fatal heart attack. What a way to go, one foot on the Exchange, and the other on the golf course. Tiffany's mother's life was less dramatic. Like Tiffany, she drank. But less.

Tiffany was proud of Bill. He was an important man. Even more important than her father. Or her brother. And hell, her brother worked just as hard as Bill did. Gloria said so. Her brother was a corporate lawyer with Wheeler, Spaulding, and Forbes, one of the oldest firms on Wall Street. But the brokerage house of Bullock and Benjamin was the most important on the Street. It made Tiffany someone. Mrs. William Patterson Benjamin IV. And she didn't mind vacationing alone. She took the children to Gstaad at Christmas, Palm Beach in February, and Acapulco for spring vacation. In summer, they spent a month at the Vineyard with Bill's mother, and then off they went to Europe; Monte Carlo, Paris, Cannes, St. Tropez, Cap d'Antibes, Marbella, Skorpios, Athens, Rome. It was divine. Everything was divine, according to Tiffany. So divine that she was drinking herself to death.

'Isn't this the most divine party you've ever seen?' Tiffany was weaving slightly and watching her friends. Marina and Kezia exchanged a rapid glance, and Kezia nodded. She and Tiffany had gone to school together. She was a nice girl too, when she wasn't drunk. It was something Kezia would not put in the column. Everyone knew she drank, and it hurt to see her like that. It wasn't something amusing to read at breakfast, like Marina's boob lift. This was different, painful. Suicide by champagne.

39

'What's next on your agenda, Kezia?' Marina lit a cigarette, and Tiffany faded back into her glass.

'I don't know. Maybe I'll give a party.' After I write that article I landed today. . . .

'Christ, you've got courage. I look at something like this and I cringe. Meg spent eight months planning it. Are you on the Arthritis Committee again this year?'

Kezia nodded. 'They asked me about doing the Crippled Children's Ball too.' Tiffany awoke at the mention of that.

'Crippled children? How dreadful!' At least she hadn't said it was divine.

'What's dreadful about it? It's as good a ball as any of the others.' Marina was quick to the fiesta's defence.

'But crippled children? I mean really, who could stand to look at them?' Marina looked at her, annoyed.

'Tiffany darling, have you ever seen an arthritic at the Arthritis Ball?'

'No . . . I don't think so. . . .'

'Then you won't see any children at the Crippled Children's Ball either.' Marina was matter-of-fact, and Tiffany seemed appeased, while something slimy turned over in Kezia's stomach.

'I suppose you're right, Marina. Are you going to do the ball, Kezia?'

'I don't know yet. I haven't decided. I'm a little tired of the benefit circuit, frankly. I've been doing that stuff for a hell of a long time.'

'Haven't we all,' Marina echoed ruefully and flicked ashes into the waiter's silent butler.

'You should get married, Kezia. It's divine.' Tiffany smiled delightedly and lifted another glass of champagne from a passing tray. It was her third since Kezia had joined them. A waltz was beginning again at the far end of the room.

'And that, my friends, is my bad luck dance.' Kezia glanced around and inwardly groaned. Where in hell was Whit?

'Bad luck? How come?'

'That's how come.' Kezia nodded quickly in the direction of the approaching Baron. He had requested the dance, and had looked high and low for her for half an hour.

'Lucky you.' Marina grinned evilly, and Tiffany did her best to focus.

'And that, Tiffany my love, is why I don't get married.'

'Kezia! Our valtz!' It was useless to protest. She nodded gracefully at her friends and departed on the arm of the Baron.

'You mean she likes him?' Tiffany looked stunned. He was really very ugly. Even drunk she knew that much.

'No, you idiot. She means that with creeps like that hounding her, who has time to find a decent guy?' Marina knew the problem only too well. She had been scouting a second husband for almost two years, and if someone halfway decent didn't hurry along pretty damn soon, her settlement would fizzle out and her tits would fall again, and she'd get waffles on her ass. She figured she had about a year to hit it lucky before the roof fell in.

'I don't know, Marina. Maybe she does like him. Kezia's a little strange, you know. Sometimes I wonder if all that money coming to her so young affected her. I mean, after all, it would affect almost anyone. It's not like you can lead a normal life when you're one of the wealthiest . . .'

'Oh for chrissake, Tiffany, shut up. And why don't you go home and sober up for a change?'

'What a rotten thing to say!' There were tears in Tiffany's eyes.

'No, Tiffany. What a rotten thing to watch.' And with that, Marina turned on her heel and vanished in the direction of Halpern Medley. She had heard that he and Lucille had just broken up. That was the best time to get them. Frightened and bruised, scared to death to manage life on their own, missing the children, lonely at night. She had three children and would be more than happy to keep Halpern busy. He was an excellent catch.

On the dance floor, Kezia was whirling slowly in the

41

arms of the Baron. Whitney was engaged in earnest conversation with a young broker with long, elegant hands. The clock on the wall struck three.

Tiffany went to sit dizzily on a red velvet banquette at the back of the room. Where was Bill? He had said something about calling Frankfurt. Frankfurt? Why Frankfurt? She couldn't remember. But he had gone out to the lobby . . . hours ago? . . . and things were beginning to whirl. Bill? She couldn't remember if he had brought her tonight, or was he out of town and had she come with Mark and Gloria? Had she . . . damn, why couldn't she remember? Let's see, she had had dinner at home with Bill and the children . . . alone with the children? . . . were the children still at the Vineyard with Mother Benjamin? . . . was. . . . Her stomach began to spin slowly with the room and she knew she was going to be sick.

'Tiffany?' It was her brother, Mark, with that look on his face, and Gloria just behind him. A wall of reproach between her and the bathroom, wherever the hell it was at whatever goddamn hotel they were in, or was this some-body's house? She couldn't remember a fucking thing, dammit.

'Mark . . . I . . .'

'Gloria, take Tiffany to the ladies' room.' He didn't waste time speaking to his sister. He simply addressed his wife. He knew the signs too well. All over the seat of the new Lincoln last time they'd driven her home. And deep within Tiffany something withered further. She knew. That was the trouble. No matter how much she drank, she always knew. She could hear the tone in their voices so clearly. That never faded.

'I . . . I'm sorry . . . Mark, Bill is out of town and if you could just drive me . . .' She belched loudly and Gloria rushed forward nervously while Mark shrank backwards with a look of disgust.

'Tiffany?' It was Bill, with his usual vague smile.

'I thought . . . you were . . .' Mark and Gloria faded into the background and Tiffany's husband took her arm and

42

escorted her as swiftly as possible from the halls where the last of the party was fading. She was too noticeable in the thinning crowd. 'I thought....' They were moving through the lobby now, and she had left her bag on the banquette. Someone would take it. 'My bag. Bill, my ...'

'That's right, dear. We'll take care of it.'

'I ... oh God, I feel awful. I have to sit down.' Her voice was barely a whisper, and her bag was forgotten. He was walking too fast, it made her feel worse.

'You just need some air.' He kept a firm grip on her arm and smiled at passersby, the director on the way to his office ... good morning ... morning ... hello ... nice to see you.... The smile never faded, and the eyes never warmed.

'I just ... I ... oh.' The cool night breeze slapped her face and she felt clearer, but her stomach rose menacingly towards her throat. 'Bill....' She turned and looked at him then, but only for a moment. She wanted to ask him a terrible question. Something was forcing her to say it. To ask. How awful. Oh God, she prayed that she wouldn't. Sometimes when she was very drunk she wanted to ask her brother the same thing. Once she had even asked her mother, and her mother had slapped her. Hard. The question always burned in her when she was this drunk. Champagne always did it to her, and sometimes gin.

'We'll just get you into a nice cosy cab, and you'll be all set, won't you dear.' He gently squeezed her arm again, like an overly solicitous headwaiter, and signalled the doorman. A cab stood with open door before them a moment later.

'A cab? Aren't you ... Bill?' Oh God, and there was the question again, trying to fight its way out of her mouth, out of her stomach, out of her soul.

'That's right, dear.' Bill had leaned over to speak to the driver. He wasn't listening. Everyone spoke over her, around her, past her, never to her. She heard him give the driver their address and she grew more confused by the moment. But Bill looked so sure. 'See you in the morning,

43

darling.' He pecked her cheek and the door slammed shut, and all she could see was the doorman's face smiling at her as the cab pulled away. She reached for the knob to open the window and frantically rolled it down ... and the question ... the question was fighting its way out. She couldn't hold it back any longer. She had to ask Bill ... William ... Billy ... they had to go back so she could ask, but the cab was lunging away from the kerb and the question sailed from her mouth with a long stream of vomit as she leaned out the window. 'Do you love me? ...'

The driver had been paid twenty dollars to get her home, and he did, without a word. He never answered the question. Nor did Bill. Bill had gone upstairs to the room he'd reserved at the St. Regis. Both girls were still waiting. A tiny Peruvian, and a large blonde from Frankfurt. And in the morning, Tiffany wouldn't even remember that she'd gone home alone. Bill was certain of that.

'Ready to go?'

'Yes, sir.' Kezia stifled a yawn and nodded sleepily at Whit.

'It was quite a party. Do you realize what time it is?'

She nodded and looked at the clock. 'Almost four. You're going to be dead at the office tomorrow.' But he was used to it. He was out almost every night in the week. Out, or at Sutton Place.

'And I can't lie in bed till noon like all of you indolent ladies.'

All of them? 'Poor, poor Whit. What a sad story.' She patted his cheek as they swept out the door and onto the deserted street. She couldn't lie in bed in the morning either. She had to start researching that new article, and wanted to be up by nine.

'Do we have anything like this on the agenda tomorrow, Kezia?' He hailed a passing cab and held the door open for her as she gathered up her blue satin skirt and settled onto the seat.

'God, I hope not. I'm out of training after the summer.'

Actually, her summer hadn't been so very different. But at least it had been blissfully devoid of the Baron.

'Come to think of it, I have a partners' dinner tomorrow night. But I think Friday there's something at the El Morocco. Are you going to be in town?' They were speeding up Park Avenue.

'As a matter of fact, I doubt it. Edward is trying to talk me into some deadly dull weekend thing with some old friends of his. They knew my father.' That was always a safe thing to say.

'Monday then. We'll have dinner at Raffles.' She smiled easily and leaned back onto his shoulder. She had lied to Whit after all. She had no plans with Edward, who knew better than to try to rope her into a weekend like the one she had described to Whit. She was going to SoHo. After tonight, she had earned it . . . and what did a little lie to Whitney matter? It was all for a good cause. Her sanity.

'Raffles on Monday sounds fine.' She'd need new material for the column by then anyway. And in the meantime, she could manage to get enough information by calling a few friends for a 'chat.' Marina was always an excellent source. And now she was going to be an excellent item as well. Her interest in Halpern Medley at the Maisonette had not gone unnoticed by Kezia. Nor had Halpern seemed indifferent to Marina. Kezia knew why Halpern was so interesting to her friend, and it was hard to blame her. Going broke was no fun, and Halpern was a most attractive remedy for what ailed her.

'I'll give you a call tomorrow or the day after, Kezia. Maybe we can sneak in a quick lunch. Lutèce, "21," we'll think of some place amusing.'

'I'm sure we will. Want to come up for a quick brandy, or coffee, or eggs or something?' It was the last thing she wanted, but she felt that she owed him something. Eggs if not sex.

'I really can't, darling. I'll be half blind at the office tomorrow as it is. I'd better get some sleep. And you too!' He wagged a finger at her as the cab drew to a halt at her door, and then kissed her ever so gently on the rim of her mouth, barely touching her lips.

'Good night, Whit. It was a lovely evening.' The preceding message was taped in Television City, Hollywood. . . .

'It's always a lovely evening with you, Kezia.' He walked her slowly to the door, and waited for the doorman to unlock it. 'Keep an eye on the papers tomorrow. I'm sure it'll be full of us. Even Martin Hallam will undoubtedly have something to say about that dress.' His eyes smiled at her appreciatively again, and he pecked her on the forehead while the doorman waited patiently. It was fascinating the way they had stopped pretending years before. A peck here and there, a grope, a feel, but she had claimed virginity long since, and he had greedily bought the story.

She waved as he walked away, and rode sleepily up to her floor. It felt good to be home. She unzipped the blue satin dress as she walked through the living room and deposited it on the couch where it could lie until Monday. Until doomsday for all she cared. What an insane way to make a living. It was like a lifetime of Halloween, trick or treat . . . getting all dressed up for a daily masquerade party to spy on your friends. This was the first 'season' when it had rankled right at the beginning. It usually took a few months to get to her. This year, the restlessness had come early.

She smoked a last cigarette, turned off the light, and it seemed as though only a few moments later the alarm was ringing. It was eight o'clock in the morning.

# CHAPTER IV

Kezia did three hours of work on the new article, outlining, sketching what she thought she knew about the women she wanted to write about, and drafting letters to key people who could tell her something more about them. It was going to be a nice solid K. S. Miller piece, and she was pleased. After that she opened her mail and sifted through it. The usual spate of invitations, a couple of 'fan' letters forwarded to her by a magazine via her agent, and a memo from Edward about some tax shelters he wanted to look into with her. None of it was interesting and she was restless. She had another article in mind; maybe that would help. A piece on child abuse in middle-class homes. It would be a hot and heavy piece if Simpson could find a market for it. She wondered if the Marshes, with their parties for a cast of thousands, ever thought of that. Child abuse. Or the slums. Or the death penalty in California. None of them were 'in' causes. If they had been, surely there would have been a benefit for them, a 'fabulous' ball, or a 'marvellous little vernissage,' something 'absolutely super' staged by a committee of beauties . . . while Marina waited for a sale at Bendel's or hunted a good knock-off at Ohrbach's, and Tiffany announced the cause as 'divine'. . . . What was happening to her, dammit? Why did it matter if Marina tried to palm off her copies as originals? So what if Tiffany was drunk every day long before noon? So fucking what? But it bothered her. Oh God, how it bothered her. Maybe a good piece of ass would calm her nerves. She was in Mark's studio by twelve-thirty.

'Wow, lady, what's with you?'
'Nothing. Why?' She stood watching him work on a gouache. She liked it. She would have liked to buy it from

47

him, but she couldn't do that, and she wouldn't let him give it to her. She knew he needed the money, and that was one commodity she was wise enough not to exchange with him.

'Well, you slammed the door, so I figured something must be bugging you.' He had given her back her keys.

'No, I'm just grumpy, I guess. Jet lag or something.' A smile broke through the anger in her eyes, and she dumped herself into a chair. 'I missed you last night. Sometimes I wish you wouldn't let me go anywhere.'

'Do I have that opinion?' He looked surprised and she laughed and kicked her shoes off.

'No.'

'That's what I thought.' It didn't seem to bother him, and Kezia was beginning to feel better.

'I like the gouache.' She looked over his shoulder as he stepped back to observe the morning's work.

'Yeah. Maybe it'll be okay.' He was demolishing a box of chocolate cookies and looking secretly pleased. Suddenly he turned to face her and slipped his arms around her. 'And what have you been up to since yesterday?'

'Oh, let's see. I read eight books, ran a mile, went to a ball, ran for president. The usual stuff.'

'And somewhere in all that bullshit lies the truth, doesn't it?' She shrugged and they exchanged a smile interspersed with kisses. He didn't really care what she did when she wasn't with him. He had his own life, his work, his loft, his friends. Her life was her own. 'Personally, I suspect that the truth is that you ran for president.'

'I just can't keep any secrets from you, Marcus.'

'No.' He said it while carefully unbuttoning her shirt. 'No secrets at all. . . . Now there's the secret I was looking for.' He tenderly uncovered one breast and leaned down to kiss it, as she slid her hands under his shirt and onto his back. 'I missed you, Kezia.'

'Not half as much as I mi sed you.' A brief flash of the evening before raced through her mind. Visions of the dancing Baron. She pulled away from Mark then and

48

smiled at him for a long moment. 'You're the most beautiful man in the world, Mark Wooly.'

'And your slave.' She laughed at him, because Mark was no one's slave and they both knew it, and then, barefoot, she darted away from him and ran behind the easel, grabbing his box of chocolate cookies as she went.

'Hey!'

'Okay, Mark, now the truth will out. What do you love more? Me or your chocolate cookies?'

'What are you, crazy or something?' He chased her behind the easel but she fled to the bedroom doorway. 'I love my chocolate cookies! What do you think?'

'Ha ha! Well, I've got them!' She ran into the bedroom and leapt onto the bed, dancing from one foot to the other, laughing, her eyes sparkling, her hair flying around her head like a flock of silky ravens.

'Give me my chocolate cookies, woman! I'm addicted!'

'Fiend!'

'Yeah!' He joined her on the bed with a gleam in his eye, took the cookies from her and flung them to the sheepskin chair, then pulled her into a tight embrace.

'Not only are you a hopeless chocoholic, Mark Wooly, but you're a sex fiend too!' She laughed the laugh of her childhood as she settled into his arms.

'You know, maybe I'm addicted to you too.'

'I doubt it.' But he pulled her down beside him, and wrapped in laughter and her long black hair, they made love.


'What do you want for dinner?' She yawned and cuddled closer to him in the comfortable bed.

'You.'

'That was lunch.'

'So? There's a law that says I can't have for dinner what I had for lunch?' He rumpled her hair, and his mouth sought her lips.

'Come on, Mark, be serious. What else do you want? Besides chocolate cookies?'

49

'Oh ... steak ... lobster ... caviar ... the usual.' He didn't know just how usual it was. 'Oh shit, I don't know. Pasta, I guess. Fettuccine maybe. Al pesto? Can you get some basil? The fresh kind?'

'You're four months late. It's out of season. How about clam sauce?'

'You're on.'

'Then I'll see you in a bit.' She ran her tongue across the small of his back, stretched once more and then hopped out of bed, just out of reach of the hand he held out for her. 'None of that, Marcus. Later. Or we'll never get dinner.'

'Screw dinner.' The light in his eyes was reviving.

'Screw you.'

'That's just what I had in mind. Now you've got the picture.' He grinned broadly as he lay on his back and watched her dress. 'You're really no fun, Kezia, but you're pretty to watch.'

'So are you.' His long frame was stretched out lazily atop the sheets. It occurred to her as she looked at him that there was nothing quite so beautiful as the bold good looks of a very young man, a very handsome young man. . . .

She left the bedroom and returned with her string bag in hand, one of his shirts knotted just under her breasts above well-tailored jeans, her hair tied in a wisp of red ribbon.

'I ought to paint you like that'

'You ought to stop being so silly. I'll get a fat head. Any special requests?' He smiled, shook his head, and she was gone, off to the market.

There were Italian markets nearby, and she always liked to shop for him. Here, the food was real. Home-made pasta, fresh vegetables, oversized fruit, tomatoes to squeeze, a whole array of sausages and cheeses waiting to be felt and sniffed and taken home for a princely repast. Long loaves of Italian bread to carry home under your arm the way they did in Europe. Bottles of Chianti dancing from hooks near the ceiling.

It was a short walk, and it was the time of day when young artists began to come out of their lairs. The end of the day, when those who worked at night began to come alive, and those who worked by day needed to stretch and walk. Later there would be more people in the streets, wandering, talking, smoking grass, drifting, stopping in at the cafés, en route to the studios of friends or someone's latest sculpture show. It was friendly in SoHo; everyone was hard at work. Companions on a shared journey of the soul. Pioneers in the world of art. Dancers, writers, poets, painters, they congregated here at the southern tip of New York, locked between the dying filth and litter of Greenwich Village and the concrete and glass of Wall Street. This was a softer place. A world of friends.

The woman in the grocery store knew her well.

'Ah signorina, comè sta?'

'Bene grazie, e lei?'

'Così così. Un po' stanca. Che cosa vorebbe oggi?'

And Kezia wandered amidst the delicious smells and chose salami, cheese, bread, onions, tomatoes. Fiorella approved of her selections. Here was a girl who knew how to buy. She knew the right salami, what to put in a sauce, how a good Bel Paese should feel. She was a nice girl. Her husband was probably Italian. But Fiorella never asked.

Kezia paid and left with the string bag full. She stopped next door to buy eggs, and down the street she went into the delicatessen for three boxes of chocolate cookies, the kind he liked best. On her way back, she strolled slowly through the ever-thickening groups on the street. The aroma of fresh bread and salami wafted around her head, the smell of marijuana hung close by, the heavy scent of espresso drifted out of the cafés, while a rich twilight sky stretched overhead. It was a beautiful September, still warm, but the air felt cleaner than it usually did, and there were pink lights in the sky, like one of Mark's early water-colours, rich in pastels. Pigeons cooed and waddled down the street, and bicycles leaned against buildings; here and there a child skipped rope.

'What'd you get?' Mark was lying on the floor, smoking a joint.

'What you ordered. Steak, lobster, caviar. The usual.'
She blew him a kiss and dropped the packages on the
narrow kitchen table.

'Yeah? You bought steak?' He looked more disappointed
than hopeful.

'No. But Fiorella says we don't eat enough salami. So I
bought a ton of that.'

'Good. She must be a trip.' Before Kezia had come into
his life, he had existed on navy beans and chocolate
cookies. Fiorella was just another part of Kezia's mystery,
one of her many gifts to him.

'She is a trip. A good trip.'

'So are you. So are you.' She stood in the kitchen
doorway, her eyes alight, a twilight glow filling the room,
and she looked back at Mark, sprawled on the floor.

'You know, once in a while I think I really love you,
Marcus.'

'Once in a while I think I love you too.'

The look they shared said a multitude of things. There was
no unpleasantness there, no pressure, no strain. No depth, but
no hassles. There was merit in that, for both of them.

'Want to go for a walk, Kezia?'

'*La passeggiata.*'

He laughed softly at the word. She always called it that.
'I haven't heard that since you went away.'

'That's what it always is to me, down here. Uptown,
people walk. They run. They go crazy. Here, they still
know how to live. Like in Europe. *Le passeggiate,* the
walks Italians take every evening at dusk, and at noon on
Sundays, in funny little old towns where most of the
women wear black and the men wear hats and white shirts,
baggy suits and no ties. Proud farmers, good people. They
check out their scene, greet their friends. They do it right,
it's an institution to them. A ritual, a tradition, and I love
it.' She looked content as she said it.

'So let's go do it.' He rose slowly to his feet, stretched
and put an arm around her shoulders. 'We can eat when
we get back.'

52

Kezia knew what that meant. Eleven, maybe twelve o'clock. First they would walk, and then they would run into friends and stop to chat on the street for a while. It would get dark and they would take refuge in someone's studio, so Mark could see the progress of a friend's latest work, and eventually the studio would grow crowded so they would all go to The Partridge for wine. And suddenly, hours later, they would be starving, and Kezia would be serving fettuccine for nine. There would be candles and music, and laughter and guitars, and joints passed around until they were tiny wisps of paper in somebody's roach clip. And Klee and Rousseau and Cassatt and Pollock would come alive in the room as their names flew among them. Paris in the days of the Impressionists must have been like that. Unloved outlaws of the art establishment banding together and forming a world of their own, to give each other laughter and courage and hope ... until one day, somebody found them, made them famous, and offered them caviar to replace the chocolate cookies. It was a shame really. For their sakes, Kezia almost hoped they would never leave the fettuccine and the dusty floors of their studios and their magic nights far behind them, because then they would wear dinner jackets and brittle smiles and sad eyes. They would dine at '21' and dance at El Morocco and go to parties at the Maisonette.

But Park Avenue was far from SoHo. A universe away. And the air was still rich with the last of summer, and the night was filled with smiles.

'Where are you off to, my love?'
'I have to go uptown to do some errands.'
'See ya later.' He wasn't paying attention to her; he was intent on a gouache.

She kissed the nape of his neck on her way past him and looked around the room with a brief, swift glance. She hated to go 'uptown.' It was as though she was always afraid she wouldn't find her way back. As though someone in her world would suspect what she'd been up to, where she had been, and might try to keep her from ever coming back here. The idea terrified her. She needed to come back, needed SoHo, and Mark, and all that they stood for. Silly really. Who could stop her from returning? Edward? Her father's ghost? How absurd. She was twenty-nine years old. Still, leaving SoHo felt like crossing the frontier into enemy territory, behind the Iron Curtain, on a scouting mission for the underground. It amused her to fantasize about it. And Mark's casual way of treating her comings and goings made it easier to float back and forth between both worlds. She laughed to herself as she ran lightly down the stairs.

It was a bright sunny morning and the subway let her out three blocks from her apartment, and the walk down Lexington Avenue and across Seventy-fourth Street was crisp. Nurses from Lenox Hill were dashing out to lunch, afternoon shoppers looked harassed, and traffic bleated angrily. Everything was so much faster here. Louder, darker, dirtier, more.

The doorman swept open the door and touched his cap. There were flowers waiting for her in the refrigerator kept by the building management for instances such as this. God forbid the roses should wilt while Madame was at the coiffeur - or in SoHo. It was the usual white box from Whit.

Kezia looked at her watch and made a rapid calculation. She had the day's calls to make on behalf of 'Martin Hallam,' snooping secretly for tidbits. And she also had the column she'd already finished which she still had to phone in to her agent. A quick bath, and then the meeting for the Arthritis Ball. First meeting of the year, and good meat for Martin Hallam. She could be back in SoHo by five, stop briefly at Fiorella's for provisions, and still be out for the nightly stroll with Mark. Perfect.

She called her service and collected her messages. A call from Edward. Two from Marina, and one from Whit, who wanted to confirm their lunch at '21' the following day. She returned the call, promised him her full attention at lunch.

54

thanked him for the roses, and listened patiently while he told her how much he missed her. Five minutes later she was in the bathtub, her mind far from Whit, and shortly thereafter she was drying herself in the big white Porthault towels discreetly monogrammed in pink. KHStM.


The meeting was at Elizabeth Morgan's house. Mrs. Angier Whimple Morgan. The third. She was Kezia's age, but looked ten years older, and her husband was trice her age. She was his third wife, the first two having conveniently died, augmenting his fortune handsomely. Elizabeth was still redoing the house. It just took 'forever to find the right pieces.'

Kezia was ten minutes late, and when she arrived, throngs of women were crowded into the hall. Two maids in crisp black uniforms offered tea sandwiches, and there was lemonade on a long silver tray. The butler was discreetly taking orders for drinks. And he was getting a lot more business than the long silver tray.

The couch and Louis XV *fauteuils* ('Imagine, eight of them, darling, from Christie's! And all in one day! You know, the Richley estate, and signed too!') were cluttered with the older women on the committee, enthroned like heads of state, clanking gold bracelets and covered with pearls, wearing 'good' suits and 'marvellous' hats, a host of Balenciaga and Chanel. They eyed the younger women carefully, criticism rich on their minds.

The room had a ceiling the height of two floors; the mantel was French, a 'marvellous' marble, Louis XVI, and the ghastly chandelier had been a wedding present from Elizabeth's mother. Fruitwood tables, an inlaid desk, an ormolu chest, Chippendale, Sheraton, Hepplewhite – it all looked to Kezia like Sotheby's the day before auction.

The 'girls' were given half an hour of grace before coming to order, and then their attention was demanded at the front of the room. Courtnay St. James was in charge.

'Well, ladies, welcome home from the summer. And doesn't everyone look just marvellous!' She was heftily poured into a navy silk suit that crushed her ample bosom and struggled over her hips. A sapphire brooch of considerable size adorned her lapel, her pearls were in place, her hat matched her dress, and three or four rings that had been born with her hands waved her demi-glasses at the 'girls' as she spoke. 'And now, let's get organized for our marvellous, marvellous fete! It's going to be at the Plaza this year.' Surprise! Surprise! The Plaza and not the Pierre. How terribly, terribly exciting!

There was a murmur among the women, and the butler silently circulated his tray at the edge of the crowd. Tiffany was first on line, and seemed to weave as she stood, smiling amiably at her friends. Kezia looked away and let her eyes comb the crowd. They were all here, all the same faces, and one or two new ones, but even the newcomers were not strangers. They had just added this committee to their myriad others. There were no outsiders, no one who didn't belong. One couldn't let just anyone work on the Arthritis Ball, could one? 'But my dear, you must understand, you do remember who her mother was, don't you?' Last year, Tippy Walgreen had tried to introduce one of her strange little friends to the group. 'I mean, after all, everyone knew her mother was half-Jewish! I mean, really, Tippy, you'll *embarrass* the girl!'

The meeting droned on. Assignments were given. Meeting schedules decided. Twice a week for seven long months. It would give the women a reason for living and a motive for drinking – at least four martinis per meeting if they caught the butler's eye often enough. He would continue his rounds, ever discreet, while the pitcher of lemonade remained almost full.

As usual, Kezia accepted her role as head of the Junior Committee. As long as she was in town, it was useful for the column to do it. And it meant nothing more than being sure that all the right debutantes came to the Ball, and that a chosen few of them were allowed to lick stamps. An honour which would enchant their mothers. 'The Arthritis Ball, Peggy? How nifty!' Nifty . . . nifty . . . nifty. . . .

The meeting broke up at five, with at least half of the women comfortably tight, but not so much so that they couldn't go home and face their husbands with the usual 'You know how Elizabeth is, she just forces it on you.' And Tiffany would tell Bill it had all been divine. If he came home. The gossip that Kezia was hearing about Tiffany these days was growing unpleasant.

The echoes she heard brought back other memories, memories that were long gone but would never quite be forgotten. Memories of reproaches she had heard from behind closed doors, warnings, and the sounds of someone violently sick to her stomach. Her mother. Like Tiffany. She hated watching Tiffany now. There was too much pain in her eyes, shoddily wrapped in 'divine' and bad jokes and that vague glazed look that said she didn't know exactly where she was or why.

Kezia looked at her watch in annoyance. It was almost five-thirty, and she didn't want to bother stopping at home to get out of the little Chanel number she'd worn. Mark would survive it. And with luck, he'd be too wrapped up in his easel to notice. If he ever got a chance to notice; at that hour it was almost impossible to catch a cab. She looked at the street in dismay. Not a vacant cab in sight.

'Want a ride?' The voice was only a few feet away, and she turned in surprise. It was Tiffany, standing beside a sleek navy blue Bentley with liveried chauffeur. The car was her mother-in-law's, as Kezia knew.

'Mother Benjamin lent me the car.' Tiffany looked apologetic. In the late afternoon sunlight, away from the world of parties and facades, Kezia saw a so much older version of her school friend, with wrinkles of sadness and betrayal around her eyes, and a sallow look to her skin. She had been so pretty in school, and still was, but she was losing it now. It reminded Kezia again of her mother. She could hardly bear to look into Tiffany's eyes.

'Thanks, love, but I don't want to take you out of your way.'

'Hell, you don't live very far . . . do you?' She smiled a

tired smile which made her look almost young again. As though being out with the grown-ups was just too much for her, and now it was time to go home. She had had just enough to drink to make her begin to forget things again. Kezia had lived in the same place for years.

'No, I don't live very far, Tiffie, but I'm not going home.'

'That's okay.' She looked so lonely, so in need of a friend. Kezia couldn't say no. Tears were welling up in her throat.

'Okay, thanks.' Kezia smiled and approached the car, forcing herself to think of other things. She couldn't cry in front of the girl, for God's sake. Cry about what? Her mother's death, twenty years later . . . or for this girl who was already halfway dead? Kezia wouldn't let herself think about it, as she sank into the gentle upholstery in the back seat. The bar was already open. 'Mother Benjamin' kept quite a stock.

'Harley, we're out of bourbon again.'

'Yes, madam.' Harley remained expressionless and Tiffany turned to Kezia with a smile.

'Want a drink?'

Kezia shook her head. 'Why don't you wait 'til you get home?' Tiffany nodded, holding the glass in her hand and gazing out the window. She was trying to remember if Bill was coming home for dinner. She thought he was in London for three days, but she wasn't sure if that was next week . . . or last week.

'Kezia?'

'Yes?' Kezia sat very still as Tiffany tried to make her mind stick to one thought.

'Do you love me?' Kezia was stunned, and Tiffany looked horrified. She had been absent-minded and it had slipped out. The question again. The demon that haunted her. 'I . . . I'm sorry . . . I . . . I was thinking of someone else. . . .' There were tears flooding Kezia's eyes now as Tiffany brought her gaze from the window to rest on Kezia's face.

'It's all right, Tiffie. It's okay.' She put her arms around her friend and there was a long moment of silence. The chauffeur glanced into the rearview mirror, then hastily averted his eyes and sat rigid, behind the wheel, patient, imperturbable and profoundly and eternally discreet. Neither of the young women noted his presence. They had been brought up to think that way. He waited a full five minutes while the women in the back seat sat hugged wordlessly and there was the sound of gentle weeping. He wasn't sure which woman was crying.

'Madam?'

'Yes, Harley?' Tiffany sounded very young and very hoarse.

'Where are we taking Miss Saint Martin?'

'Oh ... I don't know.' She dried her eyes with one gloved hand, and looked at Kezia with a half smile. 'Where are you going?'

'I ... the Sherry-Netherland. Can you drop me off there?'

'Sure.' The car had already started, and the two settled back in their seat, holding hands between fine beige kid and black suede and saying nothing. There was nothing either could say: too much would have to be said if either of them ever began to try. The silence was easier. Tiffany wanted to invite Kezia home to dinner, but she couldn't remember if Bill was in town, and he didn't like her friends. He wanted to be able to read the work he brought home after dinner, or go out to his meetings, without feeling he had to stick around and make chitchat. Tiffany knew the rules. No one to dinner, except when Bill brought them home. It had been years since she'd tried ... that was why ... that was how ... in the beginning, she had been so lonely. With Daddy gone, and Mother ... well, Mother ... and she had thought babies of their own ... but Bill didn't want them around either. Now the children ate at five-thirty with Nanny Singleton in the kitchen, and Nanny thought it 'unwise' for Tiffany to eat with them. It made the children 'uncomfortable.' So she ate alone in the dining room at seven-thirty. She wondered if Bill would be home for dinner tonight, or just how angry he would be if. . . .

'Kezia?'

'Hm?' Kezia had been lost in her own painful thoughts, and she had had a dull pain in her stomach for the last twenty minutes. 'Yes?'

'Why don't you come to dinner tonight?' She looked like a little girl with a brilliant idea.

'Tiffie . . . it . . . I . . . I'm sorry, love, but I just can't.' She couldn't do that to herself. And she had to see Mark. Had to. Needed to. Her survival came first, and the day had already been trying enough. 'I'm sorry.'

'That's okay. Not to worry.' She kissed Kezia gently on the cheek as Harley drew up to the Sherry-Netherland, and the hug they exchanged was ferocious, born of the longing of one and the other's remorse.

'Take good care, will you?'

'Sure.'

'Call me sometime soon?'

Tiffany nodded.

'Promise?'

'Promise.'

Tiffany looked old again as they exchanged a last smile, and Kezia waved once as she disappeared into the lobby. She waited five minutes and then came out and hailed a cab, and sped south to SoHo, trying to forget the anguish in Tiffany's eyes. Driving north, Tiffany poured herself one more quick Scotch.


'My God, it's Cinderella! What happened to my shirt?'

'I didn't think you'd notice. Sorry, love, I left it at my place.'

'I can spare it. It is Cinderella, isn't it? Or are you running for president again?' He was leaning against the wall, observing the day's work, but his smile told her he was glad she was back home with him.

'State senator, actually. Running for president is so

60

obvious.' She grinned at him and shrugged. 'I'll get out of this stuff and go get some food.'

'Before you do, Madam Senator . . .' He walked purposefully towards her with a mischievous grin.

'Oh?' The suit jacket was already off, her hair down, her blouse half-unbuttoned.

'Yes, "oh." I missed you today.'

'I didn't even think you'd notice I was gone. You looked busy when I left.'

'Well, I'm not busy now.' He swept her into his arms, her stockinged feet dangling over his arms, her black hair sweeping his face. 'You look pretty all dressed up. Sort of like that girl I saw in the paper while you were gone, but nicer. Much, much nicer. She looked like a bitch.' Kezia let her head fall back gently against his chest as she began to laugh.

'And I'm not a bitch?'

'Never, Cinderella, never.'

'What illusions you have.'

'Only about you.'

'Fool. Sweet, sweet fool. . . .' She kissed him gently on the mouth, and in a moment the rest of her clothes marked a path to his bed. It was dark by the time they got up.

'What time is it?'

'Must be about ten.' She stretched and yawned. It was dark in the apartment. Mark leaned out of bed to light a candle and then snuggled back into her arms. 'Want to go out for dinner?'

'No.'

'Me neither, but I'm hungry, and you didn't buy any food, did you?' She shook her head. 'I was in too much of a hurry to get home. Somehow I was more anxious to see you than to see Fiorella.'

'No big deal. We can sup on peanut butter and Oreos.'

She answered with a choking sound and a hand clasped to her throat. Then she laughed and they kissed and they made their way to the bathtub where they splashed each other generously before sharing his one purple towel. With no monogram. From Korvette's.

She was thinking, as she dried herself, that SoHo had come too late for her. Maybe at twenty it would have seemed real, perhaps then she might have believed it. Now it was fun ... special ... lovely ... Mark's, but not hers. Other places belonged to her, all those places she didn't even want, but inadvertently owned.

'Do you dig what you do, Kezia?' She paused for a long moment before answering, and then shrugged.

'Maybe yes, maybe no, maybe I don't even know.'

'Maybe you ought to figure it out.'

'Yeah. Maybe I should figure it out before noon tomorrow.' She had remembered the luncheon engagement with Whit.

'Is there some big deal tomorrow?' He looked puzzled, and she shook her head as they shared a handful of cookies and the last of the wine.

'Nope. No big deal tomorrow.'

'You made it sound like there was.'

'Nope. As a matter of fact, my love, I've just decided that when you reach my age very little is a "big deal." ' Not even you, or your lovemaking, or your sweet delicious young body, or my own bloody life. . . .

'May I quote you, Methuselah?'

'Absolutely. They've been quoting me for years.' And then in the clear autumn night, she laughed.

'What's so funny?'

'Everything. Absolutely everything.'

'I think you're drunk.' The idea amused him, and for a moment she wished that she were.

'Only a little drunk on life maybe ... your kind of life.'

'Why my kind of life? Can't this be your kind of life too? What's so different about your life and my life for christsake?'

Oh Jesus. This wasn't the time.

'The fact that I'm running for state senator, of course!'

He pulled her around to face him as she tried to laugh him off.

'Kezia, why can't you be straight with me? Sometimes

62

you give me the feeling that I don't even know who you are.' His grip on her arm troubled her, almost as much as the question in his eyes. But she only shrugged with an evasive smile. 'Well, I'll tell you, Cinderella, whoever you are, I think you're gassed.' They both laughed as she followed him into the bedroom, and she wiped two silent, unseen tears from her cheeks. He was a nice boy, but he didn't know her. How could he? She wouldn't let him know her. He was only a boy.

## CHAPTER V

'Miss Saint Martin, how nice to see you!'
    'Thank you, Bill. Is Mr. Hayworth here yet?'
    'No, but we have the table waiting. May I show you in?'
    'No, thank you. I'll wait at the fireplace.'
    The '21' Club was crammed with lunch-hungry bodies. Business executives, high-fashion models, well-known actors, producers, the gods of the publishing world, and a handful of dowagers. The Scions of Meccas. The restaurant was alive with success. The fireplace was a peaceful corner where Kezia could wait before entering the whirling currents with Whit. '21' was fun but she wasn't quite in the mood.
    She hadn't wanted to come to lunch. It was strange the way it was all getting a little bit harder. Maybe she was getting too old for a double life. Her thoughts turned to Edward. Maybe she'd see him at '21' for lunch, but he was more likely to be found at Lutèce or the Mistral. His luncheon leanings were usually French.
    'How do you suppose the children would feel about it if we took them to Palm Beach? I don't want them to feel I'm pushing out their father.' The wisp of conversation made Kezia turn her head. Well, well, Marina Walters and

Halpern Medley. Things were certainly progressing. Item One for tomorrow's news. They hadn't seen her discreetly folded in one of the large red leather chairs. The advantage of being small. And quiet.

And then she saw Whit, elegant and youthful and tanned, in a dark grey suit and Wedgewood blue shirt. She waved at him and he walked over to her chair.

'You're looking awfully well today, Mr. Hayworth.' She held out a hand to him from her comfortable seat, and he kissed her wrist lightly, then clasped her fingers loosely in his.

'I feel a lot better than I did with a jeroboam of champagne under my belt the other night. How did you weather that?'

'Very nicely, thank you. I slept all day,' she lied. 'And you?' She smiled at him and they began to thread their way towards the dining room.

'Don't make me jealous. Your sleep-ins are an outrage!'

'Ah, Mr. Hayworth! Miss Saint Martin . . .' the head-waiter led them to Whitney's customary table, and Kezia settled in and looked around. Same old faces, same old crowd. Even the models looked familiar. Warren Beatty sat at a corner table, and Babe Paley had just walked in.

'What did you do last night, Kezia?' Her smile was one he could not read.

'I played bridge.'

'You look like you must have won.'

'As a matter of fact, I did. I've been on a winning streak since I got home.'

'I'm glad for you. Me, I've been losing at backgammon consistently for the past four weeks. Bitching rotten luck.' But he didn't look overly worried, as he patted her hand gently and signalled to the waiter. Two Bloody Marys and a double steak tartare. The usual. 'Darling, do you want wine?' She shook her head. The Bloody Marys would be fine.

It was a quick lunch; he had to be back in the office at two. Now that the summer was over, it was business as usual: new wills, new trusts, new babies, new divorces, new season. It was almost like a whole new year. Like children returning to school, socialites marked the years by 'the season', and the season had just begun.

'Will you be in town this weekend, Kezia?' He seemed distracted as he hailed her a cab.

'No. Remember? I have that weekend thing with Edward.'

'Oh, that's right. Good. Then I won't feel like such a meanie. I'm going to Quogue with some business associates. But I'll call you on Monday. Will you be all right?' The question amused her.

'I'll be fine.' She slid gracefully into the cab, and smiled up into his eyes. Business associates, darling? 'Thanks for the lunch.'

'See you Monday.' He waved again as the cab pulled away, and she sighed comfortably from the back seat. Finito. She was off the hook till Monday. But suddenly, there was nothing but lies.

The weekend was perfect. Bright sunny skies, a light breeze, little pollution and a low pollen count, and she and Mark had painted the bedroom a bright cornflower blue. 'In honour of your eyes,' he told her as she worked diligently around the window. It was a bitch of a job, but when they had finished, they were both immensely pleased.

'How about a picnic to celebrate?' He was in high spirits and so was she.

She ran down to Fiorella's for provisions, while he called around to borrow a car. A friend of George's offered his van.

'Where are we going, sire?'

'Treasure Island. My own treasure island.' And he began to sing snatches of absurd songs about islands, interspersed with a great many cackles and guffaws.

'Mark Wooly, you're a madman.'

'That's cool, Cinderella. As long as you dig it.' There was no malice in the 'Cinderella'. They were too happy and it was too fine a day. And Mark had never been malicious.

He took her to a little island in the East River, a nameless gem near Randall's Island. They looped off the highway, and through litter and a bumpy little road that seemed to go nowhere, crossed a small bridge, and suddenly ... magic! A lighthouse and a crumbling castle all their own.

'It looks like the fall of the House of Usher.'

'Yes, and it's all mine. And now it's yours, too. Nobody ever comes here.' New York gazed sombrely at them from across the river, the United Nations, the Chrysler Building and the Empire State looking sleek and polite, as the happy pair lay on the grass and opened a bottle of Fiorella's best Chianti. Tugboats and ferries floated past, and they waved to captains and crewmen and laughed at the sky.

'What a beautiful day!'

'Yeah, it really is.' He put his head in her lap and she leaned down and kissed him.

'Want some more wine, Mr. Wooly?'

'No, just a slice of the sky.'

'At your service, sir.'

Clouds were gathering, and it was four in the afternoon when the first lightning flashed past the clouds.

'I think you're going to get that slice of sky you ordered. In about five minutes. See how good I am to you? Your wish is my command.'

'Baby, you're terrific.' He sprang to his feet and flung out his arms, and in five minutes it was pouring rain and lightning flashed and thunder roared, and they ran around the island together hand in hand, laughing and soaked to the skin.

When they got home, they showered together, and the hot water felt prickly on their chilled bodies. They walked naked into the new blue bedroom, and lay peacefully in each other's arms.

She left him at six the next morning. He slept like a child, his head on his arms, his hair hiding his eyes, his lips soft to her touch.

'Goodbye, my beloved, sleep tight.' She kissed him gently on one temple, and whispered into his hair. It would be noon before he awoke, and she would be far from him by then. In a different world, chasing dragons, making choices.

## CHAPTER VI

'Good morning, Miss Saint Martin. I'll tell Mr. Simpson you're here.'

'Thanks, Pat. How've you been?'

'Busy, crazy. Seems like everyone has a new idea for a book after the summer. Or a new manuscript, or a royalty cheque that got lost.'

'Yeah, I know what you mean.' Kezia smiled ruefully, thinking of her own plans for a book.

The secretary took a quick look at her desk, gathered up some papers, and disappeared behind a heavy oak door. The literary agency of Simpson, Wells, and Jones did not look very different from Edward's law firm, or Whit's office, or the brokerage house that had the bulk of her account. This was serious business. Long shelves of books, wood panelling, bronze door handles, and a thick carpet the colour of Burgundy wine. Sober. Impressive. Prestigious. She was represented by a highly reputable firm. It was why she had felt comfortable sharing her secret with Jack Simpson. He knew who she was, and only he and Edward knew of her numerous aliases. And Simpson's staff, of course, but they were unfailingly discreet. The secret had remained well guarded.

'Mr. Simpson will see you now, Miss Saint Martin.'

'Thank you, Pat.'

He was waiting for her on his feet behind the desk, a kindly man close to Edward's age, balding and grey at the temples, with a broad fatherly smile, and comforting hands. They shook hands as they always did. And she settled into the chair across from him, stirring the tea Pat had provided. It was peppermint tea today. Sometimes it was English Breakfast, and in the afternoon it was always Earl Grey. Jack Simpson's office was a haven for her, a place to relax and unwind. A place for excitement about the work she had done. She was always happy there.

'I have another commission for you, my dear.'

'Lovely. What?' She looked up expectantly over the gold-rimmed cup.

'Well, let's talk for a moment first.' There was something different in his eyes today. Kezia wondered what it was. 'This is a little different from what you usually do.'

'Pornography?' She sipped the tea and half suppressed a smile. Simpson chuckled.

'So that's what you want to do, is it?' She laughed back at him and he lit a cigar. These were from Dunhill, not Cuba. She sent him a box every month. 'Well, I'm sorry to disappoint you then. It's definitely not pornography. It's an interview.' He watched her eyes carefully. She so easily got the look of a hunted doe. There were some zones of her life where even he would not dare to tread.

'An interview?' Something closed in her face. 'Well, then I guess that's that. Anything else on the agenda?'

'No, but I think we ought to talk about this a little further. Have you ever heard of Lucas Johns?'

'I'm not sure. The name says something to me, but I can't place it.'

'He's a very interesting man. Mid-thirties, spent six years in prison in California for armed robbery, and served his sentence in Folsom, San Quentin – all the legendary horror spots one hears about. Well, he lived through them, and survived. He was among the first to organize labour unions inside the prisons, and make a lot of noise about prisoners' rights. And he still keeps a hand in it now that he's out. I gather that's his whole life; he lives for the cause of abolishing prisons, and bettering the prisoners' lot in the meantime. Even refused his first parole because he hadn't finished what he'd started. The second time they offered him parole, they didn't give him a choice. They wanted him out of their hair, so he got out and got organized on the outside. He's had a tremendous impact on the public awareness in terms of what really happens in our prisons. Matter of fact, he wrote a very powerful book on the subject when he first got out a year or two ago, can't quite remember when. It got him a lot of speaking engagements, television appearances, that sort of thing. And it's all the more amazing that he'd do that, since he's still on parole. I imagine it must be risky for him to remain controversial.'

'I would think so.'

'He served six years of his sentence, but he's not a free man. As I understand it, they have some sort of system in California called the indeterminate sentence, which means you get sentenced rather vaguely. I think in his case the sentence was five years to life. He served six. I suppose he could have served ten or twenty, at the discretion of the prison authorities, but I imagine they got tired of having him around. To say the least.'

Kezia nodded, intrigued. Simpson had counted on that.

'Did he kill anyone in the robbery?'

'No, I'm fairly certain he didn't. Just hell-raising, I think. He had a rather wild youth, from what I gathered in his book. Got most of his education in prison, finished high school, got a college degree, and a master's in psychology.'

'Industrious in any case. Has he been in trouble since he got out?'

'Not that kind of trouble. He seems to be past that now. The only trouble I'm aware of is that he is dancing a tightrope with the publicity he gets for his agitation on behalf of prisoners. And the reason for this interview now is that he has another book coming out, a very uncompromising exposé of existing conditions, and his views on the subject are sort of a follow-up to the first book, but a good deal more brutal. It's going to create quite a furore, from what I hear. This is a good time for a piece about him, Kezia. And you'd be a good one to write it. You did those two articles on the prison riots in Mississippi last year. This isn't unfamiliar territory to you, not entirely.'

'This isn't a documented piece on a news event either. It's an interview, Jack.' Her eyes sought his and held them. 'And you know I don't do interviews. Besides, he's not talking about Mississippi. He's talking about California prisons. And I don't know anything more about them than what I read in the paper, just like everyone else.' It was a weak excuse, and they both knew it.

'The principles are the same, Kezia. You know that. And the piece we've been offered is about Lucas Johns, not the California prison system. He can tell you plenty about that. You can read his first book for that matter. That'll tell you all you need to know, if you can stomach it.'

'What's he like?'

Simpson restrained a smile at the question. Maybe . . . maybe . . . He frowned and replaced his cigar in the ashtray. 'Strange, interesting, powerful, very closed and very open. I've seen him speak, but I've never met him. One gets the impression that he'll tell anyone anything about prisons, but nothing about himself. He'd be a challenge to interview. I'd say he's very guarded, but appealing in an odd way. He looks like a man who fears nothing because he has nothing to lose.'

'Everyone has something to lose, Jack.'

'You're thinking of yourself, my dear, but some don't. Some have already lost all they care about. He had a wife and child before he went to prison. The child died in a hit-and-run accident, and the wife committed suicide two years before his release. Maybe he's one of those who has already lost. . . . Something like that can break you. Or give you an odd kind of freedom. I think he has that. He's something of a god to those who know him well. You'll hear a lot of conflicting reports about him – warm, loving, kind, or ruthless, brutal, cold. It depends on whom you speak to. In his own way, he's something of a legend, and a mystery. No one seems to know the man underneath.'

70

'You seem to know a lot about him.'

'He interests me. I've read his book, seen him speak, and I did a little research before I asked you to come in and discuss this with me, Kezia. It's just the kind of piece I think you might be brilliant with. In his own way, he's as hidden as you are. Maybe it'll teach you something. And it's going to be a piece that will be noticed.'

'Which is precisely why I can't do it.' She was suddenly firm again, but for a little while she had wavered. Simpson still had hope.

'Oh? Obscurity is now something you desire?'

'Not obscurity, discretion. Anonymity. Peace of mind. None of this is new to you. We've gone over it before.'

'In theory. Not in practice. And right now you have a chance to do an article that would not only interest you, but would be an extremely good opportunity for you professionally, Kezia. I can't let you pass that up. Not without telling you why I think you ought to do it, in any case. I think you'd be a fool not to.'

'And a bigger fool yet if I did it. I can't. I have too much at stake. How could I even interview him without causing a certain "furore" myself, as you call it. From what you're telling me, he's not a man who passes unnoticed. And just how long do you think it would take for someone else to notice me? Or Johns himself, for that matter. He'd probably know who I am.' She shook her head with certainty now.

'He's not that sort of man, Kezia. He doesn't give a damn about the social register, the debutante cotillions or anything else that happens in your world. He's too busy in his own. I'd be willing to bet he's never even heard your name. He's from California, he bases himself in the Midwest now, he's probably never been to Europe, and you can be damn sure that he doesn't read the social pages.'

'You can't be sure of that.'

'I'd almost swear to it. I can sense what he is, and I already know what he cares about. Exclusively. He's a rebel, Kezia. A self-educated, intelligent, totally devoted

71

rebel. Not a playboy. For God's sake, girl, be sensible. This is your career you're playing with. He's giving a speech in Chicago next week, and you could cover that easily, and quietly. An interview with him in his offices the next day, and that's it. No one at the speech will know you, and I'm certain that he won't. There's no reason at all why K. S. Miller won't cover you adequately. And that's all he'll know or care about. He'll be much more interested in the kind of coverage you're giving him than in what you do with your private life. That's just not the sort of thing he thinks about.'

'Is he a homosexual?'

'Possibly, I don't know. I don't know what a man does during six years in prison. Nor does it matter. The point is what he stands for, and how he stands for it. That's the crux here. And if I thought, even for a moment, that writing this piece would cause you embarrassment, I wouldn't suggest it. You should know that by now. All I can tell you is that I am emphatically sure that he won't have the faintest idea about, or interest in, your private life.'

'But there's no way you can be sure of that. What if he's an adventurer, a sharp con man, who picks up on who I am, and figures out some angle where that could be useful to him? He could turn right around and have me all over the papers just for interviewing him.'

Simpson began to look impatient. He stubbed out the cigar.

'Look, you've written about events, places, political happenings, psychological profiles. You've done some excellent work, but you've never done a piece like this. I think you could do it. And do it well. And I think you should. It's a major opportunity for you, Kezia. And the point is: are you a writer or not?'

'Obviously. But it just seems terribly unwise to me. Like a breach of my personal rules. I've had peace for seven years because I've been totally, utterly, and thoroughly careful. If I start doing interviews now, and if I do this one . . . there will be others, and . . . no. I just can't.'

72

'Why not at least give it some thought? I have his last book, if you want to read it. I really think you should at least do that much before you make up your mind.'

She hesitated for a long moment and then nodded carefully. It was the only concession she would make; she was still sure she wouldn't do the piece. She couldn't afford to. Maybe Lucas Johns had nothing left to lose, but she did; she had everything to lose. Her peace of mind, and the carefully guarded secret life she had taken so long to build. That life was what kept her going. She wouldn't do anything to jeopardize it, not for anyone. Not for Mark Wooly, not for Jack Simpson, and not for some unknown ex-con with a hot 'cause'. To hell with him. No one was worth it.

'All right, I'll read the book.' She smiled for the first time in half an hour, then shook her head ruefully. 'You certainly know how to sell your arguments. Wretch!'

But Simpson knew he had not yet convinced her. All he could hope was that her own curiosity and Lucas Johns' written words would do the job. He felt in his bones that she had to do this one, and he was seldom wrong.

'Simpson, you really are a first-water wretch! You make it sound like my whole career depends on this . . . or my life even.'

'Perhaps it does. And you, my dear, are a first-water writer. But I think you're getting to a point when you have to make some choices. And the fact is that they're not going to be easy whether you make them now, over this particular article, or later, over something else. My main concern is that you make those choices, and don't just let life, and your career, pass you by.'

'I didn't think that "life" or my career was passing me by.'' She raised an eyebrow cynically, amused. It was unlike him to be so concerned, or so outspoken.

'No, you've done well until now. There has been a healthy progression, a good evolution, but only to a point. The crunch is bound to come sometime though. That moment when you can't "get by" anymore, when you can't just "organize" everything to suit all your needs. You'll have to decide what you really want, and act on it.'

'And you don't think I've been doing that?' She was surprised when he shook his head.

'You haven't had to. But I think it's time you did.'

'Such as?'

'Such as who do you want to be? K. S. Miller, writing serious pieces that could really further your career, or Martin Hallam tattling on your friends under a pseudonym, or the Honourable Kezia Saint Martin sweeping in and out of debutante balls and the Tour d'Argent in Paris? You can't have it all, Kezia. Not even you.'

'Don't be absurd, Simpson.' He was making her distinctly uncomfortable, and all over this article about an ex-convict labour agitator. Nonsense. 'You know perfectly well that the Hallam column is a joke to me,' she said, annoyed. 'I never really took it seriously, and certainly not in the last five years. And you also know that my career as K. S. Miller is what really matters to me. The deb parties and dinners at the Tour d'Argent, as you put it,' she glowered at him pointedly, 'are something I do to pass time, out of habit, and to keep the Hallam column lively. I don't sell my soul for that way of life.' But she knew too well that that was a lie.

'I'm not sure that's true, and if it is you might well find that sooner or later the price you will have to pay is your soul, or your career.'

'Don't be so dramatic.'

'Not dramatic. Honest. And concerned.'

'Well, don't be "concerned", not in that area. You know what I have to do, what's expected of me. You don't change hundreds of years of tradition in a few short years at a typewriter. Besides, lots of writers work under pseudonyms.'

'Yes, but they don't live under pseudonyms. And I disagree with you about changing traditions. You're right on one score, you don't change traditions in a few years. You change them suddenly, brutally, with a bloody revolution.'

'I don't think that's necessary.'

'Or "civilized", is that it? No, you're right, it's not civilized. Revolution never is, and change is never comfortable. I'm beginning to think you ought to read Johns' book for your own sake. In your own way, you've been in prison for almost thirty years.' His voice softened as he looked into her eyes. 'Kezia, is that how you want to live? At the expense of your happiness?'

'It isn't a question of that. And sometimes there's no choice.' She looked away from him, partly annoyed, partly hurt.

'But that's precisely what we're discussing. And there is always a choice.' Or didn't she see that? 'Are you going to live your life for an absurd "duty", to please your trustee ten years after you come of age? Are you going to cater to parents who have been dead for twenty years? How can you possibly expect that of yourself? Why? Because they died? That's not your fault for God's sake, and times have changed; you've changed. Or is this what that young man you're engaged to expects of you? If that's the case, perhaps the time will come when you'll have to choose between him and your work, and maybe you'd best face that now.'

What man? Whit? How ridiculous. And why was Simpson bringing all of this up now? He had never mentioned any of this before. Why now? 'If you mean Whitney Hayworth, I'm not engaged to him, and never will be. He could never cost me anything except a very dull evening. So you're worrying for naught on that score.'

'I'm glad to hear it. But then what is it, Kezia? Why the double life?' She sighed deeply and looked down at her hands folded in her lap.

'Because somewhere along the way they convince you that if you drop the Holy Grail for even one instant, or put it aside for a day, the entire world will collapse, and it will all be your fault.'

'Well, I'll tell you a well-hidden secret, it won't. The world will not end. Your parents will not haunt you; your

75

trustee won't even commit suicide. Live for yourself, Kezia. You really have to. How long can you live a lie?'

'Is a pseudonym a lie?' It was a weak defence, and she knew it.

'No, but the way you handle it is. You use your pseudonyms to keep two lives totally estranged from each other. Two sides of you. One is duty and the other is love. You're like a married woman with a lover, prepared to give up neither. I think that's an awesome burden to carry. And an unnecessary one.' He looked at his watch and shook his head with a small smile. 'And now, I apologize. I've railed at you for almost an hour. But these are things I've wanted to discuss with you for a very long time. Do what you want on the Johns article, but give a little thought to what we've said. I think it's important.'

'I suspect you're right.' She was suddenly exhausted. The morning had drained her. It was like watching her whole life pass before her eyes. And how insignificant it looked in review. Simpson was right. She didn't know what she'd do about the Johns piece, and that wasn't the point. The point went a great deal deeper than that. 'I'll read the Johns book tonight.'

'Do that, and call me tomorrow. I can hold the magazine off till then. And will you forgive me for preaching?'

She smiled at him, a warmer smile. 'Only if you'll let me thank you. You didn't say anything I wanted to hear, but I think I needed to hear it. I've been thinking along those lines myself lately, and this morning arguing with you was like arguing with myself. Sweet schizophrenia.'

'Nothing as exotic as that. And you're not unique; others have fought the same battle before you. One of them should have written a book on how to survive it.'

'You mean others have survived it?' She laughed over a last sip of her tea.

'Very nicely in fact.'

'And then what did they do? Run off with the elevator man to prove their point?'

'Some. The stupid ones. The others find better solutions.'

She tried not to think of her mother.

'Like Lucas Johns?' She didn't know why, but it had just slipped out. The idea was absurd. Almost funny.

'Hardly. I wasn't suggesting that you marry him, my dear. Only interview him. No wonder you made such a fuss.' Jack Simpson knew the real reasons for the fuss. She was afraid. And in his own way, he had tried to calm her fears. Only one interview . . . once. It could change so much for her – broaden her horizons, bring her out in the open, make her a writer. If only all went well. It was only because he knew the chances of her being 'found out' were so unlikely that he'd even encouraged it. She would hide forever if she got burned on this one, and he knew it. Neither of them could afford that. He had thought it all over with great care, before suggesting the article to her.

'You know, you made a great deal of sense today, Jack. I must admit, lately the "mystery" has been wearing thin. It loses its charm after a while.' And what he had said had been true. She was like a married woman with a lover. She had just never thought of it that way . . . Edward, Whit, the parties, the committees; and then Mark and SoHo and picnics on magical islands; and separate from all that, her work. Nothing fit. It was all separate and hidden, and had long since begun to tear her apart. To what and to whom did she owe her first allegiance? To herself, of course, but it was so easy to forget that. Until someone reminded her, as Jack Simpson had just done. 'Will you tolerate a hug, kind sir?'

'Not tolerate – appreciate, my dear. I would thoroughly enjoy it.' She gave him a brief squeeze and a smile as she prepared to leave.

'It's a damn shame you didn't make that speech ten years ago. It's almost a little late now.'

'At twenty-nine? Don't be foolish. Now go away, and read that book, and call me tomorrow morning.' She left him with a last wave of a brown-kid-gloved hand, and a flurry of long suede coat.

The book jacket in her hand looked unimpressive as

77

she perused it in the elevator. There was no photograph of Lucas Johns on the back, only a brief biography which told her less about him than Simpson had. It was odd, though; from what she had heard that morning, she already had a clear picture of the man. She anticipated something mean in his face, was sure he was short, stocky, hard, and perhaps overweight – and pushy as hell. Six years in prison had to do strange things to a man, and it surely couldn't add to his beauty. Armed robbery too . . . a little fat man in a liquor store with a gun. And now he was respected, and she was being offered a chance to interview him. Still, despite all the talk with Simpson, she knew she couldn't do that. He had made some good points about her life . . . but an interview with Lucas Johns, or anyone, was still out of the realm of the possible, or the wise.

She did something foolish then. She went to lunch with Edward.

'I don't think you should do it.' He was emphatic.

'Why not?' It was almost like setting a trap for him; she knew what he'd say. But she couldn't resist the urge to bait him.

'You know why not. If you start doing interviews, it's only one step away from someone catching on to what you're up to. You might get away with this one, Kezia. But sooner or later . . .'

'So you think I should hide forever?'

'You call this hiding?' He waved a hand demonstratively around the hallowed halls of La Caravelle.

'In a sense, yes.'

'In the sense you mean, I think that's wise.'

'And what about my life, Edward? What about that?'

'What about it? You have everything you want. Your friends, your comfort, and your writing. Could you possibly ask for more, except a husband?'

'That isn't on my list to Santa Claus anymore, darling. And yes, I could ask for more. Honesty.'

'You're splitting hairs. And what you'd be risking for

that kind of honesty would be your privacy. Remember the job you wanted so badly at the *Times* years ago?'

'That was different.'

'How?'

'I was younger. And that wasn't a career, it was a job, and something I wanted to prove.'

'Isn't this the same thing?'

'Maybe not. Maybe it's a question of my sanity.'

'Good heavens, Kezia, don't be ridiculous. You're all wound up with whatever nonsense Simpson levelled at you this morning. Be reasonable, the man has a vested interest in you. He's looking at it from his point of view, not yours. For his benefit, not yours.'

But she knew that wasn't true. And what she also knew now was that Edward was afraid. Even more afraid than she was. But of what? And why? 'Edward, no matter how you slice it, one of these days I'm going to have to make a choice.'

'Over an interview for a magazine? An interview with some jailbird?' He wasn't afraid, he was terrified. Kezia almost felt sorry for him as she realized what it was he so feared. She was slipping away from the last of his grasp.

'This interview really isn't the issue, Edward. We both know that. Even Simpson knows that.'

'Then what in God's name is the issue? And why are you making all these strange noises about sanity and freedom and honesty? None of it makes any sense. Is someone in your life putting pressure on you?'

'No. Only myself.'

'But there is someone in your life I don't know about, isn't there?'

'Yes.' The honesty felt good. 'I didn't know you expected to be kept informed of *all* my doings.'

Edward looked away, embarrassed. 'I just like to know that you're all right. That's all. I assumed that there was someone other than Whit.'

Yes, darling, but did you assume why? Surely not. 'You're right, there is.'

'He's married?' He seemed matter-of-fact about it.

79

'No.'

'He isn't? I was rather sure he was.'

'Why?'

'Because you're so . . . well, discreet, I suppose. I just assumed he was married, or something of the sort.'

'Nothing of the sort. He's free, twenty-three years old, and an artist in SoHo.' That ought to take Edward a while to digest. 'And just for the record, I don't support him. He's on welfare and he loves it.' She was almost enjoying herself now and Edward looked as though he might have a fit of the vapours.

'Kezia!'

'Yes, Edward?' Her voice was pure sugar.

'And he knows who you are?'

'No, and he couldn't care less.' She knew that wasn't entirely true, but she also knew he would never go to any trouble to snoop into the other side of her life. He was just curious in a boyish sort of way.

'Does Whit know about all this?'

'No. Why should he? I don't tell him about my lovers and he doesn't tell me about his. It's an even exchange. Besides, darling, Whitney prefers boys.' She had not anticipated the look on Edward's face; it was not one of total astonishment.

'Yes . . . I . . . I've heard. I wondered if you knew.'

'I do.' Their voices were quiet now.

'He told you?'

'No, someone else did.'

'I'm sorry.' He looked away and patted her hand.

'Don't be, Edward. It didn't matter to me. That sounds like a harsh thing to say, but I've never been in love with Whit. We're merely a convenience to each other. That's not very pretty to admit, but it's a fact.'

'And this other man – the artist – is it serious?'

'No, it's pleasant, and easy, and fun, and a relief from some of the pressures in my life. That's all it is, Edward. Don't worry, no one's going to run off with the piggy bank.'

80

'That isn't my only concern.'

'I'm glad to hear it.' Why did she suddenly want to hurt him? What was the point of that? But he was appealing to her, tempting her, like an overzealous agent for a resort she had hated, who insisted on luring her back. And there was no way she would go.

He didn't mention the article again until they were waiting for a cab outside the restaurant. This had been one of the rare times they had discussed her business matters in public.

'You're going to do it?'

'What?'

'The interview Simpson discussed with you?'

'I don't know. I want to give it some thought.'

'Give it a lot of thought. Weigh in your mind how much it means to you, and how high a price you're willing to pay for doing it. You might not have to pay that price, or you might well have to. But at least be prepared, know the chances you're taking.'

'Is it such a terrible chance, Edward?' Her eyes were gentle again as she looked up at him.

'I don't know, Kezia. I really don't know. But somehow, I suspect that no matter what I say, you'll do it anyway. Or maybe I can only make matters worse.'

'No. But I may have to do it.' Not for Simpson. For herself.

'That's what I thought.'


CHAPTER VII


The plane landed in Chicago at five in the afternoon, with less than an hour to spare before Lucas Johns' speech. Simpson had arranged the loan of a friend's apartment on Lake Shore Drive. The friend, an elderly widow whose

81

husband had been a classmate of Simpson's, was wintering in Portugal.

Now, as the cab circled the rim of the lake, Kezia began to feel a mounting excitement. She had finally chosen. Taken a first step. But what if it turned out to be more than she could handle? It was one thing to work over her typewriter and call herself K. S. Miller, and quite another to pull it off eye to eye. Of course, Mark didn't know who she was either. But that was different. His farthest horizon was his easel, and even if he knew, he wouldn't really care. It would make him laugh, but it wouldn't matter. Lucas Johns might be different. He might try to use her notoriety to his advantage.

She tried to shrug off her fears as the cab pulled up in front of the address Simpson had given her. The borrowed apartment was on the nineteenth floor of a substantial-looking building across from the lake. The parquet floors in the foyer echoed beneath her feet. Above her head was an elaborate crystal chandelier. And the ghostly form of a grand piano stood silent beneath a dust sheet at the foot of the stairs. There was a long mirrored hall which led to the living room beyond. More dust sheets, two more chandeliers, the pink marble of a Louis XV mantel on the fireplace glowing softly from the light in the hall. The furniture beneath the sheets looked massive, and she wandered curiously from room to room. A spiral staircase led to another floor, and upstairs in the master bedroom she drew back the curtains and pulled up the creamy silk shades. The lake stretched before her, bathed in the glow of sunset, sailboats veering lazily towards home. It would have been fun to go for a walk and watch the lake for a while, but she had other things on her mind. Lucas Johns, and what sort of man he might prove to be.

She had read his book, and was surprised that she liked the sound of him. She had been prepared to dislike him, if only because the interview had become such a major issue between her and Simpson, and Edward. But the issue was herself, and she forgot the rest as she read the book. He had a pleasant way with words, a powerful way of expressing himself, and there were hints of humour throughout the book, and a refusal to take himself seriously, despite his passion for his subject. The style was oddly inconsistent with his history, though, and it was difficult to believe that a man who had spent most of his youth in juvenile halls and jails could be so literate now. Yet here and there he slipped consciously into prison jargon and California slang. He was an unusual combination of dogmas and beliefs and hopes and cynicism, with his own flavour of fun – and more than a faint hint of arrogance. He seemed to be many different things – no longer what he once was, firmly what he had become, a successful blending that he above all respected. Kezia had envied him as she read his book. Simpson had been right. In an indirect way, the book related to her. A prison can be any kind of bondage – even lunch at La Grenouille.

Her mental image of Johns was clearer now. Beady eyes, nervous hands, hunched shoulders, protruding paunch, and thin strands of hair covering a shiny balding forehead. She didn't know why, but she knew that she knew him. She could almost see him speaking as she read the book.

A man of massive proportions was making an introduction to Lucas Johns' speech, sketching in bold strokes the labour-union problems in prisons, the rough scale of wages (from five cents an hour, to a quarter in better institutions), the useless trades that were taught, the indecent conditions. He covered the subject easily, without fire.

Kezia watched the man's face. He was setting the stage and the pace. Low-key, low-voiced, yet with a powerful impact. It was the matter-of-fact way that he discussed the horrors of the prisons that affected her most. It was almost odd that they would put this man on before Johns; it would be a tough act to follow. Or maybe not. Maybe Johns' nervous dynamism would contrast well with the first speaker's easier manner – easy, yet with an intense control. The fibre of this man intrigued her, so much so that she forgot to scan the room to assure herself that there was no one there to recognize her. She forgot herself entirely and was swept into the mood of the speech.

She took out her notebook and jotted quick notes about the speaker, and then began to observe the audience in general. She noticed three well-known black radicals, and two solid labour-union leaders who had shared their knowledge with Johns in the past, when he was getting started. There were a few women, and in the front row a well-known criminal attorney who was often in the press. It was a group that already knew the business at hand for the most part, and one that was already active in prison reform. She was surprised at the large turnout as she watched their faces and listened to the last of the introduction. The room was surprisingly still. There were no rustlings, no little movements in seats, no noisy gropings for cigarettes and lighters. Nothing seemed to move. All eyes stayed fixed on the man at the front of the room. She had been right the first time; this would be tough for Lucas Johns to follow.

She looked at the speaker again. He had the colouring of her father. Almost jet black hair, and fiery green eyes that seemed to fix people in their places. He sought eyes he knew, and held them, speaking only to them, and then moving on, covering the room, the voice low, the hands immobile, the face taut. Yet something about the mouth suggested laughter. Something about the hands suggested brutality. He had interesting hands, and an incredible smile. In a powerful, almost frightening way, he was handsome, and she liked him. She found herself watching him, probing, observing, hungry for details – the shoulders impacted into the old tweed jacket, the long legs stretched lazily out before him, the thickness of his hair, the eyes that roved and stopped, and then moved on again, until they finally sought her out.

She saw him watching her as she watched him. He held her long and hard in the grasp of his eyes, and then dropped her and let his glance move away. It had been a strange sensation, like being backed against the wall with a hand at your throat, and another stroking your hair; you wanted to cringe in fear, and melt with pleasure. She felt warm suddenly, in the room full of people, and quietly looked around, wondering why this man was taking so long. It was hardly an introduction. He had been speaking for almost half an hour. Almost as though he intended to upstage Lucas Johns. And then it dawned on her, and she had to fight not to laugh in the quiet room: this had never been an introduction. The man whose eyes had so briefly stroked hers was Johns.

## CHAPTER VIII

'Coffee?'

'Tea, if possible.' Kezia smiled up at Lucas Johns as he poured a cup of hot water, and then handed her a tea bag.

The suite showed signs of frequent guests – half-filled paper cups of coffee and tea, remains of crackers, ashtrays overflowing with peanut shells and stale cigarette butts, and a well-used bar in the corner. It was an unassuming hotel, and the suite was not large, but it was easy and comfortable. She wondered how long he had been there. It was impossible to tell if he'd made his home there for a year, of if he'd moved in that day. There was plenty to eat and drink, but nothing was personal, nothing seemed his, as though he owned the clothes on his back, the light in his eyes, the tea bag he had handed her, and nothing more.

'We'll order breakfast from downstairs.'

She smiled again over her tea, and watched him quietly. 'To tell you the truth, I'm not really very hungry. No rush. And by the way, I was very impressed by your speech last night. You seem so at ease on the stage. You have a nice knack for bringing a difficult subject down to human proportions without sounding self-righteous about what you know first-hand and your listeners haven't experienced. That's quite an art.'

'Thank you. That's a nice thing to say. I guess it's just a question of practice. I've been doing a lot of speaking to groups. Is the subject of prison reform new to you?'

'Not entirely. I did a couple of articles last year on riots in two Mississippi prisons. It was an ugly mess.'

'Yeah, I remember. The real point about the whole subject of "reform" is not to reform. I think that abolition of prisons as we know them now is the only sensible solution. They don't work like this anyway. I'm working on the moratorium on the construction of prisons right now, along with a lot of good people who organized it. I'll be heading down to Washington next.'

'Have you lived in Chicago long?'

'Seven months, as a sort of central office. I work out of the hotel when I'm here, lining up speaking engagements, and some of the other stuff I do. I wrote my new book here, just holed up for a month and got down to work. After that, I lugged the manuscript around with me and wrote the rest on planes.'

'Do you travel a lot?'

'Most of the time. But I come back here when I can. I can dig my heels in and relax here.'

Nothing about him suggested that he did that very often. He didn't seem the sort of man who would know how to stop, or when. For all the stillness, one sensed a driving force inside him. He had a very quiet way of just sitting, barely moving, his eyes watching the person he spoke to. But it was more like the cautious stance of an animal sniffing the air for signs of attack or approach, ready to spring in a moment. Kezia could sense too that he was wary of her, and not totally at ease. The humour she had seen in his eyes the night before was carefully screened now.

'You know, I'm surprised they sent a woman out to do the piece.'

'Chauvinism, Mr. Johns?' The idea amused her.

'No, just curiosity. You must be good or they wouldn't have sent you.' There was the hint of arrogance she had sensed in his book.

'I think it's mostly that they liked those two pieces I did for them last year. I suppose you could say I've skirted the subject of prisons before . . . if you'll pardon the pun.'

He grinned and shook his head. 'That's a hell of a way to put it.'

'Then call it "a view from the sidelines".'

'I'm not sure that's an improvement. You can never see from the sidelines . . . or is it that you see more clearly? But with less life. To me, it always feels better to be right in the gut of things. You either get into it, or you don't. The sidelines . . . that's so safe, such a dead way to do anything.' His eyes sparkled and his mouth smiled, but it had been a heavy message. 'Come to think of it, I've read some of your articles, I think . . . could it have been in *Playboy*?' He was momentarily bewildered; she didn't look the type for *Playboy*, not even in print, but he was sure he remembered an article not very long ago.

She nodded assent with a grin. 'It was a piece on rape. In sympathy with the man's side, for a change. Or rather on false accusations of rape, made by neurotic women who have nothing better to do except take a guy home and then chicken out, and later yell rape.'

'That's right. That's the piece I remember. I liked it.'

'Naturally.' She tried not to laugh.

'Now, now. It's funny though, I thought a man had written it. Sounded like a man's point of view. I guess that's why I expected a man to do this interview. I'm not really the kind of guy they usually send women out to talk to.'

'Why not?'

'Because sometimes, dear lady, I behave like a shit.' He laughed a deep, mellow laugh, and she joined him.

'So that's what you do, is it? Is it fun?'

He looked boyishly embarrassed suddenly and took a swallow of coffee. 'Yeah, maybe. Sometimes anyway. Is writing fun?'

'Yes. I love it. But "fun" makes it sound rather flimsy. Like something you do as a hobby. That's not the way I see it. Writing is important to me. Very. It's for real, more so than a lot of other things I know.' She felt strangely defensive before his silent gaze. It was as though he had quietly turned the tables on her, and was now interviewing her.

'What I do is important to me too. And real.'

'I could see that in your book.'

'You read it?' He seemed surprised, and she nodded.

'I liked it.'

'The new one is better.'

And so modest, Mr. Johns, so modest. He was a funny sort of man.

'This one is less emotional, and more professional. I dig that.'

'First books are always emotional.'

'You've written one?' The tables turned again.

'Not yet. Soon, I hope.' It irked her suddenly. She was the writer, had worked hard at her craft over the past seven years, and yet he had written not one but two books. She envied him. For that, and a lot of things. His style, his courage, his willingness to follow his guts and jump into what he believed in . . . but then again, he had nothing to lose. She remembered the dead wife and child then, and felt a tremor for something tender in him which must have been hidden somewhere, down deep.

'I have one more question, and then you can get into the piece. What's the "K" for? Somehow "K. S. Miller" doesn't sound like a name.'

She laughed at him, and for the briefest of moments was about to tell him the truth: *Kezia. The 'K' is for Kezia, and the Miller is a fake.* He was the sort of man to whom you gave only the truth. You couldn't get away with less, and you wouldn't have wanted to. But she had to be sensible. It would be foolish to throw it all away for a moment of honesty. Kezia was an unusual name after all, and he might see a picture of her, somewhere, someday, and the next thing you'd know. . . .

'The "K" is for Kate.' Her favourite aunt's name.

'Kate. Sensible name. Kate Miller. Kate Sensible Miller.' He grinned at her, lit another cigarette, and she felt as though he were laughing at her, but not unkindly. The look in his eyes reminded her again of her father. In odd ways they were similar . . . something about the way he laughed . . . about the uncompromising way he looked at her, as though he knew all her secrets, and was only waiting for her to give them up, to see if she would, as though she were a child playing a game and he knew it. But what could this man possibly know? Nothing. Except that she was there to interview him, and her first name was Kate.

'Okay, lady, let's order breakfast and get to work.' The fun and games were over.

'Fine, Mr. Johns, I'm ready if you are.' She pulled out the pad with the scribbled notes from the evening before, drew a pen from her bag, and sat back in her chair.

He rambled on for two hours, talking at length, and with surprising openness, about his six years in prison. About what it was like to live under the indeterminate sentence, which he explained to her: a California phenomenon which condemned men to sentences of 'five years to life' or 'three to life', leaving the term served to be determined by the parole board or the prison authorities. Even the sentencing judge had no control over the length of time a man spent in prison. Once committed to the claws of the indeterminate sentence, a man could languish in prison literally for life, and a lot of men did, forgotten, lost, long past rehabilitation or the hope of freedom until they no longer cared when they might be set free. There came a time when it didn't matter anymore.

'But me,' he said with a lopsided grin, 'they couldn't

89

wait to get rid of me. I was the ultimate pain in the ass. Nobody loves an organizer.' He had organized other prisoners into committees for better working conditions, fairer hearings, decent visiting conditions with their wives, broader opportunities for study. He had, at one time, been spokesman for them all.

He told her too of what had gotten him sent to prison, and spoke of it with surprisingly little emotion. 'Twenty-eight years old, and still stupid. Looking for trouble, I guess, and bored with the life I had. I was piss-eyed drunk and it was New Year's Eve, and well . . . you know the rest. Armed robbery, not too cool to say the least. I held up a liquor store with a gun that didn't even shoot, and got away with two cases of bourbon, a case of champagne, and a hundred bucks. I didn't really want the hundred but they handed it to me, so I took it. I just wanted the hooch to have a good time with my buddies. I went home and partied my ass off. Till I got hauled off to jail, a little after midnight. . . . Happy New Year!' He grinned sheepishly and then his face grew serious. 'It sounds funny now, but it wasn't. You break a lot of hearts when you do something like that.'

It seemed all wrong to Kezia. Admittedly it was an outrageous thing to do. But six years and his wife's life for three cases of liquor? Her stomach turned over slowly as her mind flashed back to scenes of La Grenouille and Lutèce and Maxim's and Annabel's. Hundred-dollar lunches and fortunes spent on rivers of wine and champagne. But then, at those exalted watering holes, no one ordered his champagne with a shotgun.

Luke passed gracefully over his youth in Kansas. An uneventful period, when his worst problems were his size and his curiosity about life, both of which were out of proportion with his age and his 'station in life'. Despite Simpson's warning that Luke might be closed to personal probing, Kezia found him open and easy to talk to. By the end of the morning, she felt as though she knew all about him, and she had long since stopped taking notes. It was easier to hear the soul of the man just by listening – the political views, the interests, the causes, the experiences, the men he respected and those he abhorred. She would recapture it all later from memory with more depth.

What surprised her most was his lack of bitterness. He was determined, angry, pushy, arrogant, and tough. But he was also passionate in his beliefs, and compassionate about the people he cared about. And he liked to laugh. The baritone laughter rang out often in the small living room in his suite, as she questioned him and he regaled her with stories of years long since past. It was well after eleven before he stretched and rose from his chair.

'I hate to say this, Kate, but we're going to have to stop. I'm addressing another group at noon, and I have a few things to take care of first. Can I interest you in another speech? You're a good audience. Or do you have to get back to New York?' He circled the room, putting papers and pens in his pockets, and looked over his shoulder at her with the look one reserves for a friend.

'Both really. I should get back. But I'd like to hear you talk. What's the group?'

'Psychiatrists. The subject is a firsthand report on the psychological effects of being in prison. And they'll probably want to hear how real the threat of psychosurgery in prison is. They always ask about that.'

'You mean like frontal lobotomies?'

He nodded.

'Is there a lot of that?' She was momentarily stunned.

'Even a little "of that" is too much. But I don't think it happens often. Maybe occasionally. Lobotomies, shock treatment, a lot of ugly shit.'

She nodded sombrely and looked at her watch.

'I'll go pick up my things and meet you there.'

'Are you staying at a hotel around here?'

'No, my agent got me someone's apartment.'

'That's convenient.'

'Very.'

'Want a ride?' He said it easily as they walked towards the door.

'I . . . no . . . thanks, Luke. I've got a few other stops to make on the way. I'll meet you at your speech.'

He didn't press the point, but nodded absently as they waited for the elevator. 'I'll be interested to see this piece when it comes out.'

'I'll have my agent send you tear sheets as soon as we get them.'

He left her in front of the hotel and she walked to the corner and hailed a cab. It was a nice day to walk, and if she had had more time, she would have walked all the way back to the apartment on Lake Shore Drive. It was a warm autumn day with a bright sky overhead, and when she reached the apartment building, she could see sailboats skimming over the lake.

The ghostly apartment echoed her footsteps as she ran up the stairs for her suitcase, pulled the dust sheet over the tidily made bed, and pulled down the shade. She laughed, wondering what Luke would have said if he'd seen it. It didn't fit the image of Kate. Something told her he would not have approved. Or maybe he would have been amused, and together they might have pulled the sheets from all the furniture, lit the fire, and she could have played honky-tonk on the grand piano downstairs – put a little life in the place. Funny to think of doing something like that with Luke. But he looked like a good man to have fun with, to giggle at and tease and chortle with and chase. She liked him, and he had no idea who she was. It was a safe, happy feeling, and the makings of the article already felt good in her head.

Luke's speech was interesting, and the group was receptive. She made a few notes, and nibbled absently at the steak on her plate. Luke was sitting at a long, flower-strewn table at the front of the room, and she had been seated nearby. He looked over at her now and then, with mischievous laughter in the emerald green eyes. Once, silently raising his glass towards her, he winked. It made her want to laugh in the midst of the psychiatrists' general sobriety. She felt as though she knew Luke better than anyone there, maybe even better than anyone else. He had shared so much of his story with her all morning; he had given her the peek into the inner sanctum that Simpson had prophesied she'd never get. It was a shame she could not reciprocate.

Her flight was at three, and she had to leave the luncheon at two. He had just finished speaking when she rose. He had taken his seat at the dais, the usual crowd of admirers around him. She thought about just leaving quietly, without troubling him with thanks and goodbyes, but it didn't feel right. She wanted to say at least something to him before leaving. It seemed so unkind to pry into a man's head for four hours, and then simply vanish. But it was nearly impossible to get through the crowd near his table, and when she finally did, she found herself standing directly behind him, as he spoke animatedly to someone from his seat. She put a light hand on his shoulder and was surprised when he jumped. He didn't seem the kind of man to be frightened.

'That's a heavy thing to do to someone who spent six years in the joint.' His mouth smiled, but his eyes looked serious, almost afraid. 'I get nervous about who stands behind me. By now it's a reflex.'

'I'm sorry, Luke. I just wanted to say goodbye. I have to catch my plane.'

'Okay, just a sec.' He rose to walk her out to the lobby, and she went back to her table to pick up her coat. But Luke was waylaid on the way, and he was locked into another cluster of men as she fidgeted near the door, until she couldn't wait any longer. Unkind or not, she had to go. She didn't want to miss her plane. With a last look in his direction, she slipped quietly out of the room, crossed the lobby, and retrieved her valise from the doorman as he opened the door to a cab.

She settled back against the seat, and smiled to herself.

It had been a good trip, and it was going to be a beautiful piece.

She never saw Lucas standing beneath the awning behind her, a look of storm clouds and disappointment on his face.

'Damn!' All right, Ms. Kate Miller. We'll see about that. he smiled to himself as he strode back inside. He had liked her. She was so vulnerable, so funny . . . the kind of tiny little woman you wanted to toss up in the air and catch in your arms.

'Did you catch the young lady, sir?' The doorman had seen him run.

'No.' He broke into a broad grin which bordered on laughter. 'But I will.'

## CHAPTER IX

'Called me? What do you mean he called me? I just walked in the door. And how did he know how to get hold of you?' Kezia was almost livid with rage at Simpson.

'Calm down, Kezia. He called over an hour ago, and I assume that the magazine referred him to me. There's no harm in that. And he was perfectly civil.'

'Well, what did he want?' She was stepping out of her clothes as she spoke, and the bath was already running. It was five minutes to seven, and Whit had said he'd pick her up at eight. They were due at a party at nine.

'He said he didn't feel the article would be complete unless you covered the meeting for that moratorium against prisons tomorrow in Washington. And he'd appreciate it if you'd hold off turning the piece in until you've added that to the rest. It sounds reasonable, Kezia. If you went to Chicago, you can certainly go to Washington for an afternoon.'

'When is this thing he wants me to go to?' Goddamn Lucas Johns. He was being a pest, or at least egocentric. She had written the outline for the piece on the plane, and enough was enough. Her sense of triumph was evaporating rapidly now. A man who called scarcely before she'd stepped off the plane could hardly be trusted not to pry.

'The moratorium meeting is tomorrow afternoon.'

'Hell. And if I go by plane, I'm liable to get spotted by some asshole society reporter who'll think I'm going down there for a party, and he'll try to catch a quick bit of news. And then I'm liable to end up with the paparazzi down my back.'

'That didn't happen on the way to Chicago, did it?'

'No, but Washington is a lot closer to home, and you know it. I never go to Chicago. Maybe I should drive down tomorrow, and . . . oh God, the tub! Hang on!'

Simpson waited while she went to turn off the water. She sounded nervous, and he assumed that the trip had been hectic. But it had been good for her. There was no doubt about that. She had braved it out, done the interview, and no one had recognized her, thank God. If they had, he'd never have heard the end of it. Now there were any number of interviews she could do. And Johns had certainly sounded pleased with her work. He had mentioned spending almost four hours with her. She must have handled it well, and Johns' casual references to 'Miss Miller' showed that he hadn't the faintest idea who she was. So what was her problem? Why so jumpy? She came back on the line with a sigh. 'Are you drowning over there?'

'No.' She laughed tiredly then. 'I don't know, Jack, I'm sorry I jumped on you, but it really makes me nervous to do this kind of thing so close to New York.'

'But the interview today went well, didn't it?'

'Yes. Very. But do you think the moratorium is really important to the piece, or is it that Luke Johns is on a star trip now and wants more attention?'

'I think he made a valid point when he called. It's

95

another sphere of his action, and could add a lot of strength to the piece. Atmosphere, if nothing else. It's up to you, but I don't see any harm in your going. And I know what you're worried about, but you saw for yourself in Chicago that there was no problem with that. No paparazzi, and he hasn't the faintest idea that you're anyone but K. S. Miller.'

'Kate.' She smiled to herself.

'What?'

'Nothing. Oh, I don't know. Maybe you're right. What time does the meeting start? Did he say?'

'Noon. He'll be flying in from Chicago in the morning.' She thought about it for a minute, and then nodded at the phone.

'All right, I'll do it. I suppose I could fly down on the shuttle. That's innocuous enough. And I could be back easily by tomorrow night.'

'Fine. Do you want to call Johns yourself to confirm it, or shall I? He wanted confirmation.'

'Why? So he could line up another biographer if I didn't go?'

'Now, now, let's not be nasty.' Simpson chuckled in spite of himself. There were times when she needed a good boot in the ass. 'No, he said something about picking you up at the plane.'

'Shit.'

'What?' Simpson sounded faintly shocked. He was much less used to that from her than Edward, who was of a comparable vintage but a little less proper.

'Sorry. No, I'll call him myself. And I don't want to be met at the plane. Just in case.'

'I think that's wise. And do you want me to arrange someplace for you to stay? If you want to stay at a hotel we could bill it to the magazine, along with your plane fare.'

'No, I'd rather come home. And that place you got me in Chicago was fabulous. Must be quite a home when it's in full swing.'

'Used to be . . . used to be. I'm glad you liked it. I had

96

some good times there, many years ago.' He drifted for a moment and then reverted to his business voice. 'So you'll come home tomorrow night then?'

'Damn right!' She wanted to get down to SoHo, and Mark. It had been days! And tonight she had that damn party at the El Morocco to go to with Whit. Hunter Forbishe and Juliana Watson-Smythe were announcing their engagement, as though everyone didn't already know. Two of the dullest, richest people in town, and worse luck yet, Hunter was her second cousin. The party was sure to be shitful, but at least the El Morocco was fun. She hadn't been since before the summer.

And not only were the dumb bastards getting engaged, but they had decided to have a theme for their party. Black and White. What fun it would have been to appear with George, her dancer friend from SoHo. Black and White . . . or Lucas for that matter, with his black hair to match Kezia's, and their equally white skin. How absurd – and worth a mountain of news for a year. No, she'd have to settle for Whitney, but it was a shame. Luke might have been fun at a party like that. Fun and outrageous. She laughed aloud as she sank into her bath. She would call him after she dressed, to tell him that she'd meet him in Washington tomorrow. But first she had to dress, and she needed time for a party like the one they were going to. She had long since decided what to wear for their charming soiree in black and white. The creamy lace dress was already laid out on her bed, fiercely décolleté and gently empire, with a black moire cape, and the new David Webb choker and earrings she'd bought herself last Christmas: an onyx set with a generous supply of handsome stones, diamonds of course. At twenty-nine she had stopped waiting for someone else to buy that sort of thing for her. She bought them herself.

'Lucas Johns, please.' She waited while they rang his room. He sounded sleepy when he answered. 'Luke? Kee . . . Kate.' She had almost said it was Kezia.

'I didn't know you stuttered.'

She laughed and his own laughter answered.

'I don't. I'm just in a hurry. Jack Simpson called me. I'll come down to cover that moratorium thing tomorrow. Why didn't you mention this morning that you thought I should be there?'

'I didn't think of it till after you left.' He smiled to himself as he spoke. 'I think you'll need it, though, to round out the rest. Want me to pick you up at the plane?'

'No, thanks. I'll be fine. Just tell me where to meet you.' He did and she wrote down the address, standing at her desk in the white lace dress and the black moire cape, delicate black silk sandals on her feet and one of her mother's diamond bracelets on each arm. And then she started to laugh.

'What's funny?'

'Oh, nothing really. It's just what I'm wearing.'

'And just what are you wearing, Ms. Miller?' He sounded vastly amused.

'Something terribly silly.'

'Sounds very mysterious to me. I'm not sure if you mean leather hip boots and a whip, or a rhinestone-studded peignoir.'

'A little of both. See you tomorrow, Luke.' She hung up on a last gurgle of laughter as the doorbell rang, and Whitney appeared, as crisp and elegant as ever. For him, of course, the black and white had been easy. He was wearing a dinner jacket and one of the shirts he had made four times a year in Paris.

'Where were you all day? And my ... don't you look splendid!' They exchanged their standard dry little kiss, and he held out her hands. 'Is that something new? I don't remember seeing that dress before.'

'Sort of. I don't wear it often. And I spent the whole day with Edward. We did up my new will.' They smiled at each other and she picked up her bag. Lies, lies, lies. It had never been like this before. But she knew as she swirled out to the hall that it was going to get worse. Lying to Whit,

98

lying to Mark, lying to Luke. 'Is that why you write, Kate? For fun?' She remembered Luke's question as the elevator swept them down to the lobby, and her brows knit as she thought of the look in his eyes. It had not been accusing, only curious. But no, dammit! She didn't just write for fun. It was real. But how real could anything be, when whatever you did, you draped in lies?

'Ready, darling?' Whit was waiting for her outside the elevator, and she had stood there for a moment, not moving, just looking at him, but seeing Luke's eyes, hearing his voice.

'Sorry, Whit. I must be tired.' She squeezed his arm as they walked out to the waiting limousine.

By ten she was drunk.

'Christ, Kezia, are you sure you can walk?' Marina was watching her pull her stockings up and her dress down as they stood in the ladies' room at the El Morocco.

'Of course I can walk!' But she was weaving badly and couldn't stop laughing.

'What happened to you?'

'Nothing since Luke. I mean, Duke . . . I mean breakfast dammit.' She had hardly had time to touch her lunch before catching the plane at O'Hare, and she hadn't bothered with dinner.

'Kezia, you're a nut. Want some coffee?'

'No, tea. No . . . coffee. No! Chaaaaamppagggne.' She dragged the word out and Marina laughed.

'At least you're a friendly drunk. Vanessa Billingsley is crocked out of her mind and just called Mia Hargreaves a raving bitch.' Kezia giggled and Marina lit a cigarette and sat down, while Kezia tried desperately to remember what Marina had just said. Mia called Vanessa a . . . no, Vanessa called Mia . . . if she could just hang on to it, it would be good for the column. And what had she heard earlier about Patricia Morbang being pregnant? Or was that right? Was it someone else who was pregnant? It was all so hard to remember.

'Oh Marina, it's so hard to remember it all.'

Marina looked at her with a half smile and shook her head.

'Kezia, my love, you are smashed. Well, hell, who isn't? It must be after three.'

'Christ, is it really? And I have to get up so early tomorrow. Crap.'

Marina laughed again at the sight of Kezia sprawled on the white wall-to-wall in the ladies' boudoir, looking like a child just home from school, the white lace dress frothed around her like a nightgown. the diamonds glittering on her wrists, like something borrowed from her mother to dispel the boredom of a rainy day.

'And Whit's going to be very cross if I'm drunk.'

'Tell him it's the flu. I don't think the poor bastard would know the difference.' They both laughed at that, and Marina helped her to her feet. 'You really ought to go home.'

'I think I'd much rather dance. Whit dances very nicely, you know.'

'He ought to.' Marina looked at her hard and long, but the implication of the message was lost on Kezia. She was too drunk to hear, or to care.

'Marina?' Kezia looked still more childlike as she stood watching her friend.

'What, love?'

'Do you really love Halpern?'

'No, baby, I don't. But I love the peace of mind he could give me. I've about had it with trying to make it on my own with the kids. And in another six months I'd have had to sell the co-op.'

'But don't you love him a little?'

'No. But I like him a lot.' Marina looked cynical and amused.

'But don't you love anyone? A secret lover maybe? You have to love someone.' *Don't you?*

'Do you? Well, fancy that. Do you love Whit?'

'Of course not.' Some small alarm went off in her head then. She was talking too much.

'Then who do you love, Kezia?'

'You, Marina. I love you lots and lots and lots and lots!' She threw her arms around her friend's neck and started to giggle. And Marina laughed back and gently untwined her from her neck.

'Kezia sweet, you may not love Whitney, but if I were you, I'd get him to take me home. I think you've about had it.' They walked out of the ladies' room arm in arm. Whitney was waiting just outside. He had noticed the ominous sway in Kezia's walk as she left the room half an hour before.

'Are you all right?'

'I'm wonderful!' Whit and Marina exchanged glances, and Whitney winked.

'You certainly are wonderful. And I don't know about you, darling, but I'm also wonderfully tired. I think we'll call it a night.'

'No, no, no! I'm not tired at all. Let's call it a morning!' Kezia found everything suddenly terribly funny.

'Let's call it a get-your-ass-out-of-here, Kezia, before you wind up in Martin Hallam's column tomorrow: "Kezia Saint Martin, drunk as a skunk as she left El Morocco last night with . . ." Wouldn't that be lovely?' Kezia roared with glee at Marina's warning.

'That couldn't happen to me!' Whitney and Marina laughed again and tears began to slide down Kezia's face as she giggled.

'Oh, couldn't it? It could happen to any of us.'

'But not to me. I'm . . . I'm a friend of his.'

'And so is Jesus Christ, I'll bet.' Marina patted her on the shoulder and went back to the party, while Whitney put an arm around Kezia and piloted her slowly towards the door. He had draped her black cape over his arm, and was carrying her small black beaded bag.

'It's really my fault, darling. I should have taken you to dinner before we came here.'

'You couldn't.'

'Of course I could. I left the office early today to play squash at the Racquet Club.'

101

'No you couldn't. I was in Chicago.' He rolled his eyes and placed the cape over her shoulders.

'That's right, darling. That's right. Of course you were.' She went into another fit of giggles as he gently led her outside. She patted his cheek sweetly then and looked at him strangely.

'Poor Whitney.' He was not paying attention. He was far more concerned with getting her into a cab.

He deposited her in her living room and gave her a gentle slap on the bottom, hoping to propel her into the bedroom. Alone.

'Get some sleep, mademoiselle. I'll call you tomorrow.'

'Late! Very late.' She had just remembered that she would be in Washington all day. With a terrible hangover.

'You bet "late"! I wouldn't dare call you before three.'

'Make it six!'

She giggled at him as he closed the door behind him, and she sank into one of the blue velvet living room chairs. She was drunk. Hopelessly, totally, wonderfully drunk. And all because of a stranger named Luke. And she was going to see him tomorrow.


## CHAPTER X


The print was blurred and the features were indistinct but it was definitely Kate. The way she carried herself was unmistakable, the tilt of her head, her size. The Honourable Kezia Saint Martin in what looked like some sort of black-and-white outfit. By Givenchy, the paper said, and wearing her late mother's famed diamond bracelets. Heiress to several fortunes; in steel, oil, etc. No wonder she had laughed when she called him and said she was wearing 'something funny.' It looked pretty funny to Luke too. But

102

she looked beautiful. Even in the papers. He had seen her in the papers before, but now he paid close attention to what he saw. Now that he knew her, it mattered to him. And what an odd life she must lead.

He had sensed the turmoil beneath the poise and perfection. The bird in the gilded cage was dying inside, and he knew it. He wondered if she knew it too. And what he knew most acutely was that he wanted to touch her, before it was too late.

Instead they had that damn meeting to go to, and he would have to go on playing her game. He knew that she would have to be the one to end the game of 'K. S. Miller' between them. Only she could do that. All he could do was give her the chance. But how many more chances? How many more excuses could he dream up? How many more towns? How many more meetings? All he knew was that he had to have her, however long it took. The problem was that he didn't have much time. Which made it all the more crazy.

When Kezia arrived, she found Luke in an office, surrounded by unfamiliar faces. Phones were ringing, people were shouting, messages were flying, the smoke was thick, and he hardly seemed to know she was there. He waved once and didn't look at her again all afternoon. The press conference had been rescheduled for two o'clock, and the rooms were chaotic all day long. It was six before she found a place to sit down, shoved her notebook into her bag, and gladly accepted the other half of a stranger's ham sandwich. What a day to survive with a hangover. Her head had gotten worse by the hour. Phones, people, speeches, statistics, photographs. It was all too much. Action, emotion, and pressure. She wondered how he stood it as a regular diet, with or without a hangover.

'Want to get out of here?'

'That's the best offer I've had all day.' She smiled up at him and his face softened for the first time in hours.

'Come on, I'll get you something decent to eat.'

'I really ought to get out to the airport.'

'Later. You need a break first. You look like you were hit by a truck.' And she felt it. Rumpled, tired, dishevelled. Lucas did not look much better. He looked tired and he had worn a scowl for most of the afternoon. He had a cigar in one hand, and his hair looked as though he had been running his hands through it for hours.

But he had been right. The day had been a total contrast to the two meetings she had seen in Chicago. This was the meat of it, the gut, as he called it. Impassioned, frenzied, fervent. This was more intense, less polite, and far more real. Luke seemed totally in charge here. He was almost a kind of god. There was a fierceness about him she'd only glimpsed in Chicago. The air was electric with his special kind of energy, and the toughness in him was no longer muted. But his face gentled a little as he looked at her on their way out.

'You look tired, Kate. Too much for you?' It wasn't a put-down; he looked concerned.

'No, I'm fine. And you were right. It was an interesting day. I'm glad I came down to see it.'

'So am I.' They were walking down a long busy corridor, among streams of homebound people. 'I know a quiet place where we can have an early dinner. Can you spare the time?' But his tone told her he expected her to.

'Sure. I'd like that.' Why rush back? For what? For Whitney? . . . or for Mark? But suddenly even that didn't seem so important. They walked out onto the street, and he took her arm.

'What did you do last night, by the way?' He wondered if she'd tell him.

'As a matter of fact, I got drunk. And I haven't done that in years.' It was crazy, this urge to tell him everything, without really doing so. She could have told him the whole of it, but she knew she wasn't going to.

'You got drunk?' He looked down at her with amusement all over his face. So she had gotten drunk in that black-and-white number with her mother's diamond bracelets . . . and with that faggoty-looking dude she was with no doubt scowling his disapproval. He could just see her. Drunk on champagne. Was there any other way to go?

They were walking briskly, side by side now, and she looked up at him pensively after a brief silence.

'You really care about the prison thing, don't you? I mean, in your gut.'

He nodded carefully. 'Can't you tell?'

'Yes. I can. It just amazes me a little, how much of yourself you pour into it. Seems like a lot of energy expended in one place.'

'It's worth it to me.'

'It must be. But aren't you taking a hell of a chance just being involved in these issues, and being so outspoken about them? Seems to me I've heard they can revoke a parole for less.'

'And if they do, what have I lost?'

'Your freedom. Or doesn't that matter to you?' Maybe after six years in prison it no longer mattered to him, although it seemed to her that that would only make freedom more dear.

'You miss the point. I never lost my freedom, even when I was in the joint. Oh sure, for a while, but once I found it again I kept it. It sounds corny, but no man can take your freedom from you. They can limit your mobility, but that's about all they can do.'

'All right, then let's say they try and limit your mobility again. Aren't you taking a heavy chance with the kind of agitating you do on the outside – speeches, conferences, your books, the prison labour-union issues? Seems to me like you're walking a tightrope.' Unconsciously, she was echoing Simpson's speech to her.

'Seems to me that a lot of people are. In prison and out. Maybe you're even walking a tightrope, Miss Miller. So what? It's cool as long as you don't fall off.'

'And no one pushes you off.'

'Lady, all I know is how fucked up that whole system is. I can't keep my mouth shut about it. If I did, my life wouldn't mean a damn thing to me. It's as simple as that.

105

And if I pay a price in the end, it was my own choice. I'm willing to take that chance. Besides, I'd say the California Department of Corrections is not exactly dying to invite me back for a return engagement. I gave them one giant, jumbo, A-Number-One pain in the ass.'

'You're really not afraid of getting revoked?'

'Nah. Never happen.' But he didn't look at her as he said it, and something about him seemed to stiffen. 'You like Italian food, Kate?'

'Sounds lovely. I'm not sure, but I think I'm starving.'

'Then pasta it is. Come on, let's catch that cab.' He raced across the street holding her hand, and dutifully held open the door for her, before following her inside and cramping his legs into the narrow back seat. 'Man, they must build these for midgets. And Jesus, you look so comfortable. You should thank God you're a pygmy.' He gave the driver the address of the restaurant over her outraged protests.

'Just because you're a freak of nature, Lucas Johns, does not mean you vent your problems on . . .'

'Aww, now now. Nothing wrong with being a pygmy.'

She looked at him awesomely and sniffed. 'I ought to punch you in the eye, Mr. Johns, but I'm afraid I might hurt you.'

That set the tone for the evening. Light, playful, companionable. He was easy to be with. And it wasn't until the espresso was served that they both grew more pensive.

'I like this town. Do you come down here often, Kate? I would if I lived in New York.'

'I come down once in a while.'

'What for?' He wanted her to tell him the truth. They couldn't even begin till she did.

And she wanted to tell him that she came down for parties, for balls, for dinners at the White House. For inaugurations. For weddings. But she couldn't say any of it. No matter what.

'I come down on stories occasionally, like this. Or just to see friends.' She caught a glimpse of something disappointed in his eyes, but it was fleeting. 'Don't you get tired of travelling so much, Luke?' She was once again the poised Miss Saint Martin. He was beginning to think it was hopeless.

'No, travelling is a way of life for me by now, and it's for a good cause. How about some brandy?'

'Oh God, not tonight!' She cringed at the memory of the headache that had finally left her at dinner.

'Tied one on that bad last night, huh?'

'Worse!' She smiled and took another sip of coffee.

'How come? Having a good time?'

'No. Trying to numb myself through a lousy one, and I guess I had a lot on my mind. Everything kind of got away from me.'

'Like what did you have on your mind?'

You, Mr. Johns. . . . She smiled at her own thought. 'Can I blame it on you and say it was the interview?' A look of sheer female teasing danced in her eyes.

'Sure, you can blame it on me if you want. I've been accused of a lot worse.' So she had to 'numb' herself to get through the party. Interesting. Very interesting. At least she wasn't in love with that asshole. 'You know something, Katie? I like you. You're a very nice woman.' He sat back and smiled, looking deep into her eyes.

'Thank you. I've thoroughly enjoyed the last couple of days. And should I make a terrible confession?'

'What? You flushed your notebook down the toilet back at the office? I wouldn't blame you a bit, and we could start all over. I'd like that.'

'God forbid. No, my "terrible confession" is that this was my first interview. I've always done more general pieces. But this was a new experience for me.' She wondered if all writers fell a little bit in love with the first person they interviewed. Inconvenient if the first person happened to be the tattooed lady at Ringling's.

'How come you've never done an interview before?' He was intrigued.

'Scared to.'

'Why would you be scared? You're a good writer, so that doesn't make any sense. And you're not shy.'

'Yes, I am. Sometimes. But you're difficult to be shy with.'

'Is that something I should correct?'

She laughed and shook her head. 'No, you're just fine the way you are.'

'So what's so scary about interviews?'

'It's a long story. Nothing you'd want to hear. What about you? What frightens you, Luke?'

Damn. She just wouldn't give. He wanted to stand up and shake her. But he had to look cool. 'Is this part of the interview? What frightens me?'

She shook her head, and wondered what he was thinking.

'A lot of things frighten me. Fears can create a lot of confusion. Cowardice frightens me, it can cost someone a life . . . usually someone else's. Waste frightens me, because time is so short. Otherwise, nothing much. Except women. Oh yeah, women scare me to death.'

After a moment of tension, there was laughter in his eyes again, and Kezia was relieved. For a minute she had felt him coming at her with both barrels, but she decided that was only her own paranoia. He didn't know she was lying. He couldn't possibly know, or he would have let on by now if he did. He wasn't a man to play games. She was sure of it.

'Women frighten you?' She was smiling at him again.

'They terrify me.' He tried to cower in his seat.

'Like hell they do.' She started to laugh.

'Yeah, okay. You're right.' They laughed and talked easily for another hour, as the brief tension between them eased again. She succumbed to a glass of brandy at last, and then followed it with another espresso. She wanted to sit there with him forever.

'There's a place I go to in SoHo in New York. The atmosphere reminds me of this. It's called The Partridge, and it's a funny little hangout for poets and artists and just

108

nice people.' Her face lit up as she told him about it, and he watched her talk.

'Is it an "in" place?'

She laughed out loud at the thought. 'Oh no, it's an "out" place. Very "out." That's why I love it.'

So, the lady had her haunts, did she? The places where she went to get away, where no one knew who she was, where. . . . 'Then I'd probably like it, Kate. You'll have to take me there sometime.' He slipped the suggestion in casually as he lit another cigar. 'What do you do with yourself in New York?'

'Write. See friends. Go to parties sometimes, or the theatre. I travel a bit too. But mostly, I write. I know a lot of artists in SoHo, and sometimes I hang out with them.'

'And the rest of the time?'

'I see other people . . . depends on my mood.'

'You're not married, are you?'

'No.' She shook her head decisively, as though to confirm it.

'I didn't think so.'

'How come?'

'Because you're careful, the way women are who're used to taking care of themselves. You think about what you do and say. Most married women are used to having someone else do that kind of thinking, and it shows. How's that for a classic male chauvinist remark?'

'Not bad. But it's also a very perceptive thing to say. I'd never thought of it that way, but I think you might be right.'

'Okay. Back to you now. My turn to interview.' He seemed to be enjoying it. 'Engaged?'

'Nope. Not even in love. I have a virgin soul.'

'I'm overwhelmed. If I had a hat, I'd take it off.' They both laughed again. 'But I'm not sure I believe you,' Luke went on. 'Are you trying to tell me that you don't even have an old man?' What about the faggot in the newspaper picture, baby? But he could hardly ask her about that.

'Nope. No old man.'

'Is that true?'

Her eyes rose to his then, and she looked almost hurt. 'Yes, it's true. There's someone I enjoy a lot, but I . . . I just kind of visit him . . . when I can.'

'Is he married?'

'No . . . just sort of in another world.'

'In SoHo?'

Lucas was quick to pick up on things left unsaid. She nodded again. 'Yes. In SoHo.'

'He's a lucky guy.' Luke's voice was oddly quiet.

'No, he's a funny guy actually. A nice guy. I like him. Sometimes I even like to imagine that I love him, but I don't. It's not very serious between us, and never will be. For a lot of reasons.'

'Like what?'

'We're just very different, that's all. Different goals, different views. He's quite a bit younger than I am, and headed in another direction. It really doesn't matter. Mostly, it's just that we're different.'

'Is that so bad? Being different?'

'No, but there are different kinds of "different." ' She smiled at her own words. 'In this case, different backgrounds, different interests . . . just different enough to make it *too* different, but I still like him. And what about you? An "old lady"?' The term always seemed funny to her, as though it should refer to someone's grandmother, and not his inamorata.

'Nope. No old lady. I move around too much. A few good women here and there. But I put my energy into the cause, not into my relationships. I haven't put out that kind of effort in a long time. I think the time for that is past for me. And you pay a price for the kind of work that goes into shit-kicking like this. You can't have it all ways. You have to make choices.' He said a lot of things like that. In his own way, he was a purist. And his cause came first. 'I meet a lot of good people to talk to, travelling around. That means a lot to me.'

'It means a lot to me too. People you can talk to, in

depth, are a rarity.' And he was one of those rare people.

'You're right. Which brings up a question. I'd like to look you up when I come to New York sometime, Kate. Would that be okay? We could go to The Partridge.' She smiled at him; it would be nice to see him. She felt as though she had made a new friend, and it was incredible how much of her soul she had shown him at dinner. She hadn't planned to; in fact she had planned to be rather guarded. But one forgot to be guarded with Luke. That was a very dangerous thing, and she reminded herself of it now.

'It would be fun to see you again sometime.' She was purposely vague.

'Will you give me your number?' He held out a pen and the back of an envelope. He didn't want to give her time to back off. But she made no move to retreat. In a sense, he had her cornered, and she knew it. She took the pen and wrote down her number, but not her address. There was no harm in his having the phone number.

He pocketed the envelope, paid the check, and helped her on with her jacket.

'Can I take you to the airport, Kate?' She seemed to take a long time buttoning her jacket, without looking up, and then at last she met his gaze, looking almost shy.

'That wouldn't be too much trouble?'

He pulled gently at a loose wisp of her hair, and shook his head at her. 'I'd like to.'

'That's really very nice.'

'Don't be a jerk, you're good company.'


He watched her leave, and she turned to give him a last wave at the gate. Her hand rose high above her head and impulsively she blew him a kiss as she walked away down the ramp. It had been a beautiful evening, a great interview, a marvellous day. She was feeling sentimental about the success of it, and strange about Luke.

She boarded the plane and took a seat at the front, accepting the New York and Washington papers from a

111

passing tray. Then she settled back in her seat and switched on the light. There was no one next to her whom she might disturb as she read. It was the last flight to New York, and it would be past one when she got in. She had nothing to do the following day. Work on the Lucas Johns article maybe, but that was all. She had wanted to go to SoHo to see Mark tonight, but now she wasn't in the mood. It wasn't too late. Mark would still be up. But she didn't want to see him. She wanted to be alone.

She felt a gentle sadness wash slowly over her. An unfamiliar, bittersweet feeling of having touched someone who had moved on. She knew she wouldn't see Lucas Johns again. He had the number, but he probably wouldn't have the time, and if he ever did come through town, she would probably be in Zermatt or Milan or Marbella. He would be busy for the next hundred years with his unions and his cause and inmates and moratoriums . . . and those eyes . . . he was such a good man, such a likable man . . . so gentle . . . it was hard to imagine him in prison. Hard to imagine that he'd been tough or mean, had perhaps stabbed a man in a fight in the yard. She had met a different man. A different Luke. A Luke who haunted her all the way home. He was gone for good, from her now, so she could allow herself the luxury of turning him over in her mind . . . just for tonight.

The flight was too short and she almost hated to get off the plane and fight her way through the terminal to a cab. Even at that hour La Guardia was busy. So busy that she never saw the tall, dark-haired man follow her to within yards of the cab. He watched her slide into the taxi from only a few feet away. And then, turning away to conceal his face, he looked at his watch. He had time. It would take her half an hour to get home.

And then he would call her.

112

## CHAPTER XI

'Hello?'

'Hi, Kate.' She felt a warm rush come over her at the sound of his voice.

'Hello, Lucas.' Her voice was tired and smoky. 'I'm glad you called.'

'Did you get home all right?'

'I did. It was a quiet flight. I was going to read the paper, but I didn't even bother.' He wanted to say 'I know,' but he didn't, and stifled the urge to laugh.

'What are you up to now, Ms. Miller?' There was mischief in his voice.

'Not much. I was just going to take a hot bath and go to bed.'

'Can I talk you into a drink at The Partridge? Or P.J. Clarke's?'

'Bit of a ride from your hotel in Washington, wouldn't you say? Or did you plan to walk?' She was amused at the thought.

'Yeah, I could. But it's not a bad ride from La Guardia.'

'Don't be silly. I took the last flight in.' What a madman he was to consider flying all the way up to New York for a drink.

'I know you took the last flight. But as it happens, so did I.'

'What?' And then she understood. 'You wretch! And I didn't even see you!'

'I should hope not. I almost broke my shoulder once, ducking down in my seat.'

'Lucas, you're crazy.' She laughed into his ear and lay her head on the back of the chair. 'What a perfectly nutty thing to do.'

'Why not? I have a free day tomorrow, and I was going

to take it easy anyway. Besides, I felt lousy watching you leave.'

'I felt pretty lousy leaving. I don't know why, but I did.'

'And now we're both here, and there's no reason to feel lousy. Right? So what'll we do? P. J.'s or The Partridge, or somewhere else? I'm not all that familiar with New York.'

She was still laughing and shaking her head. 'Luke, it's one-thirty in the morning. There isn't all that much we can do!'

'In New York?' He was not going to be put off that easily.

'Even in New York. You are too much. Tell you what, I'll meet you at P. J.'s in half an hour. It'll take you that long to get into the city, and I want to take a quick shower and change clothes at least. You know something?'

'What?'

'You're a nut.'

'Is that a compliment?'

'Possibly.' She smiled gently at the phone.

'Good. I'll meet you at P. J.'s in half an hour.' He was pleased with himself for what he had done. It was going to be a beautiful night. He didn't care if all she did was shake his hand. It was going to be the best night of his life. Kezia Saint Martin. It was impossible not to be impressed. But in spite of the fancy label, he liked her. She intrigued him. She was nothing like what he had imagined those women to be. She wasn't aloof and secretly ugly. She was warm and gentle and lonely as hell. He could read it all over her.

And half an hour later, there she was, in the doorway at P. J.'s, and in jeans. Not even tailor-made ones, just good old regular Levi's, with her silky black hair in two long little-girl braids. More than ever, she looked like a very young girl to him.

The bar was jammed, the lights were bright, the sawdust was thick on the floor, and the jukebox was blaring. It was his kind of place. He was having a beer, and she came over with a gleam in her eye.

'My God, you're sneaky! No one's ever followed me onto

114

a plane in my life. But what a neat thing to do!' That wasn't entirely true but she was laughing again.

She ordered a Pimm's Cup, and they stood at the bar for half an hour while Kezia glanced over his shoulder at the door. There was always the chance that someone she knew would wander in, or a group of late-night partygoers would arrive after a stop at Le Club or El Morocco, and blow the 'Kate Miller' story to pieces.

'Expecting someone, or just nervous?'

She shook her head. 'Neither. Just stunned, I guess. A few hours ago we had dinner in Washington, said goodbye at the airport, and now here you are. It's a bit of a shock.' But a pleasant one.

'Too much of a shock, Kate?' Maybe he had gone too far, but at least she didn't look angry.

'No.' She was careful with the word. 'What do you want to do now?'

'How about taking a walk?'

'That's funny, I thought of that on the plane. I wanted to go for a walk along the East River. I do that once in a while, late at night. It's a nice way to think.'

'And get killed. Is that what you're trying to do?' The idea of her walking along the river unprotected unnerved him.

'Don't be so silly, Lucas. You shouldn't believe all the myths you hear about this town. It's as safe as any other.' He glowered and finished his beer.

They began to walk slowly up Third Avenue, past restaurants and bars, and the clatter of occasional late-night traffic on Fifty-seventh Street. New York was not in any way like any other town. Not like any American city. Like a giant Rome maybe, with its thirst for life after dark. But this was bigger, more, wilder, crueller, and far less romantic. New York had its own romance, its own fire. Like a bridled volcano, waiting for its chance to erupt. They both felt the vibes of the town as they wandered its streets, out of step with its mood, refusing to feel pushed or shoved; they felt oddly at peace. They passed little groups

115

of people, and male streetwalkers carrying pug dogs and French poodles, and wearing tight sweaters and crotch-clutching jeans. Women walked lap dogs, and men lurched drunkenly towards cabs. It was a city that stayed alive round-the-clock.

They cut east on Fifty-eighth Street, and walked through the slumbering elegance of Sutton Place, sitting like a dowager next to the river. Kezia wondered for a moment if they would meet Whit, leaving his lover's apartment – if he still left it.

'What are you thinking about, Kate? You look all dreamy.'

She looked up at him and smiled. 'I guess I am. I was just letting my mind wander ... thinking about some people I know ... you ... nothing much really.' He took her hand and they walked quietly next to the river, making their way slowly north, until a question interrupted her thoughts. 'I just thought of something. Where are you going to sleep tonight?'

'I'll work it out. Don't worry about it. I'm used to arriving in cities in the middle of the night.' He looked unconcerned.

'You could sleep on my couch. You're a bit tall for it, but it's comfortable. I've slept there myself.'

'That sounds fine to me.' Better than fine, but he couldn't let her see how happy he was, or how surprised. It was all so much easier than even his wildest dreams.

They exchanged another smile and kept walking. She felt comfortable with him, and hadn't felt this peaceful in years. It didn't matter if she let him sleep on her couch. So what if he knew where she lived? In the end, what did it really matter? How long could she hide – from him, from herself, from strangers and friends? The precautions were becoming an unbearable burden. At least for one night, she wanted to see the burden aside. Luke was her friend; he wouldn't harm her, even if he knew her address.

'Do you want to go home now?' They were at Seventy-second and York.

'Do you live near here?' The neighbourhood surprised him. It was middle-class ugly.

'Not too far from here. A few blocks over and a couple more blocks up.' They headed west on Seventy-second Street, and the neighbourhood began to improve.

'Tired, Kate?'

'I must be, but I don't feel it.'

'You're probably still numb from the drunk you tied on last night.' He grinned.

'What a rotten thing to bring up! Just because I get drunk once a year . . .'

'Is that all?'

'It certainly is!'

He pulled one of the pigtails and they crossed the deserted street. Downtown, traffic would still be blaring, but here there was no one in sight. They had reached Park Avenue now, divided by neat flower beds and hedges.

'I wouldn't say you live in the slums, Katie Miller.' For a while, as they had strolled along York, he wondered if she'd take him to a different apartment to keep secret the place where she lived. Thank God, she wasn't as frightened as that. 'You must do well with your articles.' A look of open teasing passed between them, and they both started to laugh.

'I can't really complain.'

She was playing it right till the end. She wasn't going to cop to a thing. It amazed him. So secretive, and what in hell for? He pitied her for the agonies of her double life. Or maybe she didn't spend enough time on his side of the tracks to make it a strain. But there was SoHo, the place she went to 'get away.' From what? Herself? Her friends? He knew her parents were dead. What could she have to get away from? Surely not the guy he'd seen with her in the paper.

They turned a corner onto a tree-lined street, and she paused with a smile at the first door. An awning, a doorman, an impressive address.

'This is it.' She pressed the bell, and the doorman fought with the lock. He looked sleepy and his hat was tilted back on his head. It was a relief man, she observed, and all he ventured was a vague, 'Good evening.' Providentially, he couldn't remember her name.

Luke smiled to himself in the elevator. She turned the key to her apartment and pushed open the door. There was mail neatly stacked on the hall table, the cleaning woman had been there, and the place looked impeccably neat and smelled of fresh wax.

'Can I offer you some wine?'

'Champagne, I presume.'

She turned to look at him, and he was smiling gently at her, mischief in his eyes. 'It's quite a pad, baby. Class, by the barrel.' But he didn't say it cruelly; it was more like a question.

'I could tell you it's the home of my parents ... but I wouldn't want to do that.'

'Is it ... or was it?'

She raised an eyebrow. 'Nope, it's mine. I'm old enough to put together something like this for myself now.'

'As I said, you must do well with your work.'

She shrugged and smiled. She wanted to make no excuse. 'What about that wine? It's pretty lousy actually. Would you rather have a beer?'

'Yes. Or a cup of coffee. I think I'd rather have that.' She left him to put on the kettle, and he ambled after her, his voice reaching her from the doorway as she clattered cups in the kitchen. 'Hey, do you have a roomie?'

'A what?' She wasn't paying attention; she would have grown pale if she had.

'A roommate. Do you have one?'

'No. Why? Do you take cream and sugar?'

'No, thanks. Black. No roommate?'

'Nope. What makes you ask?'

'Your mail.' She paused with the kettle in her hand, and looked around at him.

'What about my mail?' She hadn't thought of that.

'It's addressed to a Miss Kezia Saint Martin.' Time seemed to stand still between them. Neither moved.

118

'Yes. I know.'

'Anyone you know?'

'Yeah.' The weight of the world seemed to fall from her shoulders with one word. 'Me.'

'Huh?'

'I'm Kezia Saint Martin.' She attempted a smile but looked almost stricken, and he tried to feign shock. Had she known him a little bit better she'd have laughed at the look in his eyes.

'You mean you're not Kate S. Miller?'

'Yeah, I'm K. S. Miller too. When I write.'

'Your pen name. I see.'

'One of many. Martin Hallam is another.'

'You collect aliases, my love?' He walked slowly towards her.

She put the kettle down on the stove, and turned deliberately away. All he could see was the dark hair and her narrow shoulders bent over.

'Yes, aliases. And lives. There are three of me, Luke. Four actually. No, five now, counting "Kate." K. S. Miller never needed a first name before. It's all more than a little schizophrenic.'

'Is it?' He was right behind her now, but he did not reach out to touch her. 'Why don't we go sit down and talk for a while?'

His voice was low and she turned to face him with a barely perceptible nod. She needed to talk, and he'd be a good man to talk to. She had to talk to someone before she went mad. But now he knew she was a liar . . . or maybe that didn't matter with Luke. Maybe he'd understand.

'Okay.' She followed him into the living room, sat primly on one of her mother's blue velvet chairs, and watched him lean back on the couch.

'Cigarette?'

'Thanks.' He lit it for her and she took a long, deep pull at the unfiltered cigarette, collecting her thoughts.

'It sounds sort of crazy when you tell someone about it. And I've never tried to tell anyone before.'

'Then how do you know it sounds crazy?' His eyes were unwavering.

'Because it is crazy. It's an impossible way to live. I know, I've tried. "My Secret Life," by Kezia Saint Martin.' She tried to laugh, but it was a hollow sound in the silence.

'Sounds like it's time you got it off your chest, and I'm handy. I'm sitting here and I've got nowhere to go and no time to be there. And all I know is that it's an insane life you seem to lead, Kezia. You deserve better than that.' Her name sounded unfamiliar on his lips, and she looked at him through the smoke. 'Worse than crazy, this must be a mighty lonely way to live.'

'It is.' She felt tears well up at the back of her throat. She wanted to tell Luke all of it now. K. S. Miller, Martin Hallam, Kezia Saint Martin. About the loneliness and the hurt and the ugliness of her world draped in gold brocade, as though they could hide it by making it pretty outside, or make their souls smell better by drenching them in perfume . . . and the intolerable obligations and responsibilities, and the stupid parties, and the boring men. And the victory of her own byline on her first serious article, and no one to share it with except a middle-aged lawyer and a still older agent. She had a lifetime to show him, a lifetime she had hidden deep in her heart, until now.

'I don't even know where to begin.'

'You said there are five of you. Pick one, and take it from there.'

Two lone tears slid down her face and he stretched out a hand to her. She took it, and they sat that way, their hands reaching across the table, the tears running slowly down her face.

'Well, the first me is Kezia Saint Martin. The name you saw on the letters. Heiress, orphan . . . isn't that a romantic vision?' She smiled lopsidedly through her tears. 'Anyway, my parents both died when I was a child, and left me a great deal of money and an enormous house, which my trustee sold and turned into a large co-op on Eighty-first

Street and Park, which I eventually sold to buy this. I have an aunt who's married to an Italian count, and I was brought up by my trustee and my governess, Totie. And of course, the other thing my parents left me was a name. Not just a name. But a *Name*. And it was carefully impressed on me before they died, and after they died, that I wasn't just "anybody." I was Kezia Saint Martin. . . . Hell, Luke, don't you read the papers?' She brushed the tears away and pulled back her hand to blow her nose on a mauve linen handkerchief, edged in grey lace.

'What in God's name is that?'

'What?'

'That thing you're blowing your nose in?' She looked at the bit of pale purple in her hand and laughed.

'A handkerchief. What do you think it is?'

'Looks like a vestment for a pint-sized priest for chrissake. Talk about fancy. Now I know you're an heiress!'

She laughed and felt a little bit better.

'And yes, I do read the papers, by the way. But I'd rather hear this story from you. I don't like to just read about people I care about.'

Kezia was momentarily confused. People he cared about? But he didn't even know her . . . but he had flown up from Washington to see her. He was there. And he looked as though what she had to say mattered to him.

'Well, every time I set foot anywhere, I get my photograph taken.'

'It didn't happen tonight.' He was trying to show her something, that she was freer than she knew.

'No, but it could have. That was just luck. That's why I was watching the doors – that, and the fact that I was afraid I'd see someone I knew, and they'd call me Kezia instead of Kate.'

'Would that have mattered so much, Kezia? If someone had blown your cover? So what?'

'So . . . I would have felt like a fool. I would have felt

121

'Frightened?' He finished for her, and she looked away.

'Maybe.' Hers was a small voice now.

'Why, love? Why would it frighten you if I knew who you really were?' He wanted to hear it from her. 'Were you afraid that I'd hurt you then? Pursue you for your money? Your name? What?'

'No ... it's ... well, possibly. Other people might want me for those things, Lucas, but I'm not worried about that with you.' Her eyes sought his squarely and she made sure he understood her. She trusted him, and she wanted him to know that. 'But the worst of it is something else. Kezia Saint Martin isn't just me. She's "someone." She has something to live up to. When I was twenty, I was considered the most eligible girl on the market. You know, sort of like Xerox stock. If you bought me, your investment was bound to go up.' He watched her eyes as she spoke and there were years of hurt embedded in them. Lucas was silent, his hand gently holding hers. 'And there was more to it than just being noticed. There was history ... good history, bad history, grandparents, my mother....' She paused and seemed to forget to go on. Lucas' voice finally stirred her.

'Your mother? What about your mother?'

'Oh ... just ... things....' Her voice was trembling and her eyes avoided his. She seemed to be having trouble continuing.

'What kind of things, Kezia? How old were you when she died?'

'I was eight. And she ... she drank herself to death.'

'I take it "things" got to her too?' He sat back for a moment and watched Kezia, whose eyes now rose slowly to his with a look of unfathomable sorrow and fear.

'Yeah. Things got to her too. She was The Lady Liane Holmes-Aubrey before she married my father. And then she was Mrs. Keenan Saint Martin. I'm not sure which must have been worse for her. Probably being Daddy's wife. At least in England she knew how it all worked. Here, things were different for her. Quicker, sharper, brasher.

She talked about it sometimes. She felt more "public" here than she had at home as a girl. They didn't jump all over her the way they do me. But then, she didn't have Daddy's fortune either.'

'Was she rich too?'

'Very. Not as rich as my father, but directly related to the Queen. Fun, isn't it?' Kezia looked away bitterly for a moment.

'I don't know, is it fun? It doesn't sound like it yet.'

'Oh, it gets better. My father was very rich and very powerful and very envied and very hated, and occasionally very loved. He did crazy things, he travelled a lot, he . . . he did whatever he did. And Mummy was lonely, I think. She was constantly spied on, written about, talked about, followed around. When she went to parties, they reported what she wore. When Daddy was away, and she danced with an old friend at a charity ball, they made a thing of it in the papers. She got to feeling hunted. Americans can be brutal that way.' Her voice trailed off for a moment.

'Only Americans, Kezia?'

She shook her head. 'No. They're all as bad. But they can be more direct about it here. They're gutsier, or less embarrassed. They show less "deference," I don't know . . . maybe she was just too frail. And too lonely. She always looked as though she didn't quite understand "why." '

'She left your father?' He was interested now. Very. He was beginning to feel something for the woman who had been Kezia's mother. The frail British noblewoman.

'No. She fell in love with my French tutor.'

'Are you kidding?' He looked almost amused.

'Nope.'

'And it made a big stink?'

'I guess so. It must have. It killed her.'

'That, directly?'

'No . . . who knows? That and a lot of other things. My father found out, and the young man was dismissed. And I guess it got to her after that. She was a traitor, and she sentenced herself to death. She drank more and more, and

123

ate less and less, and finally she got what she wanted out of it. Out.'

'You knew? About the tutor, I mean.'

'No, not then. Edward, my trustee, told me later. To be sure that the "sins of the mother would never be visited on the daughter." '

'Why do you call it a "betrayal"? Because she cheated on your father?'

'No, that would have been forgivable. The unforgivable was that she betrayed her ancestry, her heritage, her class and her breeding by falling in love – and having an affair – with a "peasant." ' She tried to laugh, but the sound was too brittle.

'And that's a sin?' Lucas looked confused.

'That, my dear, is the cardinal sin of all! Thou shalt not screw the lower classes. That applies to the women of my set anyway. For the men it's different.'

'For them it's okay to screw the "lower classes"?'

'Of course. Gentlemen have been balling the maid for hundreds of years. It's just that the lady of the house is not supposed to get laid by the chauffeur.'

'I see.' He tried to look amused but he wasn't.

'That's nice. My mother didn't see. And she committed an even worse crime. She fell in love with him. She even talked about running away with him.'

'How in hell did your father find out? Did he have her followed?'

'Of course not. He never suspected. No, Jean-Louis simply told him. He wanted fifty thousand dollars from my father not to make a scandal, not very much, all things considered. My father paid him twenty-five and had him deported.'

'Your trustee told you all this?' Lucas looked stormy now.

'Of course. Insurance. It's meant to keep me in line.'

'Does it?'

'In a way.'

'Why?'

124

'Because in a perverted way I'm afraid of my destiny. It's sort of "damned if you do, and damned if you don't." I think that if I lived my life the way I'm supposed to, I'd hate it enough to drink myself to death like my mother. But if I betray my "heritage," then maybe I'll end up like her anyway. A betrayer betrayed, in love with a two-bit low-class jerk who blackmailed her husband. Pretty, isn't it?'

'No. It's pathetic. And you really believe that crap about betrayal?'

She nodded. 'I have to. I've seen too many stories like that. I've . . . in small ways it has happened to me. When people know who you are they . . . they treat you differently, Lucas. You're no longer a person to them. You're a legend, a challenge, an object they must have. The only ones who understand you are your own kind.'

'Are you telling me they understand you?' He looked stunned.

'No. That's the whole trouble. For me, none of it works. I'm a misfit. I can't bear what I'm supposed to be. And I can't have what I want . . . I fear it anyway. I . . . oh hell, Lucas, I don't know.' She looked distraught as she folded a matchbook between her fingers.

'What happened to your father?'

'He had an accident, and not because he was heartsick over my mother. He had a healthy number of women after she died. Even though I'm sure he missed Mummy. But he was very bitter then. It seemed as though he didn't believe in anything anymore. He drank. He drove too fast. He died. Very simple really.'

'No, very complicated. What you're telling me is that a "betrayal," as you call it, of your "heritage," your world, leads to suicide, death, accidents, blackmail and heartbreak. But what does following the rules lead to? What happens if you play it straight, Kezia, and never "betray your class," as you'd put it? What happens if you just go along with their rules . . . I mean you, Kezia. What would it do to you?'

125

'Kill me slowly.' Her voice was very soft but she sounded very certain.

'Is that what's been happening to you?'

'Yes. I think so, in a small way. I still have my escapes, my freedoms. They help. My writing is my salvation.'

'Stolen moments. Do you ever take those freedoms openly?'

'Don't be ridiculous, Lucas. How?'

'Any way you have to. Just do what you want to, openly for a change?'

'I couldn't.'

'Why not?'

'Edward. The press. Whatever I did that was even the least out of line, would be all over the papers. And I mean something as simple as going out with someone "different," ' she looked at him pointedly, 'going somewhere "inappropriate," saying something unguarded, wearing something indiscreet.'

'All right, so you get bad press. And then what? Chicken Little, the sky would not fall in.'

'You don't understand, Lucas. It would.'

'Because Edward would raise hell? So what?'

'But what if he's right . . . and . . . what . . . what if I end up . . .' She couldn't say it but he could.

'Like your mother?'

She looked up, her eyes swimming in tears, and nodded.

'You wouldn't, babe. You couldn't. You're different. You're freer, I'm sure. You're probably more worldly, and maybe even more intelligent than she was. And hell, Kezia, what if you did fall in love with the tutor, or the butler, or the chauffeur, or me for that matter? So fucking what?'

She didn't answer the question. She didn't know how. 'It's a special world, Lucas,' she said finally, 'with its own special rules.'

'Yeah. Like the joint.' He looked suddenly bitter.

'You mean prison?'

He nodded quietly in answer. 'I think you may be right. A silent, invisible prison, with walls built of codes and hypocrisies and lies and restrictions, and cells padded with prejudice and fear, and all of it studded with diamonds.'

He looked up at her suddenly and laughed.

'What's funny?'

'Nothing, except that nine-tenths of the world are out there beating each other over the head to get into that elite little world of yours, and from the sound of it, they won't dig it when they get there. Not much.'

'Maybe they will. Some do.'

'But what happens to the ones who don't, Kezia? What happens to the ones who can't live with that bullshit?' He held tightly to her hand as he spoke, and her eyes rose slowly to his.

'Some of them die, Lucas.'

'And the others? The ones who don't die?'

'They live with it. They make peace with it. Edward is like that. He accepts the rules because he has to. It's the only way he knows, but it's ruined his life too.'

'He could have changed all that.' Luke sounded gruff and Kezia shook her head.

'No, Lucas, he couldn't have. Some people can't.'

'Why not? No balls?'

'If you want to call it that. Some people just can't stomach the unknown. They'd rather go down with a familiar ship than drown in unfamiliar seas.'

'Or get saved. There's always the chance that they'd find a lifeboat, or wash up on an island paradise. How about that for a surprise?'

But Kezia was thinking of something else. It was minutes before she spoke again, her eyes closed, her head resting on the back of the chair. She sounded very tired, and almost old. She wasn't entirely sure Luke understood. Maybe he couldn't. Maybe no outsider could. 'When I was twenty-one, I wanted to have a life of my own. So I tried to get a job at the *Times*. I swore to Edward that I could pull it off, that no one would bother me, that I wouldn't disgrace my name, all that bullshit. I lasted for seventeen workdays, and I almost had a nervous break-

127

down. I heard every joke, was the butt of every kind of hostility, curiosity, envy and obscenity. They even had paparazzi in the ladies' room when I had to pee. It amused them to hire me and watch the fun. And I tried, Luke, I really tried, but there was no way I could stick with it. They didn't want me. They wanted my fancy name and then to try and bring me down, just for kicks, to see if I was human too. I never came out in the open again. That was the last job anyone knew about, the last glimpse of the real me that the world out there had. From then on it was all underground, with pseudonyms, hiding behind agents, and . . . well, it's all been just the way it was when I met you. And this is the first time I've taken a chance on being found out.'

'Why did you?'

'Maybe I had to. But as far as anyone knows, I go to all the right parties, am on all the right committees, vacation in all the right places, know all the right people, and everyone thinks I'm lazy as hell. I have a reputation for partying all night and sleeping till three in the afternoon.'

'And don't you?' He couldn't suppress a grin.

'No, I do not!' She wasn't amused, she was angry. 'I work my bloody ass off, as a matter of fact. I take every decent article I can get, and I have a good name in my field. You don't get that by sleeping till three.'

'And that doesn't fit with all the "right" people? Writing isn't "right" either?'

'Of course not. It's not respectable. Not for me. I'm supposed to be looking for a husband and having my hair done, not snooping around prisons in Mississippi.'

'Or ex-cons in Chicago.' There was a hint of sadness in his eyes. She had made it all so clear now.

'Their objection would not be to whom I write about, it would be the fact that I'm betraying my heritage.'

'That again. Jesus, Kezia, isn't that notion a little out-of-date? A lot of your kind of people work.'

'Yes, but not like this. Not for real. And . . . there's more.'

'I figured that much.' He lit another cigarette and waited, and was surprised when she smiled.

'Aside from everything else, I'm a traitor. Have you ever read the Martin Hallam column? It's syndicated so you might have seen it.'

He nodded.

'Well, I write that. I started it as a kind of a fun thing, but it worked, and . . .' She shrugged and threw up her hands as he started to laugh.

'You mean you write that crazy goddamn column?'

She nodded, grinning sheepishly.

'And you rat on all your fancy friends like that?'

She nodded again. 'They lap it up. They just don't know that I'm the one who writes it. And to tell you the truth, in the last couple of years it's gotten to be a drag.'

'Talk about being a traitor! And no one suspects it's you?'

'Nope. No one ever has. They don't even know it's written by a woman. They just accept it. Even my editor doesn't know who writes it. Everything goes through my agent, and of course I'm listed as K. S. Miller on the agency roster.'

'Lady, you amaze me.' Now he looked stunned.

'Sometimes I even amaze myself.' It was a moment of light-hearted laughter after the painful start of the conversation.

'I'll say one thing, you certainly keep yourself busy. The K. S. Miller articles, the Hallam column, and your "fancy life." And no one even suspects?' He seemed dubious.

'No. And that part hasn't been easy. That's why I panicked at the idea of interviewing you. I thought you might have seen my photograph somewhere, and would recognize me, as me, not as "Kate Miller" obviously. All it would take to blow my whole trip would be one person seeing me at the wrong place at the wrong time, and zap, the whole house of cards would go down. And the truth of it is that the writing part of my life, the serious work, is the only part I respect. I won't jeopardize that for anyone, or anything.'

'But you did. You interviewed me. Why?'

'I told you. I had to. And I was curious, too. I liked your book. And my agent pressured me. He was right, of course. I can't go on hiding forever if I want a serious literary career. There are times when I'll have to take chances.'

'You took a big one.'

'Yes, I did.'

'Are you sorry?' He wanted an honest answer.

'No. I'm glad.' They smiled at each other again, and she sighed.

'Kezia. what if you told the world, *that* world, to go screw, and just openly did what you want for a change? Couldn't you at least be K. S. Miller out front?'

'How? Look at the stink it would make, what they'd say in the papers. Besides, it would muddy the waters. People would be requesting articles not because of K. S. Miller, but because of Kezia Saint Martin. I'd be back where I was eight years ago, as a gofer on the *Times*. And my aunt would have fits, and my trustee would be heartbroken, and I'd feel as though I had betrayed everyone who came before me.'

'For chrissake, Kezia. All those people are dead, or as good as.'

'The traditions aren't. They live on.'

'And all on your shoulders, is that it? You have the sole responsibility of holding up the world? Don't you realize how insane that is? This isn't Victorian England, and Jesus, that's your life you're hiding in the closet. Yours, one shot at it and it's gone. If you respect what you're doing, why not take your chances, drag it out of the closet and live it with pride? Or is it that you're too fucking scared?' His eyes burned holes in hers.

'Maybe. I don't know. I've never felt I had the choice.'

'That's where you're wrong. You always have a choice. About anything you do. Maybe you don't want a choice. Maybe you'd rather hide like a neurotic and live ten different screwed-up lives. It doesn't look worth a damn to me though, lady, I'll tell you that much.'

130

'Maybe it isn't. It doesn't look like much to me either right now. But what you don't understand is the matter of duty, obligation, tradition.'

'Duty to whom? What about yourself, dammit? Didn't you ever think of that? Do you want to sit around alone here for the rest of your life, writing in secret, and then going out to those asinine parties with that faggoty asshole?' He stopped suddenly and she frowned.

'What faggoty asshole?'

'The one I saw you with in the paper.'

'You mean you knew?'

He eyed her squarely and nodded. 'I knew.'

'Why didn't you tell me?' Her eyes blazed for a moment. She had let him so far into the inner sanctum of her life, a traitor already

'How could I tell you? "Hey, lady, before you do the next interview I'd like to tell you that I know your real name because I read about you in the paper"? So what? And I figured that you'd tell me when you were ready to, or maybe never. But if I slapped you in the face with it, you'd have run like the devil and I didn't want that.'

'Why? Afraid I might not write the article? Don't worry, they'd have sent someone else out to do it. You wouldn't have lost your story.' She almost sneered at him, and he grabbed her arm so suddenly it stunned her.

'No, but I might have lost you.'

She waited a long moment before speaking, and he still held her arm. 'Would it have mattered?'

'Very much. And what you have to decide now is whether or not you want to live lies for the rest of your days. Seems like a bummer to me ... terrified about who's going to see you when and where and with whom and doing what. Who gives a shit? Let them see you! Show them who you really are, or don't you even know, Kezia? I think that's the crux of it. Maybe K. S. Miller is as big a phony as Martin Hallam or Kezia Saint Martin.'

'Oh to hell with you, dammit!' she shouted, wresting her arm free. 'It's so goddamn easy for you to sit there and make speeches. You have absolutely nothing to lose. No one expects a damn thing of you, so how can you know what it's like? You can do anything you bloody well please.'

'Really?' His voice was quiet again and the texture of satin. 'Well, let me tell you something, Miss Saint Martin. I know about duty one hell of a lot more than you do. Only mine isn't to a bunch of upper-class mummies. My duty is to real people, guys I served my time with who have no one to speak out for them, no families to hire lawyers or remember them or give a damn. I know who they are, I remember them, sitting on their ass waiting for freedom, locked up in the hole, forgotten after years in the joint, some of them for as long as you've been alive, Kezia. And if I don't have the fucking balls to go out and do something for them, then maybe no one else will. They're my "duty." But at least they're real, and I guess I'm lucky, because I care about them. I don't just do it because I have to, or becau se I'm scared not to. I do it because I want to. I gamble my own ass for theirs, because every time I shoot my mouth off, I run the risk of winding up right back in there with them. So tell me about duty, and having something to lose. But I'll tell you one more thing before you do. And that's that if I didn't give a shit about them, if I didn't like them, or even love them, I'd say "Goodbye, Charlie" and tell them all to go fuck themselves. I'd get married again, have a bunch of kids, and go live in the country.

'Kezia, if you don't believe in the life you're leading, don't live it. It's as simple as that. Because the price you're trying to avoid paying, you're going to wind up paying anyway. You're going to wind up fucking hating yourself for wasting the years and playing games you should have outgrown years ago. If you dug that life, that would be fine. But you don't, so what are you still doing there?'

'I don't really know. Except I don't think I'm as ballsy as you are.'

'You're as ballsy as you want to be. That's bullshit.

You're just waiting for an easy way out. A petition that gives you your freedom, a man to come and take you by the hand and lead you away. Well, maybe it'll happen like that, but it probably won't. You'll probably have to do it all yourself, just like everyone else.'

She was silent in answer, and he found himself wanting to hold her. He had given her a lot to swallow in one dose, but he couldn't help himself. Now that she had opened the doors, he had to tell her what he saw. For both their sakes. But mainly for hers.

'I didn't mean to trample all over you, babe.'

'It needed to be said.'

'You could probably level some things at me that need to be said too. I see what you're going through, and you're right in a sense, it is a lot easier for me. I have an army of people waiting in the wings all the time to tell me how terrific I am. Not the parole board, mind you, but people, friends. That makes a big difference, it makes it kind of an ego trip. What you're trying to do is a lot harder. Causes carry a lot of glory, breaking away from home never does ... until later. Much later. But you'll get there. You're already more than halfway there, you just don't know it yet.'

'You think so?'

'I know so. You'll make it. But we all know it's a rough road.' As he watched her, he was once again stunned by all that he'd heard. The secrets from the depths of her soul, the confessions about her family and the insane theories about tradition and treason. It was all more than a little new to him, but intriguing nonetheless. She was the product of a strange and different world, yet a hybrid in her own way. 'Where do you think that road to freedom is going to take you, by the way – to SoHo?' He wanted to know, but she laughed at him.

'Don't be ridiculous. I have a pleasant time down there, but that's not the real thing. Even I know that. It just helps get me through the rest of the bullshit. You know, the only thing that isn't bullshit is K. S. Miller.'

133

'That's a byline, not a human being. You're the human being, Kezia. I think that's what you forget. Maybe on purpose.'

'Maybe I've had to. Just look at my life, Luke. It's nowhere, and the games are getting harder and harder to play. It's all one big long game. The game of the parties, the committees, the balls and the bullshit, the game of "artist's old lady in SoHo," the game of the gossip column. It's all a game. And I'm tired of living in a world that's so limited it can only bring itself to include about eight hundred people. And I don't fit in a scene like SoHo.'

'Why? Not your class?'

'No. Just not my world.'

'Then stop poaching on other people's worlds. Make your own. A crazy one, a good one, a bad one, whatever you want, just make it one that suits you, for a change. You make the rules. Be quiet about it if you think you have to, but at least try to respect your own trip. Don't sell out, Kezia. You're too smart for that. I think you realize yourself that you've gotten to a point where you're going to have to make some choices.'

'I know that. I think that's why I had the courage to invite you here. I had to. You're a good man, I respect you. I couldn't insult you with more lies and evasions. I couldn't insult myself like that. Not again. It's a question of trust.'

'I'm honoured.' She looked up to see if he was making fun of her, and was touched when she saw that he wasn't. 'And that makes four,' he announced.

'Four what?'

'You said there were five of you. You've just covered four. The heiress, the writer, the gossip columnist, and the tourist in SoHo. Who's number five? I'm beginning to like this.' He smiled easily again, and stretched out his legs.

'So am I. And I am not a gossip columnist, by the way. It's a "Society Editorial." ' She grinned primly.

'Forgive me, Mr. Hallam.'

'Indeed. The fifth me is your doing. "Kate." I've never told all this to anyone before. I think this marks the beginning of a new me.'

'Or the end of all the old ones. Don't just tack another role onto the list, another game. Do it straight.'

'I am.' There was tenderness in her eyes as she watched him.

'I know you are, Kezia. And I'm glad. For both of us. No . . . for you.'

'You've given me a kind of freedom tonight, Luke. That's a very special thing.'

'It is, but you're wrong about my giving it to you. I told you before that no one can take your freedom from you . . . and no one can give it back either. You manage that one all by yourself. Keep it safe.' He leaned over and kissed her on the top of her head and then moved to whisper in her ear. 'Which way's your john?'

She laughed as she looked up into his face. He was such a beautiful man.

'The john's down the hall to your left. You can't miss it, it's pink.'

'I'd be disappointed if it weren't.' His laugh was a slow rumble as he disappeared down the hall, and she went back to the kitchen to see about their coffee. Three hours had passed.

'Still want that coffee, Luke?' He was back and stretching lazily in the kitchen doorway.

'Could I trade it in for a beer?'

'Sure could.'

'Terrific, and you can keep the glass clean, thanks. No class. No class at all. You know how it is with the peasants.' He pulled the tab off the can and took a long swallow. 'Man, that tastes good.'

'It's been a long night. I'm sorry to have chewed your ear off like that, Luke.'

'No, you're not, and neither am I.' They smiled at each other again, and she sipped at a glass of white wine.

'I'll get you set up on the couch.' He nodded and took a

135

long swig of beer, as she stepped easily under the arm he had propped in the doorway.

She had the couch made up as a bed in a matter of moments.

'That ought to keep you till morning. Do you need anything else before I trot off to bed?'

What he needed would have shocked her. She was crisp and matter-of-fact again now. The lady of the house. The Honourable Kezia Saint Martin.

'Yes, as a matter of fact, I do need something before you "trot off to bed." I need a glimpse of the woman I sat here and talked to all night. You've got a poker up your ass again, my love. It's a lousy habit. I'm not going to hurt you, or rape you, or plunder your mind. I won't even blackmail you.'

She looked surprised and a little hurt as she stood across the room. 'I didn't feel you had plundered my mind. I wanted to talk to you, Lucas.'

'So what's different now?'

'I just wasn't thinking.'

'So you closed up.'

'Habit, I guess.'

'And I told you, a lousy one. Aren't we friends?'

She nodded at him, tears bright in her eyes again. It had been an emotional evening. 'Of course we're friends.'

'Good, because I think you're very special.' He crossed the room in three long strides, and gave her a hug and a kiss on the cheek. 'Good night, babe. Have a good sleep.' She stood on tiptoe and returned the kiss to his cheek.

'Thanks, and you too, Lucas. Sleep tight.'

He could hear a clock ticking somewhere in the darkened house, and there was no sound from her room. He had only been lying there for about ten minutes, and he was too keyed up to sleep. It felt as though they had talked for days, and he had been so afraid of frightening her away, of doing something to make her close the door again. That was why he was lying on the couch, and had settled

136

for a kiss on the cheek. She was not a woman you could rush at – not unless you wanted to lose her before you began. But they had come a long way in one night. He was content merely with that. He ran over the hours of talking in his mind . . . the expressions on her face . . . the words . . . the tears . . . the way she reached out for his hand. . . .

'Luke? Are you sleeping?' He had been so intent on his thoughts that he hadn't heard her bare feet pad across the carpeted floor.

'No. I'm awake.' He propped himself up on one elbow and looked at her. She was wearing a soft pink nightgown and her hair fell loose past her shoulders. 'Is anything wrong?'

'No, I can't sleep.'

'Neither can I.'

She smiled and sat down on the floor near the couch. He didn't know what to make of her reappearance. She was not always easy to read. Luke lit a cigarette and handed it to her. She took it, inhaled, and returned it.

'You did a nice thing for me tonight, Lucas.'

'What's that?' He was lying down again, gazing up at the ceiling.

'You let me talk out a lot of things that have been bothering me for years. I needed that so badly.'

And that wasn't all she needed, but the idea of dealing with that almost frightened him. He didn't want to screw up her life; she had enough on her hands.

'Luke?'

'Yeah?'

'What was your wife like?' There was a long silence and she began to regret having asked him.

'Pretty, young, crazy, like me in those days . . . and afraid. She was afraid to go it alone. I don't know, Kezia . . . she was a nice girl, I loved her . . . but it seems like a long time ago. I was different then. We did things, we never said things. It got all fucked up when I went to the joint. You have to be able to talk when something like that happens, and she couldn't. She couldn't even talk when

137

our little girl was killed. I think that's what killed her. It
knotted up inside her till she strangled on it and died. I
way she was dead before she committed suicide. Maybe
your mother.'

Kezia nodded, watching his face. He wore a farav
look, but his voice showed no emotion other than resp
for the passing of time.

'What made you ask?'

'Curious, I guess. We talked a lot about me tonight.'

'We talked a lot about me yesterday in the interview.
say we're even. Why don't you try and get some sleep?'

She nodded and he stubbed out the cigarette they 
shared, as she stood up.

'Good night, Luke.'

' 'Night, babe. See you tomorrow.'

'Today.'

He grinned at her correction, and then swatted one l
paw lazily in the direction of her bottom. 'Back-talker. (
your ass to bed now, or you'll be too tired to show me
town tomorrow.'

'Can you spend the day?'

'I plan to, unless you have something better to do.'
had never thought to ask her.

'Nope. I'm free as a bird. G'night, Lucas.' She turn
quickly in a flurry of pink silk then, and he watched her
wanting to reach out and stop her. And then it was o
before he could swallow the words.

'Kezia!' His voice was soft but urgent.

'Yes?' She turned with a look of surprise on her face.

'I love you.'

She stood very still, and neither of them moved. He
twisted on the couch, watching her face. And she lool
awed by his words.

'I . . . you're very special to me, Luke. I . . .'

'Are you afraid?'

She nodded, lowering her eyes. 'A little.'

'You don't have to be, Kezia. I love you. I won't h
you. I've never known a woman like you.'

She wanted to tell him that she had never known a man like him, but somehow she couldn't. She couldn't say anything. She could only stand there, wishing for his arms, and not knowing how to find them.

It was Lucas who went to her, quietly, wrapping himself in the sheet she'd used for his bed. He walked slowly towards her and put his arms around her, holding her close.

'Everything's okay, babe. Everything's just fine.'

'It is, isn't it?' She gazed up at him with a sunny look on her face. This was different from anything she had known. It mattered, it was serious, and to the core of her soul he knew who she was.

'Lucas . . .'

'Yeah, Mama?'

'I love you. I . . . love . . . you. . . .' He swept her up in his arms then, gently, easily, and carried her back to her room in the dark. And as he set her down, she looked up at him and smiled. It was the smile of a woman, mischievous, mysterious, and tender. 'You know something funny, Luke? I've never made love in my own bedroom before.'

'I'm glad.'

'So am I.' Their voices had sunk to whispers.

Her shyness fell away from her as she held out her arms to him, and he carefully pulled the pink silk nightgown down past her shoulders. She unravelled the sheet from his waist. His hands spent the dawn learning her body, and at last she fell asleep in his arms, as the sky was turning pale grey.

# CHAPTER XII

'Good morning, my love. What do you want to do today?'
She grinned at him with her chin on his chest.

'Oh, you know, the usual ... tennis, bridge, whatever
we're supposed to do on Park Avenue.'

'Up your nose.'

'My nose? Why my nose?'

'I love your nose. It's gorgeous.'

'You're crazy. Stark staring cuckoo, Miss Saint Martin.
Maybe that's why I love you.'

'Are you sure you love me?' She was playing a game that
women only play when they're sure.

'Absolutely certain.'

'How do you know?' She ran a finger along his neck
pensively and then let it float down his chest.

'Because my left heel itches. My mother told me I'd
know it was true love when my left heel itched. It itches. So
you must be the one.'

'Crazy nut.' He silenced her with a kiss, and she tucked
herself into his arms, and they lay side by side, enjoying the
morning.

'You're beautiful, Kezia.'

'So are you.' He had a lean, powerful body that rippled
with healthy muscles, covered by the smoothest of skin.
She bit gently at his nipple, and he swatted her small
white behind.

'Where'd you get the expensive-looking tan?'

'Marbella, of course. And in the South of France. "In
seclusion".'

'You're shitting me.' He looked vastly amused.

'I shit you not. The papers said I was "in seclusion".
Actually I went off on my own on a boat I hired in the

Adriatic, and just before Marbella I did some research for a story in North Africa. That was terrific!' Her eyes shone with the memory.

'You sure do get around.'

'Yup. I did a lot of work this summer too. Gee, Luke wouldn't it be neat if we could go to Europe together sometime? I mean the good places like Dakar and Marrakech, Camargue in France, and Brittany, and Yugoslavia. Maybe Scotland too.' She looked up at him dreamily and nibbled his ear.

'Sounds delightful, but unfortunately it'll never happen. Not for a while anyway.'

'Why not?'

'Can't. My parole.'

'What a bore.'

He threw back his head and laughed, pulling her away from his ear carefully, and looking for her lips with his mouth. They kissed hungrily and long, and when it was over he chuckled again.

'You're right, my parole is a bore. I wonder what they'd say if I told them that.'

'Let's tell them and find out.'

'I have a sneaking suspicion you would.'

She grinned wickedly at him and he pulled the sheet from her body to look at her aagain.

'You know what I love?'

'My bellybutton?'

'Better than your big mouth anyway. At least it's quiet. No, be serious for a minute . . .'

'I'll try.'

'Shut up.'

'I love you.'

'Oooh, woman, don't you ever stop talking?' He kissed her fiercely and tugged at a lock of her hair.

'I haven't had anyone to talk to in so long, never like this . . . it just feels so good I can't stop.'

'I know what you mean.' He ran a hand gently up the inside of her thigh with a passionate look in his eyes.

141

'What were you going to tell me?' She lay watching him matter-of-factly.

'Sweetheart, your timing is lousy. I was about to ravish your body again.'

'No, you weren't. You were going to tell me something.' She looked almost angelic.

'Don't be a tease. And I was going to tell you something before you interrupted me. What I was going to say is that it's incredible how last week I didn't even know you, and three days ago you appeared at one of my speeches, and two days ago I told you the story of my life. By yesterday, I had fallen in love with you. And now here we are. I didn't think things like this happened.'

'They don't. But I know what you mean. I feel like I've known you forever.'

'That's what I mean. Feels like we've been hanging out together for years. And I love it.'

'Have you ever felt like this before?'

'Women! What an impertinent question. But for your information, no, I have not. One thing's for damn sure, I've never fallen head over heels in love in three days before . . . and never with an heiress.'

He grinned at her and lit a cigar. Kezia reflected gleefully that her mother would have died. A cigar in the bedroom? Before breakfast? Good lord.

'Lucas, you know what you've got?'

'Bad breath?'

'Aside from that. You've got style.'

'What kind of style?'

'Gorgeous style, sexy style, courageous style, ballsy style . . . I think I'm crazy about you.'

'Crazy, for sure. About me, in that case I'm damn lucky.'

'So am I. Oh, Lucas, I'm so glad you're here. Imagine if I hadn't given you my phone number!' The thought appalled her.

'I'd have found you anyway.' He sounded totally confident.

'How?'

'I'd have found a way. Bloodhounds, if I'd had to. I wasn't about to let you slip out of my life in one breath. I couldn't keep my eyes off you all night at that first speech. I couldn't figure out if you were the writer who was coming to interview me.' It was delicious sharing the secrets of their first feelings, and Kezia was smiling as she hadn't in years.

'You scared me that first morning.'

'Did I? Jesus, and I tried so hard not to. I was probably ten times as scared as you were.'

'But you didn't look it. And you looked at me so pointedly, I kept thinking that you could see whatever I thought.'

'I wish to hell I could have. It was all I could do not to jump up and grab you.'

'Masher.' She rolled closer to him, and they kissed again. 'You taste of cigar.'

'Want me to go brush my teeth?'

'Later.' He smiled and rolled onto his stomach, the pink nightgown still tangled near his feet. He kissed her again and held her close in his arms, his body slowly taking hold of hers, his feet pressing her legs wide apart.


'Okay, lady, you said you'd show me the town.' He sat naked in one of the blue velvet chairs, smoking his second cigar of the day, and drinking his first beer. They had just finished breakfast. And she looked at him and started to laugh.

'Lucas, you look impossible.'

'I do not. I look extremely possible. And I feel better than hell. I told you, babe, no class.'

'You're wrong.'

'About what?'

'Having no class. Class is a question of dignity, and pride, and caring, and you happen to have lots of all three. I'm related to an absolute horde of people who have no class at all. And I met some people in SoHo who had tons of it. It's a very strange thing.'

143

'It must be.' He didn't seem to care one way or the other. 'So what are we doing today? Besides making love.'

'Hmm . . . all right, I'll show you the town.'

And she did. She arranged for a limousine, and they toured Wall Street and the Village, drove up the East River Drive and crossed Forty-second Street to Broadway, pausing at the Stage Delicatessen for cream cheese and bagels. Then they followed their route north to Central Park and swooped past the Plaza, where they stopped for a drink at the Oak Room. Back down Fifth, and up Madison past all the boutiques, and all the way uptown again, where they halted the chauffeur at the Metropolitan Museum and got out and walked in the park. It was six o'clock when they wound up at the Stanhope for drinks, fighting the pigeons for peanuts at the sidewalk cafe.

'You give a good tour, Kezia. Hey, I just thought of something. Want to meet one of my friends?'

'Here?' She looked surprised.

'No, not here, silly girl. Uptown. In Harlem.'

'Sounds interesting.' She looked at him with a long, slow smile. The idea intrigued her.

'He's a beautiful guy. Nicest dude I know. I think you'd like him.'

'I probably would.' They exchanged a sweet sunny look which reflected the warmth of the day.

'It wouldn't be too cool to go up in the limo though, would it?'

He shook his head in answer, and picked up the check. 'We can send Jeeves home, and catch a cab up.'

'Bullshit to that.'

'You want to go in the limo?' He hadn't counted on that. Certainly not for a trip up to Harlem, but maybe she didn't know how to travel any other way.

'Of course not, you dummy. We can go up on the subway. It's faster, and smarter. A lot more discreet.'

'Well, listen to her. "Discreet". You mean you take the subway?' He stood up and looked down at her face as they laughed. She was full of surprises.

144

'How do you think I used to go down to SoHo? By jet?'

'Your own private Lear, I would think.'

'But of course. Come on, Romeo, let's get rid of Jeeves, and go for a walk.' The chauffeur tipped his hat and was instantly gone, and they strolled leisurely towards the subway, where they descended into the bowels of the world, bought tokens, and shared pretzels and a Coke.

They reached the 125th Street station, and Luke held her hand as they climbed the stairs to the street.

'It's just a few blocks.'

'Come to think of it, Luke, are you sure he'll be home?'

'Nope. We're going to the place where he works and I'm sure that he'll be there. You can hardly drag him out of the damn place to feed him.'

Luke seemed broader suddenly as they walked along, and more sure of himself than he had appeared all day. His shoulders seemed to spread, his walk almost rolled, while his eyes kept careful watch on passersby. He was wearing his familiar tweed jacket, and she was in jeans. But this was still Harlem. A long way from home. For her. To him, it appeared to be something he knew. He was wary, but only he knew of what.

'You know something, Lucas? You walk differently here.'

'You'd better believe it. Brings back memories of Q.'

'San Quentin?' He nodded and they turned a corner, as Lucas looked up at a building and stopped.

'Well, baby, this is it.' They were standing in front of a decaying brownstone with a half-burnt-away sign: *Armistice House*. But it didn't look to Kezia as though it had been much of a truce.

He let go her hand and put an arm around her shoulders as they walked up the stairs. Two raucous teen-age black boys and a Puerto Rican girl came roaring out of the door, laughing and shrieking, the girl running away from the boys, but not very hard. Kezia smiled and looked up at Luke.

'So what's so different up here?'

Luke didn't smile back. 'Junkies, pushers, hookers,

pimps, street fights, shankings. Same stuff that goes on anywhere in town, in any town in the world these days . . . except the neighbourhood you live in. And don't get any fancy ideas. If you decide that you like Alejandro, don't come up here to visit after I'm gone. Give him a call, and he can come to see you. This isn't your world.'

'But it's yours?' She was almost annoyed at the speech. She was a big girl. She had survived before Luke. Though admittedly not in the middle of Harlem. 'And this is your world, I suppose?' she repeated. He didn't look like he fit any better than she did. Well, not much better.

'Used to be. But not anymore. I can deal with it though. You can't. It's as simple as that.' He held the door open for her and his tone of voice told her he meant business.

The corridor, lined with faded posters, smelled of stale urine and fresh grass. Graffiti doubled as artwork between the posters, and glass shades around light bulbs had been broken, and paper flowers hung limply from fire extinguishers. A tired sign said 'Welcome to Armistice House! We love you!' And someone had crossed out the 'love' and written 'fuck'.

Luke wove his way up a narrow staircase, keeping one hand in Kezia's, but the tenseness was leaving him now. The once-upon-a-time street fighter had come for a visit. A social call. She laughed, suddenly reminded of the legends of the Old West.

'What's so funny, Mama?' He looked at her from his great height as she came up the stairs behind him, light on her feet, smiling and happy.

'You are, Marshal Dillon. Sometimes you're an absolute riot.'

'Oh, is that so?'

'Yes, that's so.' She leaned her face towards him and he bent down to kiss her.

'I like that. I like it a lot.' He ran his hand across her behind as she joined him on the landing, and he gave her a gentle push towards a badly scarred door.

'Are you sure he's here?' Kezia felt suddenly shy.

146

'I'm sure, babe. He's always here, the dumb asshole. He spills his guts in this shithouse. His guts and his heart and his soul. You'll see.' The name on the door said 'Alejandro Vidal.' No promises, no slogans, and this time no graffiti. Only a name.

Kezia waited for Luke to knock, but he didn't. He kicked brutally at the door, and then opened it at lightning speed as he entered.

'*Qué* . . .' A slight Latino man behind a desk rose to his feet with a look of astonishment, and then began laughing.

'Luke, you bastard, how are you? I should have known it was you. For a second, I thought they were finally coming to get me.'

The small, blue-eyed, bearded Mexican looked ecstatic to see him, as Luke strode across the room and threw his arms around his friend.

It was several minutes before Luke remembered Kezia, or Alejandro even took notice, and it was just as long again before Kezia got more than a glimpse of the man, lost in Luke's bear hugs. There had been a wealth of *¿Qué pasa, hombre?*'s and a fast flurry of Mexican curses. Alejandro's pure Spanish, and the pidgin Luke had picked up in the joint. Jokes about 'twice pipes' and someone's 'short', and a variety of unintelligible dialects that were part Mexican, part prison, and pure Californian. The patois was a mystery to Kezia. And then suddenly it all stopped, and the kindest smile and softest eyes imaginable settled on Kezia's face. The smile was a slow spread from the eyes to the mouth, and the eyes were the softest blue velvet. Alejandro Vidal had the kind of face you brought your troubles to, and your heart. Almost like a Christ, or a priest. He looked shyly at Kezia and smiled.

'Hello. This rude sonofabitch will probably never remember to introduce us. I'm Alejandro.' He held out a hand and she met it with hers.

'I'm Kezia.' They shook hands with ceremony and then laughter, and Alejandro offered the room's only two chairs as he perched on his desk.

147

He was a man of average height, but of slight build, and next to Luke he was instantly dwarfed. But it wasn't his frame that caught one's attention. It was his eyes. They were tender and knowing. They didn't reach out and grab you; you went to them gladly. Everything about him was warm. His laughter, his smile, his eyes, the way he looked at them both. He was a man who had seen a great deal, but there was not a trace of the cynic about him. Only the understanding of the sorely tried, and the compassion of a gentle man. His sense of humour allowed his soul to survive what he saw. And while Luke and he made jokes for an hour, Kezia watched him. He was an odd contrast to Luke, but she liked him instantly, and knew why he was Luke's closest friend. They had met long ago in L.A.

'How long have you been in New York?' It was the first time she'd addressed him since they'd met. He had given her tea, and then succumbed to gossip and nonsense with Luke. It had been a year since they'd seen each other and there was much to catch up on.

'I've been here about three years, Kezia.'

'Seems like long enough to me,' Luke broke into the exchange. 'How much shit you gonna take around this dump, Al, before you get smart and go home? Why don't you go back to L.A.?'

'Because I'm working on something here. The only problem is that the kids we treat are outpatient instead of live-in. Man, if we had a resident facility, I could take this shabby operation a long, long way.' His eyes lit up as he spoke.

'You're treating kids with drug problems?' Kezia was interested in what he had to say. If nothing else, it might make a good story. But more than the story, she was intrigued by the man. She liked him. He was the sort of person you wanted to hug, and she had only just met him.

'Yes, drug and minor criminal histories. The two are almost always related.' He came alive as he explained the services the facility offered, showed her charts, graphs, histories, and outlines of future plans. But the real problem

148

remained: lack of control. As long as the kids went back on the streets at night, back to broken homes where a mother was turning tricks on the room's only bed, or a father was zeating his wife, where brothers shot dope in the john, and sisters took reds or sold yellows, there wasn't a lot they could do. 'The whole point is to get them out of their environment. To change the whole life pattern. We know that now, but here it's not easy.' He waved dimly at the peeling walls and amply made his point. The place was in very bad shape.

'I still think you're nuts.' But Luke was, as always, impressed with his friend's determination, his drive. He had seen him beaten, mugged, rolled, kicked, laughed at, spat on, and ignored. But no one could ever keep Alejandro down. He believed in his dreams. As Luke did in his.

'And you think you're any saner, Luke? You're going to stop the world from building prisons? Hombre, you die before you see that one happen.' He rolled his eyes and shrugged, but the respect was entirely mutual. It amused Kezia to listen to them talk. To Kezia, Alejandro spoke perfect English, but with Luke he fell into the language of the streets. A put-on, a remnant, a joke, or a bond, she wasn't quite sure. Maybe a combination of them all.

'Okay, smartass, you'll see. Thirty years from now there won't be a prison functioning in this state, or in any other state for that matter.' She caught 'loco' and 'cabeza' in answer and then Luke flipped up one finger on his right hand.

'Please, Luke, there's a lady present.' But it was all in good fun, and Alejandro seemed to have accepted her. There was the faintest hint of shyness about him. Still, he joked with her, almost as he did with Luke. 'And you, Kezia? What do you do?' He looked at her with wide-open eyes.

'I write.'

'And she's good.'

Kezia laughed and gave Luke a shove. 'Wait until you see the interview before you decide. Anyway, you're pre-

149

judiced.' They shared a smile three ways and Alejandro looked pleased for his friend. He had known immediately that this was no light-hearted fling, no one-night stand or casual friend. It was the first time he had seen Luke with a woman. Luke kept his women in bed, and went home when he wanted some more. This one had to be special. She seemed different from the others too. Worlds different. She was intelligent, and she had a certain style. Class. He wondered where Luke had met her.

'Want to come downtown for dinner?' Luke lit a cigar and offered one to his friend. Alejandro took it eagerly and then looked surprised when he lit it.

'Cubano?'

Luke nodded. Kezia laughed.

'The lady's well-supplied.'

Alejandro whistled and Luke looked momentarily proud. He had a woman who had something no one else on their block had: Cuban cigars. 'How about dinner, big Al?'

'Lucas, I can't. I'd like to, but . . .' He waved at the mountain of work on his desk. 'And at seven tonight we're having a group for the parents of some of our patients.'

'Group therapy?'

Alejandro nodded. 'Getting to the parents helps. Sometimes.'

Kezia suddenly had the feeling that Alejandro was emptying a tidal wave with a thimble, but you had to give him credit for trying.

'Dinner another time maybe. How long will you be in town?'

'Tonight. Tomorrow. But I'll be back.' Alejandro smiled again and patted his friend on the back.

'I know you will. And I'm happy for you, man.' He gazed warmly at Kezia and then smiled at them both. It felt like a blessing.

It was obvious that Alejandro hated to see them leave as much as Lucas hated to go. And Kezia felt it too.

'You were right.'

'About what?'

150

'Alejandro.'

'Yeah. I know.' Lucas had been lost in his own thoughts all the way to the subway. 'That sonofabitch is going to get himself killed up here one of these days with his goddamn groups and his fucking ideals. I wish he'd get the hell out.'

'Maybe he can't.'

'Oh yeah?' Lucas was pissed. He was worried about his friend.

'It's kind of like a war, Luke. You fight yours, he fights his. Neither of you really cares if you get sacrificed in the process. It's the end result that matters. To both of you. He's not so different from you. Not in the way he thinks. He's doing what he has to do.'

Lucas nodded, still looking disgruntled. but he knew she was right. She was very perceptive. It surprised him sometimes. For someone as dumb as she was about her own life, she had a way of putting her finger right on the spot for others.

'You're wrong about one thing, though.'

'What?'

'He isn't like me at all.'

'What makes you say that?'

'There isn't a mean bone in his body.'

'But there is in yours?' A smile started to light in her eyes. Mr. Macho was talking.

'You'd better believe it, Mama. Lots of them. You don't live through what I did, six years in the California prison system, if you're made like him. Someone turns you into a punk, and if you don't dig it, you die the next day.' Kezia was silent as they started their journey back into the subway.

'He was never in prison then?' She had assumed that he had been, because Luke was.

'Alejandro?' Luke let out a hearty bass laugh. 'Nope. All his brothers were, though. He was visiting one of his brothers at Folsom. And I dug him. When I switched to another joint, he got special permission to come and see me. We've been brothers since then. But Alejandro's not on

151

the same trip, never was. He went the other way from the rest of his family. Magna cum laude at Stanford.'

'Christ, he's so unassuming.'

'That's why he's beautiful, babe. And the dude has a heart of pure gold.'

The arriving train swallowed their words, and they rode home in silence. She tugged at his sleeve at the Seventy-seventh Street stop.

'This is us.' He nodded, smiled, and stood up. He was back to himself again, she could see it. The worry for Alejandro had faded from his face. He had other things on his mind now.

'Baby, I love you.' He held her in his arms as the train pulled away, and their lips met and held. And then suddenly he looked at her, worried again. 'Is this uncool?'

'Huh?' She didn't know what he meant, as he pulled away from her looking embarrassed.

'Well, I can dig your not wanting to wind up in the papers. I made you a lot of speeches last night, but I do understand how you feel. Being yourself is one thing, making page one is another.'

'Thank God I never do that. Page five maybe, page four even, but never page one. That's reserved for homicides, rapes, and stock market disasters.' She laughed up at him again. 'It's okay, Luke. It was "cool". Besides . . .' there was mischief in her eyes . . . 'remarkably, very few of my friends ride the subway. It's silly of them, actually. This is such a marvellous way to travel!' There was pure debutante in her voice as she fluttered her eyelashes at him, and he gave her a severe look from the top of his height.

'I'll be sure to keep that in mind.' He took her hand and swung it as they walked along with matched smiles.

'Want to pick up something to eat?' They were passing a store that sold barbecued chickens.

'No.'

'Aren't you hungry?' She was suddenly famished. It had been a long day.

'Yes. I'm hungry.'

'Well?' He was hurrying her along the street and she didn't understand, and then with a look at his face she understood. Perfectly. 'Lucas, you're awful!'

'Tell me that later.' He took her by the hand, and laughing, they ran over the subway grate, and then turned the corner towards home.

'Lucas! The doorman!' They looked like dishevelled children, running helter-skelter down the street hand in hand. They came to a screeching halt outside the door to her building. He followed her decorously inside, as they both fought to stifle giggles. They stood in the elevator like altar boys, and then collapsed in laughter in the hallway as Kezia dug for her key.

'Come on, come on!' He ran a hand smoothly under her jacket, and slid it inside her shirt.

'Stop it, Luke!' She laughed and searched harder for the elusive key.

'If you don't find the damn thing at the count of ten, I'm going to . . .'

'No, you're not!'

'Yes, I am. Right here in the hall.' He smiled and ran his mouth over the top of her head.

'Stop that! Wait . . . got it!' She pulled the key triumphantly from her bag.

'Nuts. I was beginning to hope you wouldn't find it.'

'You're a disgrace.' The door swung open and he lunged for her as they stepped inside, and swept her into his arms to carry her to their bed. 'No, Lucas, stop!'

'Are you kidding?'

She arched her neck regally, perched in his arms, looked him in the eye and bristled, but there was mirth in her eyes. 'I am not kidding. Put me down. I have to go wee-wee.'

'Wee-wee?' Luke's face broke into broad lines of laughter. *Wee-wee?*

'Yes, wee-wee.' He put her down and she crossed her legs and giggled again.

'Why didn't you say so. I mean if I'd known that . . .' His laughter filled the hall as she disappeared towards the pink bathroom.

She was back in a minute, and tenderness had replaced the spirit of teasing. She had kicked off her shoes on the way, and stood barefoot before him, her long hair framing her face, her eyes large and bright, and something happy in her face that had never been there before.

'You know something? I love you.' He pulled her into his arms and gave her a gentle hug.

'I love you too. You're something I've imagined, but never thought I'd find.'

'Neither did I. I think I'd resigned myself to not finding it, and just going on as I was.'

'And how was that?'

'Lonely.'

'I know that trip too.'

They walked silently into the bedroom and he turned down the bed as she stepped out of her jeans. Even the Porthault sheets no longer embarrassed her, they were lovely for Luke.

# CHAPTER XIII

'Lucas?'

'Yeah?'

'Are you all right?' It was dark in the bedroom and she was sitting up, looking down at him, with a hand on his shoulder. The bed was damp around them.

'I'm fine. What time is it?'

'Quarter to five.'

'Christ.' He rolled over on his back, and looked up at her, groggy. 'What are you doing up, babe?'

'I wasn't. But you had a bad dream.' A very bad dream.

154

'Don't worry about it. I'm sorry I woke you.'

He stroked one breast tenderly with his eyes half-closed, and she smiled. 'My snoring's worse, though. You got off lucky.'

But she was worried. The bed was drenched from his thrashings.

'I think I'd rather you snored. You sounded so upset. Frightened, I think.' At the last, he'd been trembling.

'Don't worry about it, Mama. You'll get used to it.'

'Do you have dreams like that often?' He shrugged in answer, and reached for his cigarettes.

'Smoke?' She shook her head.

'Do you want a glass of water?'

He laughed as he flicked out the match. 'No, Miss Nightingale, I don't. Cut it out, Kezia. What do you expect? I've been a lot of funny places in my life. They leave their mark.'

But like that? She had watched him for almost twenty minutes before waking him. He acted as though he were being tortured.

'Is that . . . is that from when you were in prison?' She hated to ask, but he only shrugged again.

'One thing's for sure. It isn't from making love to you. I told you, don't worry about it.' He propped himself up on one elbow and kissed her. But she could still see terror in his eyes.

'Luke?' Something had just occurred to her.

'What?'

'How long are you staying here?'

'Till tomorrow.'

'That's all?'

'That's all.' And then, as he saw the look on her face, he stubbed out his cigarette and drew her into his arms. 'There'll be more. This is just the beginning. You don't think I want to lose you, after it took me all these years to find you, do you?' She smiled in answer, and they lay side by side, in the dark, silent, until at last they fell asleep. Even Luke slept peacefully this time, which was rarer than

Kezia knew. Lately, since they had started following him again, he had nightmares every night.

'Breakfast?' She was pulling on the white satin robe and smiled at him crookedly as she stretched.

'Just coffee, thanks. Black. I hate to rush through breakfast and I don't have much time.' He had leaped from the bed and was already pulling on his clothes.

'You don't?' She remembered again. He was leaving.

'Don't look like that, Kezia. I told you, there'll be more. Lots more.' He patted her bottom and she slipped easily into his arms.

'I'll miss you so much when you go.'

'And I'll miss you too. Mr. Hallam, you're a very beautiful woman.'

'Oh, shut up.' She laughed, but it embarrassed her when he reminded her of the column. 'What time's your plane?'

'Eleven.'

'Shit.' He laughed at her, and ambled slowly down the hall, his large frame rolling easily in his own special gait. She watched him silently, leaning in the bedroom doorway, reflecting that it seemed as if they had been together forever – teasing, laughing, riding subways, talking late into the night, watching each other sleep and wake, and sharing a cigarette and early morning thoughts before coffee.

'Lucas! Coffee!' She set a steaming cup down on the sink for him, and tapped his shoulder through the shower curtain. It all felt so natural, so familiar, so good.

He reached around the curtain for the cup, leaned his head out and took a sip. 'Good coffee. Are you coming in?'

She shook her head. 'No, thanks. I'm a bath person myself.' Given her choice, she always preferred bathing. It was less of a shock first thing in the morning. It was all part of a ritual. Dior Bath Oil, the perfumed water just warm enough and just high enough to cover her chest in the deep pink marble tub, then emerging into warm towels

156

and her cosy white satin dressing gown, and favourite satin slippers with the ostrich plumes and the pink velvet heels. Luke grinned at her as she stood watching him, and extended an arm to invite her to join him.

'Come on in.'

'No, Luke. Really. I'll wait.' She was still in a slow, sleepy mood.

'Nope. You won't wait.' And then with an unexpected, swift, one-handed motion he slipped the robe from her shoulders, and before she could protest, he had lifted her from her feet in the crook of his arm, and deposited her in the cascade of water beside him.

'I was missing you, babe.' He grinned broadly as she spluttered and pulled the strands of wet hair from her eyes. She was naked, save for the ostrich-plumed slippers.

'Oh! You ... you ... bastard!' She pulled the slippers from her feet, tossed them out of the tub, and hit him in the shoulder with the flat of her hand. But she was fighting laughter too, and he knew it. He silenced her with a kiss and her arms went around him as he leaned down to kiss her. He shielded her from the sheets of steaming water, and she found her hands travelling down from his waist to his thighs.

'I knew you'd like it once you got in.' His eyes were bright and teasing.

'You're a miserable, rotten, oversized bully, Lucas Johns, that's what you are.' But the tone did not match the words.

'But I love you.' He oozed male arrogance and a sort of animal sensuality, mixed with a tenderness all his own.

'I love you too,' and as he closed his eyes to kiss her, she ducked him and directed the shower head high full in his face, ducking down to nip playfully at one thigh.

'Hey, Mama, watch that! Next time you might miss!' But where he feared she would bite him, she kissed him, as the shower rippled through her hair and down her back, warming them both. He pulled her up slowly, his hands travelling over her body, and their lips met as he pulled her high into his arms and settled her with legs wrapped around his waist.

'Kezia, you're crazy.'

'Why?' They were comfortably ensconced in a rented limousine, and she looked totally at ease.

'This isn't the way most people travel, you know.'

'Yeah, I know.' She smiled sheepishly at him, and nibbled his ear. 'But admit it, it's fun.'

'It certainly is. But it gives me one hell of a guilt complex.'

'Why?'

'Because this isn't my style. I don't know, it's hard to explain.'

'Then just shut up and enjoy it.' She giggled, but she knew what he meant. She had seen other worlds too. 'You know, Luke, I've spent half of my life trying to deny this way of life, and the other half giving in to it and hating it, or hating myself for being self-indulgent. But all of a sudden, it doesn't bother me, I don't hate it, it doesn't even own me anymore. It just seems like a hell of a funny thing to do, and why not?'

'In that light, it isn't so bad. You surprise me, Kezia. You're spoiled and you're not. You take this stuff for granted, and then again you laught at it like a little kid. I dig it like this. You make it fun.' He looked pleased as he lit a cigar. She had armed him with a box of Romanoff Cubans.

'I dig it like this, too. Like this, my love, it's a whole other trip.'

They held hands in the back of the limousine and JFK Airport appeared much too soon. The glass window had been up between them and the chauffeur, and Kezia pressed the button to lower the window, to remind him which terminal they wanted. Then she buzzed the window back into place.

'Sweetheart, you're a bitch.'

'That's a nice contradiction.'

'You know what I mean.' He looked briefly at the window.

'Yeah. I do.'

They exchanged the supercilious smile of people born to command, one by her heritage, the other by his soul. They rode the rest of the way in silence, holding hands. But something inside Kezia quivered at the thought of his leaving. What if she never saw him again? What if it had all been a fling? She had bared her soul to this stranger, and left her heart unguarded, and now he was going.

But in his own silence, Luke had the same fears. And those weren't his only fears. He had felt it in his gut. Cop cars were all the same, pale blue, drab green, dark tan, with a tall shuddering antenna on the back. He could always feel them, and he had felt this one. And now it was tailing them at a discreet distance. He wondered if they had followed him that night from Washington, if even on the late-night walk to her apartment, he had been tailed. They were doing that more and more lately. It wasn't just near the prisons. It was getting to be everywhere now. The bastards.

The chauffeur checked Luke's bags in for him, while Kezia waited in the car. It was only a few moments before Luke stuck his head back in the car.

'You coming to the gate with me, babe?'

'Is this like the shower or do I have a choice?' They grinned at each other with the memory of the morning.

'I'll let you use your judgment on this one. I trust mine in the shower.'

'So do I.'

He looked at his watch and her smile disappeared.

'Maybe you'd better stay here, and just go back in to the city. It would be stupid for you to get into a lot of hassles.' He shared her concern. He knew what it would do to her to have a fuss made in the papers, in case someone saw them. And he was no Whitney Hayworth III. He was Lucas Johns, and newsworthy in his own right, but not in a way

159

that would have been easy for Kezia. And what if the cops in the blue car approached him? It could ruin everything with her, might scare her off.

She held her arms out to kiss him, and he leaned towards her.

'I'm going to miss you, Lucas.'

'I'll miss you too.' He pressed his mouth down hard on hers, and she stroked the hair on the back of his head. His mouth tasted of toothpaste and Cuban cigars; it was a combination that pleased her. Clean and powerful, like Luke. Straightforward, and alive.

'God, I hate to see you go.' Tears crept close to her eyes, and suddenly he withdrew.

'None of that. I'll call you tonight.' And in a flash, he was gone. The door thumped discreetly shut, and she watched his back as he strode away. He never turned back to look, as silent tears slid down her cheeks.

She left the window to the chauffeur as it had been. Closed. She had nothing to say to him. The drive back to the city was bleak. She wanted to be alone with the cigar smoke, and her thoughts of the day and two nights before. Her thoughts rambled back to the present. Why hadn't she gone to the gate with him? What was she afraid of? Was she ashamed of him? Why hadn't she had the balls to . . .

The window sped down abruptly and the driver looked in the rearview mirror in surprise.

'I want to go back.'

'Excuse me, miss?'

'I want to go back to the airport. The gentleman forgot something in the car.' She pulled an envelope from her handbag and clutched it importantly in her lap. A flimsy excuse, the guy had to think she was nuts, but she didn't give a damn. She just wanted to get back there in time. A time for courage had come. There was no turning back now, and Luke had to know that. Right at the start.

'I'll take the next exit, miss, and double back as soon as I can.'

She sat tensely in the back seat, wondering if they would

160

get there too late. But it was hard to argue with the chauffeur's driving, as he weaved in and out of lanes, passing trucks at terrifying speeds, all but flying. They pulled up outside the terminal twenty minutes after they had left it, and she was out the door almost before the driver had brought the car to a full stop at the kerb. She darted through travelling executives, old women with poodles, young women with wigs, and tearful farewells, and breathlessly she looked up to check the gate number for the flight to Chicago.

Gate 14 E. Damn ... at the far end of the terminal, almost the last gate. She was racing, and her hair pulled free of its tight, elegant knot. Talk about a story! She laughed at herself as she pushed through people and came close to knocking down children. The paparazzi would have a field day with this - heiress Kezia Saint Martin dashing through airport, knocking people down, for a kiss from ex-con agitator Lucas Johns. She choked on a bubble of laughter as she covered the last yards of the race and saw that she had made it in time. The vast expanse of his shoulders and back was filling the open doorway at the gate. She had just made it.

'Luke!'

He turned slowly, his ticket in his hand, wondering who was in New York that he knew. And then he saw her, her hair falling free of its pins, hanging loosely over the bright red coat, her face glowing from the dash from the car. A broad grin swept over his face, and he carefully removed himself from the line of impatient travellers, and made his way to her side.

'Lady, you're crazy. I thought you'd be back in the city by now. I was just standing here thinking about you as we got ready to board.'

'I was ... halfway ... back ... to the ... city ...' She was happy and breathless as they stood looking into each other's eyes. 'But ... I ... had to ... Come back.'

'For chrissake, don't have a heart attack on me now. You okay, babe?'

She nodded vigorously and folded into his arms. 'Fine.'

He took the last of her breath away with a kiss that brought her to her toes, and a hug that threatened her shoulders and neck.

'Thank you for coming back, crazy lady.' He knew what it meant. And she glowed as she looked up at him. He knew what she was, and what the papers could do with a kiss like the one they'd just indulged in, in broad daylight, with a sea of people around them. She had come back. Out in the open. And at that moment, he knew what he had hoped, but not quite believed. She was for real. And now she was his. The Honourable Kezia Saint Martin.

'You took a hell of a chance.'

'I had to. For me. Besides, I happen to love you.'

'I knew that, even if you hadn't come back . . . But I'm glad you did.' His voice was gruff as he held her again. 'And now I have to catch that plane. I have to be in a meeting in Chicago at three.' He pulled gently away.

'Luke . . .'

He stopped and looked at her for a long moment. She had almost asked him not to go back. But she couldn't do it. She couldn't ask for something like that. And he would never have stayed . . .

'Take good care!'

'You too. We'll get together next week.' She nodded and he walked through the door at the gate. All she could see was one long-armed wave before he disappeared down the ramp.

For the first time in her life, she stayed at the airport, and watched the flight take off. It was a good feeling, watching the thin silver plane rise into the sky. It looked beautiful and she felt brand new. For the first time she could remember, she had taken her fate in her hands and publicly taken her chances. No more hiding in SoHo or vanishing somewhere near Antibes. No clandestine nothing. She was a woman. In love with a man. She had finally decided to gamble. The only hitch was that she was a novice, and she was playing with her life, without

162

knowing how high the stakes had been set. She didn't see the plain-clothesman stubbing out his cigarette near the gate. She looked straight at him, and then walked away, unaware of the threat he was to them both. Kezia was a child walking blindly into a jungle.


# CHAPTER XIV


'Where in God's name have you been?' Whit sounded annoyed, a luxury he rarely allowed himself with Kezia.

'I've been here, and for Heaven's sake, Whit, you sound like someone ripped ten inches out of your knitting.'

'I don't think that's amusing, Kezia. I've been calling you for days.'

'I had a migraine, and I put the phone on the service.'

'Oh darling, I am sorry! Why didn't you tell me?'

'Because I couldn't speak to anyone.' Except Lucas. She had spent two days entirely alone since he'd left. Two glorious days. She had needed the time alone to absorb what had happened. He had called her twice a day, his voice gruff and full of laughter and loving and mischief. She could almost feel his hands on her as they spoke.

'And how are you feeling now, darling?'

'Wonderful.' Ecstatic. That new sound crept into her voice. Even with Whit.

'You certainly sound it. And I assume you remember tonight?' He sounded prissy and irritated again.

'Tonight? What's tonight?'

'Oh for God's sake, Kezia!'

Oh shit. Duty was calling. 'Well, I can't remember. Migraines do that to me. Remind me. What's tonight?'

'The dinners for the Sergeant wedding start tonight.'

'Jesus. And which one is this?' Had she already missed some of the frivolous fetes? She hoped so.

'Tonight is the first one. Cassie's aunt is giving a dinner in their honour. Black tie. Now do you recall, my love?'

Yes, but she wished to hell she didn't. And he spoke to her as though she were retarded. 'Yes, Whit. Now I remember. But I don't know if I'm up to it.'

'You said you felt marvellous.'

'Of course, darling. But I haven't been out of bed for three days. The dinner might be quite a strain.' And it was also a must, and she knew it. She had to go, for the column if nothing else. She had had plenty of time off. She had even run roughshod over the column for the past few days. Now back to work, and reality. But how? How, after Luke? The idea was absurd. What reality? Whose? Whit's? What utter bullshit. Luke was reality now.

'Well, if you're not up to it, I suggest you explain it to Mrs. FitzMatthew,' Whit was saying petulantly. 'It's a sit-down dinner for fifty, and she'll want to know if you're planning to disrupt her seating arrangement.'

'I suppose I should go.'

'I think so.'

Asshole. 'All right, darling, I will.' There was a hint of the martyr in her voice, as she stifled a giggle.

'You're a good girl, Kezia. I was really awfully worried about where you were.'

'I was here.' And so was Luke, for a while.

'And with a migraine, poor thing. If I'd known, I'd have sent you flowers.'

'Jesus, I'm glad you didn't.' It had slipped out.

'What?'

'The smell of roses makes the headache worse.' Reprieve.

'Oh. Then it's just as well I didn't know you were ill. Well, rest up for tonight. I'll come and get you around eight.'

'Black tie or white tie?'

'I told you, black. Friday night is white tie.'

'What's Friday?' Her whole social calendar had slipped her mind.

'Those headaches do make you forgetful, don't they? Friday is the rehearsal dinner. You *are* going to the wedding, aren't you?'

The question was purely rhetorical. But he was in for a shock. 'Actually, I don't know. I'm supposed to go to a wedding in Chicago this weekend. I don't know which I should do.'

'Who's getting married in Chicago?'

'An old friend from school.'

'Anyone I know?'

'No one you know, but she's a very nice girl.'

'That's nice. Well, do what you feel best.' But the annoyance was back in his voice again. She was so tiresome at times. 'Just let me know what you decide. I had rather counted on your being at the Sergeants'.'

'We'll work something out. See you later, love.' She blew him a glib kiss and hung up the phone, pirouetting on one bare foot, the satin robe hanging open to reveal still-suntanned flesh. 'A wedding in Chicago.' She laughed over her shoulder as she walked down the hall to run her bath. Hell, it was better than a wedding. She was flying out to meet Luke.


'Good Lord, you look spectacular, Kezia!' This time even Whit looked impressed. She was wearing a filmy silk dress that draped over one shoulder *à la grecque*. It was a pale coral shade and the fabric seemed to float as she walked. Her hair was done in two long looped braids threaded with gold, and her sandals were a dull gold that barely seemed to hang on her feet. She moved freely like a vision, with coral and diamonds brilliantly at her ears and throat. But there was something about the way she moved that troubled Whit as he watched her. She was so striking tonight that it was almost unsettling. 'I've never seen you look so well, or so beautiful.'

'Thank you, darling.'

She smiled at him mysteriously as she whisked past him out the door. The scent of lily of the valley hung close to

165

her. Dior. She looked simply exquisite. And it was more than just looks. Tonight she seemed more a woman than ever before. The change would have frightened him, had they not been such old friends.

There was a butler waiting for guests in the entrance to the house of Cassie's aunt. Two parking attendants had been on hand to relieve them of Whit's car, had he not brought the limousine. Beyond the indomitable butler, Georges, who had once worked for Pétain in Paris in the 'good old days', were two maids in starched black uniforms, waiting expressionlessly to collect wraps and direct ladies to the appropriate bedroom to tend to their faces and hair before making an 'appearance'. A second butler intercepted them on their way, to begin the evening with a round of champagne.

Kezia had a white mink jacket to offer the black uniform that approached her, but no need or desire to 'fix her face'.

'Darling?' Whit held a glass of champagne out to her, and that was the last time he saw her at close range. For the rest of the evening, he caught glimpses of her, laughing at the centre of a circle of friends, dancing with men he hadn't seen on the circuit in years, whispering into someone's ear, and once or twice he thought he saw her alone on the terrace, looking out over the autumn night on the East River. But she was elusive tonight. Each time he approached, she floated away. It was damn annoying in fact, that feeling of watching a vision, or simply a dream. And people were talking about her. The men were, at least, and in an odd way that troubled him. It was what he wanted, though, or thought he did – 'Consort to The Kezia Saint Martin'. He had planned it all carefully years ago but he didn't like the taste of it lately, or the sound of her voice, or the remark she had made to him that morning. He thought they had an understanding, unspoken but mutually understood. Or was it that you had to put it to them after all? At least everyone thought he did. Kezia was good about that. She didn't care about that sort of thing anyway. Whit knew that. He was certain ... or was it ... Edward? Suddenly the idea shot into his mind and wouldn't be banished. Kezia, sleeping with Edward? And the two of them making a fool of him?

'Good evening, Whit.'

The object of his newly formed suspicions had appeared at his side. 'Evening,' he muttered.

'Beautiful party, isn't it?'

'Yes, Edward, it is. Dear Cassie Sergeant is going out in style.'

'You make her sound like a ship. Though I must say the allusion is not entirely inept.' Edward looked virtuously as their gazes fell on the more than slightly rotund form of the soon-to-be bride, poured like cement into pink satin.

'Mrs. FitzMatthew is certainly doing her best.' Edward smiled vaguely at the crowd around them. The dinner had been superb. Bongo Bongo Soup, Nova Scotia salmon, crayfish flown in from the Rockies, Beluga caviar smuggled in from France in appalling quantities ('You know, darling, France doesn't have those absurd regulations about putting all that nasty salty stuff in it. Such a frightful thing to do to good caviar!'). The fish course had been followed by rack of lamb and an almost depressing number of vegetables, salade d'endives, and soufflé Grand Marnier – after the Brie, an enormous wheel of it from Fraser Morris on Madison, the only place in town to buy it. 'And only Carla FitzMatthew could possibly have a staff equal to organizing the task of soufflé for fifty.'

'Hell of a dinner, wasn't it, Whit?'

Whit nodded grimly. He'd had more than a bit too much to drink, and he didn't like the new thoughts his mind had turned up.

'Where's Kezia, by the way?'

'You ought to know.'

'I'm flattered that you think so, Whit. Matter of fact, I haven't talked to her all evening.'

'Then save it for bed tonight.' Whitney spoke into his drink, but the words were not lost upon Edward.

'I beg your pardon?'

'Sorry ... I suppose she's here somewhere. Flitting about. Looks rather handsome tonight.'

'I'd say you could do better than "handsome", Whitney.' Edward smiled into the last of his wine, musing about Whit's comment. He didn't like the tone of Whit's voice, and he couldn't have meant what it sounded like. Besides, he was obviously plastered. 'The child looks quite extraordinary. I saw you two come in together.'

'And you won't see us going out together. How's that for a surprise?' Whitney was suddenly ugly as he leered a smile at Edward, turned on his heel and then stopped. 'Or does that please rather than surprise you?'

'If you're planning to leave without Kezia, I think you might tell her. Is anything wrong?'

'Is anything right? Good night, sir. I leave her to you. You can bid her good evening for me.'

He was instantly gone in the crowd, depositing his empty glass in Tiffany Benjamin's hand as he left. She was conveniently standing in his path to the door, and gazed rapturously into the empty glass, waving it instantly for a refill, never noticing that she now had two in her hands.

Edward watched him go, and wondered what Kezia was up to. Whatever it was, it was clear that Whit didn't like it, though why, he couldn't imagine. Polite inquiries had confirmed years of suspicion. Whitney Hayworth III was determinedly gay, though not publicly. Bit of a shabby setup for Kezia, even if she did have that boy in the Village, not that that was a comforting thought. But Whitney ... why did he have to ... you just couldn't tell with people anymore. Of course those things had gone on in his youth too, especially among the prep school boys. But it was never taken as seriously then. It was a stopgap measure, so to speak; no one thought of it as a way of life. Just a passing stage before everyone settled down, found a wife, and got married. But not anymore ... not anymore ...

'Hello, love. Why so gloomy?'

'Gloomy? Not gloomy, just thinking.' Edward roused a smile for Kezia's benefit, and she was easy to smile for. 'And by the way, your escort just left. In his cups.'

'He's been in a bad mood all day. Practically lost his temper with me on the phone this morning. He'll get over it. Probably very quickly.' They both knew that Mrs. FitzMatthew's home was within a few short blocks of Whit's lover's. Edward chose to ignore the suggestion.

'And what have you been up to?'

'Nothing much. Catching up with a few people here. Cassie's wedding certainly dragged us all out of hiding. There are people here I haven't seen in ten years. It's really a beautiful night, and a very nice party.' She swirled around him, patted his arm, and planted a kiss on his cheek.

'I thought you didn't like these gala events.'

'Once in a great while I do.' He looked at her sternly, and then felt irresistibly pulled into laughter. She was impossible, and so incredibly pretty. No, more than pretty. She was extravagantly beautiful tonight. Whitney's feeble 'handsome' had been hopelessly inadequate as praise.

'Kezia . . .'

'Yes, Edward?' She looked angelic, artlessly keeping her eyes on his, and he tried to resist the urge to smile back.

'Where have you been lately? Whitney's not the only one who hasn't been able to reach you. I was a little worried.'

'I've been busy.'

'The artist? The young man in the Village?'

Poor thing, he actually looked worried. Visions of money fleeing from her frail little hands. . . . 'Not the Village. SoHo. And no, it wasn't that.'

'Something else? Or someone else, should I say?'

Kezia could almost feel her back begin to bristle. 'Darling, you worry too much.'

'Perhaps I have reason to.'

'Not at my age, you don't.' She tucked his hand into her arm, and walked him into a circle of his friends, curtailing

169

the conversation, but not allaying his fears. He knew her too well. Something had happened. Something that had never happened before, and she was already subtly altered. He felt it. Knew it. She looked much too happy and much too calm, and as though she had finally flown free from his reach. She was gone now. She wasn't even at Carla FitzMatthews' elaborate party. And only Edward knew that. The only thing he didn't know was where she really was. Or with whom.

It was half an hour later before Edward noticed that Kezia had left the party. An inquiry here and there told him that she had left alone. It disturbed him. She was not dressed to go gallivanting around the city alone, and he wasn't sure that Whit had left her the car. Rotten little faggot, he could at least have done that much for her.

He said his goodnights and hailed a cab to take him to his own apartment on East Eighty-third but somehow he found himself giving the driver Kezia's address. He was horrified. He had never done that before. Such foolishness . . . at his age . . . she was a grown woman . . . and perhaps she wasn't alone . . . but . . . he simply had to.

'Kezia?' She answered on the first ring of the house-phone, as Edward stood in embarrassment next to the doorman.

'Edward? Is something wrong?'

'No. And I'm sorry to do this, but may I come up?'

'Of course.' She hung up and he was upstairs a moment later.

She was waiting for him in the open doorway, as he emerged from the elevator. She looked suddenly worried as she stood barefoot in her evening gown, her hair loose, and her jewellery put away. And Edward found himself feeling like a fool.

'Edward, are you all right?' He nodded and she let him into the apartment.

'Kezia . . . I . . . I'm so sorry. I shouldn't have come, but I had to make sure you'd gotten home all right. I don't like to think of you dripping in diamonds and going home unescorted.'

'Darling, darling worrywart, is that all?' She laughed softly and her face broke into a smile. 'Good God, Edward, I thought something dreadful had happened.'

'Maybe it did.'

'Oh?' Her face grew serious again for a moment.

'I think I finally became senile tonight. I suppose I should have called instead of dropping by.'

'Well, now that you're here, how about a drink?' She didn't deny that he should have called, but she was always gracious. 'Some poire, or framboise?' She waved him into a chair and went to the Chinese inlaid chest where she kept the liquor. Edward remembered it well; he had been with her mother when she had bought it at Sotheby's.

'Poire, thank you, dear.' He sank tiredly into one of the familiar blue velvet chairs, and watched her pour the potent transparent liqueur into a tiny glass. 'You really are a good sport about your old Uncle Edward.'

'Don't be silly.' She handed him the drink with a smile and sank to the floor near his feet.

'Do you have any idea how beautiful you are?' She waved the compliment away and lit a cigarette, as he sipped at his poire. She was beginning to wonder if he'd already had too much to drink. He seemed a bit doleful as the moments ticked on. And she was waiting for a phone call from Luke.

'I'm glad you're all right,' he began. And then he couldn't stop himself anymore. 'Kezia, what are you up to?' He simply had to know.

'Absolutely nothing. I'm sitting here next to you and I had been about to get undressed and do some work on the column. I want to phone it in in the morning. . . . I don't think Carla's going to like me when I do. She's too easy to poke fun at. I couldn't resist.'

Kezia was trying to keep things light but Edward looked older and more tired than she had ever seen him.

'Can't you be serious for a moment? I didn't mean what

171

you were doing right now. I meant ... well, you look different lately.'

'How lately?'

'Tonight.'

'Do I look worried, sick, unhappy, undernourished? What kind of different?' She didn't like his questioning and now she was going to turn it around on him quickly. It was high time to stop this kind of nonsense. And she didn't want any more unannounced late night visits.

'No, no, nothing like that. You look extremely well.'

'And you're worried?'

'Yes, but ... all right, all right, dammit. You know what I mean, Kezia. And you're just like your bloody father. You don't tell anyone anything until after the fact. And then everyone else has to pick up the pieces.'

'Darling, I assure you, you will never have to pick up any pieces, not for me. And since we both agree that I look rested, healthy, and well-fed, my account is not overdrawn, and I have not appeared naked at the Oak Room ... what is there to worry about?' Her voice was only a trifle sharp.

'You're being evasive.' He sighed. He didn't have a chance and he knew it.

'No, darling. I'm enjoying the right to a little privacy, no matter how much I love you, or how good a father you've been to me. I'm all grown up now, love. I don't ask if you sleep with your maid or your secretary, or what sort of things you do alone in the bathroom at night.' Something about Edward told her he'd perform rituals like that in the bathroom, where they 'belonged'.

'Kezia! That's shocking!' He looked angry and pained. Nothing went his way anymore. Not with her.

'It's no more shocking than what you're basically asking me. You just say it more gently than I do.'

'All right. I understand.'

'I'm glad.' It was high time. 'But just to put your fidgety old soul to rest, I can honestly tell you that there's nothing for you to worry about right now. Nothing.'

'Will you tell me when there is?'

172

'Would I cheat you of an opportunity to worry?'

He laughed and sat back in his chair. 'All right. I'm impossible. I know it, and I'm sorry. No . . . I'm not sorry. I like knowing that all's right with your life. And now I'll let you finish your work. You must have gotten some good items for the column tonight.' The room had been ripe with gossip. And he was embarrassed at having probed, at being in her apartment at all, at this unsuitable hour. It wasn't easy being a surrogate father. And even less so being in love with your surrogate child.

'I got some very good items, as a matter of fact, along with tales of Carla's orgy of opulence. It really is a disgrace to spend thousands on a party.'

She sounded like the old Kezia again, the one who didn't frighten him, the one he knew so well and who would always be his.

'And of course I'll include me in the gossip,' she announced with a bright smile.

'Little wretch. What are you going to say about yourself? That you looked stunningly beautiful, I hope.'

'No, well, maybe a mention of the dress. But actually I've written up Whit's charming exit.'

Was she angry? Could she possibly care? 'But why?'

'Because, to put it bluntly, the time for fun and games is over. I think it's time Whit went his way and I went mine. And Whit hasn't got the balls to do it, and maybe neither have I, so if I run something embarrassing, his friend on Sutton Place will do it for us. If he's anyone at all, he won't tolerate Whit being publicly ridiculed.'

'My God, Kezia. What did you write?'

'Nothing indecent. I'm certainly not going to make scandalous accusations in the press. I wouldn't do that to Whit. Or myself. The point is really that I haven't time to play these games after all. And it isn't good for Whit either. All I said in the column was that . . . here, I'll read it to you.' She put on a businesslike voice and went to her desk. He watched her, feeling hunger in his heart.

' "The usual lovebirds were thick in the flock; Francesco

Cellini and Miranda Pavano-Casteja; Jane Roberts and Bentley Forbes; Maxwell Dart and Courtney Williamson, and of course Kezia Saint Martin and her standby consort Whitney Hayworth III, although this couple was seldom seen together last night as they each appeared to take flight on their own. It was also noticed that in what appeared to be a fit of pique, Whitney made an early solo exit, leaving Kezia 'midst the rest of the doves, hawks, and parrots. Perhaps the elegant Whitney grows tired of following in her wake? Heiresses can be such demanding people. Also of interest in Carla FitzMatthew's baronial halls. . . ." Well, how does it sound?' She sounded suddenly chirpy and unaffected by what she had written; the business voice was put away with the column. And news was news and gossip was gossip, and Edward knew it all bored her anyway.

He looked over at her with a dubious smile. 'It sounds rather uncomfortable. Frankly, I don't think he'll like it.'

'He's not meant to. It's supposed to be somewhat demeaning. And if he doesn't have the balls to tell me to go to hell after what I'm doing to his public image, then his boyfriend will tell him he has no guts. I think this will get to him.'

'Why don't you just tell him it's over?'

'Because the only good reason I have is the one I'm not supposed to know. That, and the fact that he bores me. And hell, Edward, I don't know . . . maybe I'm cowardly. I'd rather leave it to him. With a good prod in the right direction from me. It seems as though anything I could say to him directly would be too insulting.'

'And what you said in the column is better?'

'Of course not. But he doesn't know I said it.'

Edward laughed ruefully as he finished his drink and stood up. 'Well, let me know if your plot has any effect.'

'It will. I'd bet on it.'

'And then what? You announce that in the column too?'

'No. I thank God.'

'Kezia, you confuse me. But on that note, my dear, I bid you good night. Sorry to have called on you so late.'

'I'll forgive you this time.'

The phone rang as she walked him to the door and she looked suddenly excited.

'I'll let myself out.'

'Thanks,' she smiled, pecked his cheek and ran back to her desk in the living room with a broad smile, leaving Edward to shut the door softly and wait for the elevator alone.

'Hi, Mama. Too late to call?' It was Luke.

'Of course not and I was just thinking about you.' She smiled, holding the phone.

'So was I. I miss the hell out of you, babe.'

She unzipped her dress and walked the phone into the bedroom. It was so good to hear his voice in the room again. It was almost as though he were there. She could still feel his touch . . . still . . . 'I love you and miss you. A whole bunch.'

'Good. Want to come to Chicago this weekend?'

'I was praying you'd ask.'

He laughed gruffly into her ear and took a puff on one of the Cuban cigars. He gave her the number of the flight he wanted her on, blew her a kiss and hung up.

She slipped happily out of the dress, and stood smiling for a moment before getting ready for bed. What a marvellous man Lucas was. Edward had fled entirely from her mind. As had Whit, whose call was the first she got the next morning.

## CHAPTER XV

'Kezia? Whitney.'

'Yes, darling. I know.' She knew a lot more than he did.

'What do you know?'

175

'I know that it's you, silly. What time is it?'

'Past noon. Did I wake you?'

'Hardly. I just wondered.' So, it had run in the morning's second edition. She had gotten up at the crack of dawn to phone it in.

'I think we ought to have lunch.' He sounded very crisp and very businesslike, and very nervous.

'Right this minute? I'm not dressed.' It was rotten but she was amused. He was so easy to play with.

'No, no, when you're ready, of course. La Grenouille at one?'

'How delightful. I wanted to call you anyway. I've decided to go to that wedding in Chicago this weekend. I really think I should go.'

'I think you probably should. And Kezia . . .'

'Yes, darling, what?'

'Have you seen the papers today?'

Obviously, darling. I wrote them. At least the part you mean. . . . 'No. Why? Is the nation at war? Actually, you sound quite upset.'

'Read the Hallam column. You'll understand.'

'Oh dear. Something nasty?'

'We'll discuss it at lunch.'

'All right, darling, see you then.'

As he hung up, he chewed on a pencil. Christ, he hoped she'd be reasonable. It was really getting to be a bit too much. Armand wasn't going to put up with much more of this nonsense. He had thrown the front section at Whitney at breakfast, along with a terrifying ultimatum. Above all Whit couldn't lose him. He couldn't. He loved him.

Once settled at their table at La Grenouille, their conversation was staccato but direct. Or rather, Whit's was direct, and Kezia kept quiet. It was simply that he had gotten far too attached to her, felt far too possessive about her, and knew he had no right to. She had made that much clear. And how did that make him look? And what's more, he had so little to offer her at this point in his life; he

176

wasn't even a partner in the firm, and in light of who she was . . . and it was all getting so painful for him . . . and did she understand his position at all? It was just that he knew she would never marry him, and while she would always be the love of his life, he simply had to get married and have children, and she wasn't ready and . . . oh God, wasn't it awful?

Kezia nodded mutely and gulped her Quenelles Nantua. What was a girl to do? And yes, she understood perfectly, and he was quite right of course, she was light-years away from marriage, and possibly because of the death of her parents and being an only child, she'd probably never marry, to preserve her name. And children were not something she could even faintly imagine anyway, and she felt just awful if she'd hurt him, but this was probably all for the best. For both of them. She granted him the kindness of being right. And they would always remain the 'dearest friends alive'. Forever.

Whitney made a mental note to have Effie send her flowers once a week until she was ninety-seven. Thank God, she had taken it well. And hell, maybe he had had the right idea when he suspected she had something going with Edward. You never knew with Kezia, you only sensed that there was a lot more to her than she let on to, underneath all the poise and perfection. But who gave a damn? He was free! Free of all those intolerable evenings being the man on her arm. And naturally, to recover from the 'terrible pain of it all', he wouldn't be seen socially for months . . . and he could finally live a life on Sutton Place with Armand. It was about time too. Armand had made that much clear over breakfast. After three years of waiting, he had had it. And now with Whitney humiliated in the newspapers . . . Hallam had made him sound like a puppy nipping at Kezia's skirts, and maybe it was a good thing after all. He had finally done it. No more pretence, no more Kezia. Not for him.

Kezia walked away from La Grenouille with a spring

in her step and wandered down Fifth Avenue to peek in the windows at Saks. She was going to Chicago ... Chicago ... Chicago! And she was finally free of Whit, and she had done it in the best possible way. Poor bastard, he had been ready to cry with relief. She almost hated to look so sombre about it. She wanted to congratulate him and herself. What they should have been doing was clinking champagne glasses and shouting with glee, after all the years they'd wasted putting on a show for their friends, and hell, they weren't even married. But they had been a good front for each other. A front. Thank God, she had never married him. Jesus. The very thought made her tremble.

And then another tremor went through her. It had been days, a week ... a long time ... she didn't even know how long. She hadn't even thought of him. Mark. But all in one day? In one fell swoop like that? Clean slate? Both of them? Wasn't that too much to handle? She cared a hell of a lot more about Mark than she did about Whit. Whit was in love. He had a man of his own. But Mark? God, it was like having two wisdom teeth pulled in one day.

But her feet carried her irreversibly towards the subway at Fifty-first Street and Lexington. She had to. She really had to. And she knew it.

The train bumped along on its route pointing south, and she wondered why. For Luke? But that was crazy. She hardly knew him. And what if he cancelled the weekend and never saw her again? Or what if she went to Chicago for the weekend, but he never saw her again after that? What if ... but she knew it wasn't for Luke. It was for Kezia. She had to. She couldn't play games anymore. Not with Whit, or Mark, or Edward, or anyone ... or herself. The many skins of the snake that was Kezia Saint Martin were peeling away. Now *there* would be a piece for the column.

It was a lot harder with Mark. Because she cared.
'You're going away?'

178

'Yes.' She held his eyes and wanted to stroke his hair, but she couldn't do that to him. Not to Mark.

'But that didn't make any difference this summer.' He looked hurt and confused and even younger than he was.

'It makes a difference now, though. Maybe I'll stay away for a very long time. A year, two years, I don't really know.'

'Kezia, are you getting married?' The question was suddenly blunt and she wanted to say yes, just to make it easier, but she didn't want to tell him that either. It was enough to say that she was going away. That was simpler.

'No, baby. I'm not getting married. I'm just going. And in my own way, I love you. Too much to screw you up. I'm older than you are, we both have things to do with our lives. Different things, separate things. It's time now, Marcus. I think you know that too.' He had finished the bottle of Chianti before she had finished her second glass. They ordered another.

'Can I ask you something crazy?'

'What?'

He smiled at her, hesitating; the boyish half smile she loved so much was all over his face. But that was the trouble. She loved the smile, the hair, The Partridge, and the studio. She didn't really love Mark. Not way down deep. Not the way she loved Luke. Not enough.

'Are you the chick I saw in the paper that time?'

She waited a long moment before answering. Something pounded in her ears, and then she looked at him. Straight in the eye. 'Yes. Probably. So?'

'So, I was curious. What's it feel like to be like that?'

'Lonely. Scary. Dull a lot of the time. It's not so hot.'

'Is that why you kept coming down here? Because it was dull and you were bored?'

'No. Maybe originally, just to get away. But you've been someone very special to me, Mark.'

'Was I an escape?'

Yes. But how could she tell him that? And why tell him

179

now? *Oh, please, don't let me hurt him . . . Not more than I have to.*

'No. You're a person. A beautiful person. A person I loved.'

'Loved? Not "love"?' He looked at her, tears swimming bleakly in the childlike eyes.

'Times change, Marcus. And we have to let them change, for both our sakes. It only gets ugly when people try to hang on. It's too late then. For both our sakes, I have to go.'

He nodded sadly into his wine, and she touched his face for one last time before she stood up and walked away. She half ran once she got out of the door. Mercifully, a cab was cruising down the street. She hailed it and slipped inside, so he couldn't see the tears running down her face. Nor could she see the tears on his. He never saw her again. Only in the papers, now and then.

The phone was ringing as she came through the door. She felt wrung out. It had been like two wisdom teeth after all. Four wisdom teeth. Nine. A hundred. And now what? It couldn't be Whit. Edward? Her agent?

'Hi, Mama.' It was Luke.

'Hi, love. Oh God, it's good to hear your voice. I'm beat.' She had needed the sound of him so badly . . . his touch . . . his arms . . .

'What'd you do today?'

'Everything. Nothing. It was a horrible day.'

'Christ, you make it sound like it.'

'I just "took care of business", as you'd say. I planted a nasty little piece in the column last night, designed to make Whit's lover jealous.' She had no secrets from Luke. He knew her whole life now. 'Which it did, so we had lunch and got that squared away. No more Whitney to squire me to parties.'

'You sound upset. Is that the way you wanted it?'

'Yes, that's why I did it. I just wanted to do it in some way that wouldn't ruin his ego. I felt I owed him that after

180

all these years. We played a game till the end. And then I went down to SoHo, and got that all cleared up. I feel like the bitch of the year.'

'Yeah. Those things never feel good. I'm sorry you had to deal with all that in one day.' But he didn't sound sorry, and she knew that he was relieved. It made her glad she had done it.

'It had to be done. and it's a relief. I'm just tired. And what about you, love? Busy day?'

'Not as busy as yours. What else you been up to, babe? No fancy benefit meetings?' He chuckled in the phone and she groaned. 'Now what did I say?'

'The magic word . . . oh shit. You just reminded me. I'm due at a goddamn Arthritis meeting at five, and it's already that now. Oh Fuck And Shit!' He laughed at her and she giggled.

'Martin Hallam should only hear that!'

'Oh shut up.'

'Well, I've got more good news for you. I hate to hit you with it on a day like today. You can't come to Chicago this weekend, babe. Something came up and I have to go the coast.'

'What coast?' What in hell did he mean?

'The West Coast, my love. Christ, Kezia, I hate to do this to you. Are you okay?'

'Yeah, I'm terrific.'

'Now come on, be a big girl.'

'Does that mean I can't see you?'

'Yes. It does.'

'Couldn't I fly out to meet you there?'

'No, babe, you can't. It wouldn't be cool.'

'Why not, for chrissake? Oh Luke, I had a perfectly horrible day, and now this . . . please let me come out.'

'Baby, I can't. I'm going to be organizing a heavy little business deal, you might say. It's touchy for me, and it's not a scene I want you involved in. It's going to be a rough couple of weeks.'

'That long?' She wanted to cry.

181

'Maybe. I'll see.'

She took a deep breath, and swallowed, and tried to untangle her mind. What a bitch of a day.

'Luke, will you be all right?'

He hesitated for just a moment before he said, 'I'll be fine. Now you just go to your colitis meeting, or whatever the fuck it is, and don't worry your pretty little head about me. This is one dude who can take care of himself. That much you should know.'

'Famous last words.'

'I'll let you know as soon as I'm back. Just remember one thing.'

'What?'

'That I love you.' At least there was that.

They hung up and Luke paced the length of his suite in Chicago. Shit, he was crazy to get involved with her. And now of all times, when things were starting to get hot. She was starting to depend on him, and she wanted more than he could give. He had other things to think about, the commitments he had made, the men he wanted to help, and he had his own ass to think of now, and the fucking pigs who'd been following him for weeks. Days, years, it felt as though he had always had them on his tail, like vultures swooping down on him, coming just close enough to let him know they were there, and then disappearing again behind a cloud. But he always knew they were there. He could always feel it.

He walked to the bar and poured himself a long tall bourbon in a water glass. No water, no soda, no ice, and swallowed it without putting the glass down. And then, as though he had to know, he took three long strides to the door of his suite and yanked it open with a jerk that should have pulled it off its hinges, but didn't. It shuddered briefly in his hand, and he stood there, and so did the man in the corner. He looked shocked to see Luke, and had jumped when the door opened. He was wearing a hat, and walked down the corridor trying to look like a man going somewhere, but he wasn't. He looked every

182

inch what he was, a cop on an assignment. The tail on Luke Johns.

Kezia's feet felt like lead as she stepped into the cab. The meeting was being held on upper Fifth Avenue. With a view of the park. At Tiffany's apartment. Three floors on Ninety-second and Fifth. And bourbon or scotch. No mickey-mousing around with lemonade or sherry at her place. There would also be gin and vodka for those who preferred that. At home, Tiffany stuck to Black Label.

She was standing near the door when Kezia arrived, with a double scotch on the rocks in one hand.

'Kezia! How divine! You look fabulous, and we were just getting started. You haven't missed anything!' That was for sure.

'Goodie.' Tiffany was too far gone to notice the tone of Kezia's voice or the blurry look around her eyes where her mascara had run when she'd cried. The day had taken its toll.

'Bourbon or scotch?'

'Both.'

Tiffany looked momentarily baffled. She was already drunk, and had been since noon.

'I'm sorry, love. I didn't mean to confuse you. Make it scotch and soda, but don't bother. I'll make it myself.' Kezia strode to the bar, and for this rare occasion she matched Tiffany drink for drink. It was the second time she had gotten drunk because of Luke, but at least the last time she'd been happy.

# CHAPTER XVI

'Kezia?' It was Edward.

'Hi, love. What's new?'

'That's what I wanted to ask you. Do you realize that I haven't seen or heard from you in almost three weeks?'

'Don't feel alone. No one has. I've been hibernating.' She was munching on an apple as she talked to him, with her feet on the desk.

'Are you ill?'

'No. Just busy.'

'Writing?'

'Yup.'

'I haven't seen you anywhere. I was beginning to worry.'

'Well, don't. I've been fine. I've been out a couple of times, just to keep my hand in the game for the column. But my "appearances" have been brief and sporadic, I'm sticking pretty close to home.'

'Any particular reason?' He was probing again, and she continued to munch on her apple noncommittally.

'No particular reason. Just work. And I wasn't in the mood to go out more than I absolutely had to.'

'Afraid to run into Whit?'

'No . . . well . . . maybe a little. I was more afraid to run into all the local big mouths. But actually, I've just been snowed under with work. I'm doing three articles, all with deadlines next week.'

'I'm glad you're all right then. Actually, my dear, I was wondering if you wanted to have lunch.'

She made a face and put down the apple core. Shit. 'Well, love, I'll tell you . . .' Then she started to laugh. 'Okay. I'll have lunch with you. But not at any of the usual spots.'

'My God, I do believe the girl's becoming a recluse.' He

laughed back but there was still a hint of worry in his voice. 'Kezia, are you sure you're all right?'

'Wonderful. Honest.' But she'd have been a lot happier if she could have seen Luke. They were still burning the long distance wires twice a day, but he couldn't have her around. There was still too much happening. So she had been burying herself in her work.

'All right. Then where do you want to have lunch?'

'I know a nice natural foods bar on East Sixty-third. How does that sound to you?'

'You want the truth?'

'Sure, why not?'

'Repulsive.'

She laughed at the sound of his voice. 'Be a sport, darling. You'll love it.'

'For you, Kezia . . . even a natural foods bar. But tell me the truth, is it dreadful?'

'What if it is! You order a baggie from Lutèce and bring it along.'

'Don't be absurd.'

'Then give this a try. It's really not bad.'

'Ahhh . . . youth.'

They agreed to meet at twelve-thirty, and she was already there when he arrived. He looked around, and it wasn't as bad as he'd thought. The people at the small wooden tables were a healthy mix of midtown Eastsiders. Secretaries, art directors, hippies, pretty girls in blue jeans with portfolios at their sides, boys in flannel shirts and shoulder-length hair, and here and there a man in a suit. Neither he nor Kezia stood out in their midst, and he was relieved. It was certainly not La Grenouille, but thank God it wasn't Horn & Hardart's either . . . not that there was anything wrong with their food . . . but the people. The people! They just weren't Edward's style. And one never knew what Kezia had up her sleeve. The girl had a fiendish sense of humour.

She was sitting at a corner table when he approached, and he could see that she was wearing jeans. He smiled a

185

long smile into her eyes and he leaned down to kiss her when he got to the table.

'I have missed you so, child.' He never realized quite how much until he saw her again. It was the same feeling he got every year at their first lunch after the summer. It had been almost a month this time too.

'I've missed you too, love. Hell, I haven't seen you in ages. And it's almost Halloween.' She giggled mischievously and he searched her face as he settled into a chair. There was something different about her eyes ... that same something different he had noticed the last time he'd seen her. And she was suddenly thinner.

'You've lost weight.' It was a fatherly accusation.

'Yes, but not very much. I eat funny when I write.'

'You ought to make it a point to eat well.'

'At Le Mistral perhaps? Or is it healthier to feed one's face at La Côte Basque?' She was teasing him again, not unkindly, but nevertheless with a new vehemence.

'Kezia, child, you're really too old to consider becoming a hippie.' He was teasing her back. But not entirely.

'You're absolutely right, darling. I wouldn't even consider it. Just a hard-working slave to my typewriter. I suddenly feel as though I've come into my own with my work. It's a beautiful feeling.'

He nodded silently and lit a cigar. He wondered if that's what it was. Maybe she would eventually simply retire into her work. At least it was respectable. But it didn't seem likely. And he was still troubled by the subtle alterations he sensed, but couldn't quite see. He could see that she was thinner, more angular, more intense. And she spoke differently now, as though she had finally taken her place in her beliefs, in her work. But the change went deeper than that. Much deeper. He knew it.

'Do they serve anything to drink in this place?' He looked mournfully at the menu chalked up on a board on the wall. There was no mention of cocktails, only carrot or clam juice. His stomach rebelled at the thought.

'Oh, Edward, I didn't even think of a drink for you. I

186

am sorry!' Her eyes were laughing again and she patted his hand. 'You know, I've really missed you too. But I've needed to be left alone.'

'I'd say it had done you good, but I'm not entirely sure of that either. You look as though you've been working too hard.' She nodded slowly.

'Yes, I have. I want to get into it now. And you know, it's becoming a strain to get out that damn column. Maybe I ought to retire.' Here, she felt no qualms about discussing the doings of Martin Hallam. No one would have cared.

'Are you serious about giving it up?'. The prospect troubled him. If she gave up the column, how often would he see her among the familiar faces at all the city's gala events?

'I'll see. I won't do anything rash. But I'm giving it some thought. Seven years is a very long time. Maybe it's time for Martin Halam to quit.'

'And Kezia Saint Martin?'

She didn't answer, but quietly met his eyes.

'Kezia, you're not doing anything foolish, are you, dear? I was relieved to hear of your decision about Whitney. But I rather wondered if it meant . . .'

'No. I ended it with my young friend in SoHo too. On the same day in fact. It was sort of a purge. A pogrom. And a relief, in the end.'

'And you're all alone now?'

She nodded, but what a pest he could be. 'Yes. Me and my work. I love it.' She gave him a radiant smile.

'Perhaps that's what you need for a while. But don't get all severe and intense. It wouldn't become you.'

'And why not?'

'Because you're far too pretty and far too young to waste yourself on a typewriter. For a while, yes. But don't lose yourself for too long.'

'Not "lose" myself, Edward? I feel like I've finally "found" myself.'

Oh lord, this was going to be one of those days when her face looked just like her father's. Something told him the

187

girl had made up her mind. About something, whatever it was. 'Just be cautious, Kezia.' He relit his cigar, keeping his eyes deep in hers. 'And don't forget who you are.'

'Do you have any idea how often I've heard that?' And how sick it makes me by now. 'And don't worry, darling, I couldn't possibly forget. You wouldn't let me.'

There was something hard in her eyes now, which made him uncomfortable.

'Well, shall we order?' She smiled flippantly and waved at the board. 'I suggest the avocado and shrimp omelette. It's superb.'

'Shall I catch you a cab?'

'No. I'll walk. I'm in love with this town in October.'

It was a crisp autumn day, windswept and clear. In another month it would be cold, but not yet. It was that exquisite time of year in New York when everything feels clean and bright and alive, and you want to walk from one end of the world to the other. Kezia always did, at least.

'Call me in a bit, will you, Kezia? I worry when I don't hear anything from you for weeks on end. And I don't want to intrude.'

Since when, darling? Since when? 'You never do. And thanks for the lunch. And you see . . . it wasn't so bad!' She hugged him briefly, kissed his cheek, and walked away, turning to wave as she stopped for the light at the corner.

She walked down Third Avenue to Sixtieth Street and then cut west to the park. It took her out of her way, but she was in no rush to go home. She was well ahead in her work, and it was too nice a day to hurry indoors. She took deep breaths and smiled at the pink-cheeked children on the street. It was rare to see children look healthy in New York. Either they had the greyish-green tinge of deep winter, or the hot pale sweaty look of the blistering summers. Spring came so fleetingly to Manhattan. But fall . . . fall, with its crisp crunchy apples, and pumpkins on fruit stands waiting to have faces carved on them for Halloween. Brisk winds that swept the sky clean of grey.

And people walking along with a quickened pace. New Yorkers didn't suffer in October, they enjoyed. They weren't too hot or too cold or too tired or too cross. They were happy and gay and alive. And Kezia walked in their midst, feeling good.

Leaves brushed the walks in the park, swirling about her feet. Children bounced in the carriage at the pony stand, squealing for another ride. The animals at the zoo bobbed their heads as she walked past, and the carillon began its tune as she approached. She stopped and watched it with all the mothers and children. It was funny. That was something she had never thought of before. Not for herself. Children. How strange it would be to have a little person beside you. Someone to laugh at and giggle with and wipe chocolate ice cream from his chin, and tuck into bed after reading a story, or snuggle close to as he climbed into your bed in the morning. But then, you'd have to tell him who he was, and what was expected of him, and what he'd have to do when he grew up 'if he loved you'. That was the reason she had never even remotely wanted children. Why do that to someone else? It was enough that she had to live with it for all these years. No, no children. Never.

The carillon stopped its tune, and the dancing gold animals stopped their mechanical waltz. The children began to drift away or rush towards hovering vendors. She watched them, and suddenly wanted a red balloon for herself. She bought one for a quarter and tied it to the button on her sleeve. It danced in the wind, high above her head, just below the branches of towering trees, and she laughed; she wanted to skip all the way home.

Her walk took her past the model boat pond, and at Seventy-second Street she reluctantly left the park. She ambled out slowly, the balloon bobbing as she walked behind nannies who prowled the park sedately, pushing oversized English prams covered with lace. A clique of French nurses moved like a battalion down the walk, towards an oncoming gaggle of British nannies. It amused her to watch the obvious though sugar-coated hostility

189

between the two national tribes. And she knew too that the American nurses were left to their own devices, shunned by both the British and French. The Swiss and Germans willingly kept to themselves. And the black women who cared for equally sumptuously outfitted babies did not exist. They were the untouchable caste.

Kezia waited for the traffic to ebb, and eventually wandered over to Madison to stroll past the boutiques on her way home. She was glad she had walked. Her mind wandered slowly back to Luke. It seemed forever since she had seen him. And she was trying so hard to be good about it. Working hard, being a good sport, laughing with him when he called, but something was curling up tighly inside her. It was like a small, dark kernel of sad, and no matter what she did she couldn't get rid of it. It was heavy and tight. Like a fist. How could she miss him so much?

The doorman swept open the door for her, and she pulled her balloon down low beside her, feeling suddenly silly, as the elevator man attempted not to notice.

'Afternoon, miss.'

'Afternoon, Sam.' He wore his dark winter uniform and the eternal white cotton gloves, and he looked at a spot on the wall. She wondered if he didn't ever want to turn and face the people he carted up and down all day long. But that would have been rude. And Sam wasn't rude. God forbid. For twenty-four years, Sam had never been rude, he simply took people up and down ... up ... and ... down ... without ever searching their eyes ... 'Morning, madam' ... 'Morning, Sam' ... 'Evening, sir' ... 'Good evening, Sam'. ... For twenty-four years, with his eyes rooted to a spot on the wall. And next year they'd retire him with a gold-plated watch and a bottle of gin. If he didn't die first, his eyes politely glued to the wall.

'Thank you, Sam.'

'Yes, miss.' The elevator door slipped shut behind her, and she turned her key in the lock.

She picked up the afternoon paper on the hall table, on her way in. It was her habit to keep abreast of the news, and on some days it amused her. But this was not one of those days. The papers had been full of ugly stories for weeks. Uglier than usual, it seemed. Children dying. An earthquake in Chile, killing thousands. Arabs and Jews on the warpath. Problems in the Far East. Murders in the Bronx. Muggings in Manhattan. Riots in the prisons. And that worried Kezia most of all.

But now she glanced lazily past the front page, and then stopped with one hand still on the door. Everything grew very still, she suddenly understood. Her heart stopped. Now she knew. The headline on the paper read: *Work Strike at San Quentin. Seven Dead.* Oh God . . . let him be all right.

As though in answer to the prayer she had spoken aloud, the phone came to life, and dragged her attention away from the riveting headline. Not now . . . not the phone . . . what if . . . Mechanically, she moved towards it, the paper still in one hand, as she distractedly tried to read on.

' 'Lo . . .' She couldn't take her eyes away from the paper.

'Kezia?' It didn't sound like her.

'What?'

'Miss Saint Martin?'

'No, I'm sorry, she's . . . Lucas?'

'Yes, dammit. What the hell's going on?' They were both getting thoroughly confused.

'I . . . I'm sorry, I . . . oh God, are you all right?' The sudden terror still caught in her throat, but she was afraid to say anything too precise on the phone. Maybe he was in a bad place to talk. That article suddenly had told her a great deal. Before she had suspected, but now she knew. No matter what he told her, she knew.

'Of course, I'm all right. You sound like you've seen a ghost. Anything wrong?'

'That's a fairly apt description, Mr. Johns. And I don't know if anything's wrong. Suppose you tell me.'

'Suppose you wait a few hours, and I'll tell you anything you want to know, and a lot more besides. Within reason,

191

of course.' His voice sounded deep and husky, and there was laughter peppered in with the unmistakable fatigue.

'What exactly do you mean?' She held her breath, waiting, hoping. She had just had the fright of her life, and now it sounded like ... she didn't dare hope. But she wanted it to be that.

'I mean get your ass out here, lady. I'm going crazy without you! That's what I mean! How about catching the next plane out here?'

'To San Francisco? Do you mean it?'

'Damn right, I do. I miss you so much I can hardly think straight anymore, and I'm all through out here. And it's been too fucking long since I've had my hands on your ass. Mama, this has seemed like five hundred years!'

'Oh darling, I love you. If you only knew how much I've missed you, and just now I thought ... I picked up the paper and ...' He cut her off quickly with something brittle in his voice.

'Never mind, baby. Everything's okay.' That was what she had wanted to hear.

'What are you going to do now?' She sighed as she spoke.

'Love the shit out of you and take a few days off to see some friends. But you are the first friend I want to see. How soon can you be here?'

She looked at her watch. 'I don't know. I ... what time's the next plane?' It was just after three in New York.

'There's a flight that leaves New York at five-thirty. Can you make it?'

'Jesus. I'd have to be at the airport no later than five, which means leaving here at four, which means ... I have an hour to pack, and ... screw it, I'll make it.' She jumped to her feet and looked towards the bedroom. 'What should I bring?'

'Your delicious little body.'

'Aside from that, silly.' But she hadn't smiled like this in weeks. Three weeks, to be exact. It had been that long since she'd seen him.

'How the hell do I know what you should bring?'

'Is it hot or cold, darling?'

'Foggy. And cold at night, and warm in the daytime. I think ... oh shit, Kezia. Look it up in the *Times*. And don't bring your mink coat.'

'How do you know I have one? You've never seen it.' She was grinning again. To hell with the headlines. He was all right and he loved her.

'I just figured you had a mink. Don't bring it.'

'I wasn't planning to. Any other instructions?'

'Only that I love you too goddamn much, woman, and this is the last time I let you out of my sight.'

'Promises, promises! I wish. Hey ... will you meet me?'

'At the airport?' He sounded surprised.

'Uh huh.'

'Should I? Or would it be cooler if I didn't?' It was back to that again. Being cautious, being wise.

'Screw being cool. I haven't seen you in almost three weeks and I love you.'

'I'll meet you.' He sounded ecstatic.

'You'd damn well better.'

'Yes, ma'am.' The baritone laugh tickled her ear, and they hung up. He had fought his own battles with his conscience during the last three godawful weeks, and he had lost ... or won ... he wasn't yet sure. But he knew he had to have Kezia. Had to. No matter what.

# CHAPTER XVII

The plane landed at 7.14 p.m., San Francisco time. She was on her feet before the plane had come to a full stop at the gate. And despite earnest pleadings from the stewardesses, she was one of a throng in the aisles.

She had travelled coach to attract less attention, and

she was wearing black wool slacks and a black sweater; a trench coat was slung over her arm, dark glasses pushed up on her head. She looked discreet, almost too discreet, and very well-dressed. Men checked her out with their eyes, but decided she looked rich and uptight. Women eyed her with envy. The slim hips, the trim shoulders, the thick hair, the big eyes. She was not a woman who would ever go unnoticed, whatever her name, and in spite of her height.

It was taking forever to open the doors. The cabin was hot and stuffy. Other people's bags bumped her legs. Children started to cry. Finally, they swung open the doors. The crowd began to move, only imperceptibly at first, and then in a sudden rush, the plane blurted its contents like toothpaste onto the ramp. Kezia pressed through the other travellers, and as she turned a corner, she saw him.

His head was well above all the others. His dark hair shone, and she could see his eyes from where she stood. He had a cigar in his hand. His whole being wore an air of expectation. She waved and he saw her, joy sweeping his face, and carefully he eased through the crowd. He was at her side in a moment, and swept her high off the ground in his arms.

'Mama, is it good to see you!'

'Oh Lucas!' She grinned in his arms, and their lips met in a long, hungry kiss. Paparazzi be damned. Whatever they saw, they could have. She was finally back in his arms. The other travellers moved round them like water around rocks in a stream, and there was no one left by the time they moved on.

'Let's get your bags and go home.'

They gave each other the smile usually exchanged by people long used to sharing one bed and took the escalator down to the baggage claim, her small hand clasped firmly in his large one. People caught sight of them and watched them go hand in hand. Together, they were the sort of people you notice. With envy.

'How many bags did you bring?'

'Two.'

'Two? We're only staying three days.' He laughed and gave her another hug. And she tried not to show the flash of pain in her eyes. Three days? That was all? She hadn't asked him before. But at least it was that much. At least they were together again.

He plucked her bags from the turntable like a child snatching furniture out of a dollhouse, propped one suitcase under his arm, grasped the other by the handle in the same hand, and kept his other arm around Kezia, squeezing her tight.

'You haven't said much, Mama. Tired?'

'No. Happy.' She looked up at him again, and nestled in close. 'Christ, it's been such a long time.'

'Yeah, and it won't ever be that long again. It's bad for my nerves.' But she knew it might be that long again. Or longer. It might have to be. That was the way his life was. But it was over now. Their three-day honeymoon had just begun.

'Where are we staying?' They were waiting outside for a cab. And so far, so good. No cameras, no reporters; no one even knew she had left New York. She had made one brief call saying that was taking two days off from the column before she'd call in to report. They could run some of the extra tidbits she hadn't had room for in the column that week. That would tide them over until she got her mind back on Martin Hallam again.

'We are staying at the Ritz.' He said it with grandeur as he tossed her bags into the front seat of a cab.

'Is that for real?' She laughed as she settled back in his arm.

'Wait till you see it.' And then he looked worried. 'Baby, would you rather stay at the Fairmont or the Huntington? They're a lot nicer, but I thought you'd worry about . . .'

'Is the Ritz more discreet?' He laughed at the look on her face.

195

'Oh yeah, Mama. It sure is discreet. That's one thing I like about the Ritz. It is *discreet!*'

The Ritz was a large fading grey house in the heart of the mansions of Pacific Heights. It had once been an elegant home, and now housed castoffs; little old ladies and fading old men, and circulating in their midst the occasional 'overflow' of houseguests from the sumptuous homes nearby. It was an odd mixture, and the decor was the same: crooked chandeliers with dusty prisms, fading red velvet chairs, flowered chintz curtains, and here and there an ornate brass spitoon.

Luke's eyes danced as he led her inside towards a twittering old woman who hovered nervously at the desk. She wore a cup of braided hair over each ear, and her false teeth looked as though they would glow in the dark.

'Good evening, Ernestine.' And the beauty of it was that she looked like an Ernestine.

'Evening, Mr. Johns.' Her eyes took in Kezia with approval. She was the sort of guest they liked. Well-dressed, well-heeled, and well-polished. After all, this was the Ritz!

He led her into a decaying elevator run by a tiny old man who hummed 'Dixie' to himself as they rose, swaying, to the second floor.

'Usually, I walk. But I thought I'd give you the full show.'

A sign in the elevator announced breakfast at seven, lunch at eleven, and dinner at five. Kezia giggled, holding tight to his hand.

'Thank you, Joe.' Luke gently patted his back and picked up the bags.

'Carry the bags for you, sir?'

'No, thanks.' But he quietly slipped a bill into the man's hand, and led Kezia down the hall. It was carpeted in dark red, and the walls were lined with elaborate sconces. 'To your left, babe.' She followed his nod to the end of the hall. 'Wait till you see the view.' He fitted his key in the lock, turned it twice, set down the bags, and

196

then pulled her close. 'I'm so glad you came out. I was afraid you'd be busy or something.'

'Not for you, Luke. After all this time, you must be joking! Well, are we going to stand here all night?'

'Nope. We sure as hell aren't.' He picked her up easily, and carried her over the threshold into a room that made her gasp and then laugh. She had never seen so much blue velvet and satin all in one place.

'Luke, it's a riot. And I love it.' He set her down with a smile, and she looked at the bed with wide eyes. It was a huge four-poster with blue velvet hangings and a blue satin spread. There were blue velvet chairs and a blue satin chaise longue, an old-fashioned dressing table, a fireplace, and a flowered blue rug that had seen better days. And then she noticed the view.

It was a dark expanse of bay, lit on the other side by the hills of Sausalito, the lights on the Golden Gate twinkling as traffic sped by.

'Luke, what a fabulous place!' Her face glowed.

'The Ritz. At your feet.'

'Darling, I love you.' She walked into his arms and kicked off her shoes.

'Lady, you couldn't love me half as much as I love you. Not even a quarter.'

'Oh shut up.'

His mouth came down gently on hers and he lifted her onto the blue satin bed.


'Hungry?'

'I don't know. I'm so happy I can't think.' She rolled sleepily onto her side, and kissed him on the side of his neck.

'How about some pasta?'

'Mmmm . . . sure . . .' But she made no move to get up. It was one in the morning, her time, and she was content where she lay.

'Come on, Mama, get up.'

'Oh God, not a shower!' He laughed and slapped her on the behind as he pulled back the sheets.

'If you don't get up in two minutes, I'll bring the shower to you.'

'You wouldn't dare.' She lay with her eyes stubbornly closed and a sleepy smile on her face.

'Oh wouldn't I?' He was looking down at her, love and tenderness rich in his eyes.

'Christ, you would. You're such a meanie. Can't I take a bath instead of a shower?'

'Take whatever you want, but get up off your ass.' She opened her eyes and looked up at him, without moving an inch.

'In that case, I'll take you.'

'After we eat. I didn't have time for lunch today and I'm starving. I wanted to wrap everything up before you got out.'

'And did you?' She sat up on one elbow and reached for a cigarette. This was the opening she had been waiting for, and suddenly there was tension in her voice, mirrored in his eyes.

'Yeah. We wrapped everything up.' The faces of the dead men flashed through his head.

'Lucas ...' She had never directly asked him, and he had not yet volunteered.

'Yeah?' Everything about him seemed suddenly guarded. But they both knew.

'Should I mind my own business?' He shrugged and then slowly shook his head. 'No. I know where you're going, Mama. And I guess it's your business to ask. You want to know what I've been up to out here?' She nodded. 'But you already know, don't you?' He looked almost old and very tired as he spoke. The holiday atmosphere had suddenly faded.

'I think so. I think I knew without knowing, but then this afternoon ...' Her voice trailed off. This afternoon? Only then? It seemed years ago. 'This afternoon I saw the paper, and the headline ... the San Quentin work strike, that was your doing, wasn't it, Luke?' He nodded very slowly. 'What will they do to you for that, Lucas?'

'Who? The pigs?'

'Among others.'

'Nothing. Yet. They can't pin anything on me, Mama. I'm a pro. But that's part of the problem, too. I'm too much of a pro. They can never pin anything on me, and one day they're going to screw me royally. Out of vengeance.' It was a first warning.

'Can they do that?' She looked shocked, but not really as though she understood.

'They can if they want to. Depends how badly they want to. Right now, I figure they're pretty pissed.'

'And you're not scared, Lucas?'

'What would that change?' He smiled a cynical little smile, and shook his head. 'No, pretty lady, I'm not scared.'

'Are you in danger, Lucas? I mean real danger?'

'You mean my parole, or other kinds of danger?'

'Either.'

He knew that she had to know, so he answered her. More or less. 'I'm not in real danger, babe. There are some very angry people involved, but the ones who're the most pissed are the least sure I had anything to do with it. That's the way I run things. The parole pricks won't even try to do anything to me for a while, and by then they'll have cooled off. And any of the hotheads involved in the strike who don't dig my views are too pissy-eye scared of me to even flip me the bird. So, no, I'm not really in danger.'

'But you could be, couldn't you?' It hurt her to think of it, to realize it . . . to admit it. She had known that about him from the first. But now she was in love with him. It was different. She didn't want him to be some hotshot troublemaker. She wanted him to lead a peaceful life.

'What are you thinking of? You looked a thousand miles away for a minute there. You didn't even hear me answer your question.'

'What was your answer?'

'That I could be in danger crossing the street, so why

get paranoid now? You could be in danger. You could get kidnapped for a fat ransom. So? So why go crazy about could I be in danger, or could I not be in danger. I'm sitting here, I'm fine, I love you. That's all you need to know. Now what were you thinking?'

'That I wish you were a stockbroker or an insurance agent.' She grinned and he let out a burst of laughter.

'Oh Mama, have you got the wrong number!'

'All right, so I'm crazy.' She shrugged in momentary embarrassment and then looked at him seriously again. 'Luke, why do you still get involved in the strikes? Why can't you let it go? You're not in prison anymore. And it could cost you so much.'

'Okay. I'll tell you why. Because some of those guys make three cents an hour for the work they do in there. Backbreaking work, in conditions you wouldn't let your dog live in. And they have families, wives and children just like the rest of the world. Those families are on welfare, but they wouldn't have to be if the poor bastards inside could earn a decent wage. Not even a high wage, just a decent one. There's no reason why they shouldn't be able to put some money aside. They need it as much as everyone else. And they work for their bread. They work damn hard. So, we set up work strikes. We design them so that the system we use can be implemented by inmates at any prison. Like this one. Folsom is going to be pulling almost the same thing, with some minor alterations in style. Probably next week.' He saw the look on her face and then shook his head. 'No. They don't need me for that one, Kezia. I did my bit here.'

'But why in hell do you have to be the one to do it?' She sounded almost angry and it surprised him.

'Why not?'

'Your parole for one thing. If you're on parole, then you still "belong" to the State. Your sentence was five to life, wasn't it?'

'Yeah. So?'

'So they own you for life, officially. Right?'

200

'Wrong. Only for another two and a half years, when my parole runs out, smartass. Sounds like you've been doing some reading on the subject.' He lit another cigarette and avoided her eyes.

'I have, and you're full of shit with your two and a half years. They could revoke your parole any time they want to, and then they've got you for life again, or another five years.'

'But Kezia ... why would they want to do that?' He was trying to pretend he didn't know.

'Oh for chrissake, Luke. Don't be naive, or is that just for my benefit? For agitation in the prisons. That's got to be in violation of your parole agreement. You don't need me to tell you that. And I'm not as dumb as you think.' She had been doing more reading than he'd anticipated. And this was a tough one to argue. She was right on the money.

'I never thought you were dumb, Kezia.' His voice was subdued. 'But neither am I. I told you, they could never pin this work-strike thing on me.'

'Who says so? What if one of the people you do this stuff with says something? Then what? What if some asshole just gets fed up and kills you? Some "radical", as you put it.'

'Then we worry. Then. Not now.' She was silent for a moment, her eyes bright with tears.

'I'm sorry, Lucas. I can't help it, though. I do worry.' And she knew she had good reason to. Lucas was not about to give up his work in the prisons, and he was in danger. They both knew it.

'Come on, Mama, let's forget this and go eat.' He kissed her on the eyes and the mouth, and pulled her firmly by both arms. He had had enough heavy talk for a while. The tension between them eased away slowly, but Kezia's fears were not over. She only knew that she was fighting a losing battle if she hoped to make him give up what he was doing. He was a born gambler. She just hoped he'd never lose.

They were downstairs in the lobby again half an hour later.

'Where are we going?'

'Vanessi's. Best pasta in town. Don't you know San Francisco?'

'Not very well. I was here as a child, and once about ten years ago for a party. But I didn't see very much. We had dinner someplace Polynesian, and stayed at a hotel on Nob Hill. I remember the cable car, and that's about it. I was out here with Edward and Totie.'

'That doesn't sound like much fun. Jesus, you don't know this town at all.'

'Nope. But now I've seen the Ritz, and you can show me the rest.' She hugged his arm and they exchanged a peaceful smile.

Vanessi's was crowded, even at ten. Artists, writers, newspaper people, an after-theatre crowd, politicians, and debutantes. It was jammed with a fair sampling of everything there was in town. And Luke had been right. The pasta was great. She had gnocchi, and he had fettuccine, and for dessert they shared an unforgettable zabaglione.

She sat back with her espresso and took a lazy look around.

'You know, it kind of reminds me of Gino's, in New York, only better.'

'Everything in San Francisco is better. I'm in love with this town.'

She smiled at him and took a sip of the hot coffee.

'The only trouble is that the whole city goes dead at midnight.'

'Tonight I think I might too. Christ, it's already two-thirty in the morning, my time.'

'Are you beat, babe?' He looked almost worried. She was so small and looked so fragile. But he knew she was a lot tougher than she looked. He had already glimpsed that.

'No. I'm just relaxed. And happy. And content. And that bed at the Ritz is like falling asleep on a cloud.'

'Yeah. Isn't it though?' He reached across the table and took her hand, and then she saw him glance at something over her shoulder with knit brows. She turned around to see what it was. It was only a table of men.

'People you know?'

'In a way.' His whole face had hardened, and his hand had seemed to lose interest in hers. It was a group of five men, with short, well-trimmed hair, double-knit suits, and light ties. They looked faintly like gangsters.

'Who are they?' She turned to face him again.

'Pigs.' He said it matter of factly.

'Police?'

He nodded. 'Yeah, special detail investigators, assigned to digging up trouble for people like me.'

'Don't be so paranoid. They're just having dinner here, Luke. Like we are.'

'Yeah. I guess so.' But they had dampened his mood, and shortly after, they left.

'Luke ... you have nothing to hide. Do you?' They were walking down Broadway now, past the barkers at all the topless bars. But the table of cops still weighed on their minds.

'No. But that guy who was sitting at the end of the table has been on my ass since I got into town. I'm getting sick of it.'

'He wasn't following you tonight. He was having dinner with his friends.' The group of policemen had shown no interest in their table. 'Wasn't he?' Now she was worried too. Very.

'I don't know, Mama. I just don't like their trip. A pig is a pig ... is a pig.' He licked one end of a cigar, lit it, and looked down at her face. 'And I'm a sonofabitch to throw my bad vibes on you. I just don't like cops, baby. That's the name of the game. And let's face it, I've been playing heavy games with the strike at San Quentin. Seven guards were killed during the three weeks.' For a moment, he wondered if he had been wrong to stick around.

They wandered into porn bookstores, watched tourists on the street, and finally ambled onto Grant Avenue, cluttered with coffeehouses and poets, but the police stayed on their minds, however little they showed it to each other. And Luke was once again aware of being tailed.

Kezia tried to lighten his mood by playing tourist.

'It looks rather like SoHo, only more funky somehow. You can tell it's been around for a while.'

'Yeah, it has. It's the old Italian neighbourhood, and there are a lot of Chinese. And kids, and artists. It's a good scene.' He bought her an ice cream cone, and they took a cab to the Ritz. It was four in the morning for Kezia by then, and in the arms of her lover she slept like a child. Something troubled her only faintly as she drifted off to sleep – something about police ... and Luke ... and spaghetti. They were trying to take away his spaghetti ... or ... she couldn't figure it out. She was too tired. And much, much too happy.

She had fallen asleep as he watched her, a smile on his face as he stroked the long black hair that rippled past her naked shoulders and down her back. She looked so beautiful to him. And he was already so goddamn in love with her.

How was he ever going to tell her? He slipped quietly out of bed after she fell asleep, and went to look at the view. He had blown it, blown all his own rules. What a fucking stupid thing to do. He had no right to someone like Kezia. He had no right to anyone until he knew. But he had wanted her, had to have her – as an ego trip at first because of who she was. And now? Now it was all different. He needed her. He loved her. He wanted to give her something of himself ... even if only the last golden hours before sunset. Moments like that don't come every day, at most they come once in a lifetime. But now he knew he would have to tell her. The question was, how?

# CHAPTER XVIII

'Lucas, you're a beast!' She groaned as she turned over in bed. 'For God's sake, it's still dark.'

'It's not dark, it's just foggy. And breakfast in this joint is at seven.'

'I'll go without.'

'No, you won't. We have things to do.'

'Lucas ... please ...' He watched her struggle out of sleep. His hair was combed, his teeth were brushed, his eyes were bright. He had been up since five. He had a lot on his mind.

'Kezia, if you don't get off your ass, I'll keep you on it all day. And then you'll be sorry!' He ran his hand smoothly from her breast to her belly.

'Who says I'll be sorry?'

'Don't tempt me. But come on, babe. I want to show you the town.'

'In the middle of the night? Can't it wait a few hours?'

'It's seven-fifteen.'

'Oh God, I'm dying.'

And then, laughing at her, he picked her up out of bed, and deposited her in the bathtub of warm water he had run while she slept.

'I figured you wouldn't be up to a shower this morning.'

'Lucas, I love you.' The hot water lulled her gently, as she lay looking sleepily into his eyes. 'You spoil me. No wonder I love you.'

'I figured there had to be a reason. And don't take too long. They close the kitchen at eight, and I want some food in my stomach before I drag you around town.'

'Drag me, eh?' She closed her eyes and sank deeper into the tub. It was an ancient bathtub that stood high off the floor on gold-leaf claw feet. It would have been large enough for both of them.

They breakfasted on pancakes and fried eggs and bacon. And for the first morning in years, Kezia didn't even bother to read the paper. She was on holiday, and she didn't give a damn what the world had to say. 'The world' would only complain, and she was not in the mood for complaints. She felt too good to be bothered with that.

'So where are you taking me, Lucas?'

'Back to bed.'

'What? You got me up, just to go back to bed?' She looked incensed and he laughed.

'Later. Later. First, we take a look at the town.'

He drove her through Golden Gate Park and they walked around its lakes and kissed in hidden corners under still-flowering trees. Everything was still green and in bloom. The rusty look of the East in November was so different, and so much less romantic. They had tea in the Japanese Garden, and then drove out to the beach before driving back through the Presidio to look out over the bay. She was having a ball: Fisherman's Wharf, Ghiradelli Square, The Cannery. . . .

They ate fresh crab and shrimp at the stands at the wharf, and revelled in the noise of Italian vendors. They watched old men playing boccie in Aquatic Park, and she smiled watching one very old man teach his grandson how to play. Tradition. Luke smiled too, watching her. She had a way of seeing things that he had never thought of before. She always had a sense of history, of what had come before and what would come later. It was something to which he'd never given much thought. He lived with his feet firmly planted in *now*. It was an exchange they gave to each other. She gave him a sense of her past, and he taught her to live where she was.

As the fog lifted, they left their borrowed car down at the wharf, and took the cable car to Union Square. It made her laugh as they rolled down the hills. For the first time in her life she felt like a tourist. Usually she moved across a regulated map between familiar houses in cities she had known all her life, from the homes of old friends to the homes of other old friends, wherever she was, the world over. From one familiar world to another. But with Luke being a tourist was fun. Everything was. And he loved the way she enjoyed what he showed her. It was a fun town to show – pretty, and easy, and not too crowded at that time of year. The rugged natural beauty of the bay and the hills made a pleasing contrast to the architectural treasures of the town: skyscrapers all politely herded downtown, the gingerbread Victorians nestled in Pacific Heights, and the small colourful shops of Union Street.

They drove over the Golden Gate Bridge just because she wanted to see it 'up close', and she was enchanted.

'What a handsome piece of work, isn't it, Luke?' Her eyes scanned far above to its spires piercing the fog.

'So are you.'

They dined that night at one of the Italian restaurants on Grant Avenue. A place with four tables for eight, where you sat next to strangers, and made friends as you shared soup and broke bread. She talked to everyone at their table; this was new to her too. Luke grinned as he watched her. What would they have said if they had known she was Kezia Saint Martin? The idea made him laugh more. Because they wouldn't have known. They were plumbers and students, bus drivers and their wives. Kezia Saint Who? She was safe. With him, and with them. That pleased him; he knew that she needed a place where she could play, without fear of reporters and gossip. She had blossomed in the brief time since she'd flown into town. She needed that kind of peace and release. He was glad it was something he could give her.

They stopped for a drink at a place called Perry's on Union Street, before going home. It reminded her a bit of P. J.'s in New York. And they decided to walk home from there. It was a pleasant walk over the hills, dotted with small parks along the way. The foghorns were bleating at the edge of the bay, and she kept stride beside him, holding his hand.

'God, Luke. I'd love to live here.'

'It's a good place. And you don't even know it yet.'

'Not even after today?'

'That's just the tourist stuff. Tomorrow we see the real thing.'

They spent the next day driving north on the coast. Stinson Beach, Inverness, Point Reyes. It was a rugged coastline that looked much like Big Sur farther south. Waves crashing against the cliffs, gulls and hawks soaring high, long expanses of hills, and sudden sweeps of beaches, unpopulated and seeming almost to be touched by the hand of God. Kezia knew what Luke had meant. This was a far cry from the wharf. This was real, and incredibly beautiful, not merely diverting.

They had an early dinner in a Chinese restaurant on Grand Avenue, and Kezia was in high spirits. They were seated in a little booth with a curtain drawn over the doorway and you could hear giggles and murmurs in other booths, and beyond, the clatter of dishes and the tinkling sound of Chinese spoken by the waiters. Kezia loved it, and it was a restaurant Luke knew well, one of his favourite hangouts in town. He had been there the night before she arrived, to tie up the loose ends about the strike at San Quentin. It was an odd thing, talking about dead men and inmates over fried wonton. It seemed immoral somehow, when he gave it much thought, but mostly he didn't. They had learned to accept what they lived with. The realities of men in prison, and the cost of changing that system. It cost some men their lives. Luke and his friends were the generals, the inmates were the soldiers, the prison administrators the enemy. It was all very simple.

'You're not listening to me, Lucas.'

'Hm?' He looked up to see Kezia watching him with a smile.

'Something wrong, darling?'

'Are you kidding? How could there be?' She was watching his eyes, and he pushed thoughts of San Quentin from his mind, but something was bothering him. A sense of foreboding, of ... something. He didn't know what. 'I love you, Kezia. It was a beautiful day.' He wanted to chase the painful thoughts away, but it was getting harder to do.

'Yes, it was. You must be tired from all that driving though.'

'We'll get a good night's sleep tonight.' He chuckled at the thought and leaned forward for a kiss.

It wasn't until they left that he saw the same face he had seen too often during the weeks he'd spent in San Francisco. As he looked around and saw the man darting back into one of the booths with a newspaper under his arm, it was suddenly too much for him.

'Wait for me up front.'

'What?'

'Go on. I have some business to take care of.'

She looked suddenly surprised, and frightened by the expression on his face. Something had happened to him; it was as if a dam had broken, or like the moment before an explosion ... like ... it was frightening to watch.

'Go on, dammit!' He gave her a firm shove towards the front of the restaurant and headed quickly back towards the booth he had seen the man enter. It took him only a moment to reach it, and he pulled back the aged, fading curtain with such force that it tore at the top. 'Okay, sweetheart, you've had it.' The man looked up from his newspaper with an overdone expression of unknowing surprise, but his eyes were wary and quick.

'Yes?' He was greying at the temples but he looked almost as solid as Luke. He sat poised in his seat, like a tiger ready to pounce.

'Get up.'

'What? Look, mister ...'

'I said get up, motherfucker, or didn't you hear me?' Luke's voice was as sweet and smooth as honey but the

209

look on his face was terrifying, and as he spoke, he lifted the man from his seat with a hand on each lapel of his ugly plaid double-knit sportcoat. 'Now what is it exactly that you want?' Luke's voice was barely more than a whisper.

'I'm here for dinner, Mack, and I suggest you lay off right now. Want me to call the cops?' The man's eyes were menacing and his hands were starting to come up slowly and with well-trained precision.

'Call the cops . . . you fucking . . . whatcha got, a radio in your pocket, motherfucker? Listen, man, I'm having dinner with a lady and I don't dig being tailed night and day, everywhere I go. It makes me look bad, got that? Nice and clear?' And then he gasped. Luke's victim had removed both of Luke's hands from his lapels and delivered a swift punch to his middle all in one flashing gesture.

'That'll make you look worse, Johns. Now how about going home like a nice boy, or you want me to run you in for attempted assault? That'd look good to your parole board, wouldn't it? You're just fucking lucky they don't get you with a murder beef one of these days.' There was hatred in his voice.

Luke caught his breath and looked up into the man's eyes. 'Murder? They'd have a bitch of a time sticking me with that. A lot of things, but not murder.'

'What about the guards at Q. last week, or don't they count? You might as well have killed them yourself, instead of having your punks do the job.' The conversation was still carried on in an undertone, and Luke lifted one eyebrow in suprise as he stood up slowly and painfully.

'Is that to what I owe the honour of your company everywhere I go? You're trying to stick me with the murder of those Bulls in Quentin?'

'No. That's not my problem. Not my detail. And believe it or not, babyface, I don't like tailing you any more than you like having me on your ass.'

'Watch out, you may make me cry.' Luke picked up a glass of water from the table and took a long swallow. 'So what's with the tail?' Luke put down the glass and watched him carefully, wondering why he hadn't punched the man back. Jesus, he was getting soft ... dammit ... she was changing everything, and that could really cost him.

'Johns, you may find it hard to believe, but you're bring tailed for protection.'

Luke answered with a shout of cynical laughter. 'How sweet. Whose protection?'

'Yours.'

'Really? How thoughtful. And just who do you think is going to hurt me? And just exactly why do you care?' He looked doubtful; they could have thought of a better story.

'I don't care, and that's upfront, but the assignment is to follow you until further notice and keep my eyes open for assailants.'

'Bullshit.' Luke was angry now. He didn't like the idea. 'Is it bullshit?'

'Sure it is. Oh, what the fuck do I know?' That was all he needed, with Kezia around. Shit.

'The word is that some of the hothead left-wing reform groups don't like your trip, don't like you floating in and out of their scene like some kind of visiting hero. They want your ass, man.'

'Yeah? Well, let's put it this way: if they ask for it, I'll call you. Till I do, I can do without company.'

'I could do without you too, but we don't have a choice. Nice place for dinner though. Great egg rolls.'

Lucas shook his head with a look of restrained aggravation and shrugged. 'Glad you liked it.' He paused for a long moment in the doorway then and watched the man who had punched him. 'You know something, man? You're a lucky motherfucker. You'd hit me like that some other time and I'd have pulverized you. And enjoyed it.' They eyed each other for a long moment and the other man shrugged and folded his newspaper.

'Suit yourself. But that would buy you a one-way ticket back to the joint. Save us all a lot of trouble if you ask me. But anyway, watch your ass, man. Somebody's out to get you. They didn't tell me who, but it must've been a hot tip because they had me out on the street an hour later.'

Luke started to leave the booth then, and suddenly turned with a question in his eyes. 'You guys tailing anyone else?' That might tell him something.

'Maybe.'

'Come on, man, don't tell me half-assed stories without telling me the rest!' There was fire in his eyes again and the other man nodded his head slowly.

'Yeah. Okay. We're tailing some other dudes.'

'Who?'

The cop heaved a slow sigh, looked at his feet and then back at Luke. There was no point playing games and they both knew it. And he felt that he had already pushed Luke as far as he should, farther possibly. Lucas Johns was not a man you played with. He looked up slowly, and reeled off the names expressionlessly.

'Morrissey, Washington, Greenfield, Falkes, and you.'

'Jesus.' The five of them were the all-time heavies in prison agitation. Morrissey lived in San Francisco, Greenfield in Vegas. Falkes had come out from New Hampshire, but Washington was local and the only black in the group. All radicals of a kind, but none of them heavy left-wingers. They just wanted to fight for their ideals, and change a system that should have died years ago. None of them had wild illusions about changing the world. Washington took the most flak from those who opposed them. The black factions thought he should be fighting with them; he wasn't enough of a rebel for them. But Luke thought he was the best of both worlds.

'You're tailing Frank Washington?'

'Yeah.' The plainsclothesman nodded.

'Then you better tail him good.' The other man nodded knowingly, and Luke turned his back and left.

212

Kezia was waiting nervously at the front door.

'Are you all right?'

'Of course I'm all right. Why shouldn't I be?' He wondered if she had heard something, or worse yet seen. Remarkably, no one had walked by during the brief fracas and the waiters had been too busy to notice the intensity of the subsequent exchange.

'You were gone for so long, Lucas. Is something wrong?' She searched his face but found nothing.

'Of course not, I just saw someone I know.'

'Business?' Her face had the intense look of a wife.

'Yes, silly lady, business. I told you. Now mind your own, and let's go back to the hotel.' He gave her a fierce hug and walked her out into the night fog with a smile. She knew something was amiss, but he covered it well. There was never anything she could put her finger on. And Luke was going to see that it stayed that way.

But the next morning over breakfast there was no mistaking that something was very wrong. She had awakened him this time, after ordering a sumptuous breakfast for them to share. She shook him gently with a kiss after the tray had been delivered to the room.

'Good morning, Mr. Johns. It's time to get up, and I love you.' He rolled over with a sleepy smile and half-opened eyes, and pulled her down to kiss him.

'Sure is a nice way to start the day, Mama. What are you doing up so early?'

'I was hungry, and you said you had a lot to do today, so I got up and got organized.' She sat on the edge of the bed with a smile.

'Want to come back to bed and get unorganized again?'

'Not until after breakfast, hot pants. Your eggs'll get cold.'

'Jesus, you're practical. Such a cold-hearted woman.'

'No. Just hungry.' She patted his behind, kissed him again, and got up to take the covers off their breakfast.

'Boy, that smells good. Did they send up the paper too?'

'Yes, sir.' It was neatly folded on the tray, and she

213

picked it up and unfolded it, handing it to him with a small curtsy. 'At your service, monsieur.'

'Lady, how did I live without you before?'

'With difficulty, undoubtedly.' She smiled at him again and turned to pour him a cup of coffee. When she looked up she was shocked by the expression on his face. He was sitting naked on the side of the bed, with the newspaper open on his lap, and tears starting down his face, contorted with anger and grief. His hands were clenched in fists.

'Lucas? Darling, what is it?' She went to him hesitantly and sat down next to him, searching the headlines quickly to see what had happened. It was the main feature in the paper: *Ex-Priest Prison Reformer Shot and Killed*. The killing was thought to have been done by a radical left-wing group, but the police were not yet sure. Joseph Morrissey had been shot eight times in the head while leaving his house with his wife. The photographs on the front page showed a hysterical woman leaning over the shapeless form of the victim. Joe Morrissey. His wife was reported to be seven months pregnant.

'Shit.' It was the only sound she heard from Luke as she ran a hand gently around his shoulders, with tears running from her own eyes. They were tears for the man who had died, and tears of fear for Luke. It could have been Lucas.

'Oh darling. I'm so sorry.' They seemed such empty words, for what she felt. 'Did you know him well?'

He nodded silently and then closed his eyes. 'Too well.'

'What do you mean?' Her voice was a whisper.

'He was my front man. Remember, I told you I never go into the prisons, and no one can pin anything on me?'

She nodded.

'Well, they can't pin anything on me because of guys like Joe Morrissey. He was a chaplain in four of the joints before leaving the priesthood. He stuck around with some of the hard-core reformers after that. And he fronts for the heavies. Mostly me. And now ... we killed him. I killed him. Goddamn fucking . . .' He got up and walked angrily across the room, wiping the tears from his face. 'Kezia?'

'Yes?' Her voice was a frightened little sound from across the room.

'I want you packed and dressed right now. And I mean *right now*. I'm getting the hell out of here.'

'Lucas . . . you're afraid?'

He hesitated for a moment and then nodded. 'I'm afraid.'

'For me? Or yourself?'

He almost smiled then. He was never afraid for himself. But this was no time to get her involved. 'Let's just say I want to be smart. Now come on, baby. Let's get moving.'

'You're leaving too?' She was talking to his back now though.

'Later.'

'What are you going to do before that?' She was suddenly terrified. Oh God, what if they killed him?

'I'm going to take care of business, and then get my ass back to Chicago tonight. And you're going to go to New York, like a nice girl, and wait there. Now shut up and get dressed, dammit!' He turned towards her with an attempted snarl, but then his face softened as he saw the look of terror on her face. 'Now, Mama, come on. . . .' He walked back across the room and took her in his arms as she began to cry again.

'Oh Lucas, what if . . .'

'Shhh . . .' He held her tight and kissed the top of her head gently. 'No "what if", Mama. Everything's going to be cool.'

Going to be cool? Was he out of his mind? Someone had just been killed! His front man, for chrissake. She looked at him with shock in her eyes and he pulled her gently up off the bed.

'Now I want you to get ready.' Too many people could figure out where he was staying. And Kezia was one gold mine he didn't want in his pocket if someone was laying

215

for him. Maybe killing Morrissey was just a warning. Some warning. His stomach turned over again at the thought.

She started to get dressed while throwing things into her suitcase and casting sidelong glances at Luke. He suddenly looked so businesslike, so foreign to her, so angry.

'Where will you be today, Lucas?'

'Out. Busy. I'll call you when I get to Chicago. And you're not going to a birthday party for chrissake. Just put on some clothes. Hurry up.'

'I'm almost ready.' And a moment later she was, looking very sober, with large dark glasses concealing the lack of makeup.

He looked at her for a long moment, tension rippling through his body, and then nodded. 'Okay, lady. I'm not going to ride with you. I'm going to call a cab, and get the hell out of here. You're going to wait in Ernestine's office downstairs and wait for a cab with her. She will take you to the airport.'

'Ernestine?' Kezia looked surprised. The proprietress of the Ritz didn't look the sort to play nursemaid to grown guests. And Luke was wondering about it himself. But he figured that for fifty bucks she'd do almost anything.

'That's right. Ernestine. Go to the airport with her. And get on the first goddamn plane out. I don't give a shit if it stops fifteen times on the way to New York. But I want you out of here. I don't want you hanging around the airport. Is that clear?' She nodded silently. 'It damn well better be, 'cause Kezia, I'm not kidding. I'll tear your hide off if you fool around somewhere. *Get out of this town!* Is that clear? I'm sorry I brought you here in the first place.' And he looked it.

'I'm not sorry. I'm glad. And I love you. I'm just sorry your friend . . .' Her voice trailed off and her eyes grew large as she looked at him, and he softened. He took her in his arms again, once more torn between wanting her and knowing he shouldn't take her down with him. But he needed her too much.

216

'You're quite something, lady.' He kissed her quietly and then straightened up. 'Get ready to go, Mama. I'm going to tell Ernestine to get you out of here within five minutes, and I'll be calling to check. I'll call you in New York tonight. But it may be late. I want to get back to Chicago before I start playing around making phone calls.'

'You'll be okay today?' But it was a pointless question and she knew it. Who knew if he'd be okay? What she really wanted to ask him was when she'd see him again, but she didn't dare. She just watched with large damp eyes as he quietly closed the door to the room. A moment later she saw him leave the hotel in a cab. And ten minutes later, she and Ernestine did the same. Kezia got very drunk on the flight back to New York.

# CHAPTER XIX

It had been over a week since she'd left him in San Francisco. Now he was back in Chicago and calling her two or three times a day. But there had been a raw fibre of terror in her gut since she'd left him. He said everything was fine, and he'd be in New York any day. But when? And how was he really? She was aware of a guarded quality to his speech when he called. He didn't trust his phone. And this was far worse than the last time they'd been apart. Then she had only been lonely. Now she was afraid.

She was desperately trying to keep her time, and her mind, as filled as she could. She had even suggested to Luke that she do a piece on Alejandro.

'On that fleabag centre he runs?'

'Yes. Simpson says he might have a market for it. I think I'd like to do it. Think Alejandro would agree?'

'He'd love it, and a little publicity might help him get funds.'

'All right. I'll get busy on it.' Either that or go crazy, sweetie pie.


'Okay, now what do I do? I've never been interviewed before.' She laughed at the nervous look on his face. He was such a nice man, with a good sense of humour.

'Well, Alejandro, let's see. Actually, you're only my second personal interview. Usually, I go about it quietly. Kind of sneaky.' She looked like a kid in her pigtails and jeans. But a clean kid. That was rare in those halls.

'Why sneaky? Are you afraid of what you write?' His eyes opened wide. It surprised him. She was so direct; it seemed unlike her to go through any back doors.

'It's mostly because of the crazy life I lead. Luke covered it fairly accurately. I am one way, and live a number of other ways.'

'And what's Luke to you, Kezia? Is he real?'

'Very. It's my old life that isn't real. Never was. And it's even less so now.'

'You don't like it?'

She shook her head in silent answer.

'That's too bad.'

'I'm almost ashamed of it, Alejandro.'

'Kezia, that's crazy. It's part of you. You can't deny it.'

'But it's so ugly.' She toyed with a pencil and looked at her hands.

'It can't all be ugly. And why "ugly"? To most people that life looks pretty good.' His voice was very soft.

'It's an empty life, though. It takes everything out of you, and doesn't put anything back. It's pretence and games, and people cheating on each other, and lying, and thinking how many thousands of dollars to spend on a dress, when they could be putting it into something like this. It just doesn't make a hell of a lot of sense to me. I guess I'm a misfit.'

'I'm afraid I don't know much about that world.'

'You're better off.'

'And you're silly.' He reached out and touched her face, pulling her chin up until her eyes met his. 'It's part of you, Kezia. A nice part. A gracious part. You really think you'd be so much better off living up here like this? People lie and cheat and steal here too. They shoot junk. They fuck their children. They beat their mothers and their wives. They get frustrated and angry. They don't have time to learn the things you know. Maybe you should just take that knowledge and use it well. Don't waste your time feeling bitter or sad for the years before this. Just use it well now.'

She smiled at him for a long moment. He made sense. And he was right. Her world had given her something. It was a part of her life. 'I think I hate it so much because I'm afraid I'll get stuck there in the end. It's like an octopus, and it won't let you go.'

'Baby, you're a big girl now. If you don't want it, all you have to do is walk away. Quietly. Not with a bazooka in one hand and a grenade in the other. No one can stop you. Haven't you figured that out yet?' He looked surprised.

'I guess not. I never felt I had a choice.'

'Sure you do. We all have choices. We just don't see them sometimes. Even I have a choice, in this "shithouse" as Luke calls it. Any time it gets me down, I can walk out. But I don't.'

'Why don't you?'

'Because they need me. And I love it. I feel like I *can't* walk out, but the point is, I can. I just don't want to. Maybe you didn't want to walk out of your world either. Maybe you still don't want to. Maybe you're not ready to yet. Could be you feel safe there. And why not? It's familiar. And familiar is easy. Even if it's the shits, it's easy, because you know it. You never know the hell that is going to be out there.' He gestured vaguely with one arm as she nodded. He understood very well.

'You're right. But I think I'm ready to leave the womb

219

now. I also know that until now I haven't been ready. That's embarrassing to admit. Seems like at my age, I should have all that behind me, and be all squared away.'

'Bullshit. That takes a hell of a long time. I was thirty before I had the balls to leave my little Chicano world in L.A. and come here.'

'How old are you now?'

'Thirty-six.'

'You don't look it.' She was surprised.

'Maybe not, *querida*, but I sure as hell feel it.' He laughed his soft velvety laugh, and the warm Mexican eyes danced. 'Some days I feel eighty.'

'I know what you mean. Alejandro . . .' Her face grew serious.

'What, babe?' He thought he knew what was coming.

'You think Luke's okay?'

'In what way?' Oh God, don't let her ask. He couldn't tell her. Luke had to do that himself, if he hadn't already . . . but he should have by now.

'I don't know. He's so . . . well . . . so bold, I guess that's the right word. He just does what he does and that's it. I worry about his parole, about his safety, his life, everything. But he doesn't seem to.' She wasn't looking at him and he watched her hands; they were nervous and taut, playing games with her pen.

'No, he doesn't worry about his parole, or his ass, or much of anything. That's just Luke.'

'Do you think he's going to get his ass in a jam one day? Like maybe killed?' She couldn't help thinking of Morrissey. Her eyes came back to him, full of questions, and fear.

'If he has problems, Kezia, he'll tell us.'

'Yeah. The day before the ceiling comes down.' She had learned that much about him. He never said a word till the last minute, about anything. 'He doesn't give one much warning.'

'No, Kezia. He doesn't. That's just his way.'

'One has to respect it, I suppose.'

220

He nodded very quietly, and wanted to reach out and touch her hand. But he couldn't. All he could do was talk to Luke. He thought it was time.

'And that, my friend, ought to finish the story. Thank you.' With a sigh, she sat back in the chair in Alejandro's office. It had been a long day. They'd been talking for hours.

'You think you've got it all?' He looked pleased. She was fun to work with. Lucas was one hell of a lucky man, *and* he knew it.

'All, and then some. Can I lure you downtown for dinner? You ought to have something to make up for my picking your brain all afternoon.'

He smiled at the thought. 'I don't know about that. Hell, Kezia, if you get us some decent publicity for this place, it might change a lot of things. Community acceptance, if nothing else. That's been one of our biggest problems. They hate us worse up here than they do at City Hall. We get it at both ends.'

'It really seems like that.'

'Maybe your story will change the trend.'

'I hope so, love. I really hope so. So, what about dinner?'

'You're on. I'd take you to dinner up here, but Lucas would kill us both. I don't think he wants you hanging around this part of town.'

'Snob.'

'No, for once in his life he's using his head. Kezia, he's right. Don't just come up here like it's the cool thing to do. It isn't. It's dangerous. Very.'

She was amused at their collective concern. The two rough guys protecting the delicate flower. 'Okay, okay. I get the message. I got a whole speech from Luke on the phone. He wanted me to come up here today in a limo.' She laughed.

'Did you?' Alejandro's eyes grew wide. Talk about heat from the neighbourhood!

221

'Of course not, you ass. I came up by subway.' He answered her laugh with his own. They had fallen into the easy banter and jovial insults of friends, and she was glad. He was a very appealing man. Deeply sensitive, and at the same time fun. Above all, what struck her again about him was his kindness. And he was right about her too. Her past was a part of her life. The grandeur, the money . . . running away from it wouldn't solve anything. She was tempted to with Luke, and that wouldn't do it. She was Kezia Saint Martin and he was Lucas Johns and they loved each other. He couldn't become another Whit, and she was no street girl. They had come from different places and met when the time was right. But now what? What about the future? She hadn't figured that one out yet. She hadn't figured that out at all. And maybe neither had Luke.

'Hey, Kezia, tell you what . . . how about dinner down in the Village?'

'Italian?' It was all she ever ate with Luke, and pasta was coming out of her ears. She had cooked spaghetti for him the night before.

'No. Fuck Italian. That's Luke's trip. Spanish! I know a great place.' She laughed at him and shook her head.

'Don't you guys ever eat hamburgers or hot dogs or steak?'

'No way. Right about now I'd sell my soul for a burrito. You don't know what it does to a Mexican to live in this town. Everything's kosher or pizza.' He made a face and she laughed again as she followed him out.


'Tell the truth. It's fantastic, isn't it?' She had settled on a tostada while he ate paella.

'I've got to admit, it's not bad. And it's a change from fettuccine.'

'This place is run by a Mexican bandit, and his old lady's from Madrid. Great combination.'

She smiled and sipped at her wine. It had been a nice evening. She enjoyed Alejandro's company and it took the edge off her yearning for Luke. All she wanted to do was go home and wait for his call.

'Kezia . . .' Alejandro seemed to hesitate.

'Yeah?'

'You're good for him. You're the best thing he's ever had. But do me a favour . . .' He paused again.

'What, love?' How she liked this funny Mexican man. He cared so much about everything. The kids at his centre, his friends, and especially Luke. And now her.

'Please don't get hurt. He lives a hard life. It's a long way from home for you. Lucas is a gambler. He plays and he pays. But if he loses . . . you'll pay too. Through the teeth, kid – worse than anything you know.'

'Yeah. I know.' They sat silent for a moment in the light of the candle on their table, and thought their own thoughts.

And when Alejandro took her home, Luke was waiting for her in the living room.

'Lucas!' She ran into his arms and was instantly swept off the ground. 'Oh darling, you're home!'

'You'd better believe it! And what's this lecherous Mexican bandit doing with my woman?' But there was no fear in his eyes, only delight at having Kezia in his arms again.

'We did the interview today.' Her words were muffled as she buried her face in his chest. She held him as tightly as a child would, clutching all her security in those arms, in those shoulders, in that man.

'I wondered where you were. I got home two hours ago.'

'You did?' She looked more childlike than ever, the days of worry slipping away from her like rain. Alejandro stood by and watched the scene with a smile. 'We had dinner at a nice little Spanish place in the Village.'

'Oh God, he took you to that place? How bad is the heartburn?'

She grinned up at him again as she slid out of her shoes and stretched, a look of mischief coming into her eyes. Lucas was home and he was safe!

223

'Not bad. And it was lovely. Alejandro is very good to me.'

'Best dude I know.' Lucas sprawled on the couch with an appreciative look towards his friend, who was getting ready to leave them.

'Don't you want some coffee, Alejandro?'

'Nope, I'll leave you lovebirds alone.'

'Smart man, Al. She has some packing to do anyway. We're leaving for Chicago in the morning.'

'We are? Oh Lucas, I love you! How long are we staying?' This time she wanted to know how long they had.

'How about till Thanksgiving?' He looked at her happily through half-closed eyes.

'Together? Three weeks? Lucas, you're crazy! How can I stay away that long? The column . . .' Oh shit.

'You do it in the summer, don't you?' She nodded.

'Yeah, but I cover things over there, and there's no one here in the summer.' He laughed, and she looked a question into his eyes.

'What's so funny?'

'The way you say "no one". Can't you cover a couple of posh parties in Chicago?'

'Yeah. I guess I could.' And she wanted to go. Oh God, how she wanted to go!

'Then why don't you? And maybe I can wind things up there in less than three weeks. There's no reason why I can't work out of New York. What the hell . . . and all I really need is a week there to work out some things. I can commute, if I have to.'

'Could we both commute?' Her eyes were filled with stars.

'Sure we could, Mama. The two of us. I made up my mind on the plane coming back here tonight. I told you it would never be like that last stint again, and it won't be. I can't stand it without you.'

'Lucas, my love, I adore you.' She bent quickly to kiss him.

'Then take me to bed. Good night, Alejandro.'

Their friend chuckled to himself as he let himself out. Lucas was asleep before she turned the lights out. She looked at him, sound asleep on his side. Lucas Johns. Her man. The hub of her life. And here she was, following him from town to town like a gypsy. It was fun, she loved it, but she knew that sooner or later she'd have to make some decisions ... the column ... she hadn't been to a party in weeks ... and now she was off to Chicago ... and what then? But at least Lucas was with her. And safe. Who cared about parties? She had been afraid for his life.


CHAPTER XX


'Kezia, when are you coming back?'

She had been on the phone long-distance to Edward in New York for over half an hour. 'Probably some time next week. I'm still working on that story out here.' And she had appeared at two social galas, but it was harder out here. This wasn't her town. It took a lot more research to come up with the dirt. 'Besides, darling, I'm enjoying Chicago.' That confirmed the worst of his suspicions. She sounded so happy. And she was not the sort to be thrilled by Chicago; it was not her milieu. Too Midwest, too American, too Sears Roebuck, and not enough of the rarefied air of Bergdorf's and Bendel's. There had to be someone in Chicago. Someone new? He only hoped it was someone worthwhile. And respectable.

'I saw your last article in *Harper's*. Nice piece. And I heard from Simpson the other day that you've got something coming out in a few weeks in the Sunday *Times*.'

'I do? Which one?'

225

'Something about a drug rehabilitation centre in Harlem. I didn't know you'd done that.'

'That was just before I left town. Save it for me when it comes out.' But suddenly there was an unspoken awkwardness between them. They both felt it.

'Kezia, are you all right?'

And now it was back to that again. 'Yes, Edward, I'm fine. Honest. We'll have lunch next week when I get back, and you can see for yourself. I'll even meet you at La Côte Basque.'

'Dear lady, how kind you are.'

She laughed at him and they hung up after a few moments of business: they had some new tax shelters to discuss.

Luke looked up from his reading with a quizzical eye.

'Who was that?' He knew it had to be Edward or Simpson.

'Edward.'

'You can tell him you'll have lunch with him sooner. If you want.'

'Are you sending me back?' They had been gone for ten days.

'No, you jerk.' He grinned at the look on her face. 'I just thought we'd go back tomorrow. You've got your work to consider, and I have to commute to D.C. for the rest of the week. There's a series of closed meetings for the moratorium that I want to attend, and I can catch another speaking engagement or two down there. Washington seems to love me.' The checks had been coming in with pleasing regularity. 'I just thought we'd settle down in New York for a couple of weeks.'

She laughed at him, relieved. 'Are you sure you can stand staying any place for that long?'

'I'll sure try.' He slapped her behind as he walked to the bar and poured himself a bourbon and water.

'Luke?' She was lying on the bed, looking pensive.

'Yeah?'

'What am I going to do about the column?'

226

'That's up to you, babe. You've got to make up your own mind on that. Do you dig writing it?'

'Once in a while. But not lately. Not for a long time, in fact.'

'Then maybe it's time to quit, for your own sake. But don't give it up for me. Do what you want. And if you've got to stick around New York covering fancy parties, then you do that. You've got to take care of your business too. Don't forget that.'

'I'll see how I feel about it after next week. I'll do my usual thing when we go back to New York. Then I'll see how it feels.' With Luke commuting to Washington, she'd have plenty of time to hit her old circuit.


After four days in New York, she had been to the opening of a play, the closing of a theatre, two lunches for ambassadors' wives, and a charity fashion show. Her feet hurt, her mind ached, and her ears were numbed by the constant flow of idle gossip. Who gave a damn? Kezia didn't. Not any more.

'Lucas, if I ever hear the word "divine" again, I think I'm going to throw up.'

'You look tired.' She looked more than tired. She looked drained, and she felt it.

'I am tired, and I hate all that fucking shit.' She had even made it to a meeting of the Arthritis Ball that day. Tiffany had passed out in the john. And she couldn't even use it for the column. The only good piece of information she'd picked up was that Marina and Halpern were getting married. But so what? Who cared?

'What are we doing this weekend?' If he told her that they were going to Chicago, she would have a fit of hysterics. She didn't want to go anywhere, except bed.

'Nothing. Maybe I'll go up and see Al. Want to have him for dinner?' He was sitting on the edge of the bed and looked as tired as she.

'That, I would love. I'll cook something here.' He smiled at the domestic exchange and she picked up on

227

what he was thinking. 'It's neat, isn't it, Luke? Sometimes I wonder if you love it all as much as I do. I've never lived like this before.'

He grinned at her, knowing how true that was.

'You know what I mean.'

'Yes, I do. And I probably love it even more than you do. I'm beginning to wonder how I survived without you before this.' He slipped into bed beside her, and she turned off the light. He had his own keys to the apartment, and used the answering service as his, she had cleaned out a closet for him, and the maid had finally even smiled at him. Once. She called him 'Mister Luke.'

'You know something, darling? We're lucky. Incredibly lucky.' She was pleased with herself, as though she had caught a falling star in her hands.

'Yes, baby, we are.' Even if only for now. . . .


'Well, gentlemen, I propose a toast to the demise of Martin Hallam.'

'Lucas, what does she mean?' Alejandro looked puzzled and Luke looked at her curiously. This was the first he had heard of it.

'Kezia, does this mean what I think?'

'Yes, sir. It does. After seven years of writing the Martin Hallam column, I quit. I did it today.'

Luke looked at her, shocked. 'What did they say?'

'They don't know yet. I told Simpson today, and he's going to handle the rest. They'll know tomorrow.'

'Are you sure?' It wasn't too late to reverse the decision.

'I have never been so sure in my life. I don't have the time for that garbage any more. Or the inclination to waste my time doing it.' She saw a strange look pass between Luke and Alejandro, and wondered why no one seemed impressed. 'Well, you two are certainly a lousy audience for my big announcement. Phooey on both of you.'

Alejandro smiled and Luke laughed.

'I guess we're just kind of shocked, babe. And I suddenly wondered if you're doing it because of me.'

'Not really, darling. It's my decision. I don't want to have to go to those shitty parties for the rest of my life. You saw how tired I was this week. And for what? It's just not my thing any more.'

'Have you told Edward?' He looked worried, and Alejandro was looking daggers at him.

'No. I'll call him tomorrow. You're the first two to know after Simpson. And you're a couple of creeps.'

'I'm sorry, baby. It's just sort of a shock.' He lifted his glass to her then, a nervous smile on his face. 'To Martin Hallam then.' Alejandro raised his glass in response, but his eyes never left Lucas' face.

'To Martin Hallam. Rest in peace.'

'Amen.' Kezia drained her glass in one gulp.


'No, Edward. I'm sure. And Simpson agrees. It's a diversion I don't really have time for any more. I want to stick with serious writing.'

'But it's such a drastic step, Kezia. You're used to the column. Everyone's used to it. It's become an institution. Have you given this decision adequate thought?'

'Of course I have. For months. And the fact is, darling, that I don't want to be an "institution." Not that kind of institution. I want to be a writer, a good one, not a gossip-monger amongst fools. Really, darling, you'll see. It's the best possible decision.'

'Kezia, you're making me nervous.'

'Don't be ridiculous. Why?' She swung her foot as she sat at her desk. She had called him right after Luke left the house for a morning of meetings. At least Luke had come around, after the first shock. And Simpson had applauded the decision, and said it was high time.

'I wish I knew why you make me nervous. I think it's because I get the feeling I don't know what you're up to, not that it's really any of my business.' But he wanted it to be. That was the rub.

229

'Edward, you're going to make yourself senile worrying about nothing.' He was beginning to annoy her. Constantly.

'What are you doing for Thanksgiving?' It was almost an accusation.

'Going away.' But he didn't dare ask where. And she didn't volunteer the information. They were going back to Chicago.

'All right, all right. Dammit, Kezia, I'm sorry. It's just that, in my mind, you will always be a child.'

'And I will always love you, and you will always worry too much. Over nothing.'

He had made her uncomfortable, though. After they hung up, she sat silently and wondered. Was she crazy to stop writing the column? At one time, it had been so important to her. But not any more. But still . . . was she losing touch with who and what she was? In a way, she had done it for Luke. And for herself. Because she wanted to be free to move around with him, and besides, she had outgrown the column years ago.

But suddenly, she wanted to discuss it with Luke. He was gone for the day. She could call Alejandro, but she hated to bother him. It was a queasy feeling, like leaving the dock in the fog, headed for an unknown destination. But she had made her decision. She would live by it. Martin Hallam was dead. It was a simple decision really. The column was over.

She sat back at her desk and stretched, and decided to go for a walk. It was a grey November day, and there was a nip of winter in the air. It made her want to throw a long wool scarf around her neck and run to the park. She felt suddenly free of an old wearisome burden. The weight of Martin Hallam had finally slipped from her shoulders.

Kezia grabbed an old sheepskin jacket from her closet and slipped tall black custom-made boots under her carefully pressed jeans. She dug a small knitted red cap from the pocket of her jacket, and took a pair of gloves from a shelf. She felt new again now. A writer of anything she wanted, not a scavenger of social crumbs. A small smile hovered on her lips, and there was a mischievous gleam in her eye as she headed for the park, with long strides. What a marvellous day, and it wasn't even lunchtime yet. She thought about buying a picnic to eat in the park, but decided not to bother. Instead, she bought a small bag of hot roasted chestnuts from an old gnarled man pushing a steaming cart along Fifth Avenue. He grinned at her toothlessly and she waved at him over her shoulder as she walked away. He was sweet really. Everyone was. Everyone suddenly looked as new as she felt.

She was well into the park and halfway through the chestnuts when she looked ahead and saw the woman trip and fall on the kerb. She had spun out into the street close to the clomping feet of an ageing horse pulling a shabby hansom carriage through the park. The woman lay very still for a moment, and the driver of the carriage stood and pulled at the horse's reins. The horse seemed not even to have noticed the bundle near his hoofs. She was wearing a dark fur coat and her hair was very blond. It was all Kezia could see. She frowned and quickened her pace, shoving the chestnuts into her pocket, and then breaking into a trot as the driver of the hansom jumped from his platform, still holding the reins. The woman stirred then, knelt and lurched forward, into the horse's legs this time. The horse shied, and his owner pushed the woman away. She sat down heavily on the pavement then, but mercifully free of the horse's legs at last.

'What the hell'sa matta wi'youse? Ya crazy?' His eyes bulged furiously as he continued to back his horse away and stare at the woman. Kezia could only see the back of her head, as she shook her head mutely. He mounted his platform then, and clucked his horse back into motion, with a last flick of his middle finger at the still-seated woman, and a 'Stupid bitch!' His passengers were obscured beyond a scratched and smoky window in the carriage, and the ancient horse continued plodding, so

231

used to his route that bombs could have shattered near his feet and he would have continued in the well-worn groove he had travelled for years.

Kezia saw the woman shake her head fuzzily and kneel slowly on the pavement. She ran the last few steps then, wondering if the woman had been hurt, and what had caused her to fall. The dark fur coat was fanned out behind her now, and it was obvious that it was a long and rather splendid mink. Kezia heard a dry little cough from the woman just as she reached her, and then she saw her turn her head. What she saw made her stop, shocked by who it was and how stricken she looked. It was Tiffany, her face gaunt yet swollen, her eyes puffy, yet her cheeks were pulled inward, with painful lines near her eyes and mouth. It wasn't yet noon, and she was already drunk.

'Tiffany?' Kezia knelt beside her and smoothed a hand over her hair. It was uncombed and dishevelled and there was no makeup on the ravaged face. 'Tiffie ... it's me. Kezia.'

'Hi.' Tiffany seemed to look somewhere past Kezia's left ear, unknowing, unseeing, uncaring. 'Where's Uncle Kee?'

*Uncle Kee.* Jesus, she meant Kezia's father. Uncle Kee. She hadn't heard that in so long ... Uncle Kee ... Daddy ...

'Tiffie, are you hurt?'

'Hurt?' She looked up vaguely, seeming not to understand.

'The horse, Tiff. Did it hurt you?'

'Horse?' She wore the smile of a child now, and seemed to understand. 'Oh, horse. Oh, no, I ride all the time.' She stood up shakily then, and dusted off her hands and the front of her long black mink coat. Kezia looked down and saw torn grey stockings and one bruised black suede Gucci shoe. The coat gaped a little and Kezia caught a glimpse of a dressy black velvet skirt and a white satin shirt, with several rows of large grey and white pearls. It was no outfit to be roaming the park in, nor was it an

232

outfit for that time of day. Kezia wondered if she'd been home the night before.

'Where are you going?'

'To the Lombards'. For dinner.' So that was where she'd been. Kezia had been invited there too, but had turned down the invitation weeks ago. The Lombards. But that had been last night. What had happened since?

'How about if I take you home?'

'To my house?' Tiffany looked suddenly wary.

'Sure.' Kezia tried to put an easy tone in her voice, while holding Tiffany up firmly by one elbow.

'No! Not my house! No. . . .' She bolted from Kezia's grip then and stumbled, and was instantly sick at Kezia's feet and over her own black suede shoes. She sat down on the pavement again and began to cry, the black mink trailing sadly in her own bile.

Kezia felt hot tears burn her eyes as she reached down to her friend and tried to pull her up again.

'Come on, Tiffie . . . let's go.'

'No . . . I . . . oh God, Kezia . . . please . . .' She clutched at Kezia's denim-clad legs, and looked up at her with eyes torn by a thousand private demons. Kezia reached gently down to her and pulled her up again, as she saw a cab swoop around the bend from which the hansom cab had appeared only moments before. She held up a hand quickly and hailed it, and then pulled Tiffany closer. 'No!' It was the anguished wail of a heartbroken child, and Kezia felt her friend trembling in her arms.

'Come on, we'll go to my place.'

'I'm going to be sick.' She closed her eyes and sank toward Kezia again, as the cabbie darted out and threw open the door.

'No, you're not. Let's get in.' She managed to slide Tiffany onto the seat and gave the driver her own address as she rolled down both windows to give her friend air. It was then that she noticed that Tiffany wasn't carrying a handbag.

'Tiffie? Did you have a bag?' The girl looked around

233

blankly for a moment and then shrugged, letting her head fall back onto the seat as both eyes closed and the air rushed in over her face.

'So what?' The words were so low Kezia had barely heard her.

'Hm?'

'Handbag ... so what?' She shrugged, and seemed almost to fall asleep, but a moment later her hand blindly sought Kezia's and gripped it tightly as two lone tears squeezed down her face. Kezia patted the thin cold hand and looked down with horror at the large pear-shaped emerald flanked by diamond baguettes. If someone had taken Tiffany's handbag, he had missed the best part. The thought made Kezia shudder. Tiffany was ripe prey for anyone. 'Walked ... all ... night....' The voice was almost a painful croak, and Kezia found herself wondering if it wasn't more likely 'drank' all night. It was obvious she hadn't gone home after the Lombards.

'Where did you walk to?' She didn't want to get into a heavy conversation in the cab. First she'd put Tiffany to bed, call her home and tell the housekeeper that Mrs. Benjamin was fine, and then they'd talk later. No drunken hysterics in the cab.... The cabbie might decide he had a hot story and ... Christ, that Kezia did not need.

'Church ... all night ... walking ... slept in church....' She kept her eyes closed and seemed to drift off between words. But the grip on Kezia's hand never slackened. It was only a few minutes before they drew up in front of Kezia's building, and with no explanations required or proffered, the doorman helped Kezia get Tiffany into the elevator, and the elevator man helped get her inside. The apartment was empty; Luke was out, and the cleaning woman wasn't due. Kezia was grateful for the solitude as she led her friend into the bedroom. She didn't want to explain Luke, even in Tiffany's current state. She had taken a hell of a chance bringing her there, but she couldn't think of any place else.

Tiffany sat sleepily on the edge of Kezia's bed and looked around. 'Where's Uncle Kee?'

Her father again ... Christ. 'He's out, Tiff. Why don't you lie down, and I'll call your place and tell them you'll be home later.'

'No! ... Tell them.... Tell.... Tell her to go to hell!' She began to sob then and shake violently from head to foot. Kezia felt a cold chill run up her spine. Something about the words, the tone of voice ... something ... it had struck a chord in her memory, and she suddenly felt frightened. Tiffany was looking at her now with wild eyes, shaking her head, tears pouring down her face. Kezia stood near the phone and looked at her friend, wanting to help, but fearing to go near her. Something inside Kezia turned over.

'Shouldn't I tell them something?' The two women stayed that way for a moment, with Tiffany slowly shaking her head.

'No ... divorce....'

'Bill?' Kezia looked at her stunned.

Tiffany nodded.

'Bill asked for a divorce?'

She nodded yes and then no. And then she took a deep breath. 'Mother Benjamin.... She called last night ... after the Lombards' dinner. Called me a ... a ... lush ... an alcoholic ... a ... the children, she is going to take the children, and make Bill ... make Bill ...' She gasped, choking back more sobs, and then retched briefly, but dryly.

'Make Bill divorce you?'

Tiffany gasped again and nodded while Kezia continued to look on, still dreading to go near her.

'But she can't "make" Bill divorce you, for Christ's sake. He's a grown man.'

But Tiffany shook her head and looked up with empty, swollen eyes. 'The trust. The big trust. His whole life ... depends ... on it. And the children ... their trust ... He ... she could ... he would ...'

'No, he wouldn't. He loves you. You're his wife.'

'She's his mother.'

'So what, dammit? Be reasonable, Tiffany. He's not going to divorce you. . . .' But suddenly Kezia wondered. Would he? What if the bulk of his fortune depended on it? How much did he love Tiffany? Enough to sacrifice that? As Kezia watched her, she knew Tiffany was right. Mother Benjamin held all the cards. 'What about the children?' But she saw the answer in Tiffany's eyes.

'She . . . she . . . they . . .' She was racked by fresh sobs, and clutched the bedspread beneath her as she fought to finish. 'She has . . . them. . . . They were gone last night after the . . . Lombards' dinner . . . and . . . Bill . . . Bill . . . in Brussels . . . she said . . . I . . . oh God, Kezia, someone help me please. . . .'

It was a death wail and Kezia found herself trembling as she stood across the room and finally, painfully, slowly began to walk toward her friend. But it was like hearing it again . . . hearing it . . . things began to come back to her. There were tears on her own face now and there was this horrible, terrible urge to slap the girl sitting filthy and broken on her bed . . . an urge to just sweep her away, to shake her, to . . . oh God, no. . . .

She was standing in front of her and the words seemed to rip through her soul, as though they were someone else's, hurled by and at a long vanished ghost. 'Then why are you such a fucking drunk, dammit . . . why . . . why?' She sank down on the bed beside Tiffany then, and the two women held each other tight as they cried. It seemed like years before Kezia could stop, and this time it felt as though Tiffany were comforting her. There was a time-lessness about the arms veiled by black mink. They were arms that had held Kezia before. Arms that had heard those words before, twenty years before. Why?

'Jesus. I'm . . . I'm sorry, Tiffie. It . . . you brought back something so painful for me.' She looked up to see her friend nodding tiredly, but looking more sober than she had in an hour. Maybe in days.

'I know. I'm sorry. I'm a bad trip all around.' The tears continued to fan out from her eyes, but her voice sounded almost normal.

'No, you're not. And I'm so sorry about the kids, and about Mrs. Benjamin. What a stinking thing to do. What are you going to do?'

She shrugged in answer, looking down at her hands.

'Can't you fight it?' But they both knew otherwise. Not unless she cleaned up radically overnight. 'What if you go to a clinic?'

'Yeah, and when I come out, she'll have a grip on those kids that will never loosen, no matter how sober I get. She's got me, Kezia. She's got my soul ... my heart ... my ...' She closed her eyes again then, and the look of pain on her face was intolerable. Kezia put her arms around her again. She seemed so thin and frail, even in the thick fur coat. There was so little one could say. It was as though Tiffany had already lost. And she knew it.

'Why don't you lie down and try to get some sleep?'

'And then what?' Her eyes were almost haunting.

'Then you can take a bath, have something to eat, and I'll take you home.'

'And then?' There was nothing Kezia could say. She knew what the other girl meant. Tiffany stood up slowly and walked shakily to the window. 'I think it's time I went home.'

She seemed to be looking far beyond and far away, and Kezia berated herself silently for the wave of relief that she felt. She wanted Tiffany out of her house. Before Luke came home, before she fell apart again, before she said something that brought even one instant of horror back, she wanted her gone. Tiffany made her unbearably nervous. She frightened her. She was like a living ghost. The reincarnation of Liane Holmes-Aubrey Saint Martin. Her mother ... the drunk.... She did not argue with Tiffany.

'You want me to take you home?' But she found herself hoping not.

Tiffany shook her head and brought her gaze back from the window with a small, gentle smile, and quietly shook her head. 'No. I have to go alone.' She walked out of the bedroom, through the living room, and stopped at the front door, looking back at Kezia hovering uncertainly in the bedroom doorway. Kezia wasn't sure if she should let her leave alone, but she wanted her to. She just wanted her to go home. To go away. Their eyes held for a moment, and Tiffany lifted one hand in a mock military salute, pulled her coat more tightly around her, and said, 'See ya,' just as they had when they were in school. 'See ya,' and then she was gone. The door closed softly behind her, and a moment later Kezia heard the elevator take her away. She knew she had no money to go home with, but she knew that Tiffany's doorman would pay for the cab. The very rich can travel almost anywhere empty-handed. Everyone knows them. Doormen are delighted to pay for their cabs. They double their money in tips. Kezia knew Tiffany was safe. And at least she was out of her house. There was a heavy scent left hanging in the air, a smell of perfume mixed with perspiration and vomit.

Kezia stood at the window for a long time, thinking of her friend, and her mother, loving and hating them both. After a while, the two seemed to blend into one. They were so much alike, so ... so ... It took a long hot bath and a nap to make Kezia feel human again. The excitement and the freedom of the morning, of ditching that damn column, was tarnished by the agony of seeing Tiffany sprawled in the street at the feet of that horse, shouted at by the hansom cab driver, puking and crying and wandering lost and confused ... and screwed over by her mother-in-law ... bereft of her children, with a husband who didn't give a damn. Hell, he probably would let his mother talk him into a divorce. And it probably wouldn't take much talking. It made Kezia's stomach turn over again and again, and when at last she lay down for a nap she slept badly, but at least when she awoke,

238

things looked better again. Much better. She looked up to see Luke standing at the foot of the bed. She glanced at the clock by her bed. It was much later than she'd thought.

'Hi, lazyass. What did you do? Sleep all day?' She smiled at him for a moment and then grew serious as she sat up and held out her arms. He leaned over to kiss her and she nuzzled his neck.

'I had kind of a rough day.'

'An assignment?'

'No. A friend.' She seemed unwilling to say more. 'Want something to drink? I'm going to make some tea. I'm freezing.' She shivered gently and Luke looked at the window and the night sky beyond.

'No wonder, with the windows open like that.' She had opened all of them wide, to banish the smell. 'Make me some coffee, babe?'

'Sure thing.' They exchanged a haphazard kiss and a smile, and she took the newspaper from the foot of the bed where he'd left it when he leaned over to kiss her hello.

'That girl in the paper anyone you know?'

'Who?' She was wandering barefoot through the living room now, yawning as she went.

'The socialite on the front page.'

'I'll look.' She flicked on the kitchen light, and looked down at the paper in her hands. The room spun around as she did. 'It ... it ... I ... oh God, Lucas, help me ...' She slid slowly down the side of the doorway, staring at the photograph of Tiffany Benjamin. She had jumped from the window of her apartment shortly after two. '*See ya ... see ya. ...*' Suddenly the words rang in her ears. 'See ya.' With that little salute they had done all through school. Kezia scarcely felt Luke's arms around her as he led her to the couch to sit down.

# CHAPTER XXI

'Do you want me to come with you?' Kezia shook her head as she zipped up the black dress and then slipped on the black alligator shoes she had bought the summer before in Madrid.

'No, love, thanks. I'll be okay.'

'Promise?'

She smiled at him as she put on her mink hat. 'Swear.'

'I'll say one thing, you sure as hell are looking fancy.'

He looked at her appreciatively and she smiled again.

'I'm not sure that I'm supposed to.' But she knew that she looked just right. She was trying to decide if she should wear her mink coat or her black Saint Laurent. She decided on the black.

'You look fine. And listen, lady, if it gets too heavy for you, you split, right?'

'I'll see.'

'That's not what I said.' He walked to the mirror and pulled her around to face him. He still didn't like the look in her eyes. 'If it gets heavy, you come home. Either that, or I come with you.' He knew that was out of the question. Tiffany's funeral was going to be one of the 'events' of the season. But all he wanted to know was that Kezia knew the score. It wasn't her fault Tiffany had committed suicide. She had not killed Tiffany. She had not killed her mother. She had done her best. They had been over it and over it and over it, and he wanted to be sure that she wouldn't backslide now. It was a bitch of a thing to happen but it wasn't her fault. She slid quietly into his arms as they stood in front of the mirror, and she held him tighter than usual.

'I'm glad you're here, Lucas.'

'So am I. Now do I have that promise from you?' She nodded silently and held her face up to him to kiss, which he did with a vengeance.

'Goodness, at that rate, Mr. Johns, I may never leave here in the first place.'

'That would suit me just fine.' He ran a hand inside the V-neck of her dress and she backed off with a giggle.

'Lucas!'

'At your service, madam.'

'You're awful!'

'Awful horny!' He was eyeing her with a smile as she clipped on simple pearl earrings. He knew he was being irreverent, but it lightened the mood. He tried to sound casual as he sat down and watched her put on lipstick and a last dab of perfume. 'Is Edward going with you?' She shook her head and picked up the black alligator bag and short white kid gloves. The thick black and white silk scarf from Dior provided the only brighter spot to her outfit.

'I told Edward I'd met him there. And stop worrying about me. I'm a big girl, and I'm fine, and I love you and you take care of me better than anyone in this world.' She faced him with a smile that looked more like the Kezia who could take care of herself and he began to feel better.

'Jesus, you look good. If you weren't in a hurry . . .'

'Lucas, you're all talk.' She had turned away and was crossing the living room on her way to get her coat, when he came up silently behind her and picked her up off her feet.

'All talk am I? Listen here, wench . . .'

'Lucas! Lucas dammit, put me down! Lucas!' He spun her around back down to the ground and she fell giggling and breathless into his arms as he chuckled. 'You are the worst, most miserable, impossible . . .' He met her lips with his own and after a moment she pushed him gently away with a look both happy and sad on her face. 'Luke . . . I have to go.'

241

'I know.' He was sober now too, and helped her on with her coat. 'Just take it easy.' She nodded, kissed him, and was gone.

The church was already filled when she got there, and Edward was waiting discreetly near a door. He signalled silently to her, and she joined him, slipping a hand inside his arm.

'You look lovely.' His voice was a whisper and she nodded, as he tightened his grip on her arm. They were ushered up the main aisle, and Kezia tried not to see the casket draped in a blanket of white roses. Mother Benjamin sat piously in the front pew with her widower son and his two children. Kezia felt the breath catch in her throat as she saw them, and she wanted to scream 'Killer!' at the bowed head of her friend's mother-in-law. 'Killer! You killed her, with your fucking threats of divorce and taking the children . . . you . . .'

'Thank you.' She heard Edward's subdued voice as the usher showed them to a pew near the middle. Whit was standing three pews ahead.

He looked thinner, and suddenly more openly effeminate in an over-tailored Cardin suit that clutched at his waist, and seemed to hang too closely across his back. She suspected the suit had been a gift from his friend. It was not the sort of thing Whit would have bought for himself.

Marina was there too, with Halpern, looking embarrassingly happy in spite of the setting. They were getting married at New Year's in Palm Beach. Marina looked as if her troubles were over.

Kezia found it hard not to cast the eye of Martin Hallam about, looking for people, tidbits, stories. But she couldn't hide behind him any more. Now he was dead too. And she was simply Kezia Saint Martin, mourning her friend. The tears ran freely down her face as they carried the casket down the aisle, to the maroon limousine that waited outside. Two policemen had been detailed to redirect traffic around the long snaking line of limousines, not a single one of which was rented. It was all the real thing. And as was to be expected, an army of press lay in wait for the mourners as they left.

It was hard to believe that it was all over. They had had so much fun in school, had written to each other from their respective colleges. Kezia had been Tiffany's maid of honour when she married Bill, had laughed at her when she was pregnant. When did the end start? When did the drinking make her a drunk? Was it then, after the first baby? Or after the second? Was it later? Had she been before? The awful part was that now it seemed as though she had always been that way, always lurching, vague, dropping 'Divine's like rabbit pellets everywhere she went. It was this Tiffany that leapt to mind, the drunken, vomiting, confused Tiffany ... not the funny girl in school ... that mock salute at the door that last day ... that ... see ya ... see ya ... see ya. ...

Kezia found herself staring blankly at the backs of people's heads and felt Edward guiding her slowly out of the pew. It was a long wait at the line where she shook hands with assorted relatives. Bill looked officious and solemn, dispensing small smiles and understanding nods like an undertaker instead of a husband. The children looked confused. Everywhere people were looking around, checking out who was there, what they had worn, and clucking and shaking their heads over Tiffany ... Tiffany the drunk ... Tiffany the lush ... Tiffany the ... friend. And it was all so much like Kezia's mother's funeral that it was unbearable. Not only to her, but to Edward. He looked grey when they left the church at last. Kezia took a deep breath, patted his hand and looked up at the sky.

'Edward, when I die, I want you to see to it that I'm tossed into the Hudson, or something equally simple and pleasant. If you do one of these numbers for me, I'll haunt you for the rest of your life.' She was not entirely joking. But Edward looked at her with an unhappy expression.

'I hope I won't be around to worry about it. Do you want to go to the cemetery?' She hesitated for a moment,

243

and then shook her head, remembering her promise to Luke. This had been bad enough.

'No, I don't. Are you going?'

He nodded painfully.

'Why?' Because he ought to. She knew the answer too well. That's what killed people like Tiffany. Ought to's.

'Really, Kezia. One ought . . .' She didn't wait to hear the end of it. She merely leaned over, kissed his cheek, and started down the steps.

'I know, Edward. Take care.'

He had wanted to ask her what she was doing later, but he never got the chance, and he didn't want to impose on her. He never did. It didn't seem right to trouble her. She had her own life to live, but it had been such a wretched day. Such a bad day for him. It all reminded him so much of Liane. Of that godawful, unbearable day when. . . . He watched Kezia slip easily into a cab, and wiped a tear quickly from his cheek. He was smiling a small, appropriate smile when she looked back at him from the rear window.


'How was it?' Luke was waiting for her with hot tea.

'Horrible. Thanks, darling.' She took a sip of the tea before she took off the black Saint Laurent coat, and with her free hand pulled the dark mink hat from her head. 'It was ghastly. Her mother-in-law even had the bad taste to bring the kids.' But Kezia had been at her mother's funeral too. Maybe that was just the way things had to be. As painful as possible to make them seem real.

'Do you want to go out to dinner, or have something sent in?'

She shrugged, not really caring. Something was bothering her. Everything was.

'Baby, what's wrong? Did it hit you that hard? I told you. . . .' He looked at her unhappily.

'I know. I know. But it's upsetting . . . and maybe something else is bothering me. I don't know what. Maybe it's seeing all those fossils who still think they own

244

me. Maybe it's growing pains. I'll be okay. I'm probably just depressed about Tiffany.'

'You sure it's not something else?' He was troubled, more than she knew.

'I told you, I don't know. But it's no big deal. There have just been a lot of changes lately ... quitting the column ... you know. It's time to grow up, and that's never easy.' She tried to smile but his eyes didn't answer.

'Kezia, am I making you unhappy?'

'Oh, darling, no!' She was horrified. What a ridiculous thought. And what the hell had he been worrying about all afternoon, she wondered. He looked lousy.

'Are you sure?'

'Of course I'm sure. I'm positive, Lucas. Really.' She leaned over to kiss him and saw sadness in his eyes. Maybe it was compassion for her, but what she saw touched her deeply.

'Are you sorry about having given up the column?'

'No, I'm glad. Honestly glad. It just feels odd when things change. Makes one insecure. It does me, anyway.'

'Yeah.' He nodded and stayed silent for a long time as she finished her tea, her coat now tossed on a chair, the black dress she wore making her look more severe. He watched her and it was a long time before he spoke again. There was an odd note in his voice when he did. The bantering of earlier in the day was gone.

'Kezia ... there's something I have to tell you.'

She looked up, all innocence, trying to smile. 'What is it, love?' And then she joked, 'You're secretly married and have fifteen children?' She spoke with the confidence of a woman who knows that there are no secrets ... only one.

'No, you jerk. I'm not married. But there's something else.'

'Give me a hint.' But for once she didn't look worried. It couldn't be important or he wouldn't be bringing it up now. He knew she was upset about Tiffany.

'Babe, I don't know any way to tell you, except to put it to you straight. But I have to tell you. It just can't wait

245

any more. I'm up for a revocation hearing.' The words fell into the room like a bomb. Everything smashed and then stopped.

'A what?' She couldn't have heard him correctly ... couldn't have. She was dreaming. This was one of his nightmares and she'd overheard by mistake.

'A hearing. I'm up for a hearing. About my parole. They want to revoke me for conspiracy to provoke disturbances in the prisons. In other words, agitation.'

'Oh God, Lucas. . . . Tell me you're joking.' She closed her eyes and sat very still, as though she were waiting, but he could see her clenched hands shake in her lap.

'No, babe, I'm not kidding. I wish I were, but I'm not.' He reached out and took both her small hands in his. Her eyes opened slowly, drowning in tears.

'How long have you known?'

'There's been a threat of it for a while. Since before I met you, in fact. But I never believed it would happen. I got confirmation of the hearing today. What really did it, I think, was the San Quentin work strike. They got pissed enough to grab my ass this time.' That, and kill Morrissey.

'Jesus. What'll we do?' Her face looked limp as the tears flowed in silence. 'Can they prove you were involved in that strike?'

He shook his head in answer, but he didn't look encouraged. 'No. But that's why they're so pissed. Now they'll try to get me on anything they can. But we'll do our damnedest. I have a good lawyer. And I'm lucky. A few years ago, you couldn't have an attorney at hearings to revoke your parole. Just you and the board. So, cheer up, things could have been worse. We have a good lawyer, we have each other. And they can't object to our life-style, it's as clean as they come. We'll just have to do what you do with these things. Wait it out till the hearing, and then put up a good fight.'

But they both knew that the key issue was neither the fight, nor his life-style. He was accused of agitation. And

246

it was all true. 'Come on, Mama, hang tough.' He leaned over to kiss her, taking her into his arms, but her body was stiff and unyielding, her face bent as the tears continued to flow. He saw her knees shake as he looked down at her lap. He felt as though he had killed her. And in a way, he was right.

'When is the hearing?' She expected to hear that it was the next day.

'It's still more than six weeks away. January eighth, in San Francisco.'

'And then what?'

'What do you mean, "and then what?" ' She was sitting so still that she frightened him.

'What if they make you go back?'

'That won't happen.' His voice was deep and subdued.

'But what if it does, dammit, Luke?' Her shriek of pain and fear slashed through the silence.

'Kezia, it won't!' He lowered his voice and tried to calm her, while fighting his own desperation. This was not at all what he'd planned. But what could he expect? He should have known this from the beginning. He had led her gently away from her home, into his, and now he was sitting there telling her that their house might burn down. The look in her eyes made her an orphan again. And her pain was his doing. He felt the weight of it like a cement sack around his heart.

'Darling, it's not going to happen like that. And if it does – and that's only an "if" – then we live with it. We both have the balls to do that. If we have to.' He knew he did. But did she? Not the way she looked then.

'Lucas . . . no!' Her voice was a barely audible whisper.

'Baby, I'm so sorry. . . .' There was nothing more he could say. The thing that he'd feared for so long had finally happened. Only the joke of it was that before Kezia he hadn't feared it in the same way. Hadn't feared it at all. He had regarded it as a potential price to pay, a possible inconvenience. He had had nothing to lose . . . and now he had it all . . . and it was all on the line. And she had to pay the price with him. But she had to be told. Alejandro had told him that for weeks, and he had stalled, and evaded, and lied to himself. There was no lying now. The notice lay crumpled in a ball on the desk. They had taken the matter out of his hands . . . and now look at the mess. . . . He lifted her chin gently with one hand, and sought her lips tenderly with his. It was all he could give her, what he felt, what he was, how he loved her. They still had another six weeks. If no one murdered him first.

## CHAPTER XXII

For Thanksgiving, they had hot turkey sandwiches in their room at the hotel in Chicago. The revocation hung over their heads, but they had fought hard to ignore it. They rarely discussed it, except once in a while, late at night. They had six weeks till the hearing, and Kezia was determined not to let the threat of it ruin their life. She fought for gaiety with an almost unbearable determination. Lucas knew what was happening to her, but there was so little he could do. He couldn't wish the hearing away. His own nightmares were back, and he didn't like the way Kezia looked. She was already losing weight. But she was game. She made the same old jokes, they had a good time. They suddenly made love two and three times a day, sometimes four, as though to stock up on what they might lose. Six weeks was so short. When they went back to New York, there were only five left.

'Kezia, you don't look well. You don't look well at all.'
'Edward, my darling, you're driving me mad.'
'I want to know what you're up to.' The waiters

swished past them and poured more Louis Roederer champagne.

'You're prying.'

'YES, I am.' He looked sour, and old. She looked tired, and far older than she had so briefly before.

'All right. I'm in love.'

'I assumed that much. And he's married?'

'Why do you always assume that the men I go out with are married? Because I'm discreet? Hell, I have a right to be that, I've learned that much over the years.'

'Yes, but you don't have a right to indulge in sheer folly.'

No, just a right to misery, darling, and shitty rotten luck. Right, Edward? Of course. Or is it just a right to duty and pain? 'Folly, in this case, dear Edward, is a beautiful man whom I adore. We have more or less lived and travelled together for more than two months now. And just before Thanksgiving, we found out ... that ...' Her voice caught and her heart trembled as she wondered what she was doing ... 'We found out that he's sick. Terribly sick.'

Edward's face suddenly looked pinched. 'What sort of sick?'

'We're not sure.' She was into it now. She almost believed it herself. It was easier than the truth, and it would get him off her back for a while. 'They're attempting treatment, and at this point he has about a fifty-fifty chance of living. Which is why I don't "look well." Satisfied?' Her voice was ripe with bitterness, her eyes dulled with tears.

'Kezia, I'm so sorry. Is he ... is he ... anyone I know?'

Not on your ass, sweetheart. She almost wanted to laugh. 'No, he isn't. We met in Chicago.'

'I wondered about that. Is he young?'

'Young enough, but he's older than I am.' She was quiet now. In a way she had told him the truth. Sending Lucas back to prison would be like condemning him to

249

death. Too many men hated or loved him, he was too well known, had stirred up too much. San Quentin would kill him. Someone would. If not an inmate, a guard.

'I don't know what to say.' But his face said what his words couldn't. There was a ghost in his eyes. The ghost of Liane Saint Martin. 'This man ... is he ... would ... does he come to New York?' He was groping for a criterion that Kezia wouldn't leap at in fury but there were none. Where did he go to school? What does he do? Where does he live? Who is he? Kezia would have exploded at any of those questions. But he wanted to know. Had to. He owed it to her ... to himself.

'Yes, he comes to New York. He's been here with me.'

'He stays in your apartment?' He suddenly remembered her saying that they had lived together. My God, how could she?

'Yes, Edward. In my apartment.'

'Kezia ... is he ... is he ...' He wanted to know if this was someone decent, respectable, not some fortune hunter, or ... or 'tutor,' but he simply couldn't ask, and she wouldn't have let him. Edward felt as though he was on the verge of losing her forever. 'Kezia. . . .'

She looked at him then with tears on her cheeks and quietly shook her head. 'Edward ... I ... I can't do this today. I'm sorry.' She kissed him gently on the cheek then, picked up her handbag, and slid to her feet. He didn't stop her. He couldn't. He merely watched her retreat towards the door and clenched his hands very tightly for a moment before signalling for the check.

In the bitter cold of the winter afternoon, she rode the subway to Harlem. Alejandro was the only one who could help. She was beginning to panic. She had to see him.

She walked quickly from the subway to the centre, oblivious of how she looked in the long red Paris coat and the full white mink hat. She didn't give a damn how she looked. On the streets where she slalomed between garbage cans and scampering children, they looked at her as if she were a strange apparition, but the wind was bitingly cold and there was snow in the air. No one had time to be bothered. They left her alone.

There was a girl in Alejandro's office when Kezia arrived, and they were laughing. Kezia paused in the doorway. She had knocked, but their laughter had muffled the sound.

'Al, are you busy?' It was rare that she called him by the nickname Luke used.

'I ... no ... Pilar, will you excuse me?' The girl bounced from the chair and scraped past Kezia with a look of wonderment in her eyes. Kezia looked like a vision fresh out of *Vogue*, or someone in a movie.

'I'm sorry to break in on you like this.' Her eyes looked agonized beneath the white fur.

'It's all right. I was ... Kezia?'

She had crumbled into tears in front of his eyes, and now she stood there, broken, holding out both arms, her handbag askew on the floor, the last of her control dissolved.

'Kezia ... *pobrecita* ... babe ... take it easy ...'

'Oh, Christ, Alejandro.... I can't stand it!' She let herself fall into his arms and buried her face on his shoulder. 'What can we do? They're going to take him back. I know it.' She sniffed and pulled away to see his eyes. 'They will, won't they?'

'They might.'

'You think they will too, don't you?'

'I don't know.'

'Yes, you do, godammit. Tell me! Somebody tell me the truth!'

'I don't know the truth, damn you!'

She was shouting and he was shouting still louder. The walls seemed to echo with what they had both penned up – fear and anger and frustration.

'Yeah, maybe they will take him back. But for chrissake, lady, don't give up till they say it. What are you going to do? Let yourself die now? Give him up? Destroy yourself? Wait till you hear, for chrissake, then figure it out.' The room had been full of his voice and she could hear tears creeping up on him too, but she was quiet. He had brought her back to her senses, to a point of control.

'Maybe you're right. I'm just so fucking scared, Alejandro. I don't know what to do to hang on anymore. . . . I get this rising panic like bile in my guts.'

'There's nothing you can do, except try to be reasonable and hang in. Try not to panic.'

'What if we run away? Do you think that they'd find him?'

'Yes, eventually, and then they'd kill him on sight. Besides, he'd never do that.'

'I know.' He came close to her again and held her in his arms. She was still wearing the coat and fur hat, and her face was streaked with mascara and tears. 'The worst of it is that I don't know what to do to help him, how to make it easier for him. He's under so damn much strain.'

'You can't change that. All you can do is stand by him. And take care of yourself. It's not going to help anyone if you fall apart. Remember that. You can't give up your whole life for him, or your sanity. And Kezia . . . don't give up yet. Not till they say the word, if they do, and not even then.'

'Yeah.' She nodded tiredly at him and leaned back against the desk. 'Sure.'

'I didn't know you were a quitter.'

'I'm not.'

'Then don't act like one. Get your shit together, woman. You've got a rough road ahead, but nobody said it was the end of the road. It isn't to Luke.'

'Okay, mister big mouth, I get your point.' She tried to muster a smile.

'Then start acting like you ain't going to quit. That big dude loves you one hell of a lot.' And then he walked back to her and hugged her again. 'And I love you too, little one . . . I do too.' Tears started to squeeze from her eyes again and she shook her head at him.

'Don't be nice to me, or I'll cry again.' She laughed through her tears and he rumpled her hair.

'You're looking mighty fancy, lady. Where've you been? Shopping?' He had just noticed.

'No. To lunch with a friend.'

'It couldn't have been heroes and Cokes from the look of it.'

'Alejandro, you're nuts.' But they shared the moment of honest laughter, and he reached for his coat on the back of the door.

'I'll take you home.'

'All the way downtown? Don't be silly!' But she was touched at the thought.

'I've done enough here for one day. Want to play hooky with me?' He looked young as he made the offer, his eyes dancing, his smile that of a playful boy.

'As a matter of fact, that sounds just fine.'

They walked away from the centre arm in arm, her red coat linked with his drab army surplus jacket and hood. He gave her a squeeze and she laughed into the warm eyes. She was glad she had come up to see him. She needed him, differently but almost as much as she needed Luke.

They got off the subway at Eighty-sixth Street and stopped in one of the German coffeehouses for a cup of hot chocolate 'mit schlag': great clouds of whipped cream. An oom-pah-pah band was doing its best, and outside, Christmas lights were already blinking hopefully. They said nothing of the revocation, but talked of other times. Christmas, California, his family, her father. It was funny; she had thought about her father a lot lately, and wanted to share it with someone. It was so hard to talk to Luke now; every conversational path led them back to the tangled emotional maze of the revocation.

'Something tells me you're a lot like your father, Kezia. He doesn't sound all that much of a conformist either, if you scratch the surface a little.'

She smiled at the melting whipped cream on her hot chocolate. 'He wasn't. But he had a nice way of pulling it all off,

253

judging from what I've been told and what I remember. I suspect he wasn't as compelled to make choices.'

'Those were different times. He didn't have the same choices. That might have had something to do with it. What's your trustee like?'

'Edward? He's lovely. And solidly to the bone everything he was brought up to be. And I think he's lonely as hell.'

'And in love with you?'

'I don't know. I never gave it much thought. I don't think he is.'

'I'll bet you're wrong.' He smiled and took a swallow of the warm sweet drink, his lips frothed with the cream. 'I think there's a lot you don't see, Kezia. About yourself and your effect on other people. You're naive in that sense.'

'Is that so?' She smiled at him. He was nice to be with. And she had needed someone to talk to. Years ago, she had talked so well with Edward, but not now. In an odd way, Alejandro was replacing him now. It was Alejandro she had turned to, when she couldn't talk to Edward, or even Luke. Alejandro who gave her solace and fatherly advice. And then she had a funny thought. She looked up, and giggled. 'And I suppose you're in love with me too?'

'Maybe so.'

'You nut.' She knew he didn't mean it, and they sat back and listened to the pounding of the old-fashioned music. The restaurant was crowded but they sat apart from the noise and the movement, as isolated as the old men reading German newspapers alone at their tables.

'What are you guys doing for Christmas?'

'I don't know. You know Luke. I don't think he's made up his mind. Or if he has, he hasn't told me. Are you staying here?'

'Yeah. I wanted to go home to L.A., but I've got too much to do at the centre, and the trip is expensive. There's a facility I want to check out in San Francisco, though. Maybe next spring.'

254

'What kind of facility?' She lit a cigarette and relaxed in her chair. The afternoon had metamorphosed into something delightful.

'They call them therapeutic communities out there. Same as the centre, except the patients live in, which gives you a much better chance of success.' He looked at his watch and was surprised at the time. It was just after five. 'Want to join us for dinner?'

He shook his head regretfully. 'No. I'll leave you two lovebirds in peace. Besides, there's a "little piece" of my own I want to check into, closer to home.' He cackled evilly, and she chuckled.

'Havoc in Harlem? Who is she?'

'A friend of a friend. She works at a day-care centre and probably has big tits, bad breath and acne.'

'You've got something against big tits?' She grinned again.

'Nope. Just the other two. But it's a type. There are two or three like that who work at the centre. And yeah, I'm a snob. About women.' He signalled for the check.

Kezia laughed at him. 'How come you don't have an old lady?' She had never asked him before.

'Either because I'm too ugly, or too mean. I'm not quite sure which.'

'Bullshit. What's the real story?'

'Who knows, *hija*. Maybe my work. You were right way back when – Luke and I have a lot in common that way. The causes come first. That's hard for a woman to live with, unless she's got a heavy trip of her own. Anyway, I'm picky.'

'I'll bet you are.' And therein most likely lay the truth. Because he was assuredly neither ugly, nor mean. She found him strangely attractive, and cherished the relationship that had blossomed between them. 'So what's with this lady tonight?'

'I'll see.' He was gently evasive, but Kezia was curious.

'How old is she?'

'Twenty-one, twenty-two. Something like that.'

255

'I hate her already.'

'You should worry.' He looked up at the porcelain skin framed by the white fur hat. Her eyes stood out like sapphires.

'Yeah. But I'm staring at thirty. That's a far cry from twenty-two.'

'And you're a lot better off.' She thought about it for a moment and nodded. Twenty-two hadn't been very much fun. It had started to be, though, after she began writing. Before that, it was the shits. Unsure of where she was going, what she was doing, and who she wanted to be, while having to present an outward appearance of unshakable certainty and poise.

'You should have known me ten years ago, Alejandro. You would have laughed.'

'You think I was better off at that age?'

'Probably. You were freer.'

'Maybe, but still not very cool. Hell, ten years ago I wore a crew cut cemented into place with "greasy kid stuff." Talk about funny! And I'll bet you weren't wearing a crew cut.'

'No. A pageboy. And pearls. I was adorable. The hottest thing on the market. Come and get it, ladies and gentlemen, one untouched, unused, near-perfect heiress. She walks, she talks, she sings, she dances. Wind her up and she plays "God Bless America" on the harp.'

'You played the harp?'

'No, dummy. But I did everything else. I was absolutely "mahvelouss," but not very happy.'

'So now you're happy. That's a lot to be grateful for.'

'I am.' Her thoughts flew back to Lucas . . . and the hearing. Alejandro watched the transitions in her eyes, and moved quickly to bring her back to the easy chatter of the last hour.

'How come you don't play the harp? Aren't heiresses supposed to?' He was all innocence.

'No, that's angels. They're the ones who play the harp.'

'You mean they're not the same thing?'

She threw back her head and laughed at the thought. 'No, darling. They are most emphatically not the same thing. I do play the piano, though. That's a prerequisite for your heiress wings. A few play the violin, but most of us tackle the piano at an early age, and give it up by the time we're twelve. Chopin.'

'I still kind of wish you could play the harp.'

'Up your ass, Mr. Vidal.' She grinned and he feigned shock.

'Kezia! And you're an heiress? How shocking! Up my ... what?'

'You heard me, mister. Now come on, let's go home. Lucas will worry.' They slipped into their coats, he left the tip on the table, and they walked out into the cold air, arm in arm. The afternoon had been well spent. She felt restored.

When they got home, Luke was waiting in the living room, bourbon in hand and with a smile on his face.

'Well, what have you two been up to?' He liked to see them together, but Kezia noticed something pinched about his eyes. Jealousy?

'We went out for a cup of hot chocolate.'

'A likely story. But I'll forgive you both. This time.'

'That's big of you, darling.' Kezia walked to his side and bent to kiss him.

He pulled a cigar out of his pocket and winked at Alejandro, as he slid his arm around her waist. 'Why don't you get our friend a beer?'

'Probably because he'd throw up after all the hot chocolate he drank ... mit schlag!' She grinned over at Alejandro.'

'What's that?' Luke's voice sounded unusually loud. As though he was terribly nervous.

'Whipped cream.'

'Puke. Nah, get him a beer.'

'Lucas ...' She wondered suddenly if he had something to say to Alejandro, he looked so odd – and a little bit crocked.

257

'Go on.'

Kezia looked at him strangely and then turned to Alejandro. 'You want a beer?'

Their friend threw up both hands and shrugged. 'No, but with a dude that size, who argues?' All three of them laughed and Kezia vanished into the kitchen.

She called back over her shoulder as she flicked on the light. 'I'll make you coffee. I can't stand the idea of beer after all that good chocolate.'

'Right on.' Alejandro sounded distracted as he answered and Kezia wondered what was afoot. Lucas had the look of a small boy. Or the look of a man with a secret. She grinned to herself, wondering if it was something to do with her. Maybe a present, something silly, an outing, a dinner. Luke was like that. She wouldn't allow herself to wonder if it was something to do with the hearing. It couldn't be. He looked much too pleased with himself, and a little bit punchy.

She went back to the living room a few moments later with the coffee. Two cups. Luke looked as if he could use one.

'Look at that, man, she wants to sober us up.' Luke's tone was jovial, but Alejandro didn't look as if he needed sobering. He looked tense and unhappy, as though something drastic had happened in the moments she was out of the room. Kezia looked at his face, then at Luke's, and then she put down the two cups and sat down on the couch.

'Okay, sweetheart, game's over. What's up?' Her voice was light and nervous and brittle, and her hands had begun to tremble. It was something to do with the hearing. It wasn't anything fun after all. Now she could tell. 'What's wrong?'

'Why the hell should something be wrong?'

'For one thing,' she cast a glance away from him, and apologetically at their friend, 'if you'll forgive me,' and then she turned back to Luke, 'because you're drunk, Lucas. How come?'

'I am not.'

'You are. And you look scared. Or pissed. Or some-thing. And I want to know what the hell's happening. You told Al, now tell me.'

'What makes you think I told Al anything?' Now he looked visibly nervous, and Kezia was beginning to look angry.

'Look, dammit! Don't play games with me. I'm having just as tough a time coping with all this crazy bullshit as you are. Now tell me! What's wrong?'

'Oh, for chrissake. Will you listen to that, Al?' He looked around at them both with a plastic smile on his face, and crossed one leg over the other and then back again, while Alejandro looked very upset.

Kezia looked from Lucas to him. 'Okay, Alejandro, will you tell me what's going on?' Her voice was rising to an uncomfortable level, nearing hysteria. But Lucas broke in with a look of impatience, and pushed himself forcefully out of his chair, growing instantly pale as he stood.

'Just keep it together, Mama. And I'll tell you myself.' But as he turned to face her the room swam, and he sank almost to his knees. Alejandro rushed to his side and took the half-empty glass from his hand. Most of the bourbon had sloshed into the carpet, and Luke's face was now frighteningly pale.

'Take it easy, brother.' He supported him with one arm, as Kezia rushed to his side.

'Lucas!' Her eyes were frantic as Luke sat down heavily on the floor next to her, and rested his head on his knees. He was drunk and in shock. But slowly he turned his face towards her with a gentle expression.

'Mama, it's no big deal. Someone tried to shoot me today. They missed by an inch.' He closed his eyes on the last words, as though afraid of her eyes.

'Someone what?' She held his face with both her hands and slowly he looked up at her again. It had not yet registered in her face.

'Someone tried to kill me, I guess, Kezia. Or scare the

259

piss out of me. Either way, but everything's cool. I'm just a little punchy, that's all.'

She thought instantly of Morrissey now, and knew Lucas had too. 'My God ... Lucas ... who did it?' She was sitting next to him, trembling, and her stomach felt as though it were riding a wave.

'I don't know who. Hard to tell.' He shrugged and suddenly looked very tired.

'Come on, man, let's get you to bed.' Alejandro helped him slowly to his feet, and he wasn't sure if he should be supporting Lucas or Kezia. She looked almost worse. 'Can you make it, Luke?'

'Are you kidding? I'm not hurt, man. I'm gassed.' He chuckled proudly for a moment, as he walked into the bedroom. Alejandro shook his head with a worried frown on his face, as Kezia settled Luke against the pillows. 'For chrissake, Kezia, I'm not dying. Don't overdo it. And get me another drink, will you?'

'Should you?'

He laughed at the question and crossed both eyes with a grin. 'Oh Mama, should I!' The smile she returned to him was her first in ten minutes, but she could feel her knees shaking as she sank onto the edge of the bed.

'My God, Lucas, how did it happen?'

'I don't know. I went up to talk to some guys in Spanish Harlem today, and we were walking down the street after the meeting and whap, someone almost winged me. The motherfucker must have been aiming for my heart, but he took lousy aim.'

Kezia sat staring at him in shocked disbelief. It could have been like Morrissey. He could have been dead. There were chills on her spine as she thought of it.

'Anyone else knew about the meeting?' Alejandro looked frightened as he continued to stand there and look at his friend.

'A few people.'

'How few?'

'Not few enough.'

'Oh God, Lucas . . . who did it?' Suddenly Kezia's head was bowed, and she was sobbing as she sat there. Luke leaned forward and circled her with his right arm, pulling her towards him.

'Come on, baby, take it easy. It could have been anyone. Just some crazy kid out for a laugh. Or maybe someone who knew me. Could have been some heavy-weight right-winger up there who doesn't dig prison reform. Could have been some pissed off left-winger who doesn't think I'm enough of a "brother". What the hell difference does it make? They tried. They didn't get me. I'm okay. You're okay. I love you. So . . . no big deal, please. Okay?' He sank back on the pillows then with a dazzling smile. But neither Kezia nor Alejandro was swayed by the bravado.

'I'll get you another drink.' Alejandro left the room, and had a drink of his own in the kitchen. Shit. It was coming to that now. And with Kezia in the picture. Terrific. He heaved a long sigh as he walked back to the bedroom with a tall glass of straight bourbon for Luke. Kezia was crying again when he walked in, but this time softly. The two men exchanged a long look over her head and Luke nodded slowly. It had been quite a day. And they were both wondering if it was going to be like this all the way till the hearing. It could have been a cop for all they knew, and they both realized it, even though they didn't tell that to Kezia. But the reality was that Lucas was popular only with those he worked with on the outside or the men in prison all over the country who benefited directly from all he did. Not many others really understood. And as loved as he was, he was equally hated.

'I'm going to hire you a bodyguard.' She looked up with a sniff, as Luke took a long sip of his bourbon and Alejandro sat down in a chair near the bed. She was still sitting near Luke.

'No, you're not, pretty lady. No bodyguard, no bullshit. This happened once. It won't happen again.'

'How do you know?'

'Baby, don't push me. Let me run this show. All I want from you is your beautiful smile and your love.' He patted her hand and took a long sip of bourbon Alejandro had handed him. 'All I want from you is what you already give me.'

'Yeah, and not my advice.' She said it sadly, her shoulders sagging. 'Why don't you let me hire a body-guard?'

'Because I already have one.'

'You hired someone?' Why didn't he tell her anything anymore?

'Not exactly. But I've been followed by the cops for a while now.'

'By the cops? Why by them?'

'Why the hell do you think, Mama? Because they think I'm a threat.' It put an aspect on things that she didn't like. And it suddenly brought home to her that in a sense Luke was considered an outlaw, and that in living with him, she was on that same ill-favoured side of the law. She somehow hadn't totally absorbed her position in all this before. 'And don't kid yourself, sweetheart, it could just as well have been a cop who tried to get a piece of me today.'

'Are you serious?' Her face grew even paler. 'Would they do that to you, Luke?'

'Damn right. If they thought they could get away with it, they'd do it in a hot second. And enjoy it.'

'Oh God.' The police taking potshots at Luke? They were supposed to give decent citizens protection. But that was the whole point. And Kezia finally knew it. To the cops, Lucas wasn't 'decent'. He was only that in her eyes, and Al's, and his friends', not in the eyes of the rednecks, and the Adult Authority, and the law.

Luke exchanged a rapid look with Alejandro, who slowly and unhappily shook his head. Bad things were coming. He could feel it. 'But I'll tell you one thing, Kezia. I don't want any bullshit from you. You do exactly what I tell you from now on. No visits to Al up in Harlem, no traipsing through the park alone, no disappearing into the subway. Nothing except what I tell you you can do. Is that clear?' He was wearing the face of a general again as he said it. 'Is it?'

'Yes, but . . .'

'No!' He was roaring now. 'Just listen to me for once in your life, damn you! Because if you don't, you goddamn stupid naive asshole . . . because if you don't,' his voice began to tremble and Kezia was shocked to see tears in his eyes, 'maybe they'll get you instead of me. And if they did . . .' His voice began to crack and grow soft as he lowered his eyes, 'if they did . . . I couldn't . . . take it. . . .' She went to him with tears on her own cheeks as she put her arms around him and let him rest his head on her chest. They stayed like that for what seemed like hours, with Luke crying in her arms, and what she did not know was that he was torturing himself for what he was doing to her. Oh God . . . how could he have done this to a woman he loved . . . Kezia. . . . At last he fell asleep in her arms as they sat there, and when Kezia slid him down onto the pillow and turned off the light, she suddenly remembered Alejandro sitting in the chair. She turned to find him, but he was long since gone, with heartaches of his own, and no Kezia whose arms he could cry in. And like Luke, the tears that he cried were for her.

## CHAPTER XXIII

Lucas put down the phone with a look of dismay, and Kezia instantly knew.

'Who was it?' But she didn't need to ask. She knew, whatever the name, whatever the city, it didn't really matter. He always wore that face, and sounded the way he had, for calls about prisons. But now, when Christmas was so close. . . .

'It was one of my crazy friends out in Chino.'

'And?' She wasn't letting him off the hook.

'And . . .' He ran a hand through his hair and bit the end of a cigar that had been lying on the desk. It was almost midnight and he had been strolling the house in his shorts, barefoot and bare-chested. And . . . they want me to come out. Think you can handle that, Mama?'

'You mean come out with you?' It was the first time he had asked her.

'No, I mean stay here. I'll be back by Christmas. But . . . it looks like they need me. Or at least they think they do.' There was something gruffer in his voice, pure macho, all man. And a vibrant chord of excitement that ran through his words, no matter how careful he was to conceal it. He loved what he did. The meetings, the men, the riots, the cause. He loved getting back at the 'pigs', and helping his brothers. It was what he lived for. And there was no room for Kezia in that world. It was a world of men who had lived without women for long enough to know that they could do without them, if they had to. They had a hard time learning to include them again. And this was one place where Luke wouldn't budge. He wouldn't have considered taking her with him, not for a moment. Not when there was danger involved. Not after last time in San Francisco. Not after he'd almost been shot. She knew she had been crazy to hope that he was inviting her this time. He wasn't.

'Yes, I can handle it, Luke. But I'll miss you.' She tried to keep the sadness from her voice, and the terror, but he knew. She looked at him and shrugged. 'So it goes. You're sure you'll be home by Christmas?'

'As sure as I can be. They're afraid riots might start. But I think we'll probably get everything straightened out before that happens.' Maybe. If. She wondered if he really wanted to, or if he'd rather play with the fireworks. But she knew that wasn't fair. 'I'm sorry, Mama.'

'Me too, but I'll be okay.' She walked over to him and slid her arms around his neck. She kissed him gently on

264

the back of the head and smelled the fresh richness of the
cigar. He was going to 'war'. Again. 'Lucas . . .' She
hesitated about saying it, but she had to.

'What, babe?'

'You're crazy to do this now. With the hearing
pending. And . . .' She was afraid to voice all her fears,
but he knew them. He had the same ones.

'Oh Christ, Kezia, don't start that.' He pulled away
from her and stood up to walk across the room, half
naked and puffing on his cigar, with a ferocious look on
his face. 'You just be sure you take care of yourself. And
what fucking difference does it make what I do now, with
the backlog of bullshit they're going to throw at me at the
hearing anyway? I've been doing this kind of thing since I
got out of the joint. You think one more time will make a
difference?'

'Maybe.' She stood very still and kept her eyes on his.
'Maybe this one time could make the difference between
revocation and freedom. Or between living and dying.'

'Bullshit. And anyway . . . I have to, that's all.' He
slammed the door to the bedroom and she wondered how
close she was to the truth. He had no right to do this to
her, jeopardize his own life and hers with it. If this trip
cost him his freedom, or his life, what did he think it
would do to her, or didn't he think? The bastard. . . .

Kezia followed him into the bedroom and stood looking
at him as he pulled a suitcase out of his closet. She
watched him with fire in her eyes, and a lead weight on
her heart.

'Lucas . . .' He didn't answer. He knew. 'Don't go . . .
please, Luke . . . not for me. For you.' He turned to look
at her then, and without exchanging another word with
him, she knew she had lost.

It was the twenty-third before Kezia got the call she
had feared. He would not be home for Christmas. He'd be
gone for at least another week. Four men had already
died in the Chino strike, and the last thing on his mind
was Christmas, or home. For one brief moment Kezia

found herself wanting to tell him what a bastard he was, but she couldn't. He wasn't. He was simply Luke.

She didn't want to admit to Edward that she was going to spend Christmas alone. It was such a lonely admission, an admission of defeat. He would have tried to be sweet to her, and insisted she spend it with him in Palm Beach, which she would have hated. She wanted to spend the holiday with Luke, not with Edward or Hilary. She had toyed with the idea of flying out to California to surprise him, but she knew she wouldn't have been welcome. When he was involved in his work, that was it. He wouldn't have been amused or pleased by the gesture, and he probably wouldn't have been able to spend any time with her anyway.

So she was alone. With a stack of engraved invitations, and red and green inked notes suggesting she stop by for a drink, or drop in on the city's 'best' holiday parties, the sort of invitations people would have given right arms and eyeteeth for. Eggnog, punch, champagne, caviar, pâté, amusing little stocking gifts from Bendel's or Cardin. The cotillions were in full swing, if she wanted to check out the season's debs, which she didn't. There was a rash of charity balls, a white tie party at the Opera, and a skating fete at Rockefeller Centre to celebrate the alliance of Halpern Medley and Marina Walters. The El Morocco would be alive with the holiday spirit. Or there was always Gstaad or Chamonix ... Courchevelles or Klosters ... Athens ... Rome ... Palm Beach. But none of it appealed. None of it.

After mulling it all over in cursory fashion, Kezia decided it would be less lonely to be alone, than to be lost in the midst of empty hilarity. She was not feeling very festive. She thought briefly about inviting some friend over to help her spend Christmas day, but she never got up enough steam to ask anyone in particular, and could think of no one she really wanted to ask ... only Lucas. And the others would be busy with whatever they had planned, just as right now they were busy at Bergdorf's and Saks buying shocking pink slippers and parrot green robes, or drinking rum in the Oak Room, or helping their mothers 'get ready' in Philadelphia or Boston or Bronxville or Greenwich. Everyone was bound to be somewhere, and she was actually alone. She and an army of doormen and maintenance men, each of whom had received his Christmas dues. The superintendent discreetly left a mimeographed sheet in the mail around the fifteenth of December. Twenty-two names, all waiting for bribes. Merry Christmas.

It was the afternoon of the twenty-fourth, and Kezia had nothing to do. She walked the length of the apartment in her cream satin robe, and smiled to herself. There was a mist of snow on the ground outside.

'Merry Christmas, my love.' The whispered words were for Lucas. He had kept his word and called every day, and she knew he'd call again later. Christmas by telephone. It was better than nothing. But not much. The silver-wrapped boxes on her desk were for him – a tie, a belt, a bottle of cologne, a briefcase, and two pairs of shoes. A collection of mundane gifts, except that she knew they would all make him laugh. She had explained all the 'in' symbols to him when they first met, like translating the language of the country she lived in. Status-ese. The Dior ties, the Gucci shoes, the Vuitton luggage, and its ugly LV's plastered all over the mustard and mud coloured surface. It had made him laugh when she told him. 'You mean those guys all wear the same shoes?' She had laughed back, nodding, and explained that the women wore them too. One style for the women, and one for the men. Varied styles would have created insecurity, so there was just one. One had a choice of colours, of course. It was all terribly, terribly original, wasn't it? But it had become a standard joke with them, and neither of them could keep a straight face anymore as they passed a pair of Guccis on the street, or a Pucci dress on a woman. The Pucci-Gucci Set. It was something else they shared from their private vantage point. So that's what she had bought him for Christmas. A Pucci tie, a Gucci belt, Monsieur Rochas cologne (which she actually decided she liked quite a lot), a Vuitton briefcase, and the indomitable Gucci shoes in black leather, standard model, and of course, a duplicate pair in brown suede. She smiled to think of him opening them all, and the look on his face.

But her smile deepened as she thought of the real presents she had bought him, the ones hidden in the pocket of the Vuitton case. Those were the ones that mattered to her, and would undoubtedly matter to him. The signet ring with the dark blue stone carved with his initials, and her initials and the date engraved in tiny letters on the inside of the setting. Carefully wrapped in tissue paper was a leather-bound book of poems that had been her father's, and had occupied a place of honour on his desk for as long as Kezia could remember. It made her happy to know that now it would be Luke's. It meant a great deal to her. It was a tradition.

She drank a cup of hot chocolate as she stood looking out at the snow. It was cold out, very cold, the way only New York and a few other cities can be. The kind of chill that makes you feel as though you've been slapped when you walk out the door. The freezing winds swept your legs and brushed your cheeks like steel wool, and the ice on the windowsill was frozen in patterns of lace.

The phone rang as she stood alone in the silent room. It could be Luke. She dared not ignore it.

'Hello?'

'Kezia?' It wasn't Luke's voice, and she wasn't quite sure whose it was. There was the merest hint of an accent. 'What are you doing here?'

'Oh, Alejandro!'

'Who were you expecting? Santa Claus?'

'In a way. I thought it might be Luke.'

He smiled at the comparison. Only she could come up with that. 'I had a suspicion you'd be here. I saw the papers, and have an idea of what it must be like in Chino.

I figured he wouldn't want you out there. So what are you up to? Ten thousand parties?'

'No. Nary a one. And you're right. He didn't want me out there. He's too busy.'

'That, and it's not a cool scene.' Alejandro was grave.

'No. But it isn't a cool scene for him either. He's a fool to get sucked into that now. It'll just add more fuel to their fires at the hearing. But Luke never listens.'

'So what else is new? What are you doing for Christmas?'

'Oh, I think I'll hang my stocking up on the fireplace and put out cookies and a glass of milk for Santa, and . . .'

'Milk? *Qué* horror!'

'And what would you suggest?'

'Tequila, of course! Jesus, if that poor sonofabitch has to drink milk all over the world, it's a wonder he bothers with the trip.'

She laughed at him and switched on some lights. She had been standing in the early darkness of the winter dusk.

'Do you suppose it's too late to pick up some tequila?'

'Baby, it's never too late for that!'

She laughed again at the earnest sound of his voice. 'And what are you up to for Christmas? More work at the centre?'

'Yeah, some. It's better than sitting at home. Christmas with my family is always a big deal. It kind of depresses me to be away from all that, unless I keep busy. How come you're not going to all those big fancy parties?'

'Because that would depress me. I'd rather be alone this year.' She was thinking of the hearing on the eighth again. It was strange though, lately things with Luke had seemed nearly normal. The first shock of the hearing was gone. It almost didn't seem real. Just a meeting they would have to go to, nothing more. Nothing could touch the magic circle around Kezia and Luke. Certainly not a hearing.

'So you're sitting around there all by yourself?'

269

'Sort of.'

'What do you mean "sort of"?'

'Well, okay. Yeah. I am all by myself. But it's not like I'm crying my eyes out. I'm just enjoying being peaceful at home.'

'Sure. With presents for Luke all over the house, and a Christmas tree you haven't bothered to decorate, and not answering the phone, or only when you think it might be Luke. Listen, lady, that's one stinking way to spend Christmas. Am I right?' But he knew he was. He knew her by now.

'Only partially, Father Alejandro. Boy, you sure like to lecture!' She laughed at the tone of his voice. 'And the presents for Luke are not "all over the house", they're neatly stacked on my desk.'

'And what about the tree?'

'I didn't buy one.' Her voice was suddenly meek.

'Sacrilege!'

She laughed again and felt silly. 'All right. I'll go buy one. And then what do I do?'

'You don't do anything. Do you have any popcorn?'

'Hmmm . . . yes. As a matter of fact, I do.' There was still some left from the last time she and Luke had made popcorn in the bedroom fireplace at three in the morning.

'Okay. Then cook up some popcorn, make some hot chocolate or something, and I'll be there in an hour. Or do you have other plans?'

'Not a thing. Just waiting for Santa.'

'He'll be on the subway and down in an hour.'

'Even if I don't have tequila in the house?' She was teasing him; she was glad he was coming.

'Don't worry. I'll bring my own. Imagine not having a tree!' Friendly outrage crept into his voice. 'Okay, Kezia. See you later.' He already sounded busy as he hung up the phone.

He arrived an hour later with an enormous Scotch pine dragging behind him.

270

'In Harlem, you get them cheaper, particularly on Christmas Eve. Down here this would cost you twenty bucks. I got it for six.' He looked chilled and ruffled and pleased. It was a beautiful tree; it stood a head taller than he, and its branches reached out furrily when he pulled off the ropes that had bound them. 'Where'll I put it?' She pointed to a corner, and then unexpectedly reached up and kissed his cheek.

'Alejandro, you are the best friend in the world. It's a beautiful tree. Did you bring your tequila?' She hung his coat in the closet and turned back to look at the tree. Now it was beginning to look like Christmas. With Luke not planning to come home, she hadn't done any of the things she usually loved. No tree, no wreath, no decorations and very little Christmas spirit.

'My God, I forgot the tequila!'

'Oh no . . . how about cognac?'

'I'll take it.' He smiled at the offer with obvious pleasure.

She poured him a glass of cognac, and went to ferret out the box of Christmas tree ornaments from the top shelf of a closet. They were old ones, some of which had been her grandfather's. She took them out tenderly, and held them up for Alejandro to see.

'They look pretty fancy to me.'

'No, just old.'

She joined him in a glass of cognac and together they strung lights and hung baubles until there were none left in the box.

'It really looks beautiful, doesn't it?' Her face lit up like a child's, and he reached over and gave her a hug. They sat side by side on the floor, their cognac glasses and a huge crystal bowl full of popcorn beside them.

'I'd say we did a damn good job.' He was a little merry from the drinks, and his eyes looked soft and bright.

'Hey . . . you want to make a wreath?' She had just thought of the ones she had made every year as a child.

Make one? With what?'

'All we need is a branch from the tree . . . and some fruit . . . and . . . let's see, wire. . . .' She was looking around, getting organized. She went to the kitchen and came back with a knife and some scissors. 'You cut off a branch, one of the lower ones in the back so it won't show. I'll get the rest.'

'Yes, ma'am. This is your show.'

'Wait till you see.' The light in his eyes had been contagious and now hers shone too, as she gathered what they would need. They were going to have Christmas! In a few minutes, it was all spread out on the kitchen table. She wiped her hands on her jeans, rolled up the sleeves of her sweater, and set to work, as Alejandro watched, amused. She looked a lot better than she had two hours before. She had looked so lost and sad when he arrived, and he hadn't liked the sound of her voice on the phone. He had cancelled a date, a dinner, and two promises to "drop in," but he owed this one to Luke. And to Kezia. It was crazy; there she was in her fancy apartment, with all her millionaire friends, and she was alone on Christmas. Like an orphaned child. He wasn't about to let it stay that way either. He was glad he had cancelled his plans and come down. For a moment, he hadn't been sure she would let him.

'You going to make a fruit salad?' She had apples, pears, walnuts, and grapes spread out near the branch.

'No, silly. You'll see.'

'Kezia, you're crazy.'

'I am not . . . or maybe I am. But I know how to make a wreath anyway. I used to make ours every year.'

'With fruit?'

'With fruit. I told you, you'll see.' And he did. With deft fingers, she tied the branch together with wire, and then carefully wired each piece of fruit and attached it to the wreath. The finished product looked like something in a Renaissance painting. The thick pine branch was covered with a neat circle of fruit, the nuts scattered here and there, the whole thing held together with an invisible

272

network of fine wire. It was a handsome ornament, and Alejandro loved the look on her face. 'See! Now where'll we put it?'

'On a plate? It still looks like a fruit salad to me.'

'You're a barbarian.'

He laughed and pulled her into his arms. It was warm and comfortable there.

'You'd never get away with a wreath like that in a poor neighbourhood. It'd be picked clean in an hour. But I will admit . . . I like it. It's a beautiful wreath – for a fruit salad.'

'Asshole.'

'Yup. That's me.' But she was still comfortably lodged in his arms as they spoke. She felt safe there; she liked it. She pulled reluctantly away after a few moments, and their eyes met with laughter.

'What about some dinner, Kezia? Or are you serving the wreath?'

'You take one bite out of that and I'll brain you! One of my friends' brothers did that one year and I cried for a week.'

'He must have been a sensible kid, but I can't stand women in tears. We'd better go get a pizza.'

'On Christmas?' She was shocked.

'Well, they don't sell tacos in this part of the world, or I would have suggested that. Can you suggest anything better?'

'I certainly can!' She still had the two Rock Cornish game hens she had been saving for Luke's Christmas dinner, just in case he came home. 'How about a real Christmas dinner?'

'How about saving that for tomorrow? Will the invitation still be good?'

'Sure? Why . . . do you have to go now?' Maybe he was in a hurry, and thus the suggestion of pizza. Her face suddenly fell, and she tried to look as though nothing had happened. But she wanted him to stay. It had been such a nice evening.

'No, I don't have to go. But I just had an idea. Want to go skating?'

'I'd love it.'

She put another sweater on over the one she already wore, thick red wool socks, brown suede boots, and buried herself in a lynx jacket and hat.

'Kezia, you look like someone in a movie.' She had the kind of beauty which appealed to him. Luke was a damn lucky man.

She told the answering service when they'd be back, in case Lucas called, and together they braved the biting night air. There was no wind, only a bitter frost which seared the lungs and eyes.

They stopped for hamburgers and hot tea, and she laughed as he told her of the chaos of Christmas in a Mexican home. A thousand children underfoot and all the women cooking, their husbands drunk, and parties in every home. She told him the things she had liked about her Christmases as a child.

'You know, I never got the purple-sequined gold dress.' She still looked almost surprised. She had seen it in a magazine when she was six, and had written all about it to Santa.

'What did you get instead? A mink coat?' He said it teasingly, without malice.

'No, darling, a Rolls.' She looked down her nose at him from beneath the big furry hat.

'And a chauffeur, of course.'

'No, I didn't get him till I was seven. My own, of course, with two liveried footmen.' She giggled at him again from under the hat. 'Shit, Alejandro, they used to drop me three blocks from school when I was a kid, and then follow me. But I had to walk the last bit of the way because they didn't think it was cool for me to arrive at school with a chauffeur.'

'That's funny. My parents felt the same way. I had to walk too. It's really rough what kids have to go through, isn't it?' His eyes laughingly mocked her.

274

'Oh shut up'

He threw back his head and laughed. Plumes of frost flew from his mouth in the cold night air.

'Kezia, I love you. You are really one crazy lady.'

'Maybe I am.' She was thinking of Lucas.

'Man, I wish I had bought some tequila. It's gonna be colder than shit on the ice.' She giggled at him then, looking like a child with a secret. 'I'm glad you think it's so funny. Me, I'm not wearing fur, and if I fall on my ass, which I will, I'll wind up with a good case of frostbite.' She giggled again, and with a white cashmere mittened hand pulled a flat silver flask from her pocket. 'What's that?'

'Instant insulation. Cognac. The flask was my grandfather's.'

'The dude was no dummy. That's a mighty thin flask. Hell, you could wear that in your suit and no one would spot it . . . pretty cool.' Arm in arm, they walked into the park, and began to sing 'Silent Night.' She unscrewed the cap on the flask and they each took a sip before she put it back in her pocket, feeling much better. It was one of those rare nights in New York when the city seemed to shrink. Cars had all but disappeared, buses seemed quieter and fewer, people were no longer rushing and actually took the extra second or two to smile at passersby. Everyone was either at home or away, or hiding from the fierce winter cold, but here and there groups were walking or singing. Kezia and Alejandro smiled at the other couples they passed, and now and then someone joined in their songs. By the time they got on the ice at the skating rink they had all but exhausted their collective knowledge of Christmas carols, and had had several sips from the flask.

'That's what I like, a woman who travels equipped. A flask full of cognac. Yep, you are crazy . . . but good crazy, definitely good crazy.' He sailed past her on the ice with a broad grin, intending to show off, and winding up instead on his ass.

'Mister, I think you're drunk.'

'You ought to know, you're my barman.' He grinned at her good-humouredly as he got up.

'Want some more?'

'No. I just joined A.A.'

'Party pooper.'

'Lush.'

They laughed at each other, sang 'Deck the Halls,' and skated a few turns arm in arm. The rink was almost deserted, and the other skaters shared in the Christmas spirit. The piped music was merry and light, carols intermingled with waltzes. It was a beautiful night. And it was past eleven before they decided the 'd had enough. Despite the cognac, their faces were numb from the cold.

'How about midnight mass at Saint Patrick's? Or would that be a bad trip? You're not Catholic, are you?'

'Nope. Episcopal, but I have nothing against Saint Patrick's. Your mass isn't that different from ours. I'd really enjoy it.' There was a moment of worry in her face, as she thought of missing a call from Luke. But the prospect of church appealed to her, and Alejandro swept her along. He suspected what she'd been thinking. And going home to sit by the phone would negate all they'd done. It was turning into a passable Christmas, and he wasn't going to let her spoil it. Even for Luke.

They walked down a deserted Fifth Avenue, past all the ornate window dressings, the lights and the trees. It had a carnival air. Saint Patrick's was jammed, hot, and smelled strongly of incense. They wedged their bodies in way at the back of the church; they could not approach the front pews, short of standing on shoulders and walking on heads. People had come from miles. Midnight mass at Saint Patrick's was a tradition for many.

The organ was somber and majestic, the church dark except for the light shed by thousands of candles. It was a high mass, and one-thirty when they got out.

'Tired?' He held her arm as they made their way down the steps. The cold air was a shock after the scented warmth of the church.

'More like sleepy. I think it's the incense.'

'Of course the cognac and the skating have nothing to do with it.' His eyes laughed at her, but kindly.

He hailed a cab, and the doorman at her place lurched his way to the door.

'Looks like he's been having a good time.'

'So would you if you raked in as much money as he and the other guys do. They each get an envelope from everyone in the building.' She thought of what Alejandro must make at the centre and cringed at the comparison. 'Want to come up for a drink?'

'I shouldn't. . . .' He knew she was tired.

'But you will. Come on, Al, don't be a drag.'

'Maybe I'll just stay for a minute, and have a bite of the fruit salad.'

'Touch my wreath and you'll regret it! And don't say I didn't warn you!' She brandished the nearly empty flask at him and he ducked. They giggled sleepily as they walked out of the elevator arm in arm. The apartment was warm and cozy and the tree looked pretty all lit up in the corner. She went out to the kitchen, as he sat down on the couch.

'Hey Kezia!'

'What?'

'Make that another hot chocolate!' He had had more than enough cognac, and so had she.

'I was.'

She came out with two steaming cups covered with rapidly dissolving marshmallows, and they sat side by side on the floor, looking up at the tree.

'Merry Christmas, Mr. Vidal.'

'Merry Christmas, Miss Saint Martin.' It was a solemn moment, and for what felt like a very long time neither spoke. Their thoughts were drifting separately to other people, other years, and in their own ways, they each found their minds wandering back to Luke and the present.

'You know what you ought to do, Alejandro?'

'What?' He had stretched out on the floor, his eyes

closed, his heart warm. He was growing very fond of her and he was glad he had made a change of plans. This was turning into a beautiful Christmas. 'What should I do?'

'Sleep on the couch. It seems stupid for you to go all the way uptown at this hour. I'll give you some sheets and a blanket and you can stay here ' And then I won't have to wake up in an empty house tomorrow morning, and we can giggle and laugh, and go for a walk in the park. Please, please stay . . . please. . . .

'Wouldn't it be a pain in the ass for you if I stay?'

'No. I'd love it.' The look in her eyes said she needed his presence there, and he didn't know why, but he needed that too.

'Are you sure?'

'Very sure. And I know Lucas won't mind.' She knew she could trust him, and it had been such a nice evening that now she desperately didn't want to be alone. It was Christmas. It had finally dawned on her. Christmas: a time for families and friends and people you love. A time for children and big sloppy dogs to come lumbering into the house and play with the wrappings from the gifts that were being opened. Instead, she had sent Edward a set of colourless books for his library, and French place mats from Porthault to Aunt Hil, to add to the towering stack already in her London linen closets. And in turn, Hilary had sent her perfume, and a scarf from Hardy Amies. Edward had given her a bracelet that was too large and not her style. And Totie had sent her a hat that she'd knitted, that didn't go with anything Kezia owned, and might possibly have fit her when she was ten. Totie had aged. Hadn't they all? And the exchange of gifts had all been so meaningless this year, by mail, via stores, to people she owed by ritual and tradition, not really by heart. She was glad she and Alejandro had not tried to drum up gifts for each other that night. They had given each other something far better. Their friendship. And now she wanted him to stay. Aside from Luke, it suddenly felt as though he were her only friend.

278

'Will you stay?' She looked down at him lying on the floor beside where she sat.

'With pleasure.' He opened an eye, and held out a hand for one of hers. 'You may be crazy, but you're still a beautiful lady.'

'Thank you.'

She kissed him gently on the forehead, and went down the hall to get him some sheets. A few minutes later, she gently closed the door to the room with a last whispered 'Merry Christmas,' which meant 'thanks.'

## CHAPTER XXIV

Kezia had been out shopping. She had stopped sitting in her apartment, just waiting for Luke. It had been driving her crazy. So she foraged around Bendel's and wandered through the boutiques on Madison Avenue for an hour that afternoon, and when she opened the door, Luke's suitcase was spilling its contents nervously across the floor, brush, comb, razor, rumpled shirts, sweaters lying about, two broken cigars tangled with a belt, and one shoe, whose mate was missing: Lucas was home.

He waved at her from the desk as she walked in. He was on the phone, but a broad grin spread over his face, and she walked swiftly to his side, matching his smile, and wrapped her arms around his broad shoulders. It felt so good just to hold him again. He felt so big and so beautiful, his hair smelled fresh and felt like silk under her hand. Black silk, and soft on his neck. He hung up the phone and turned around in his chair to hold her face in his hands and look into the eyes that he loved.

'God, you look good to me, Mama.' There was something fervent in his eyes and his hands were almost rough.

'Darling, how I missed you!'

'Baby, me too. And I'm sorry about Christmas.' He buried his face in her chest, and gently kissed her left breast.

'I'm so glad you're home . . . and Christmas was lovely. Even without you. Alejandro took care of me like a brother.'

'He's a good man.'

'Yes, he is.' But her thoughts were far from Alejandro Vidal. They were filled with the man she was looking at. Lucas Johns was her man. And she was his woman. It was the best feeling she knew. 'Oh Jesus, but how I missed you, Lucas!' He laughed with pleasure at the catch in her voice, and pulled her off her feet, standing up and sweeping her into his arms like a child. He kissed her firmly on the mouth, said not a word, and walked her straight into the bedroom as she giggled. He marched right over the suitcase, the clothes, the cigars, kicked the bedroom door shut with his foot, and made his presence rapidly and amply known. Lucas was very much home.

He had brought her a turquoise Navajo bracelet of elaborate and intricate beauty, and he laughed at the Christmas presents she gave him . . . and then grew silent over the book that had been her father's. He knew what it must have meant for her to give it to him, and he felt something hot at the back of his eyes. He only looked up at her and nodded, his eyes quiet and grave. She kissed him gently, and the way their lips met told them both what they already knew, how much he loved her, and she him.

He was back at the phone in an hour, bourbon in hand. And half an hour later he announced that he had to go out. When he did, he didn't come back to the apartment until nine, and then got back on the phone again. When he finally got to bed at two in the morning, Kezia had long since gone to sleep. He was up and dressed when she awoke the next morning. These were hectic days. And tense ones. And now there were always plainclothesmen wherever Luke was. Even Kezia spotted them now.

'Jesus, darling, I feel like I didn't even get to talk to you yesterday. Are you already going out now?'

'Yeah, but I'll be back early today. I just have so much to do, and we've got to get back out to San Francisco in three days.' Three days. Where had she gotten the idea that they would be spending time alone in New York? Time to walk in the park, and talk, to lie in bed at night and think aloud, time to smile at the fire, and giggle over popcorn. It wasn't going to be like that at all. It already wasn't. The hearing was less than a week away now, and at his insistence, she was sticking close to home. He had been adamant about that. He had enough to think about without worrying about her.

He left ten minutes later, and the promise that he'd be back early went by the wayside. He walked in at ten that night, looking tired and nervous and worn, reeking of bourbon and cigars, with dark rings under his eyes.

'Luke, can't you take one day off? You need it so much.' He shook his head as he threw his coat over the back of a chair. 'Just an afternoon? Or one evening?'

'Goddammit, Kezia! Don't press me! I have too fucking much to do as it is.' Gone the dream of peace before the hearing. There would be no peace, no time alone, no rest, no candlelight dinners. There would be Luke coming and going, looking ravaged, up at dawn, drunk by noon, and sober again and spent by the end of the evening. And nightmares when he finally allowed himself a few hours of sleep.

A canyon had opened between them, a space around him which she couldn't even begin to approach. He wouldn't let her.

On their last night in New York she heard Luke's key in the door and turned in her seat at the desk. He looked pathetically tired, and he was alone.

'Hi, Mama. What's doing?'

'Nothing, love. You look like you had a bitch of a day.'

'Yeah, I did.' The smile was old and rueful, the lines around his eyes had deepened noticeably in the last few days. Luke sagged visibly in his chair. He was beat.

'Want a drink?' He shook his head. But tired as he was, there was a familiar light in his eyes. It was as though the old Luke had finally come home ... the one she'd waited weeks, and now days for. He was worn out, exhausted, but sober and alone. She went to him and he put his arms around her.

'I'm sorry I've been such a sonofabitch.'

'You haven't been. And I love you ... a whole bunch.' She looked down into his face, and they smiled.

'You know, Kezia, the funny thing is that no matter how hard you run, you can't run away from it. But I got a lot done. I guess that's something at least.' It was the first hint he'd given her that he was scared too. It was like a train heading straight for their life, and their feet were rooted to the tracks while it just kept coming at them ... and coming and coming and coming ... and ...

'Kezia ...'

'Yes, love?'

'Let's go to bed.' He took her by the hand, and they walked quietly into the bedroom. The Christmas tree still stood tall in a living room corner, shedding needles all over the floor, the branches beginning to droop dryly from the weight of the ornaments. 'I wanted to take that down for you this week.'

'We can do it when we get back.' He nodded and then stopped in the doorway, looking at something over her head, but still holding her hand.

'Kezia, I want you to understand something. They might take me away at the hearing. I want you to know that, and accept it, because if that happens, it happens, and I don't want you falling apart.'

'I won't.' But her voice was shaken and tiny.

'Noblesse oblige?' His accent was funny and she smiled. The words meant 'Nobility obliges'; she'd grown up with it all of her life. The obligation to keep your chin up, no

282

matter who sawed off your legs at the knee; the ability to serve tea with the roof coming down around your ears; the charm of developing an ulcer while wearing a smile. Noblesse oblige.

'Yeah, noblesse oblige, and partly something else maybe.' Her voice was strong again now. 'I think I could keep it together because I love you as much as I do. Don't worry. I won't fall apart.' But she didn't understand it either, nor could she accept it. It couldn't happen to them. And maybe it wouldn't . . . or maybe it would.

'You're a beautiful lady, sweet Kezia.' He put his arms around her again, and they stood in the doorway for a long, long time.

## CHAPTER XXV

Their mood on the plane was almost hysterically festive. They had decided to travel first-class.

'First-class all the way. That's my girl.' He was prominently carrying his new Vuitton briefcase, and ostentatiously wearing the brown suede Gucci shoes. They had agreed that the brown suede were the wealthier looking.

'Lucas, pull your feet in.' She giggled at him; he was deliberately dangling one foot in the aisle.

'Then they won't see my shoes.' He lit a cigar from the new shipment from Romanoff, and flapped the Pucci tie in her face.

'You're a nut, Mr. Johns.'

'So are you.' They exchanged a honeymoon smooch and the stewardess looked over and smiled. They were a good-looking couple. And so happy they were almost ridiculous.

'Want some champagne?' He was fumbling around in his briefcase.

'I don't think they'll serve it till we're off the ground.'

'That's their business, Mama. Me, I bring my own.' He grinned broadly at her.

'Lucas, you didn't!'

'I most certainly did.' He pulled out a bottle of vintage Moët et Chandon and two plastic glasses, also a small tin of caviar. In four months he had developed a fondness for much of her way of life, while still keeping his own view and perspective. Together they filtered out the best of both worlds and made it their own. Mostly, the 'posh' things amused him, but there were certain things he truly liked. Caviar was one of them. And so was pâté. The Gucci shoes were a lark, and she knew that's how he'd feel, which was why she had bought them.

'Want some champagne?' She nodded, smiling, and reached out for one of the two plastic glasses.

'What are you looking so funny about?'

'Who, me?' And then she started to laugh, and leaned over and kissed him. 'Because I brought some too.' She opened her tote bag, and pointed at the bottle lying on the top. Louis Roederer, though not quite as vintage a year as his Moët. But still, not a bad one. 'Darling, aren't we chic?'

'It's a wine-tasting party!' Stealthily they guzzled champagne and devoured the caviar; they necked during the movie, and traded old jokes, which got sillier by the hour and the glass. It was like leaving on a vacation. And he had promised her that he would be all hers the next day. No appointments, no meetings, no friends. They would have the day to themselves. She had taken reservations at the Fairmont, just for the hell of it; a suite in the tower, for a hundred and eighty-six dollars a day.

The plane landed smoothly in San Francisco, just before three o'clock. They had the rest of the afternoon and the evening before them. Their rented limousine was waiting, and the chauffeur took their baggage stubs, so they could head for the car. Luke was as anxious as Kezia to avoid any publicity. This was no time for that.

284

'Do you think they noticed my shoes?'

She looked down at them pensively for a moment. 'You know, maybe I should have bought them in red.'

'Maybe I should have made love to you during the movie. No one would have seen.'

'How about in the car?' She settled back on the seat, and automatically pressed the button to raise the glass between their seat and the chauffeur's. He was still hunting for their bags.

'Baby, that may cut out the sound track, but if we're going to make love he'll still get a wide-angle view.'

She laughed with him at the thought. 'Want some more champagne, Lucas?'

'You mean there's more left?' She nodded, smiling, and produced the remaining half bottle of Roederer. They had polished off the Moët et Chandon. He produced the plastic glasses from his briefcase, and they poured another healthy round.

'You know, Lucas, we really have a great deal of class. Or is it panache? Possibly . . . style.' She was thinking it over, the glass tilted slightly in one hand.

'I think you're drunk.'

'I think you're gorgeous, and what's more, I think I love you.' She made a passionate lunge at him, and he groaned as her champagne flew at the window, and his splashed on the floor.

'Not only are you drunk, but you're a sloppy drunk. Just look at the Honourable Miss Kezia Saint Martin.'

'Why can't I be Kezia Johns?' She sank back into the corner with her empty champagne glass, and waited for him to refill it, a pout taking over her face. He eyed her curiously for a long moment and cocked his head to one side.

'Are you serious or drunk, Kezia?' This was important to him.

'Both. And I want to get married.' She looked as though she were going to add, 'And so there!' but she didn't.

'When?'

'Now. Let's get married now. Want to fly to Vegas?' She brightened at the thought. 'Or is it Reno? I've never gotten married before. Did you know I'm an old maid?' She smiled primly, as though she had revealed a marvellous secret.

'Jesus, baby, you're shitfaced.'

'I most certainly am not! How dare you say such a thing?'

'Because I've been supplying the champagne. Kezia, be serious for a minute. Do you really want to get married?'

'Yes. Right now.'

'No. Not right now, you nut. But maybe later this week. Depending on ... well, we'll see.' The accidental reference to the impending hearing had gone over her head, and he was grateful for that. She was thoroughly plastered.

'You don't want to marry me.' She was getting close to champagne-induced tears, and he was trying hard not to laugh.

'I don't want to marry you when you're drunk, stupid. That's immoral.' But there was a special smile on his face. My God, she wanted to marry him. Kezia Saint Martin, the girl in the papers. And here he was in a limo wearing Gucci shoes, on his way to a suite at the Fairmont. He felt like a kid with ten electric trains. 'Lady, I love you. Even if you are shitfaced.'

'I want to make love.'

'Oh God.' Luke rolled his eyes, and the chauffeur slid into his seat behind the wheel. A moment later the car pulled away from the kerb. Neither of them had seen the unmarked car drive up behind them. They were being followed again, but by now they were used to it. It was a fixture.

'Where are we going?'

'To the Fairmont, remember?'

'Not to church?'

'Why the fuck would we want to go to church?'

'To get married.'

'Oh, that kind of church . . . Later. How about getting engaged?' He looked at the signet ring on his hand again. He had been so pleased with the gift. But she saw the look in his eyes, and anticipated what he had in mind.

'You can't give me that. I gave it to you. That would be Indian giving, not a proper engagement . . . an Indian engagement? In any case, I don't believe it would be for real.' She looked haughty and was listing badly to one side.

'I don't believe you're for real, Mama. But okay, if this one won't do it, let's stop and get a "proper" engagement ring. What would you consider proper? I hope it's something smaller than a ten-carat diamond.'

'That would be vulgar.'

'That's a relief.' He grinned at her, and she dropped the haughty look for a smile.

'I think I'd like something blue.'

'Oh. Like a turquoise?' He was teasing, but she was too drunk to see it.

'That would be pretty . . . or a lapis patchouli. . . .'

'I think you mean lapis lazuli.'

'Yes, that's who I mean. Sapphires are nice too, but they're too expensive, and they crack. My grandmother had a sapphire that . . .' He shut her up with a kiss, while pressing the button to lower the window separating them from the chauffeur.

'Is there a Tiffany's here?' He knew all the right names now. For a man who hadn't known the difference between a Pucci and a lap dog four months ago, he had learned the private dialect of the upper classes with astonishing speed. Bendel's, Cartier's, Parke Bernet, Gucci, Pucci, Van Cleef, and of course . . . Tiffany, everyone's favourite supermarket for diamonds. And comparable stones . . . undoubtedly, they would have something blue, other than turquoise.

'Yes, sir. There's a Tiffany's here. On Grant Avenue.'

'Then take us there before the hotel. Thanks.' He

287

rolled the window back into place. He had learned that one too

'My God, Lucas, we're getting engaged? For real?' Tears sprang to her eyes as she smiled.

'Yes, but you're going to stay in the car. The papers would really love this one. Kezia Saint Martin gets engaged at Tiffany's, and the bride was noticeably inebriated.'

'Noticeably shitfaced,' she corrected.

'Excuse me.' He gently relieved her of the empty glass she'd been holding, and kissed her. They rode into town sitting close together in the back of the car, his arm around her, a beatific smile on her face, and a look of peace on his that hadn't been there for weeks.

'Happy, Mama?'

'Very.'

'Me too.'

The driver stopped in front of the grey marble façade of Tiffany's on Grant Avenue, and Luke gave her a hasty kiss and dashed from the car, with a sobering admonition that she stay there.

'I'll be right back. Don't leave without me. And don't under any circumstances get out of the car. You'd fall flat on your ass.' Then, as an afterthought, he stuck his head in the window and wagged a finger at her slightly hazed eyes. 'And stay out of the champagne!'

'Go to hell!'

'I love you too.' He gave her a quick wave over his shoulder as he dashed into the store. It seemed like only five minutes before he was back.

*Show me what you got!* She was so excited she could hardly sit still. Unlike other women at her age, this was the first time she'd gotten engaged.

'I'm sorry, baby. They didn't have anything I liked, so I didn't get anything.'

'Nothing?' She looked crushed.

'No . . . and to tell you the truth, they didn't have a thing I could afford.'

'Oh shit.'

'Darling, I'm sorry.' He looked crestfallen and held her close.

'Poor Lucas, how awful for you. I don't need a ring, though.' She suddenly brightened and tried to keep the disappointment out of her voice, but she was so tipsy that it was hard to keep it all in control.

'Do you suppose we could get engaged without a ring?' He sounded almost humble.

'Sure. I now pronounce thee engaged.' She waved an imaginary wand at him, and smiled happily into his eyes. 'How does it feel?'

'Fantastic! Hey, far out! Look what I found in my pocket!' He pulled out a dark blue velvet cube. 'It's something blue, isn't that what you wanted? A blue velvet box.'

'Oh you . . . you! You did get me a ring!'

'No. Just the box.' He dropped it into her lap and she snapped the lid open and gasped.

'Oh Lucas, it's gorgeous! It's . . . it's incredible! I love it!' It was an emerald-cut aquamarine with a tiny diamond chip set on either side. 'It must have cost you a fortune. And oh darling, I love it!'

'Do you, babe? Does it fit?' He took it from the box for her and carefully slipped it on her finger. Doing that was a heady feeling for both of them, as though when it reached the base of her finger something magic would happen. They were engaged. Christ, what a trip!

'It fits!' Her eyes danced as she held out her hand, looking at the ring from every possible angle. It was a beautiful stone.

'Shit. It looks like it's loose. Is it too big?'

'No, it isn't. No, it isn't! Honest!'

'Liar. But I love you. We'll get it sized tomorrow.'

'I'm engaged!'

'Hey, that's funny, lady. Me too. What's your name?'

'Mildred. Mildred Schwartz.'

'Mildred, I love you. That's funny though, I thought

289

your name was Kate. Didn't it used to be?' He had a tender light in his eye, remembering the first day he'd met her.

'Isn't that what I told you when we met?' She was a little too drunk to be sure.

'It was. You were already a liar way back then.'

'I already loved you then, too. Right away, just about.' She sank back into his arms again, with her own memories of their first days.

'You loved me then?' He was surprised. He thought it had taken longer. She had been so evasive at first.

'Uh huh. I thought you were super. But I was scared you'd find out who I was.'

'Well, at least now I know. Mildred Schwartz. And this, my love, is the Fairmont.' They had just pulled up in the driveway, and two porters approached to assist the chauffeur with their bags. 'Want me to carry you out?'

'That's only when you get married. We're only engaged.' She flashed the ring at him with a smile which enchanted him.

'Please forgive the impertinence. But I'm not sure you can walk.'

'I beg your pardon, Lucas. I most certainly can.' But she wove badly when her feet touched the pavement.

'Just keep your mouth shut, Mama, and smile.' He picked her up in his arms, nodded to the porters and mentioned something about a weak heart, and a long plane trip, while she quietly nibbled his ear. 'Stop that!'

'I will not.'

'You will, or I'll drop you. Right here. How'd you like a broken ass for an engagement present?'

'Up your ass, Lucas.'

'Shh ... keep your voice down.' But he wasn't much more sober than she; he only held it a mite better.

'Put me down, or I'll sue you.'

'You can't. We're engaged.' He was halfway through the lobby with Kezia in his arms.

'And it's such a pretty ring too. Lucas, if you only knew how much I love you.' She let her head fall onto his shoulder and studied the ring. He carried her easily, like a rag doll, or a very small child.

'Due to Mrs. Johns' weak heart, and her weakened condition from the flight,' would they send the registration forms up to the room? The couple rode quickly up in the elevator, with Kezia carefully propped up in a corner. Luke watched her with a grin.

'I'll walk to the room, thank you.' She looked at him imperiously, and tripped as she got out of the elevator. He caught her before she fell, and he offered her his arm, trying hard to keep a straight face.

'Madam?'

'Thank you, sir.' They walked gingerly down the hall, with Luke supporting most of her weight, and at last arrived at the room.

'You know what's funny, Lucas?' When she was drunk, she had the voice of Palm Beach, London, and Paris.

'What, my dear?' Two could play that game.

'When we came up in the elevator, I felt like we could see the whole world, even the sky, the Golden Gate Bridge . . . everything. Is that what being engaged does to you?'

'No. It's what being in a glass elevator does to you, when it runs along the outside of the building, and you ride in it when you're drunk. You know, sort of like special effects.' He gave her his most charming smile.

'Go to hell.'

The porter was waiting for them in the door of the suite, and Luke tipped him solemnly and closed the door behind him.

'And I suggest that you lie down, or take a shower. Probably both.'

'No, I want to . . .' She walked slowly towards him, an evil gleam in her eye, and he laughed.

'As a matter of fact, Mama, so do I.'

'Hey, lady, it's a beautiful day.'

'Already?'

'It has been for hours.'

'I think I'm going to die.'

'You're hung over. I ordered coffee for you.' He smiled at the look on her face. They had made matters worse with a third bottle of champagne after dinner. It had been a night for lengthy celebration. Their engagement. It was more than a little mad. He knew only too well that by the following day he could be in jail, which was why he hadn't jumped at the thought of Reno or Vegas. But that was one thing he wouldn't do to her. If they revoked him, that was it. He wasn't going to take her down with him, as his wife. He loved her too much to do that to her.

She struggled with the coffee, and felt better after a shower.

'Maybe I'm not going to die after all. I'm not quite sure yet.'

'You never know with a weak heart like yours.'

'What weak heart?' She looked at him as though he were crazy.

'That's what I told them when I carried you into the lobby.'

'You carried me?'

'You don't remember?'

'I don't remember being carried. I do remember feeling like I was flying.'

'That was the elevator,.

'Jesus. I must have really been bombed.'

'Worse than that. Which reminds me ... do you remember getting engaged?'

'Several times.' She grinned wickedly and ran a hand up his leg.

'I mean with a ring, you lewd bitch. Shame on you!'

'Shame on me? If I remember correctly ...'

'Never mind that. Do you remember getting engaged?'

But her face softened as she saw how earnest he was. 'Yes, darling, I remember. And the ring is incredible.' She flickered it at him, and they both smiled as she kissed him. 'It's a magnificent ring.'

'For a magnificent woman. I wanted to buy you a sapphire, but they were waaaaaayyyy over my head.'

'I like this better. My grandmother had a sapphire that . . .'

'Oh not that again!' He started to laugh and she looked surprised.

'I already told you?'

'Several times.' She grinned and shrugged her slim shoulders. She was wearing only his ring. 'Now, are we going to sit here all day, making love and being lazy, or are we going to go out?'

'Do you suppose we ought to go out?' But she looked as if she liked the first idea better.

'It might do us good. We can come back for more of this later.'

'Is that a promise?'

'Do you usually have to force me, my love?'

'Not exactly.' She smiled primly and walked to the closet. 'Where are we going?'

'What do you want to do?'

'Can we go for a drive? I'd love that. Up the coast, or something nice and easy like that.'

'With the chauffeur?' The idea didn't have much appeal. Not with the chauffeur.

'No, silly, alone of course. We can rent a car through the hotel.'

'Sure, babe, I'd like that too.'

She was forking out vast sums of money for this trip. The suite at the Fairmont, the first-class seats on the trip out, the limousine, the elaborate room service meals, and now yet another car, for his pleasure. She wanted it all to be special. She wanted to soften the blow of the hearing, or at least provide some diversion from the reason they were there. Underneath the holiday air was the kind of gaiety one produces for a child who is dying of cancer – circus, puppet shows, dolls, colour TV, Disneyland, and ice cream all day long, because soon, very soon . . . Kezia longed for the days of their first trip to San Francisco, for their early days in New York. This time nothing was natural; it was all terribly luxurious, but it wasn't the same. It was forced.

The concierge rented a car for them, a bright red Mustang with a stick shift that pleased Luke. He roared up the hills on his way to the bridge.

It was a pleasant drive for a sunny winter afternoon. It was never very cold in San Francisco. There was a brisk breeze, but the air was warm, and everything around them was green, a far cry from the barren landscape they'd left.

They drove all afternoon, stopped here and there at a beach, walked to the edge of the cliffs, sat on rocks and talked, but neither spoke of what weighed on their hearts. It was too late to talk and there was nothing to say. The hearing was too close. They had both said it all, in all the ways they knew how, with their bodies, with gifts, with kisses, with looks. All they could do now was wait.

A light green Ford trailed them all day long, and it depressed Luke to realize they were being followed that closely. He didn't say anything to Kezia, but something in her manner led him to suspect that she knew too. There was more than a faint air of bravado, of each trying to reassure the other, by pretending not to see all the terrors around them ... or simply the passing of time. The hearing was right in front of their faces, and Lucas noticed that the cops stuck much closer now, as though they thought he'd suddenly bolt and run. But to where? He knew enough not to run. How long could he have gotten away with something like that? Besides, he couldn't have taken Kezia. And he couldn't have left her. They had him; they didn't have to breathe down his neck.

They stopped for dinner at a Chinese restaurant on their way back, and then went to the hotel to relax. They had to meet Alejandro's plane at ten o'clock that night.

The plane was on time and Alejandro was among the first through the doors.

'Hey, brother, what's your hurry?' Lucas stood lazily propped against the wall.

'It must be New York. It's getting to me. How's it going, man?' Alejandro looked worried and tired, and felt suddenly out of place when he saw the look on their faces, happy, relaxed, with windburn tans and pink cheeks from the sun. It was almost as though he had come out for no reason. What could be wrong in the lives of two people who looked like that?'

'Hey! Guess what?' Kezia's eyes glowed. 'We're engaged!' She held out the ring for his inspection.

'Beautiful. Congratulations! We're going to have to drink to that!' Luke rolled his eyes and Kezia groaned.

'We did that one last night.'

' "We", my ass. She did. Shitfaced to the gills.'

'Kezia?' Alejandro looked amused.

'Yop, on champagne. I drank about two bottles all by myself.' She said it with pride.

'From your flask?'

She laughed at the memory of Christmas and shook her head, as they went to claim his bags. They had brought the limousine; the Mustang had been returned.

The banter in the car on the way into the city was light and easy, bad jokes, silly memories, Alejandro's account of his trip, complete with a woman in labour and another woman who had smuggled her French poodle aboard under the coat and then threatened hysterics when the stewardess tried to take the dog away.

'Why do I always get on those flights?'

'You should try flying first-class.'

'Sure, brother, you bet. Hey, what's with the fruity brown shoes?' Kezia laughed and Lucas looked pained.

'Man, you ain't got no class at all. They're Guccis.'

'Look like fruit shoes to me.' The three of them laughed and the car pulled up in front of the hotel.

'It's not much, but we call it home.' Luke was in high spirits as he waved grandly to the towering palace that was the Fairmont.

'You guys certainly travel in style.' They had offered him the couch in the living room of their suite. It pulled out to make an extra bed.

'You know, Al, they've got a little old guy who walks around in the lobby just making "F"'s in the sand in the ashtrays.' Alejandro rolled his eyes, and the three of them chuckled again. 'It's the little things that make the difference.'

'Up your ass, man.'

'Please, not in front of my fiancée.' Luke looked mock prim.

'You guys really engaged? For real?'

'For real.' Kezia confirmed it. 'We're going to get married.' There was steel in her voice, and hope, and life, and tears, and fear. They would get married. If they got the chance.

None of them mentioned the hearing and it wasn't until Kezia started to yawn that Luke began to look serious.

'Why don't you go on to bed, babe? I'll be in, in a bit.' He wanted to talk to Alejandro alone, and it was easy to know what about. Why couldn't he share his fears with her? But it wouldn't do to look hurt. It wouldn't have served any purpose.

'Okay, darling. But don't stay up too late.' She kissed him gently on the neck and blew a kiss to Alejandro. 'Don't get too drunk, you guys.'

'Look who's talking.' Luke laughed at the thought.

'That's different. I was celebrating my engagement.' She tried to look haughty, but started to laugh as he swatted her behind and gave her a kiss.

'I love you. Now beat it.'

' 'Night, you guys.'

She lay awake in their bed and watched the line of light under the bedroom door until three. She wanted to go out there, to tell them that she was scared shitless, too, but she couldn't do that. She couldn't do it to Luke. She had to keep a stiff upper lip. Noblesse oblige, and all that shit.

She saw the next morning that Luke hadn't gone to bed all that night. At six in the morning, he had finally fallen asleep where he sat, and Alejandro had quietly laid down on the couch. They all had to be up by eight.

The hearing was at two, and Luke's attorney was due at the Fairmont at nine for a briefing. It would probably be the first time that Alejandro would hear it all straight. Luke had a way of clouding the issues, to spare his friends fear. And he knew that Kezia wouldn't let herself speak what she thought. Alejandro got nothing from Kezia now, and nothing from Luke except bullshit and bravado. The only real thing he had heard was to 'take care of Kezia, in case.' And that was going to be no easy task. That girl was going to take it harder than hell if he fell.

For a brief moment before he went to sleep, Alejandro almost wished that he hadn't come. He didn't want to see it. Didn't want to watch it happen to Luke, or see Kezia's face when it did.

# CHAPTER XXVI

The attorney arrived at nine, bringing tension with him. Kezia greeted him with a formal 'good morning', and made the introduction to 'Our friend, Mr. Vidal.' She poured coffee and commented what a beautiful day it was. That's when things started to go sour. The attorney gave a terse little laugh that set Kezia's nerves on edge. She was suspicious of him anyway. He was renowned for his skill at hearings like Luke's, for which he charged five thousand dollars. Lucas had insisted on paying it himself with his savings. He had set aside money for that, 'just in case'. But Kezia didn't like the man's style – over-

297

confident, overpaid, and overbearing. He assumed far too much.

The attorney looked around the room and felt the chill vibes from Kezia, and then made matters worse by putting his foot in his mouth. She was a most unnerving young woman.

'My father used to say on mornings like this, "Could be a beautiful day to die".' Her face grew ashen and taut and Luke gave her a look that said 'Kezia, don't blow it!' She didn't, for Luke's sake, but she smoked twice as much as she ordinarily did. Luke made no pretense: at nine in the morning, he was drinking bourbon straight up. Alejandro chain-drank cold coffee. The party was over.

The meeting lasted two hours, and at the end of it they knew nothing more than they had before. No one did. There was no way to know. It all depended on the Adult Authority and the judge. No one could read their minds. Lucas was in danger of being revoked for instigating 'unrest' in the prisons, agitating, and basically meddling in what the parole board and prison authorities felt was no longer his business. They had the right to revoke him for less, and there was no denying Luke's agitating. Everyone knew of it, even the press. He had been less than discreet in the years he'd been out. His speeches, his book, his meetings, his role in the moratorium against prisons, his hand in prison labour strikes across the country. He had gambled his life on his beliefs, and now they'd have to see what the price was. Worse, under the California indeterminate sentence laws, once he was revoked, the Adult Authority could keep him for as long as they liked. The attorney's 'probably not more than two or three years' only added to their collective gloom. No one held out much hope. For once, not even Luke. And Kezia was silent.

The lawyer left them shortly after eleven, and they agreed to meet at the courthouse at one-thirty. Until then, they were free.

'Want to have lunch?' It was Alejandro's suggestion.

'Who can eat?' Kezia was having increasing trouble playing the game. She had never looked as pale, and suddenly she wanted to call Edward or Totie, even Hilary, or Whit. Someone ... anyone ... but someone she knew well. This was like waiting in a hospital corridor to find out if the patient would live ... and what if ... what if he didn't ... what if ... oh God.

'Come on, you guys, let's go out.' Luke had the situation in control, except for the almost imperceptible tremor of his hands.

They had lunch at Trader Vic's. It was nice, it was pretty, it was 'terribly posh' as Luke said, and the food was probably excellent, but none of them noticed. It didn't feel right. It was all so fancy, so overdone, so false, and such a goddamn strain to keep up the pretense of giving a damn where they ate. Why the Fairmont and Trader Vic's? Why couldn't they just eat hot dogs, or have a picnic, or go on living after today? Kezia felt a weight settle over her like a parachute dipped in cement. She wanted to go back to the hotel to lie down, to relax, to cry, to do something, anything but sit in this restaurant eating a dessert she couldn't even taste. The conversation droned on; all three of them talked, saying nothing. By the time the coffee was served, they had sunk into silence. The only sound was of Luke, drumming the fingers of one hand softly on the table. Only Kezia heard; she felt the sound rippling through her like a triphammer pulse. She felt wired to the marrow of his bones, to his brain, to his heart. If they took him, why couldn't they take them together?

Alejandro looked at his watch, and Luke nodded.

'Yeah. It's about that time.' He signalled for the check and Alejandro made a gesture to reach for his wallet. With a sharp look in his eyes, Luke shook his head. And this wasn't a day to argue with him. He left the money on the small wicker platter the waiter had left with the bill, and they pushed the table away. Kezia felt as though she could hear a drum roll as they walked outside to the limousine. She felt like a costar in a B movie. They couldn't be real people, this couldn't be an hour before Luke's hearing, it couldn't be happening to them. None of it seemed real. And then, as the limousine rolled them inexorably away, she started to laugh, almost hysterically.

'What's funny?' Luke was tense, and Alejandro was silent now. Her laughter rang out jarringly. There was something shattering about it, something unbearably painful. It wasn't real laughter.

'Everything's funny, Luke. All of it. It really is, it . . . I . . . it's all so absurd.' She laughed on, until he took her hand and held it too hard. Then she stopped, tears suddenly trying to rush into the space where the laughter had been. It was all so absurd, all those ridiculous people at Trader Vic's – they'd be going to a concert after lunch, or the hairdresser, or to board meetings, or I. Magnin's, or to tea parties and dressmakers . . . leading their perfectly normal lives. But what could be normal, that, or this? None of it made any sense. The laughter tried to bubble back into her mouth, but she wouldn't let it. She knew that if she laughed again she would cry, and maybe even howl. That was what she wanted to do. Howl like a dog.

They drove west into the pale afternoon sun, and then south on Van Ness Avenue, past used cars and new cars and the blue plastic of the Jack Tar Hotel. The ride seemed to go on forever. People were busy, were running, were going, were living, and all too soon the dome of City Hall loomed before them. It stuck out like a proud gilded onion, a dowager's tit, noble and overdressed in patina and gold. Terrifying. City Hall. And within so few feet, other limousines were beginning to arrive for the symphony at the Opera House. Nothing made any sense.

Kezia felt vague and confused, almost drunk, though she'd had only coffee. And only the steadying presence of Luke on one side and Alejandro on the other kept her feet moving. Up the steps, through the doors, into the building, past the people . . . oh God . . . oh God, no!

'I need a pack of smokes.' Luke strode away from them and they followed, through the vast marble halls and under the dome. He walked with the determined rolling gait she knew so well, and silently she reached for Alejandro's hand.

'You okay, Kezia?'

She answered with a question in her eyes: *I don't know. Am I?*

'Yes.' She gave him a small wintry smile and looked up at the dome. How could ugly things happen here? It looked like Vienna or Paris or Rome, the columns and friezes and arches, the lofty swoop of the dome, the echo, the gold leaf. The day was really here. January eighth. The hearing. She was nose to nose with it now. Brutal reality.

She held tight to Luke's hand as they rode up in the elevator, and she stood as close to him as she could . . . closer . . . tighter . . . nearer . . . more. . . . She wanted to slip inside his skin, bury herself in his heart.

The elevator stopped on four, and they followed the corridors to the law library where the attorney had said he would meet them. They passed a courtroom, and suddenly Luke pushed her aside, almost thrusting her at Alejandro.

'What . . .'

'Fucking bastards.' Luke's face was suddenly angry and red, and Alejandro understood before she did. They quickened their pace, and he put an arm around her shoulders.

'Alejandro, what . . .'

'Come on, babe, we'll talk about it later.' The two men exchanged a look over her head, and when she saw the television cameras waiting, she knew. So that was it. Lucas was going to make news. Either way.

They detoured the reporters unnoticed, and slipped into the law library to wait. The attorney joined them after a few minutes, a thick file in his hand, a tense look on his face. But something about his demeanor impressed Kezia more than it had at the hotel.

301

'Everyone ready?' He tried to look jovial and failed dismally.

'Now? Already?' It wasn't two o'clock yet, and Kezia was beginning to panic, but Alejandro still had a tight grip on her shoulders. Luke was pacing in front of a book-lined wall.

'No. It'll be a few minutes. I'll meet you back here, and let you know when the judge is in court.'

'Is there any other way into the courtroom?' Alejandro was troubled.

'I . . . is . . . why?' The attorney looked puzzled.

'Have you walked past the courtroom yet?'

'No. Not yet.'

'It's crawling with reporters. Television cameras, the works.'

'The judge won't let them inside. Not to worry.'

'Yeah. But we'll still have to walk through them.'

'No, we won't.' Luke was back in their midst. 'Or Kezia won't in any case, if that's what you're worried about, Al.'

'Lucas, I most certainly will!' Small as she was, she looked as though in the heat of the moment she might hit him.

'You will not. And that's that.' This was no time to argue with him. The look on his face made that much clear. 'I want you here. I'll come and get you when it's over.'

'But I want to be in there with you.'

'On TV?' His voice dripped irony, not kindness.

'You heard what he said. They won't be in court.'

'They don't need to be. They'll get you coming and going. And you don't need that. And neither do I. I am not going to argue with you, Kezia. You're staying here in the library, or you can go back to the hotel. Now. Is that clear?'

'All right.'

The attorney left them, and Luke began to pace again, and suddenly he stopped and walked slowly towards her,

302

his eyes fixed on hers, everything about him familiar and dear. It was as though the barbed wire had gone from his spine. Alejandro sensed the mood and moved slowly towards a distant row of maroon and gold books.

'Baby . . .' Luke was only a foot away from her, but he didn't reach out to touch her, he only looked, watching her, as though counting every hair on her head, every thread in her dress. He took in all of her, and his eyes bore through to her soul.

'Lucas, I love you.'

'Mama, I have never ever loved you more. You know that, don't you?'

'Yes. And you know how much I love you?'

He nodded, his eyes still digging deep.

'Why are they doing this to us?'

'Because I decided to take my chances a long time ago, before I knew you. I think I'd have done it differently if I'd known you all along. Maybe not. I'm a shitkicker, Kezia. You know it. I know it. They know it. It's for a good cause, but I'm a thorn in their side. I've always thought it was worth it, if I could change something for the better . . . but I didn't know then that I'd be doing this to you.'

'Is it still worth it, for you, not counting me?' Even without considering her, how could it have been now? But his answer surprised her.

'Yes.' His eyes didn't waver, but there was something sad and old about them that she had never seen before. He was a man paying a heavy price, even if they didn't revoke him. It had already cost him a great deal.

'It's worth it even now, Lucas?'

'Yes. Even now. The only thing I feel like shit about is you. I should never have dragged you through it. I knew better right at the start.'

'Lucas, you're the only man I've ever loved, maybe the only human being I've ever loved. If you hadn't "dragged me through this," my life would never have been worth a good goddamn. And I can live with what's happening.

303

Either way.' For a moment she was as powerful as he; it was as though his strength had filled her to catalyze her own.

'And what if I go?'

'You won't.' I won't let you. . . .

'I might.' He seemed almost detached, as if he was ready to go if he had to.

'Then I'll handle that too.'

'Just handle yourself, little lady. You're the only woman I've ever loved like this. I won't let anything destroy you. Not even me. Remember that. And whatever I do, you've got to know that I know what's best. For both of us.'

'Darling, what do you mean?' Her voice was a whisper. She was afraid.

'Just trust me.' And then, without another word, he bridged the last foot between them, pulled her into his arms and held her breathlessly close. 'Kezia, right now I feel like the luckiest man in the world. Even here.'

'Just the most loved.' There were tears brushing her lashes, as she buried her face in his chest. Alejandro was forgotten, the law library had faded around them. The only thing they had that mattered and was real was each other.

'Ready?' The lawyer's face looked like a vision from a bad dream. Neither of them had heard him coming. Nor had they seen Alejandro watching them with tears streaming down his face. He wiped them away as he walked towards them.

'Yeah. I'm ready.'

'Lucas . . .' She clung to him for a moment, and he pushed her ever so gently away.

'Take it easy, Mama. I'll be back in a minute.' He gave her a lopsided smile and squeezed her hand tight. She wanted so desperately to reach out to him, to keep him from going, to stop it, to hold him close and never let him go. . . .

'We'd best be . . .' The attorney looked pointedly at his watch.

'We're going.' He signalled to Alejandro, gave Kezia a last ferocious squeeze, and strode to the door, his attorney and his friend right behind him. Kezia was standing where he had left her.

'Lucas!' He turned at the door as her voice echoed in the silent rows of books. 'God be with you!'

'I love you.' His three words rang in her ears as the door whooshed slowly closed.

There was no sound, not even that of a clock ticking. Nothing. Silence. Kezia sat in a straight-backed chair and watched a sliver of sunlight asleep on the floor. She didn't smoke. She didn't cry. She only waited. It was the longest half hour of her life. Her mind seemed to doze like the sun on the floor. The chair was uncomfortable but she didn't feel it. She didn't think, didn't feel, didn't see, didn't hear. Not even the footsteps that finally came. She was numb.

She saw his feet pointing at hers before she saw his face. But they were the wrong feet, the wrong shoes, a different colour and too small. Boots . . . Alejandro . . . where was Luke?

Her eyes ran up the legs until they reached his face. His eyes were dark and hard. He said nothing, only stood there.

'Where is Lucas?' The words were small and precise. Her whole body had stopped. And he answered all in one breath.

'Kezia, they revoked him. He's in custody.'

'What?' She flew to her feet. Everything had started again, only now it was all going too fast instead of too slowly. 'My God, Alejandro! Where is he?'

'He's still in the courtroom. Kezia, no . . . don't go . . .' She was on her way to the door, her feet racing over the grey marble floor. 'Kezia!'

'Go to hell!' She flew out the door just as he caught her arm. 'Stop it, damn you! I have to see him!'

'Okay. Then let's go.' He held her hand tightly in his,

305

and hand in hand they ran down the hall. 'He may be gone now.'

She didn't answer, she only ran faster, her shoes beating like her heart, pounding the floor as they ran. The reporters had already thinned out. They had their story. Lucas Johns was on his way back to Quentin. So it goes. Poor sonofabitch.

Kezia shoved her way past two men blocking the door of the courtroom, and Alejandro slipped in beside her. The judge was leaving the bench, and all she could see was one man, sitting quietly, alone, his back to her, facing straight ahead.

'Lucas?' She slowed to a walk and approached him slowly. He turned his head towards her, and there was nothing on his face. It was a mask. A different man than she knew. An iron wall with two eyes. Two eyes that held tears, but said nothing.

'Darling, I love you.' She had her arms around him then, and he leaned slowly against her, letting his head rest on her chest, letting his weight go, his whole body seeming to sag. But his arms never moved to go around her, and then she saw why. He was already in handcuffs. They hadn't wasted much time. His wallet and change lay on the table before him, and among them were the keys to the New York apartment, and his ring, the one she had given him for Christmas. 'Lucas, why did they do it?'

'They had to. Now you go home.'

'No. I'll stay till you go. Don't talk. Oh Christ, Lucas . . . I love you.' She fought back the tears. He would not see her cry. He was strong, so was she. But she was dying inside.

'I love you too, so do me a favour and go. Get the hell out of here, will you?' The tears had gone from his eyes and she covered his mouth with her own as her answer. She was bending towards him, her thin arms and small hands trying to envelop the whole of his body, as though he were a child and had grown too big for her lap. Why had they done it? Why couldn't she take this away from him? Why couldn't she have bought them? Why? All this pain and the ugliness and the handcuffs . . . why was there nothing she could do? Fucking goddamn parole board, and the judge and . . .

'Okay, Mr. Johns.' There was a nasty inflection on the 'Mr.,' and the voice came from right behind her.

'Kezia, go!' It was the command of a general, not a plea from the defeated.

'Where are they taking you?' As her eyes flew open wide with anger and fear, she felt Alejandro's hands on her shoulders, pulling her back.

'To county jail. Alejandro knows. Then to Quentin. Now get the fuck out of here. Now!' He rose to his full height and faced the guard who was about to lead him away.

She stood on tiptoe briefly and kissed him, and then almost blindly she let Alejandro lead her out of the court. She stood for a moment in the hall, and then as though in a distant vision far off down the hall she saw him go, a guard on either side, his hands shackled in front of him. He never looked back and it seemed as though, long after he was gone, she felt her mouth open, and a long piercing sound filled the air. A woman was screaming but she didn't know who. It couldn't be someone she knew. Nice people don't scream. But the sound wouldn't end and someone's arms were holding her tight, as flashbulbs began to explode in her face and strange voices assailed her.

And then suddenly she was flying over the city in a glass cage, and after that she was led into a strange room and someone put her to bed and she felt very cold. Very cold. A man piled blankets on her, and another man with funny glasses and a moustache gave her a shot. She started to laugh at him because he looked so funny, but then that terrifying sound came back again. The woman was screaming. What woman? It was a long, endless howl. It filled the room until all the light was squeezed out of her eyes and everything went black.

# CHAPTER XXVII

When Kezia woke up, Alejandro was sitting in the room with her, watching her. It was dark. He looked tired and rumpled and was surrounded by empty cups. He looked as though he had spent the night in the chair, and he had.

She watched him for a long time; her eyes were open and it was hard to blink. Her eyes felt bigger than they ever had before.

'You awake?' His voice was a hoarse whisper. The ashtrays were filled to the brim.

She nodded. 'I can't close my eyes.'

He smiled at her. 'I think you're still stoned. Why don't you go back to sleep?'

She only shook her head, and then tears washed the too-open eyes. Even that didn't help her to close them. 'I want to get up.'

'And do what?' She made him very nervous.

'Go pee pee.' She giggled and choked on fresh tears.

'Oh.' The smile was brotherly and tired.

'You know something?' She looked at him curiously.

'What?'

'You look like hell. You stayed up all night, didn't you?'

'I dozed. Don't worry about me.'

'Why not?' She staggered out of bed and headed for the john, pausing in the doorway. 'Alejandro, when can I see Luke?'

'Not till tomorrow.' So she already remembered. He had been afraid that he would have to start from scratch after the shot they'd given her the night before. It was now six in the morning.

'You mean today or tomorrow?'

'I mean tomorrow.'

'Why can't I see him till then?'

'County only has two visiting days. Wednesday and Sunday. Tomorrow is Wednesday. Them's the rules.'

'Bastards.' She slammed the bathroom door and he lit another cigarette. He was into his fourth pack since the night had begun. It had been one hell of a night. And she still hadn't seen the crap in the papers. Edward had called four times that night. He'd seen the news in New York. He was half out of his mind.

When she came back, she sat on the edge of the bed and lit a cigarette from his pack. She looked tired, haggard, and pale. The tan seemed to have instantly faded, and dark rims framed her eyes all the way around, like purple eye shadow gone wild.

'Lady, you don't look so hot. I think you ought to stay in bed.' She didn't answer, but only sat there, smoking and swinging her foot, her head turned away from him.

'Kezia?'

'Yeah?' She was crying again when she turned to face him, and she felt like a very small child melting into his arms. 'Oh God, Alejandro. Why? How can they do this to us? To him?'

'Because sometimes it happens that way. Call it fate, if you want.'

'I'd call it fucked.' He smiled tiredly and then sighed.

'Babe . .' She had to know, but he hated to tell her.

'Yeah?'

'I don't know if you remember, but the newspaper boys took a bunch of pictures as they led Luke away.' He held his breath and watched the look on her face. He could see that she didn't remember.

'Those shits, why couldn't they leave him his last shred of dignity? Miserable, rotten . . .'

Alejandro shook his head. 'Kezia . . . they took pictures of you.' The words dropped like a bomb.

'Of me?'

He nodded.

'Jesus.'

'They just thought you were his old lady, and I had Luke's attorney call them and ask them not to run the pictures or your name. But by then, they knew who you were. Somebody spotted the pictures when they were developing them. That's a lot of bad luck.'

'They ran the pictures?' She sat very still.

'Out here, you're page one. Page four in New York. Edward called a few times last night.' Kezia threw back her head and started to laugh. It was a nervous, hysterical laugh, and not the reaction he had expected.

'Man, we really bought it this time, didn't we? Edward must be dying, poor thing.' But she didn't sound very sympathetic. She sounded distracted.

'That's putting it mildly.' Alejandro almost felt sorry for the man. He had sounded so stricken. So betrayed.

'Well, you plays, you pays, as they say. How bad are the pictures?'

About as bad as you could get. She had been hysterical when the photographers had spotted them. Alejandro pulled the evening edition of the *Examiner* from under the bed and held it out to her. On the front page was a photograph of Kezia collapsing in Alejandro's arms. She cringed as she saw it, and glanced at the text. 'Socialite heiress Kezia Saint Martin, secret girlfriend of ex-con Lucas Johns, collapses outside courtroom after . . .' It was worse than they had feared.

'I think Edward is mainly concerned with what kind of shape you are in now.'

'My ass, he is. He's having a heart attack over the story. You don't know Edward.' She sounded almost like a child afraid of her father. It seemed odd to Alejandro.

'Did he know about Luke?'

'Not like this he didn't. Actually, he knew I had interviewed him, and he also knew there's been someone important in my life for the last few months. Well, sooner or later, I guess it had to come out. We were lucky till now. It's a bitch that it had to be like this though. Have the papers called since?'

'A few times. I told them there was no story, and you were flying back to New York today. I thought that might get them off your back, and they'd keep busy watching the airport.'

'And the lobby.'

He hadn't thought about that. What an insane way to live.

'We'll have to call the manager and arrange to get out of here. I want to move to the Ritz. They won't find us there.'

'No, but you can count on some coverage tomorrow if you want to see Luke at the jail.'

She stood up and faced him, an icy look in her eyes. 'Not "if", Alejandro, "when". And if they want to be pigs about it, fuck them.'


The day slipped by in a haze of silence and cigarette smoke. Their move to the Ritz passed uneventfully. A fifty dollar 'gift' to the manager encouraged him to show them out through a back door, and keep his mouth shut about it later. Apparently, he had. There were no calls for them at the Ritz.

Kezia sat lost in her own thoughts, rarely speaking. She was thinking of Luke, and how he had looked when they led him away . . . and before that, how he had looked in the law library. He had been a free man then, for those last precious moments.

She called Edward from the Ritz and struggled through a brief, anguished conversation with him. They both cried. Edward kept repeating, 'How could you do this?' He left the words 'to me' unspoken, but they were there, nevertheless. He wanted her to fly home or let him fly out. He exploded when she refused.

'Edward, please, for God's sake, don't do this to me. Don't pressure me now!' She shouted through her tears and wondered briefly why they kept throwing guilt at each other. Who cared 'who was doing what to whom'. It had been done unto Kezia, and Luke, but not by Edward.

311

And Kezia had done nothing to Edward, not intentionally. They were all caught in the teeth of a maniacal machine, and no one could help it, or stop it.

'You have to come home, Kezia! Think of what they'll do to you out there.'

'They've already done it, and if it's in the papers in New York it won't make any difference where I am. I could fly to Tangiers for chrissake, and they'd still want a piece of the action.'

'It's really unbelievable. I still don't understand ... and Kezia ... good God, girl, you must have known this would happen to him. That story you told me about his being sick ... this was what you meant, wasn't it?' She nodded silently at the receiver and his voice came back sharper. 'Wasn't it?'

'Yes.' Her voice sounded so small, so broken and hurt.

'Why didn't you tell me?'

'How could I?' There was a long moment of silence when they both knew the truth.

'I still don't understand how you could involve yourself. You said in your own article about him that there was a possibility of this. How ...'

'Oh shut up, damn you, Edward, I did. That's all, I did. And stop clucking like a bloody mother hen about it. I did, and I got hurt, we both got hurt, and believe me, he's hurting one hell of a lot more sitting in jail right now.' There was deadly silence and Edward's voice came back with a measured venom that was totally foreign to him ... except for once before.

'Mr. Johns is used to jail, Kezia.' She wanted to hang up on Edward then, but she didn't quite dare. Severing the connection would sever something more, something deeper, and she still needed that tie, maybe only a little bit, but she needed it. Edward was all she had in a way, except Luke.

'Do you have anything else to say?' Her voice was almost as vicious as his had been a moment before. She was willing to kick at him, but not dismiss him entirely.

'Yes. Come home. Immediately.'

'I won't. Anything else?'

'I don't know what it will take to bring you to your senses, Kezia, but I suggest you make an effort to become rational as quickly as possible. You may regret this for a lifetime.'

'I will, but not for the reasons you think, Edward.'

'You have no idea how something like this can jeopardize . . .' His voice trailed off unhappily. For a moment he hadn't been speaking to Kezia, but to the ghost of her mother, and they both knew it. Now Kezia was certain. Now she knew why he had told her about her mother and the tutor. Now she knew it all.

'Jeopardize what? My "position"? My "consequence", as Aunt Hil would say? Jeopardize my chances of finding a husband? You think I give a damn about all that now? I care about Luke, Edward. I care about Lucas Johns. I love him!' She was shouting again.

Three thousand miles away, silent tears were sliding down Edward's face. 'Let me know if there's anything I can do for you.'

It was the voice of her attorney, her trustee, her guardian. Not her friend. Something had finally snapped. The gap between them was broadening to a frightening degree, for both of them.

'I will.' They exchanged no goodbye and Edward severed the connection. Kezia sat for a long moment holding the dead phone in her hands, while Alejandro watched her.

Tears of farewell slid down her cheeks. That had been two in two days. In one way or another, she had lost the only two men she had ever loved, since her father. Three lost men in a lifetime. She knew that somehow she had just lost Edward. She had betrayed him. What he had sought most to prevent had finally come.

Edward, sitting in his office, knew it too. He walked solemnly to the door, locked it carefully, walked back to his desk, and flicked the switch on his intercom,

313

informing his secretary in the driest of tones that he did not want to be disturbed until further notice. Then, having carefully put aside the mail on his desk, he lay his head down on his arms and broke into heart-rending sobs. He had lost her ... lost them both ... and to such unworthy men. As he lay there he wondered why the only two women he had ever loved had such a brutal flaw in their characters ... the tutor ... and now this ... this ... jailbird ... this nobody! He found himself shouting the word, and then, surprised at himself, he stopped crying, lifted his head, sat back in his chair, and stared at his view. There were times when he simply did not understand. No one played by the rules anymore. Not even Kezia, and he had taught her himself. He shook his head slowly, blew his nose twice, and went back to his desk to look over the mail.

Jack Simpson was sympathetic when he called her. But Kezia's agent didn't help matters by feeling guilty for introducing her to Luke. She assured him that he'd given her the best gift of her life, but the tears in her voice didn't console either of them.

Alejandro tried to coax her into a walk, but she wouldn't move, and sat in the hotel room with the shades drawn, smoking, drinking tea, coffee, water, scotch, scarcely eating, just thinking, her eyes filling with tears, her hands shaking and frail. She was afraid to go out now, afraid of the press and afraid of missing a phone call from Luke.

'Maybe he'll call.'

'Kezia, he can't call from county jail. They won't let him.'

'Maybe they will.'

It was pointless to argue with her; it was almost as though she didn't hear. And whatever she heard, she didn't listen to. The only sounds that penetrated were her own inner voices, and the echoes of Luke.

It was midnight before Alejandro finally got her to bed.

314

'What are you doing?' She could see his outline in the chair in the corner. Her voice sounded strangely odd.

'I thought I'd just sit here for a while. Will it keep you from sleeping?' She wanted to reach out in the darkness and touch his hand. She couldn't find the words again, all she could do was shake her head and cry. It had been an unbearable day, not as tense as the previous day, but more wearing. The endless pressure of pain.

He heard muffled sobs in the pillow and came closer to sit on the edge of the bed. 'Kezia, don't.' He stroked her hair, her arm, her hand, as her body shook with sobs. She was keening for Luke. 'Oh baby ... little girl, why did this happen to you?' She was so unprepared, so unused to anything she could not control, and she had seen nothing like this. There were tears in his own eyes again, but she couldn't see them.

'It didn't happen to me, Alejandro. It happened to him.' The voice was bitter and tired through her tears.

He stroked her hair for what seemed like hours, and at last she fell asleep. He smoothed the covers around her, and touched her cheek ever so gently. She looked young again as she slept; the anger had left her thin face. The bitterness of what can happen to a life out in the big, bad, ugly world had come as a shock to her. She was learning the hard way, with her heart, and her guts.

He heard her knock gently on his door, and raised his head from the pillow. Sleep had taken a long time to come to him the night before, and now it was only five after six.

'Who is it?'

'Me. Kezia.'

'Is anything wrong?'

'I just thought maybe we should get up.' Today was the day she was going to see Lucas. Alejandro smiled tiredly as he got up to open the door, pulling on his pants as he went.

'Kezia, you're crazy. Why don't you go back to sleep

315

for a while?' She was standing there in a blue flannel nightgown and her white satin robe, her feet bare, her hair loose and long and dark. Her eyes looked alive again in the much too pale face.

'I can't sleep and I'm hungry. Did I wake you?'

'No, no, of course not. I always get up at six. In fact, I've been up since four.' He looked at her chidingly and she laughed.

'Okay, okay. I get the message. Is it too early to get you some coffee, and me some tea?'

'Sweetheart, this ain't the Fairmont. Do you really want to get moving that bad?'

She nodded. 'How soon can I see him?'

'I don't think they let you visit till eleven or twelve.' Christ, they could have had another four hours of sleep. Alejandro silently mourned the lost hours. He was half dead.

'Well, we're up now. We might as well stay up.'

'Wonderful. That's just what I wanted to hear. Kezia, if I didn't love you so much, and if your old man weren't such a fucking giant, I think right about now I'd kick your ass.'

She smiled delightedly at him. 'I love you too.'

He grinned at her, sat down, and lit a cigarette. She already had one in her hand, and he saw that the hand was still shaking, but aside from that and the pale, pointed look of her face, she looked better. Some sparkle had come back to her eyes, a hint of life and the old Kezia. The girl was a fighter for sure.

He vanished into the bathroom and came out with combed hair, brushed teeth, and a clean shirt.

'My, don't you look pretty.' She was wide awake and full of teasing this morning. It was a far cry from the condition she'd been in the morning before. At least that was a relief.

'You're just looking for trouble this morning, aren't you? Hasn't anyone ever told you not to bug a man before his first cup of coffee?'

'*Pobrecito!*'

He flipped her the finger and she laughed at him.

'And now that you've dragged me out of my warm bed, I suppose you're going to take two hours to dress.' He waved at the nighgown and robe.

'Make that five minutes.'

She was as good as her word. She was moving very quickly this morning, like a kid waiting for her first trip to the circus, up at dawn, nervous, jumpy, and already tired by breakfast. And they still had five hours to kill before they could see Luke.

Alejandro's thoughts drifted constantly to Luke now. How was he taking it? Was he all right? What was he thinking? Was he already back to the jailhouse living, the cold indifference of lost hopes, or was he still Luke? And if he had already reverted to what he'd once been, how big a shock would it be for Kezia? And how would she adjust to the visit? Alejandro knew it only too well, but he knew that she didn't. Visiting through a thick glass window, speaking on a static-ridden phone, with Luke wearing a filthy rumpled orange overall that would barely reach to his elbows and knees. He would be living in a cell with half a dozen other men, eating beans and stale bread and an imitation of meat, drinking coffee grinds and shitting with no toilet paper. It was one hell of a place to take Kezia, visiting with pimps and hookers and thieves and distraught mothers and hippie girls who would bring ragged children in their arms or on their backs. There would be noise and stench and agony. How much could she take? How far into this world would Luke lead her? And now it was on *his* back. It was Alejandro's baby. Taking care of Kezia.

There was a knock on his door that broke into his thoughts. Kezia again. Dressed and ready to go.

'Boy, you sure look gloomy as hell.'

His thoughts must have showed. 'Morning is not my best hour. I can't say the same for you, though. You look pretty sharp for tea at a truck stop.' She was, as usual,

317

expensively dressed. And there was a brittle cheeriness about her which was beginning to make him nervous. What if she cracked?

'Shouldn't we call a cab?' They had dispensed with the limousine when they checked into the Ritz, again with an oversized tip to buy the chauffeur's silence.

'We can walk. I know a place a few blocks away.'

They headed south in the damp air, and crept down the steep hills hand in hand.

'It's really such a beautiful city, isn't it, Al? Maybe we can go for a walk later today.'

He hoped not. He hoped Luke would tell her to get her ass on a plane to New York. By the end of the week, Luke would be back in Quentin, and there was no point in her staying for that. She couldn't visit him until she got clearance anyway, and that could take weeks. And sooner or later, she'd have to go home. Better sooner than later.

The truck stop was full but not crowded; the room was warm, and the jukebox was already alive. The aroma of coffee mingled with the odour of tired men, cigarette smoke and cigars. She was the only woman in the place, but invited only a few uninterested glances.

Alejandro made her order breakfast, and she made a face. He was unyielding. Two fried eggs, bacon, hash browns, and toast.

'For chrissake, Alejandro, I don't eat that much for dinner.'

'And you look it. Skinny upper-class broad.'

'Now don't be a snob.' She ate one piece of bacon, and played with the toast. The untouched eggs stared up at her like two jaundiced eyes.

'You're not eating.'

'I'm not hungry.'

'And you're smoking too much.'

'Yes, Daddy. Anything else?'

'Up yours, lady. Listen, you'd better take care of yourself, or I'll squeal to the boss.'

'You'd tell Lucas?'

318

'If I have to.' A flicker of worry flashed through her eyes.

'Listen, Alejandro, seriously. . . .'

'Yes?' He laughed at the way she was beginning to squirm.

'I'm serious. Don't upset Luke about anything. If he saw it, that hideous picture in the paper will be bad enough.'

Alejandro nodded, sobered, no longer teasing. They had both seen the small item on page three of the *Chronicle* that morning: Miss Saint Martin had not yet returned to New York; it was assumed that she was 'hiding' somewhere in the city. There was even some speculation about whether she had been hospitalized for nervous collapse. She had certainly looked well on her way to it in the pictures. But they also suggested that if she were in town, she'd probably show up on a visiting day to see Luke, 'unless Miss Kezia Saint Martin has pulled strings for private visiting privileges with Mr. Johns.'

'Gee, I never thought of that.'

'Want to give it a try? It may spare you some hassles with the press. It seems pretty clear they'll be watching for you on visiting days.'

'So let them. I'll go on the same day as everyone else, and visit just like everyone else does.'

Alejandro nodded. The remaining hours until visiting began to grind by. It seemed like weeks before it was a quarter to twelve.

# Chapter XXVIII

'Ready to go?' She nodded and picked up her handbag. 'Kezia, you're amazing.' She looked like an extremely pretty young woman without a care in the world. The makeup helped, but it was the way she carried herself, the mask she had slipped into place.

'Thank you, sir.' She looked tense but beautiful, and totally different from the sobbing woman he'd held in his arms in the City Hall corridor two days before. She was every inch a lady, and every ounce in control.

Only the tremor of her hands gave her away. If it weren't for that, she would have looked completely unruffled. Alejandro mused as he watched her. So that's what it was, the hallmark of class, to never show what you feel, as though you've never known a moment of sorrow. Just comb your hair, put it back in an elegant little knot, powder your nose, smack a smile on your face, and speak in a low subdued voice. Remember to say 'thank you' and 'please' and smile at the doorman. The mark of good breeding. Like a show dog, or a well-trained horse.

'Are you coming, Alejandro?' She was in a hurry to leave the hotel.

'Christ, woman, I can hardly keep my mind straight, and you stand there like you're going to a tea party. How do you do it?'

'Practice. It's a way of life.'

'It can't be healthy.'

'It's not. That's why half the people I grew up with are now alcoholics. The others live on pills, and in a few years a whole bunch of them will drop dead from heart attacks. Some of them have already managed to die.' A vision of Tiffany flashed through her mind. 'You cover up all your life, and one day you explode.'

'What about you?' He was following her down the hotel's ill-lighted stairs.

'I'm okay. I let off steam with my writing. And I can be myself with Luke . . . and now you.'

'No one else?'

'Not till now.'

'That's no way to live.'

'You know, Alejandro,' she said, when she had climbed into the cab, 'the trouble with pretending all the time is that eventually you forget who you are, and what you feel. You become the image.'

'How come you didn't then, babe?' But, as he watched her, he wondered. She was frighteningly cool.

'My writing, I guess. It helps me spill the grief in my guts. Gives me a place where I can be me. The other way, keeping it all in, sooner or later rots your soul.' She thought once more of Tiffany. That's what had happened to her, and others in the course of the years. Two of Kezia's friends had committed suicide since college.

'Luke'll feel better when he sees you, anyway.' And that was worth something. But Alejandro knew why she had worn the well-tailored black coat, the black gabardine slacks, the black suede shoes. Not for Lucas. But to make sure that the next picture in the paper showed her with it all in control. Elegant, uptight, and distinguished. There would be no collapse at the jail.

'You think there'll be press when we get there?'

'I don't think so, I know it.'

There was. Kezia and Alejandro got out of the cab at the front entrance of 850 Bryant Street. The Hall of Justice. It was an unimpressive grey building with none of the majesty of City Hall. Outside, a pair of sentries from the *Examiner* scouted her arrival. Another pair were pacing at the building's rear entrance. Kezia had a nose for them, like Luke did for police. She clung tightly to

Alejandro's arm while looking as though she barely held it, and quietly pulled her dark glasses over her eyes. There was a faint smile on her face.

She brushed quickly past a voice calling her name, while a second reporter spoke into a pocket-sized transmitter. Now they knew what lay ahead. Alejandro studied her face as a guard searched her handbag, but she looked surprisingly calm. A photographer snapped their picture, and with bowed heads they stepped quickly into an elevator in the salmon marble halls. It struck Kezia, as the doors closed, that the walls were the same colour as the gladioli at Italian funerals, and she laughed.

On the sixth floor, Alejandro led her quickly through another door and up a flight of strangely drafty stairs.

'A breeze from the River Styx perhaps?' There was irony and mischief in her voice. He couldn't get over it. Was this the Kezia he knew?'

She kept the glasses in place and he took her hand as they waited in line. The man in front of them smelled and was drunk, the black woman in front of him was obese and crying. Farther up the line, a few children were wailing and a bunch of hippies leaned back against the wall, laughing. They stood in a long thin line on the stairs, one by one reaching a desk at the top. Identification of visitor, name of inmate, and then a little pink ticket with a window number and a Roman numeral indicating a group. They were in Group II. The first group had already been herded inside. The stairs were crowded but there were no reporters in sight.

They moved inside, to a neon-lit room which boasted another desk, two guards, and three rows of benches. Beyond it they could see a long hall lined with windows, along which ran a shelf with a telephone every few feet, and a stool to sit on as you visited. It was awkward and uncomfortable. Group I was in the midst of its visit, destined to last five minutes or twenty, depending on the mood of the guards. Faces were animated, women giggled and then cried, inmates looked urgent and determined

322

and then let their faces relax at the sight of a three-year-old son. It was enough to tear your heart out.

Alejandro glanced at Kezia uncomfortably. She looked undaunted. Nothing showed. She smiled at him and lit another cigarette. And then suddenly the photographers swarmed them. Three cameramen and two reporters, even the local rep from *Women's Wear* was with them.

Alejandro felt a wave of claustrophobia engulf him. How did she stand it? The other visitors looked astonished and some backed away while others pressed forward to see what was happening. Suddenly, there was chaos, with Kezia in the eye of the storm, dark glasses in place, mouth set, looking stern but unshakably calm.

'Are you under sedation? Have you spoken to Luke Johns since the hearing? Are you. . . . Did you. . . . Will you. . . . Why?' She said nothing, only shaking her head.

'I have no comment to make. Nothing to say.' Alejandro felt useless beside her. She remained in her seat, bowed her head, as though by not seeing them, they might disappear. But then unexpectedly, she stood up and spoke to them in a low, subdued voice.

'I think that's enough now. I told you, I have nothing to say.' A burst of flashes went off in her face, and two guards came to the rescue. The press would have to wait outside, they were disrupting the visiting. Even the inmates having visits had stopped talking and were watching the group around Kezia and the flashes of light that went off every few seconds.

A guard called her aside to the desk, as the photographers and reporters reluctantly exited. Alejandro joined her, realizing he hadn't said a word since the onslaught began. He felt lost in the stir. He had never even thought of dealing with something like that, but she handled it well. That surprised him. There had been no trace of panic, but then again it wasn't new to her either.

The head guard leaned close to them and made a suggestion. A guard could accompany them when they left. They could take an elevator straight into the police garage in the basement, where a cab could be waiting. Alejandro leapt at the idea, and Kezia gratefully agreed. She was even paler than she had been, and the tremor in her hands was now a steady fluttering. The paparazzi attack had taken its toll.

'Do you suppose I might see Mr. Johns in a private room somewhere up here?' She was rapidly abandoning her determination to shun special favours. The curious crowd was becoming almost as oppressive as the press. But her request was denied. Nevertheless, a young guard was assigned to hover nearby.

A voice called out the end of the first visit, and guards ushered Group I into a cage where they could wait for the elevator without disturbing the next group. It was strange to watch the difference in faces as they left – pained, shocked, silent. Their moment of laughter had ended. Women clutched little slips of paper with orders, requests: toothpaste, socks, the name of a lawyer a cellmate had suggested.

'Group Two!' The voice boomed into her thoughts, and Alejandro took her elbow. The pink slip of paper in her hand was crumpled and limp, but they checked it for the number of the window where they'd visit Luke.

There would be other visitors at close range on either side, but the promised guard was standing beside them. It seemed like a very long wait. Ten minutes, maybe fifteen. It felt endless. And then they came. From behind a steel door, a line of dirty wrinkled orange suits, unshaven faces, unwashed teeth, and broad smiles. Luke was fifth on the line. Alejandro took one look at his face and knew he was all right, and then he watched Kezia.

Unconsciously, she got to her feet as she saw him, stood very straight, to her full tiny height, a blistering smile on her face. Her eyes came alive. She looked incredibly beautiful. And she must have looked even better to Luke. Their eyes met and held and she almost danced on the spot. Until finally he got to the phone.

'Why's the goon standing behind you?'

324

'Lucas!'

'All right, the *guard*.' They exchanged a smile.

'To keep away the curious.'

'Trouble?'

'Paparazzi.'

Luke nodded. 'Someone said there was a movie star out here, and a lot of reporters took her picture. I take it that's you?'

She nodded.

'Are you okay?'

'I'm fine.' He didn't question that, and she wouldn't have confessed to being other than "fine," if he had. His eyes momentarily sought Alejandro, who nodded and smiled.

'That picture of you in the paper was the shits, Mama.'

'Yeah, it was.'

'I freaked out when I saw it. Looked like you were having a stroke.'

'Don't be a jerk. And I'm all back together now.'

'Did that scoop hit New York?'

She nodded again.

'Jesus. You must have heard about it from Edward.'

'You might say that. But he'll survive.' She smiled ruefully.

'Will you?'

She nodded as he searched her face.

'What did he say?'

'Nothing unexpected. He was just worried.'

'What a bitch for you to have to go through that on top of everything else.' It was odd the way they were talking, as though they were sitting side by side on the couch.

'Bullshit. Besides, Lucas, we've really been lucky till now. It could have happened long before this.'

'Yeah, but we could have gotten press coverage in a lot better circumstances.'

She nodded and smiled, anxious to turn to other subjects. They had so little time.

325

'Are you all right, darling? Really?'

'Baby, I'm used to this shit. I'm A-I okay.'

'We're still engaged, you know, Mr. Johns.'

'Mama, I love you.'

'I adore you.' Her whole face glowed as she melted into his eyes.

They discussed legal technicalities, and he gave her a list of calls to make, but basically he had taken care of all his own business before they came out for the hearing. He had known what the chances were, better than she had.

The rest of their visit was spent on banalities, jokes, teasing, sarcastic descriptions of the food, but he looked surprisingly well. The grimness was not unfamiliar to him. He spoke to Alejandro for a few minutes, and then pointed back at Kezia. She removed an earring again and picked up the phone as Luke looked over his shoulder towards a voice she couldn't hear.

'I think this is going to be it. Visiting is about over.'

'Oh.' A dim light flickered in her eyes. 'Luke . . .'

'Listen, babe, I want you to do something for me. I want you to go back to New York tonight. I already told Alejandro.'

'Lucas, why?'

'What are you going to do here? Hang out till I get to Q, and then wait three weeks till I get clearance for visits, and see me once a week for an hour? Don't be an ass, babe. I want you at home.' Besides, it was safer. Even though now, she wasn't really in danger. Now that he was on ice, all the factions warring against him would be appeased. Kezia was of no real interest. Still, he didn't want to take chances with her.

'Go to New York, and then what, Luke?'

'Do what you do, Mama. Write, work, live. You're not in here, I am. Don't forget that.'

'Lucas, you . . . darling, I love you. I want to stay here in San Francisco.'

She was fierce, but he was more so. 'You're going. I'm

leaving for Quentin on Friday. And I'll put the forms in for you to visit. When they get processed, you can come back. Figure about three weeks. I'll let you know when.'

'Can I write to you?'

'Does a bear shit in the woods?' He grinned at her.

'Lucas!' The tenseness broke into laughter. 'You must be all right.'

'I am. So you be fine too. And tell that idiot friend of mine that he'd better take care of you or he'll be one dead Mexican when I get out.'

'How charming. I'm sure he'll be thrilled.'

And then it was suddenly over. A guard called something on Luke's side of the glass wall, and another guard told them they'd had it on the visitors' side. She felt Alejandro's hand on her arm, and Lucas stood up.

'That's it, Mama. I'll write.'

'I love you.'

'I love you, too.' The entire world seemed to stop with those words. It was as though he placed them one by one in her heart via his eyes. He said them, and held her close with a look, and then gently he put down the phone. Her eyes never left him as he walked back through the door, and this time he looked back, with a jaunty grin and a wave. She answered with a wave and her most valiant smile. And then he was gone.

The guard who had stood behind them now took them aside and showed them the way to the separate elevator. A cab had been called and was already waiting in the garage. There were no reporters in sight. In a moment, they were in the cab and speeding from the building and Luke. They were alone again, Alejandro and Kezia, and now she had nothing to look forward to. The visit was over. And his words rang in her ears, as his image filled her mind's eye. She wanted to be alone just then, with the dreams of the recent and distant past. The still new aquamarine sparkled on her trembling hand as she lit a cigarette and fought for control.

'He wants us to go back to New York.' She spoke to

Alejandro without looking at him and her voice sounded hoarse.

'I know.' He had expected a fight. It surprised him to hear her say it so bluntly. 'Are you up to the trip?' It would be best if she was, to just get the hell out and let her pick up the pieces at home, and not at the Ritz.

'I'm fine. I think there's a plane at four. Let's catch it.'

'We'll have to run like the devil.' He looked at his watch, and she discreetly blew her nose.

'I think we can make it.' Her voice kept him a thousand miles away, and it was the last time they spoke until they boarded the plane.

## CHAPTER XXIX

The voice on the phone had grown familiar and dear.

'I'm hungry. Any chance that you'll feed me?' It was Alejandro. They had been back in New York for a week. A week of constant calls from him, unexpected visits, small bunches of flowers, problems he supposedly needed her help to resolve, ruses and excuses and tenderness.

'I suppose I might drum up some tuna surprise.'

'That's what they eat on Park Avenue? Shit, I eat better uptown. But the company's not as good there. Besides, I've got a problem.'

'Another one? Bullshit. Honest, love, I'm okay. You don't have to come down here again.'

'What if I want to?'

'Then I shall rejoice at the pleasure of seeing you.' She smiled into the phone.

'So formal. And serving tuna surprise yet. Any news from Luke?'

'Yep. Two great big fat letters. And a visiting form for me to fill out. Hallelujah! Fifteen more days and then I can visit.'

'Keep your shirt on. Did he say anything else? Or just a lot of corny shit I don't want to hear?'

'Lots of that. And he also said he was in a four-by-nine cell with another guy. Sounds cosy, doesn't it?'

'Very. Any other good news?' He didn't like the sound of her voice when she told him. Bitterness had begun to replace grief.

'Nothing much otherwise. He said to send you his love.'

'I owe him a letter. I'll do it this week. And what did you do today? Write anything sexy?'

She laughed at the thought. 'Yeah, I wrote a very sexy book review for the Washington *Post*.'

'Fantastic. You can read it to me when I get there.'

He arrived two hours later, with a small plant and a bag of hot chestnuts.

'How are things at the centre? Mmm ... yummy ... have another one.' She was shelling the hot nuts in her lap in front of the fire.

'The centre's not bad. It's been worse.' But not much. He didn't want to tell her that now. The way things were going, he'd be gone in a month, maybe two. But she'd had enough of her own changes recently, without having to listen to his.

'So what's this alleged problem you want to discuss with me?'

'Problem? Oh! *That* problem!'

'Liar ... but you're a sweet liar. And a good friend.'

'All right. I'll confess. I just wanted an excuse to see you.' He hung his head like a kid.

'Flattery, dear Alejandro ... I adore it.' She grinned up at him and tossed him another chestnut. He watched her as she leaned her back against a chair, warming her feet by the fire. There was a smile on her lips. But the spark had gone dead in her eyes. Daily, she was looking worse. She had lost a lot of weight, she was deathly pale, and her hands still shook almost constantly. Not a lot, but enough. He didn't like it. He didn't like it at all.

'How long has it been since you've been out, Kezia?'

'Out of what?'

'Don't play dumb with me, asshole. You know what I mean. Out of this house. Outdoors. In the fresh air.' He eyed her directly, but she avoided his gaze.

'Oh that. Actually, not for a while.'

'How long is a while? Three days? A week?'

'I don't know, a couple of days, I guess. Mainly, I've been worried about being swarmed by the press.'

'Bullshit. You told me three days ago that they didn't call anymore, and they haven't been hanging around the building. The story is dead, Kezia, and you know it. So what's keeping you home?'

'Lethargy. Fatigue. Fear.'

'Fear of what?'

'I haven't figured that out yet.'

'Look, babe, a lot of things have changed for you, and very brutally and suddenly at that. But you have to get back to doing something with yourself. Go out, see people, get some air. Hell, go shopping if that's what turns you on, but don't lock yourself up in here. You're beginning to turn green.'

'How terribly chic.' But she had gotten the point.

'Want to go for a walk now?'

She didn't, but she knew that she ought to. 'Okay.'

They wandered towards the park in silence, holding hands, and she kept her eyes down. They were almost at the zoo before she spoke.

'Alejandro, what am I going to do?'

'About what?' He knew, but he wanted to hear it from her.

'My life.'

'Give yourself time to adjust. Then figure it out. It's still much too fresh. In a sense, you're in shock.'

'That's what it feels like. Like I'm wandering around in a daze. I forget to eat. I forget if the mail has come, I can't remember what day of the week it is. I start to work, and then my mind wanders and I look up and it's two hours later and I haven't finished the sentence I was typing. It's crazy. I feel like one of those little old ladies who burrow into their houses, and someone has to keep reminding them to put the other stocking on, and to finish their soup.'

'You're not that bad yet. You cleaned up those chestnuts pretty quick.'

'No. But I'm getting there, Alejandro. I just feel so vague . . . and so lost . . .'

'All you can do is be good to yourself, and wait till you feel more yourself.'

'Yeah, and in the meantime I look at his stuff in the closet. I lie in bed, and wait to hear his key in the door, and I kid myself that he's in Chicago and he'll be back in the morning. It's driving me goddamn nuts.'

'No wonder. Look, babe, he's not dead.'

'No. But he's gone. And I've come to rely on him so much. In thirty years, or ten adult ones anyway, I've never relied on a man. But with Luke, I let myself go, I tore down all the walls. I leaned all over him, and now . . . I feel like I'm going to fall over.'

'Now?' He tried to tease her a little.

'Oh shut up.'

'All right, seriously. The fact is that he's gone and you're not. You're going to have to pick up your life. Sooner or later.'

She nodded again, dug her hands deeper into her pockets, and they walked on. They had reached the horse carriages at the Plaza before she looked up.

'It must be quite a hotel,' Alejandro said. In a way, it reminded him of the Fairmont.

'Haven't you ever been in it? Just for a look?' She was surprised when he shook his head.

'Nope. No reason to. This isn't exactly my part of town.' She smiled at him and slipped her hand through his arm.

'Come on, let's go in.'

'I'm not wearing a tie.' The idea made him nervous.

'And I look like a slob. But they know me. They'll let us in.'

'I bet they will.' He laughed at her, and they marched up the steps to the Plaza, looking as though they had decided to buy the place on a lark.

They walked past the powdered dowagers eating pastry to the strains of violins in the Palm Court, and Kezia guided him expertly down the mysterious halls. They heard Japanese, Spanish, Swedish, a flurry of French, and the music that reminded Alejandro of old Garbo movies. The Plaza was more grandiose than the Fairmont, and much more alive.

They stopped at a door while Kezia peeked inside. The room was large and opulent with the endless oak panelling that had given it its name. There was a long elaborate bar, and a lovely view of the park.

'Louis?' She signalled to the headwaiter as he approached with a smile.

'Mademoiselle Saint Martin, *comment ça va! Quel plaisir!*'

'Hello Louis. Do you suppose you could squeeze us into a quiet table? We're not dressed.'

'*Aucune importance.* That is not a problem!' He assured them so magnanimously that Alejandro was convinced they could have arrived stark naked, and possibly should have.

They settled at a small table in the corner, and Kezia dug into the nuts.

'Well, do you like it?'

'It's quite something.' He looked a bit awed. 'Do you come here a lot?'

'No. I used to. As much as one can. Women are only allowed in at certain times.'

'A stag bar, eh?'

'You're close. Rhymes with ...' She giggled. 'Fags, darling, fags. I suppose you might say this is the most elegant gay bar in New York.' He laughed in answer and took a look around. She was right. There were a number of gay men scattered here and there - a very large number as he took a second look. They were by far the most elegant men in the room. The others all looked like solid businessmen, and dull.

'You know, Kezia, when I look around a place like this, I know why you wound up with Luke. I used to wonder. Not that there's anything wrong with Lucas. But I'd expected you to hang out with some Wall Street lawyer.'

'I tried that for a while. He was gay.'

'Jesus.'

'Yeah. But what did you mean when you said "when you look around a place like this"?'

'Just that the men in your set don't knock me out.'

'Oh. Well, they don't knock me out either. That was always the trouble.'

'And now what? You go back to the old world?'

'I don't know if I can, or why I should bother. I think most likely I'll wait for Luke to get out.' He didn't say anything, and they ordered another round of scotch.

'What about your friend Edward? Have you made peace with him?' Alejandro still shuddered at the memory of the half-crazed voice on the phone at the Fairmont after the hearing.

'After a fashion. I don't think he'll ever really forgive me for the scandal. It makes him feel like a failure, since in a sense he brought me up. But at least the papers have cooled it. And people forget. I'm already old news.' She shrugged and took another swallow of scotch. 'Besides, people let me get away with a lot. If you have enough money they call you eccentric and think you're amusing. If you don't have the bucks they call you a perverted pig and an asshole. It's disgusting, but it's true. You'd be aghast at some of the things my friends get away with. Nothing as mundane as my "outrageous" love affair with Luke.'

'Do you care if people get upset about Lucas?'

'Not really. It's my business, not theirs. A lot has changed in the last few months. Mostly me. It's just as well Edward, for instance, had this illusion of me as a child.'

Alejandro wanted to say 'So do I,' but he didn't. She had that quality about her; it had something to do with her size and her seeming fragility.

They left after their third round of scotch, on equally empty stomachs, both high as kites.

'You know what's funny?' She was laughing so hard she could barely stand up, but the cold air had sobered them both a little.

'What's funny?'

'I don't know . . . everything is . . .' She laughed again, and he wiped tears of cold and mirth from his eyes.

'Hey, you want a buggy ride?'

'Yes!' They piled aboard and Alejandro instructed the driver to take them to Kezia's. It was a cosy carriage with an old raccoon lap robe. They snuggled under it and giggled all the way home, insulated by the raccoon and the scotch.

'Can I tell you a secret, Alejandro?'

'Sure. I love secrets.' He held her close so she wouldn't fall out. That was as good an excuse as any.

'I've been drunk every night since I got back.'

He looked at her through his own haze of scotch and shook his head. 'That's dumb. I won't let you do that to yourself.'

'You're such a nice man. Alejandro, I love you.'

'I love you too.'

They sat side by side and rode the rest of the way to her house in silence. He paid for the hansom cab and they rode up to her apartment, giggling in the elevator.

'You know, I think I'm too drunk to cook.'

'Just as well. I think I'm too drunk to eat.'

'Yeah. Me too.'

'Kezia, you should eat. . . .'

'Later. Want to come to dinner tomorrow?'

'I'll be there. With a lecture.' He tried to look grave but couldn't master the expression and she laughed at him.

'Then I won't let you in.'

'Then I'll huff and I'll puff and I'll blow ...' They both collapsed in the kitchen with mirth, and he tipsily kissed the tip of her nose. 'I've got to go. But I'll see you tomorrow. And make me a promise?'

'What?' All of a sudden he had looked so serious.

'No more drinking tonight, Kezia. Promise?'

'I ... uh ... yeah ... okay.' But it was a promise she was not planning to keep.

She saw him to the elevator, and waved cheerily as the door closed, before coming back to the kitchen and bringing out the rest of last night's fresh bottle of scotch. She was surprised that there was only an inch or so left.

It was odd, but as she poured what was left into a tumbler with one ice cube, the vision of Tiffany's funeral flashed into mind. It was a dumb way to die, but the others all left such a big mess. At least drinking wasn't messy ... not really ... not very ... or was it? She didn't really give a damn, as she smiled to herself and drained the full glass.

The phone was ringing but she didn't bother to answer it. It couldn't have been Luke. Even drunk she knew that much. Luke was away on a trip ... in Tahiti ... on a safari ... and there were no phones there ... but he'd be back at the end of the week. She was sure of it. Friday. And let's see ... what was today? Tuesday? Monday? Thursday! He'd be home tomorrow. She opened a fresh bottle. Bourbon this time. For Lucas. He'd be coming home soon.

## CHAPTER XXX

'Child, you look awfully thin.'

'Marina just called it "divinely svelte". She and Halpern just walked by.' The wedding had been held over the New Year's holiday in Palm Beach.

Edward slid onto the banquette beside her. It was their first lunch in almost two months. And now she looked so different it shocked him.

Her eyes were sunken into her head, her skin looked taut on her cheekbones, and there was not even lustre where once there had been fire. What a price she had paid. And for what? It still horrified him, but he had promised her not to discuss it. That was the condition on which she'd accepted his invitation to lunch. And he wanted so much to see her. Maybe there was still a chance to regain what they'd lost.

'Sorry I was late, Kezia.'

'Not to worry, love. I had a drink while I waited.' And that was new too. But at least she was still impeccably groomed. Even more so than usual, in fact. She looked almost formal. The mink coat she so seldom wore was thrown over the back of a chair.

'Why so dressed up today, my dear? Going somewhere after lunch?' Normally, she played it down, but not today, and the rare appearance of the mink coat surprised him.

'I'm turning over a new leaf. Coming home to roost, as they say.' Luke's letter that morning had insisted that she at least try her old stamping grounds again. It was better than sitting home sulking – or drinking, a new habit he didn't know about. But she had decided to try his advice. That was why she had accepted the luncheon with Edward, and dragged out the fur coat. But she felt like an ass. Or like Tiffany, trying to dress up disaster with breath mints and fur.

'What do you mean by "turning over a new leaf"?' He didn't dare mention the Luke Johns affair, she might have walked out on the spot. And he was afraid of that. He signalled the waiter to order their usual Louis Roederer champagne. The waiter looked harassed but showed he understood, with a smile.

'Oh, let's just say that I'm making an effort to be a nice girl, and see some of my old friends.'

'Whitney?' Edward was a little taken aback.

'I said I was being nice, not ridiculous, darling. No, I just thought I'd "come back" and take a look around.' The champagne arrived, the waiter poured, Edward tasted and nodded approval. The waiter poured again for both of them, and Edward lifted his glass in a toast.

'Then allow me to say welcome home.' He wanted to ask if she had learned her lesson, but he didn't dare. Perhaps she had, though . . . perhaps she had. And in any case, her little misadventure had certainly aged her. She looked five years more than her age, particularly in a simple lilac wool dress and her grandmother's remarkable pearls. And then he noticed the ring. He glanced at it and nodded approval. 'Very pretty. Something new?'

'Yes. Luke got it for me in San Francisco.' Something pinched in his face again. Bitterness. Anger.

'I see.' There was no further comment, and Kezia finished her drink while Edward sipped his champagne.

'How is the writing these days?'

'It'll do. I haven't written anything I like in a while. And yes, Edward, I know. But looking at me like that won't change a damn thing. I know all about it.' She was suddenly sick of the constant arch in his brows. 'That's right, darling, I'm not writing as well as I should. I've lost twelve pounds since you last saw me, I lock myself up at home because I'm terrified of reporters, and I look ten years older. I know all about it. We both know I've had a rough time. And we both know why, so stop looking so fucking shocked and disapproving. It's really a dead bore.'

'*Kezia!*'

'Yes, Edward?'

He realized then from the look in her eyes that she had had more to drink than he'd thought. He was so stunned that he half turned in his seat and eyed her intensely.

'Okay, darling, what now? Is my mascara on crooked?'

'You're drunk.' His voice was barely a whisper.

'Yes, I am,' she whispered back with a bitter little

smile. 'And I'm going to get drunker. How's that for a fun day?' He sat back in his seat with a sigh, searching for the right words to say, and then he saw her. The reporter from *Women's Wear Daily*, eyeing them from across the room.

'Damn.'

'Is that all you can say, love? I'm turning myself into an alcoholic and all you can think of is "damn"?' She was playing with him now, evilly, meanly, but she couldn't help herself. She was shocked when she felt his grip on her arm.

'Kezia, that woman from *Women's Wear* is over there and if you do anything, anything to catch her attention or antagonize her, I'll ... you'll regret it.' Kezia laughed a deep-throated laugh and kissed his cheek. She thought it was funny, and Edward felt the sinking feeling of events slipping away from him, out of control. She wanted to bait everyone; she didn't want to 'come home'. She didn't even know where home was. And she was worse than Liane had ever been. So much more brazen, so much stronger, tougher, more wilful ... and so much more beautiful. He had never loved her more than now, at this instant, and all he wanted to do was shake her, or slap her. And then make love to her. Right in the middle of La Grenouille if he had to. The ideas suddenly running through his mind shocked him, and he shook his head as though to clear it. As he did, he felt Kezia patting his hand.

'Don't be afraid of silly old Sally, Edward, she won't bite you. She just wants a story.' He found himself wondering if they should leave now, before they had lunch. But that might make a scene too. He felt trapped.

'Kezia. . . .' He was almost trembling with fear, and all he could do was take her hand in his, look into her eyes and pray that she'd behave herself and not create a scene. 'Please.' Kezia saw the pain in his eyes, and it was like scalding oil on her soul. She didn't want to see his feelings, not now. She couldn't handle her own, let alone his.

'All right, Edward. All right.' She looked away, her voice subdued again, and noticed the *WWD* reporter making little notes on a pad. But there would be no further story. Only that they had been seen. She was not going to make trouble. They'd all had enough. 'I'm sorry.' She said it with the sigh of a child, leaning back against the banquette, as relief swept over Edward. It made him feel tender again.

'Kezia, why can't I help you?'

'Because nobody can.' There were tears trembling on her lashes. 'Just try to accept that there isn't a hell of a lot you can do for me right now. The present is what it is, and the past happened, and the future . . . well, I don't see it too clearly right now. Maybe that's the trouble.' She often found herself wondering now if this was what Tiffany had felt. As though someone had stolen the future. They had left her the large emerald ring and the pearls, but no future. It was hard to explain it to Edward. He was always so certain of everything. It made him seem far away too.

'Do you regret the past, Kezia?' But he looked up with horror at the reaction in her eyes. He had said the wrong thing again. Lord, it was hard to talk to the girl. Crucifixion over lunch.

'If you are referring to Lucas, Edward, of course I don't regret it. He's the only decent thing that's happened to me in the last ten or twenty, or maybe even thirty years. What I regret is the revocation. There's nothing I can do about it now. There's nothing anyone can do. You can't appeal a revocation of parole. It's totally pointless.'

'I see. I didn't realize you were still that involved in this . . . this problem. I thought that after . . .'

She cut him off, with a look of extreme aggravation.

'You thought wrong. And just so you don't die of the shock if you see it in the papers, I'm going back out there shortly.'

'What in God's name for?' He was speaking to her

339

*sotto voce* so no one would hear, but Kezia was speaking in her normal voice.

'To visit him, obviously. And I told you, I don't want to discuss it. And do you know something, Edward? I'm finding this entire subject inappropriate with you, and this lunch unbearably boring. As a matter of fact, darling, I think I've about had it.' Her voice was rising to an unpleasant timbre, and Edward could feel himself squirm inside the starch in his collar. He was hating every minute of it. She drained her glass, looked around the room for a minute, and then looked back at him strangely.

'Kezia, are you all right? You looked rather pale for a moment.' He looked terribly worried.

'No, really, I'm fine.'

'Shall I have them get you a cab?'

'Yes, maybe I ought to go. To tell you the truth, it's a hell of a strain. That bitch from *Women's Wear* has been watching us since we sat down, and all of a sudden I feel like the whole goddamn place is watching me to see what kind of shape I'm in. It's all I can do not to stand up and tell them all to go fuck themselves.'

Edward blanched. 'No, Kezia. I don't think you ought to do that.'

'Oh hell, darling, why not? For a laugh?'

She was playing with him again, and so cruelly. Why? Why did she have to do that to him? Didn't she know that he cared? That it tore him apart to see her this way . . . that he was not made merely of white shirts and dark suits . . . that someone lived inside the elegant tailoring, a heart . . . a body . . . a man. Tears burned his eyes and there was a gruffness in his voice as he quietly stood and took Kezia's arm. He looked different now, and she sensed it too. The games were over.

'Kezia, you're leaving now.' She could hardly hear his words, but she could have read his tone from across the room. She was being dismissed like a naughty child.

'Are you very angry?' She whispered it to him as he helped her into her mink. She was frightened now. She had only wanted to play ... wanted to ... hurt. They both knew it.

'No. Only very sorry. For you.' He guided her towards the door, keeping a firm grip on her elbow. She was going to have no chance to misbehave between the table and the door. The fun was over. And she felt oddly submissive at his side. He cast a few frosty smiles left and right as they made their way out. He didn't want anyone to think there was trouble, and Kezia looked dreadful.

They stood for a moment at the cloakroom while he waited for the girl to retrieve his coat and homburg.

'Edward, I ...' She had started to cry now and held tightly to his arm.

'Kezia, not here.' Enough was enough. He couldn't bear it anymore.

She swept the tears away with one hand gloved in black suede, and tried out a wintry smile.

'Where are you going from here? Home to lie down, I hope.' And get hold of yourself. He didn't say it, but it was in his eyes, as he settled the homburg into place.

'Actually, I was going to show up at the Arthritis Ball meeting today. But I don't know if I'm up to it.'

'I don't think you are.'

'Yes. But I haven't been there in so long.' And now there's Tiffany's place to fill as the local socialite lush. ... Motherfucking old bags. Oh God, what if she said ... what if ... what if. ... She felt a rush of heat follow the wave of pale green and wondered if she was going to faint or throw up. That would make a story for *WWD*.

Edward took charge of her elbow again and led her out to the street. The cold air seemed to restore her. She took a deep breath and felt better.

'Do you have any idea what it's like to watch you do this to yourself? And for ... for ...' Her eyes sought his but he couldn't stop himself anymore. 'For nothing. For that ... that no one. Kezia, for God's sake, stop now. Write to him, tell him you don't want to see him again. Tell him. ...'

Her words stopped him cold. 'Are you telling me this is a choice?' She stood still, watching him.

'What do you mean?' He felt ice trickle slowly down his back.

'You know exactly what I mean. Is this a choice, Edward? Your friendship or his love?'

No, little girl, my love or his. But he couldn't say that to her.

'Because if that's what you're saying ... then I'm saying goodbye.' She held out her arm before he could answer and stopped a cab that was passing. It came to a screeching halt just beyond the canopy.

'No, Kezia, I ...'

'See you soon, darling.' She pecked at his cheek before he could regain his composure and slipped quickly into the cab. Before he knew it she was gone. Gone. '... then I'm saying goodbye.' How could she? And so heartlessly, without any emotion in her eyes.

But what he didn't know was that she couldn't give up Luke. Not for anyone. Not even for him. Luke was her route to escape from the world that had haunted her. Luke had shown her the way out; now she had to stick with him. She couldn't turn back. Not even for Edward. And alone in the cab, she wanted to die. She had done it. She had killed him. Killed Edward. It was like killing her father ... like killing Tiffany again. Why did someone always have to get mutilated, Kezia wondered as she drove uptown, fighting back sobs. And why Edward? Why him? He only had her, and she knew it. But maybe it had to be. She couldn't leave Luke, and if it was a question of loyalty ... Edward could take it. He was so sturdy. He would always weather what had to be borne. He was good about those things. He understood.

Kezia did not know that he would spend the rest of the day walking, looking into faces, looking at women, and thinking of her.

The cab drew up outside the Fifth Avenue address

Kezia had given. She was right on time for the meeting. The committee would be beginning to gather. She thought of their faces as she paid the driver the fare. ... All those faces ... and mink coats ... and sapphires ... and emeralds ... and ... she felt a wave of panic sweep over her. The lunch with Edward had left her drained, and she didn't feel able to cope. She paused for a moment before going inside the building. And then she knew. She couldn't go in. The prying eyes at La Grenouille had been bad enough. But at least they had to keep their distance. The women on the committee didn't, and they'd be all over her in an instant, with snide questions and sneering asides. And of course they had all seen the newspaper photographs of her collapsing in court, and read every word of the story. It was simply too much to handle.

The snow crunched beneath her feet as she walked to the corner to hail another cab and go home. She wanted to flee. She had unthinkingly walked back into the insanity of her life before Luke. And even for a day it unnerved her. From cab to cab, from luncheon to meeting to nowhere to nothing to drink to drank to drunk. She wondered what in God's name she was doing.

It was snowing and she was hatless and without boots, but she pulled the mink coat tightly around her and sank her gloved hands into her pockets. It was only a twelve-block walk to her house, and she needed the air.

She trudged all the way home, her suede shoes soaking wet on her feet, her hair damp, and when she got home her cheeks were aflame and her legs felt icy and numb, but she felt alive and sober again. She had pulled her hair from its knot and let it fall around her shoulders, gathering a mantilla of snow.

The doorman rushed to her side with his half-broken umbrella as he saw her loom from the snow and darkness, and she laughed as he approached.

'No, no, Thomas. I'm fine!' She felt like a child again, and the sodden shoes didn't matter at all. It was the sort

343

of performance that would have won her days of scolding as a child. Totie might even have reported her to Edward for something like that. But Totie was a thing of the past now, as was Edward. She had seen that today. She could walk in the snow all night now if she wanted. It didn't really matter. Nothing did. Except Luke.

But at least the buzzing sound had left her head, her shoulders didn't feel quite so heavy, her spirit felt clean. Even the drinks had been washed away by the cold and the snow.

The doorbell rang just as she peeled off her stockings and struck her cold feet under the hot water tap in the tub. They tingled and hurt and turned red. She debated answering the door, and decided rapidly not to. It was obviously just the elevator man with a package; had it been a visitor they would have called from downstairs for permission to send someone up. But the bell was persistent, and finally she dried her feet in one of the big monogrammed towels, and ran to the door.

'Yes? Who is it?'

'Cesar Chavez.'

'Who?'

'It's Alejandro, you dummy.'

She pulled open the door. 'Good lord, you look like Frosty the Snowman. Did you walk?'

'All the way.' He looked terribly pleased with himself. 'I think I love New York after all. When it snows anyway. Isn't it great?'

She nodded with a broad smile of agreement. 'Come on in.'

'I was hoping you'd say that. They rang from downstairs for ages, but you didn't answer. The guy said you were home, and I must have looked honest or cold, because he let me come up.'

'I had the water running in the tub.' She looked down at her bare feet which were now almost purple from the return of circulation after the shock of the tub. 'I walked home too. It felt great.'

'What happened? Couldn't find a cab?'

'Nope. I just felt like walking. It was sort of a crazy day, and I needed to unwind.'

'What happened?' He looked faintly worried.

'Nothing much. I had one of those unbearably fancy lunches with Edward, and it was a hell of a strain. Between his dismal failure at not looking disapproving, and the stares of the rest of the people there, not to mention a *Women's Wear* reporter creeping up on us . . . I got a bad case of the freaks. And then to make matters worse, I took myself off to a benefit meeting, and flaked out before I walked in the door. That's when I decided to walk home.'

'Sounds like you needed it.'

'Yeah. I just can't play the old games anymore. I can't even begin to tackle the double life nonsense again, and I won't do it. That life just doesn't suit me. I'd rather be here by myself.'

'Are you telling me to leave?'

'Don't be a jerk.'

He chuckled, and she took his sopping wet coat, and hung it on the kitchen door.

'I must admit, that whole trip sounds pretty bad.'

'Worse . . . but dahling, how divine you look, isn't that the wet look by Cardin . . . oh, and your ring!' She picked up the hand where he had a large rough Indian turquoise. 'But the ring is David Webb of course . . . his nnneeewwww collection, daaahhhling? Ah, and of course sneakers by Macy's. What an exquisite idea!' She made a face and rolled her eyes. 'I mean, Jesus, Alejandro, how can anyone breathe under all that shit?'

'Wear a snorkel?'

'You're impossible. I'm being serious.'

'Forgive me.' He settled down on the couch after having dumped his sneakers with his coat in the kitchen. 'Hell, you used to live that life fairly successfully, didn't you?'

'Sure. As long as I was sneaking around on subways to

345

meet my lover in SoHo, or flying off to meet Luke in Chicago. Besides, I had to do all that dumb shit for the column.'

'Bullshit. You didn't just "have to," you wanted to, or you wouldn't have done it.'

'That's not necessarily true. But in any case, I don't want to do it anymore, and I won't. Besides, everyone knows I won't play the game now, so why try to pretend? But the point is what do I do now? I don't fit there, and Luke's not here, which leaves me feeling . . . aimless, I guess is the best way to put it. Any suggestions?'

'Yeah. Make me a cup of hot chocolate. Then I'll solve all your problems.'

'That's a deal. Want some brandy in it?'

'Nope. I'll take it straight, thanks.' He didn't want to give her an excuse to start drinking. She didn't need much of an excuse, but he thought she might balk at drinking alone. He was right.

'You're not much fun, but in that case I'll have mine straight too. I think I've been drinking too much lately.'

'No kidding. When did you figure that out? After A.A. called you with a free subscription, or before?'

'Don't be nasty.'

'What do you want me to do? Keep my mouth shut till you wind up with cirrhosis?'

'That sounds fine.'

'Jesus, Kezia, that's not even funny. You really piss me off!' And he looked it as she vanished into the kitchen.

She appeared a few minutes later with two steaming mugs of hot chocolate. 'And how was your day?'

'Stinking, thanks. I had a minor altercation with my board of directors. At least they thought it was minor. I almost quit.'

'You did? How come?'

'The usual garbage. Allotment of funds. I got so annoyed I told them I was taking two days off.'

'That must have pleased them. What are you going to do with the two days?'

'Fly out to San Francisco with you to see Luke. When are you going?'

'Good lord, Alejandro! Can you do that?' She was delighted, but he had just spent so much money coming out with them to the hearing.

'Sure I can do it. But not in first-class. Are you willing to sit with the peasants at the back of the bus?'

'I think I can stand it. Do you play backgammon? I can bring my small set.'

'How about poker?'

'You're on. To tell you the truth, I'm glad you're coming. . . . I was thinking about it this morning, and I think I'm scared to death of this trip.'

'Why?' That surprised him.

'San Quentin. It sounds so awful. And I've never been any place like it.'

'It's not exactly a joy ride, but it's not a dungeon either. You'll be okay.' But just to be sure, he was going. Luke had urgently requested that he come out with her. And Alejandro knew he wouldn't ask unless there was a damn good reason. Something was happening.

'Listen, are you coming out just because you figured I was afraid to do it alone?' The idea amazed her.

'Don't be so egocentric. He happens to be my friend too.' She blushed faintly and he tugged at a lock of the rumpled black hair. 'Besides, after what I've seen you come through, I have the feeling that if they were firing M-16's over your head, you'd just tighten your earrings, put on your gloves, and march right on in.'

'Am I as bad as all that?'

'Not bad, baby - impressive. Goddamn impressive. And by the way, while we're out there I want to interview for a job at a therapeutic community I mentioned to you once.'

'You're serious about looking for a new job?' So much was changing.

'I don't know yet. But it's worth looking into.'

'Well, whatever your reasons, I'm glad we're going out

347

there together. And Luke will be so pleased to see you. What a super surprise for him!'

'When are we going?'

'When can you get away from the centre?'

'Pretty much any time I want.'

'How about tomorrow night? I got a letter from Luke this morning that said I'll be cleared in two days. So tomorrow night would be just right, for me anyway. How about you?'

'Sounds perfect.'

They settled back with their hot chocolate, and snuggled into the couch, telling old stories and talking about Luke. She laughed again as she hadn't in weeks, and at midnight she lured him into almost an hour of dice.

'You know what I can't handle anymore?'

'Yeah, dice. Lady, you play lousy.' But she loved it, and he was having a good time too.

'No, shut up. I'm being serious.'

'Excuse me.'

'Really, I am. The thing that I can't handle is the pressure of pretence, and that whole way of life I grew up with is pretence to me now. I can't talk openly about Luke without creating a scandal. I can't show anyone that I hurt. I can't even be me. I have to be The Honourable Kezia Saint Martin.'

'Maybe that's because you happen to be the Honourable Kezia Saint Martin. Ever think of that?' He rolled the dice in his hands.

'Yes, but I'm not "that" Kezia Saint Martin. Not anymore. I'm me. And I keep worrying, thinking I'm going to blurt it all out or call someone an asshole, or throw a quiche Lorraine in somebody's face.'

'Sounds like fun. Why not try it?' She roared with laughter as they sat in front of the fire, her legs tucked under her.

'Someday I might just try it. But that, my friend, would be the ultimate grand finale. Can't you see it in

*Time* magazine? "Kezia Saint Martin flipped out at a party on Friday and threw a lemon meringue pie that sprayed five guests. The victims of Miss Saint Martin's temporary insanity were the Countess von . . ." et cetera, et cetera, et cetera.'

'Do they serve lemon meringue pies at those parties?' He looked faintly curious.

'No. I guess I'd have to settle for baked Alaska.'

He chuckled at the thought, and reached out and stroked her now dry hair. It was warm from the fire.

'Kezia, love, you've got to gain back some weight.'

'Yeah. I know.' They shared a small tender smile, and then with a gleam in his eyes, he rolled the dice in his hands, blew on them and threw, closing both eyes.

'Snake eyes, or bust!'

Kezia chuckled at the results, pinched his nose, and whispered in his ear, 'In that case, Mr. Vidal, it's bust. Hey, you asshole, open your eyes.' But instead he reached out unexpectedly and swept an arm around her waist. 'What are you doing, you nut?' His face was barely a breath away from hers, and she thought it was funny. It wasn't funny to him.

'What am I doing? Making an ass of myself of course.' He opened both eyes and made a clown's face, checked out the dice and shrugged, but there was a hint of pain in his eyes. How dense could she be? But it was, perhaps, for the best.

He got to his feet and stretched slowly in front of the fire, watching the flames lick at the logs. He had his back to the still chuckling Kezia. 'You know what, little one? You're right. I can't stand the pressure of pretence anymore either.'

'It's a bitch, isn't it?' She was sympathetic as she munched on a cookie. It was the first time in weeks that she hadn't had a drink all evening.

'Yeah . . . it's a bitch. "The pressure of pretence," how well you put it.' She thought he was referring to his job.

'I'm an expert on the subject.' But she wasn't in the

349

mood to be serious. Not with him; they had had too happy an evening. 'What brought that into your mind?' The words were garbled in cookie crumbs. She looked up but his back was still turned to her.

'Nothing. Just a thought.'

## CHAPTER XXXI

They travelled in coach and the flight was dull. The movie was one Kezia had already seen with Luke, and Alejandro had brought some professional journals to read. They spoke during the meal, but the rest of the time he left her alone. He knew how tense she was, and this time he was not amused when she brought out the flask.

'Kezia, I don't think you should.'

'Why not?' She looked almost hurt.

'Drink what they serve you, that ought to be enough.' He wasn't preaching, but he sounded very firm. The tone of his voice embarrassed her more than his words, and she put it away. When the drinks came around, she ordered one scotch, and turned down the second.

'Satisfied?'

'It's not my life, sister. It's yours.' He went back to his reading, and she to her own thoughts. He was an odd man at times. Independent, lost in his own doings, and then at other times he took such pains with her. She more than suspected that he was making the trip mostly for her, to be sure she would be all right, and he could have lost his job for that.

They had made reservations at the Ritz, and she felt a thrill of excitement ripple through her as they drove towards the city. The skyline began to show as they cleared the last bend, and then suddenly there it was. The new modern cathedral on Gough, the brown licorice

350

silhouette of the Bank of America building, and the lick of fog rolling in from the bay. She realized now how she had longed to see it again. The bay, and the Golden Gate Bridge, with Sausalito and Belvedere and Tiburon twinkling like a forest of Christmas trees at night, if there wasn't too much fog. And if there was, she would close her eyes, breathe deeply of the fresh sea air, and listen to the lonely bleating of the fog horns. She knew that when she heard them again, Lucas would be listening to them too.

Alejandro watched her as they drove, and it touched him to see her like that. Excited, tense, combing the city with her eyes as though looking for something precious she had left there.

'You love this town too, don't you, Kezia?'

'Yes, I do.' She sat back and looked at it with pleasure, as though she had built it herself.

'Because Luke brought you here?'

'Partly. But it's something else too. Just the town, I guess. It's so damnably pretty.' He smiled and looked over at her.

'Damnably, huh?'

'Okay, okay, so make fun of me. All I know is that I'm happy here.' Despite the brutal things that had happened there, she loved it. It had something no other city she knew had. Her thoughts drifted back to Luke again, and she couldn't suppress a smile. 'You know, it's incredible, I've come three thousand miles to see him for an hour.'

'And something tells me you'd have come six thousand miles if you'd had to.'

'Maybe even twelve.'

'Even twelve? Are you sure?' He was teasing again, and she liked it. He was an easy companion.

'Alejandro, you're a pest. But a nice pest.'

'I love you too.'

It was one in the morning in San Francisco, and four in the morning for them, but neither of them was sleepy.

'Want to go out for a drink, Alejandro?'

'No, I'd rather go for a ride.'

'The temperance society at my beck and call. How delightful.' She set her mouth primly and he laughed. 'Mind your own business. After we drop off the stuff at the hotel, let's go down to the bay.' They had rented a car at the airport and Alejandro was driving.

'At your service, madam. Isn't that what you're used to?'

'Yes and no. But one thing's for sure. I'm not used to remarkable friends like you. You really are amazing.' Her voice had grown very soft. 'I don't think anyone's ever done as much for me as you have. Not even Edward. He used to watch over me, but we were never this at ease with each other. I love him, but very differently. He always expected so much of me.'

'Like what?'

'Oh ... to be everything I was born to, and more, I suppose.'

'And you are.'

'No, not really. The computer must have blended it all differently in me. Some of the pieces don't fit, by his standards.'

'You miss the point. It's your head that matters, your soul, your heart.'

'No, love. You miss the point. It's the parties you go to, the clothes you wear, which committees you belong to.'

'You're crazy.'

'Not anymore. But I used to be.' She was suddenly serious, but the moment fled as they arrived at the Ritz. Ernestine, wearing a green plaid flannel bathrobe, checked them in, looking faintly disapproving to see Kezia with Alejandro, and not Luke. But their separate rooms at opposite ends of the hall seemed to appease her. She padded back to bed, and they went back outside to the car.

'To the bay!' He was as excited as she.

'Thank you, Jeeves.'

'Certainly, madam.' They giggled together, and let the

352

car bump over the hills on Divisadero Street. It felt like a roller coaster as the sharp swoops and drops lifted them off the seat.

'Want to stop for a taco?'

She smiled in answer and nodded her head. 'Me, I get turned on by the bay. You, it's the tacos. Welcome home.'

'And not a pizza in sight.'

'Don't they have pizza out here?'

He made a face in response. 'Yes, but we keep them under control. Not like New York. One of these days, a mad onslaught of crazed pizzas will take over the town.' He made fierce monster faces and she laughed.

'You're a nut. Good heavens, look at that car!' They rolled into a drive-in food place on Lombard, and waiting at the window was a hot rod with the back all jacked up. 'You'd think they'd fall on their faces.'

'Of course not. What a beauty ... vrooommm ... rooom!' He made the appropriate sounds and grinned broadly. 'Haven't you ever seen one like that?'

'Not that I can remember – and I daresay I'd remember – except maybe in a movie. What a horror!'

'Horror? It's a beauty! Wash your mouth out with soap!'

She was laughing and shaking her head. 'Don't tell me you had one like that! I'd be shocked!'

'Well, I did. A lowrider special. My first car. After that I screwed up my image and got a secondhand VW. Life was never the same.'

'It sounds tragic.'

'It was. Did you have a car as a kid?' She shook her head, and his eyes opened wide in disbelief. 'You didn't? Christ, all kids in California have cars by the time they're sixteen. I bet you're lying. I'll bet you had a Rolls. Come on, tell the truth!' She giggled, furiously shaking her head, as they drove up to the window to order their tacos.

'I'll have you know, Mr. Vidal, that I did not have a Rolls! I borrowed a crumbling old Fiat when I stayed in Paris, and that was it. I've never owned a car in my life.'

'What a disgrace. But your family had one, right?' She nodded. 'Aha! And it was . . .' He waited.

'Oh, just a car. You know, four wheels, four doors, steering column, the usual stuff.'

'You're telling me it was a Rolls?'

'It was not.' She grinned at him broadly and handed him the tacos that had just appeared at the window. 'It was a Bentley. But my aunt has a Rolls, if that makes you feel any better.'

'Much. Now hand over those tacos. You may have come three thousand miles to see your old man. I came for the tacos. A Bentley . . . Jesus.' He took a bite of his taco and sighed rapturously. Kezia leaned back in her seat and began to unwind. It was comfortable being with him; she didn't have to pretend. She could just be herself.

'You know something funny, Alejandro?'

'Yeah. You.' He was into his third taco.

'No, I'm being serious.'

'Yeah? How come?'

'Oh, for chrissakes, put a taco in you and you get all full of yourself.'

'No, I get gas.'

'Alejandro!'

'Well, I do. Don't you ever get gas? Or is that bred out of you?'

She blushed as she laughed. 'I refuse to answer that question on the grounds that . . .'

'I'll bet you fart in bed.'

'Alejandro, you're awful. That's a highly unsuitable remark.'

'*Pobrecita.*' He was a ceaseless tease when he was in a good mood, but she liked it. He had been so quiet on the plane, but now the atmosphere was festive again.

'What I was trying to tell you, Mr. Vidal, before you got outrageous . . .'

'Outrageous? Fancy that!' He had switched from tacos to root beer and took a long swallow.

'What I'm trying to tell you . . .' she lowered her voice,

354

'is that the weird thing is, I have really come to need you. Isn't that strange? I mean, I'd be totally lost without you. It's so nice knowing you're around.'

He was silent, with a distant look in his eyes. 'Yeah. I feel that way too,' he said, finally. 'It feels funny when I don't see you for a couple of days. I like knowing you're okay.'

'It's nice to know that you care. I guess that's what I feel, and it feels good. And I worry that maybe someone's killed you on the subway when you don't call.'

'You know, that's one of the things I like best about you.'

'What?'

'Your unfailing optimism. Your faith in the human race ... killed on the subway. ... Asshole. Why would I get killed on the subway?'

'Everyone else does. Why shouldn't you?'

'Gee. Terrific. You know what I think, Kezia?'

'What?'

'That you fart in bed.'

'Oh, so we're back on that again, are we? Alejandro, you're a shit. And a rude, outrageous shit at that! Now drive me to the bay. And what's more I do *not* fart in bed!'

'You do!'

'I don't!'

'You do!'

'Ask Luke!'

'I will!'

'You dare!'

'Aha! Then he'd tell me the truth, wouldn't he! You do!'

'I do not! Damn you!'

The debate continued as he backed out of the drive-in, and finally dissolved in gales of their laughter. They chuckled and giggled and teased the remaining few blocks to the bay, and then they fell silent. It lay stretched before them like a bolt of darkest blue velvet, and there was a veil of fog high overhead, not low enough to obstruct the view from across the bay, but just enough so that it sat suspended on the spires of the bridge. A foghorn hooted sadly far off in the distance, and the lights around the rims of the shore sparkled.

'Lady, one of these days I'm going to move back here.'

'No, you won't. You're in love with your work at the centre in Harlem.'

'That's what you think. That bullshit is getting to be more than I want to have to deal with every day. People just don't get as crazy out here. You never know, maybe that interview I have lined up out here will pan out.'

'And then what?'

'We'll see.'

She nodded pensively, unnerved by the idea that he might leave New York. But it was probably just talk, to let off some steam. She decided to ignore what he had said. It was safer that way.

'When I see it like this, I want to stop time and stay in this moment forever.'

'Crazy girl. Don't we all wish we could do that. Did you ever come down here at dawn?' She shook her head. 'It's much better then. This city is like a beautiful woman. It changes, it has moods, it gets all grey and baggy-eyed, and then turns beautiful and you fall in love with her all over again.'

'Alejandro, who do you love?' She hadn't thought of that since the day they'd shared hot chocolate in Yorkville. He was almost always alone, or with her.

'That's a strange question.'

'No, it's not. Isn't there someone? Even an old flame from the past?'

'No, none of those. Oh, I don't know, Kezia. I love a lot of people. Some of the kids I work with, you, Luke, other friends, my family. A whole bunch of people.'

'And too many. It's so safe to love lots of people. It's a lot harder to love just one. I never did . . . until Luke. He taught me so much about that. He isn't afraid of that the

356

way I was ... and maybe you are. Isn't there even one woman you love, as a woman? Or maybe a few?' She had no right to ask, and she knew it, but she wanted to know.

'No. Not lately. Maybe one of these days.'

'You ought to give it some thought. Maybe you'll meet someone out here sometime.' But deep in her heart, she hoped he wouldn't. He deserved the best sort of woman there was, one who could give him back all that he gave. He deserved that, because he gave so much. But secretly, she knew that she hoped he wouldn't find her just yet. She wasn't ready to lose him. Things were so lovely just as they were. And if he had someone, she would lose him; it would be inevitable.

'What are you thinking about, little one? You look so sad.' He thought he knew why, but he didn't.

'Just silly stuff drifting through my head. Nothing much.'

'Don't worry so much. You'll see him tomorrow.'

She only smiled in response.


# CHAPTER XXXII


They saw it as they rounded a bend on the freeway. San Quentin. Across a body of water, a finger of the bay that had poked its way inland, it stood at the water's edge, looking ugly and raw. Kezia kept it in view the rest of the way, until finally it vanished again as they left the freeway and followed an old country road around a series of bends.

The mammoth fortress that was San Quentin took her breath away when they saw it again. It seemed to stand with its body jutting into her face, like a giant bully or an evil creature in a hideous dream. One felt instantly dwarfed beneath the turrets and towers, the endless walls that soared upwards, dotted only here and there by tiny windows. It was buillt like a dungeon, and was the colour of rancid mustard. It was not only fearsome, but it reeked of anger and terror, loneliness, sorrow, loss. Tall metal fences topped with barbed wire surrounded the encampment, and in all possible directions stood gun towers manned by machine-gun-toting guards. Guards patrolled the entrance, and people emerged wearing sad faces, some drying their eyes with bits of handkerchief or tissue. It was a place one could never forget. It even boasted a long dry moat, with still active drawbridges to the gun towers that kept the guards safe from potential 'attack.'

As she looked at the place, Kezia wondered how they could be so fearful. Who could possibly get free of that place? Yet now and then people did. And seeing the place made her suddenly know why they'd try anything, even death, to escape. It made her understand why Luke had done what he had to help the men he called his brothers. Prisoners of places like that had to be remembered by someone. She was only sorry it had been Luke.

She also saw a row of tidy houses with flowers beds out front. The houses stood inside the barbed wire fences, in the shadow of the gun towers, at the feet of the prison. And she guessed, accurately, that they were the houses of guards, living there with their wives and their children. The thought made her shudder. It would be like living in a graveyard.

The parking lot was rutted with potholes and strewn with litter. There were only two parking spaces left when they got there, and a long line of people snaked past the guardhouse at the main gate. It took them two and a half hours to reach the head of the line, where they were superficially searched and then herded on to the next gate, to have their pockets ransacked again.

The gun tower stood watchfully over them as they walked into the main building to sit with the rest of the visitors in a smoke-filled, overheated waiting room that looked like a train station. There were no sounds of laughter in that room, no whispered snatches of conversation, only the occasional clinking of coins in the coffee machine, the whoosh of the water fountain or the brief spurt of a match. Each visitor hugged to himself his own fears and lonely thoughts.

Kezia's mind was filled with Luke. She and Alejandro hadn't spoken since they entered the building. There was nothing to say. Like the others, they were preoccupied with the business of waiting. Another two hours on those benches . . . and it had been so long since she'd seen him, touched his hand, his face, kissed him, held him, or been held the way only Luke knew how to hold her. Kisses are different when they come from such a great height, or that's how it had seemed. Everything was different. He was a man she could look up to, in myriad ways. The first man she had looked up to.

In all, she and Alejandro waited almost five hours, and it felt like a dream when a voice on the intercom squawked out his name.

'Visit for Johns . . . Lucas Johns. . . .' She sprang to her feet and ran to the door of the room where they would visit. Luke was already there, filling the doorway, a quiet smile on his face. He stood in a long, barren grey room, whose only decor was a clock. There were long refectory tables with inmates on one side and visitors on the other, while guards wandered and patrolled, their guns displayed prominently. One could kiss hello and goodbye, and hold hands during the visit. That was all. The whole scene had an eerie unreality to it, as if this couldn't exist, not for them. Luke lived on Park Avenue with her, he ate with a fork and a knife, he told jokes, he kissed her on the back of the neck. He didn't belong here. It didn't make sense. The other faces around them looked ragged and fierce, angry and tired and worn. But now so did Luke. Something had changed. As she walked into his arms, she felt a wave of claustrophobic terror seize her throat . . . they were lost in the bowels of that tomb . . . but once in Luke's arms, she was safe. And the rest seemed to fade. She was oblivious of all but his eyes. She completely forgot Alejandro beside her.

Luke swept her up in his arms and the force of his embrace flushed the air from her chest in one breath. He held her aloft for a moment, not releasing his grip, and then gently set her down, hungrily seeking her lips once again. There was a quiet desperation about him, and his arms felt thinner. She had felt bones in his shoulders where weeks before there had been so much flesh. He was wearing blue jeans and a workshirt, and coarse shoes that looked too small for his feet. They had shipped the Guccis and everything else back to New York. Kezia had been there when the package arrived, everything crumpled, and his shirt badly torn. It gave you an idea of how it had come off his back. Not with a valet, but at the point of a gun. At the time she had cried, but now there were no tears. She was too glad to see him. Only Alejandro had tears in his eyes as he watched them, a radiant smile sweeping over her face, hiding the panic, and a look of intense need in the eyes of his friend. After a moment, Luke's gaze swept over her head, and acknowledged Alejandro. It was a look of gratitude Alejandro didn't remember seeing before. Like Kezia, he saw that something was different, and he remembered the urgent plea in Luke's letters to come out with Kezia. Alejandro knew something was coming, but he didn't know what.

Luke led Kezia by the hand to one of the long refectory tables, and went around to his side to sit down, while Alejandro took another chair next to her. She smiled even more as she watched Luke take his seat.

'Jesus, it's so good to just watch you walk. Oh, darling, how I've missed you.' Luke smiled quietly at her and gently touched her face with his work-roughened hand. The callouses had come back quickly.

'I love you, Lucas.' She said the words carefully, like three separate gifts she had wrapped for him, and his eyes shone strangely.

'I love you too, babe. Do me a favour?'

360

'What?'

'Take your hair down for me.' She smiled and quickly pulled out the pins. There was so little pleasure she could give him, each minute gesture suddenly meant so much more. 'There, that's better.' He stroked the silky softness of her hair, and looked like a man running his hands through diamonds or gold. 'Oh Mama, how I love you.'

'Are you all right?'

'Can't you tell?'

'I'm not sure.' But Alejandro could. He could tell a lot more than either of them, each was so blinded by what he wanted to see. 'I guess you look okay, but you've gotten thin.'

'Look who's talking. You look like shit.' But his eyes said she looked better than that. 'I thought you told me you were going to take care of her, Al.' He looked from one to the other, and at last there was a hint of long-forgotten laughter back in his eyes. He looked almost like Lucas again.

'Listen, man, do you know how hard this woman is to push around?'

'You're telling me!' The two men laughed and exchanged an old familiar smile. And Luke's eyes lit up as he looked at Kezia again. She held so tightly to his hands that her fingers ached until they were numb.

It was an odd visit, full of conflicting vibrations. Luke seemed to have a passionate and hungry need for Kezia, which was amply mutual. Yet, there was a rein on him somewhere. She sensed it, and didn't know what it was. A hesitation, a withdrawal, and then he would say something and she would feel the floodgates open again.

Suddenly the hour was over. The guard signalled, and Luke stood up quickly and led her back to the front of the room for their one regulation farewell kiss.

'Darling, I'll be back as soon as they'll let me.' She was thinking of staying out for the week, and coming back to see him again. But right now she was nervous at the sight of the guard, and Alejandro seemed to edge closer. It was all happening too fast. She wanted more time with Lucas . . . the moments had flown by.

'Mama . . .' Luke's eyes seemed to devour every inch of her face. 'You won't be coming back here.'

'Are they transferring you?'

He shook his head. 'No. But you can't come back anymore.'

'That's ridiculous. I . . . aren't the papers in order?' She was suddenly terrified. She had to come back again. She needed to see him. They had no right to do this.

'The papers are in order. For today. But I'm taking you off my visiting list tonight.' His voice was so low she could barely hear it. But Alejandro could, and he knew what Lucas was doing. Now he understood why Luke had wanted him to come out.

'Are you mad? Why are you taking me off your list?' Hot tears burned her eyes and she clung to his hands. She didn't understand. She hadn't done anything wrong. And she loved him.

'Because you don't belong here. And this is no life for you. Baby, you've learned a lot in the last few months, and done a lot of things you'd never have done if you hadn't met me. Some of it was good for you, but this isn't. I know what this does, what it'll do to you. By the time I get out, you'd be burnt out. Look at you now, thin, nervous . . . you're a wreck. Go back to what you have to do. And do it right.'

'Lucas, how can you do this?' The tears began to roll down her face.

'Because I have to . . . because I love you . . . now be a good girl, and go.'

'No, I won't. And I'll come back. . . . oh Lucas! Please!' Luke's eyes sought Alejandro's over her head and there was a barely perceptible nod. Luke bent quickly to kiss her, squeezed her shoulders, and then quickly turned and took a step towards the guard.

'Lucas! No!' She reached out her arms, ready to cling to him, and he turned back to her with a face carved in stone.

'Stop it, Kezia. Don't forget who you are.'

'I'm nothing without you.' She stepped towards him and looked into his eyes.

'That's where you're wrong. You're Kezia Saint Martin, and you know who she is now. Treat her well.' And then with a nod at the guard, he was gone. An iron door swallowed the man she had loved. He never turned back for a last look or another goodbye. He had said nothing to Alejandro as he left. He hadn't had to. The short nod at the end said it all. He was committing her into his care. He would know that she was safe and that was all he could do. It was all he had left to give.

Kezia stood in the visiting area, numb, unaware of the eyes that turned towards her. It had been an agonizing scene for the few who had overheard it. It made the men squirm, and their visitors blanch. It could have happened to them, but it didn't. It happened to her.

'I . . . Alej . . . I . . . could . . .' She was disoriented, stunned, lost.

'Come on, love, let's go home.'

'Yes, please.' She seemed to have shrunk in those last shattering minutes. Her face looked frighteningly pale. This time he knew there was no point in asking how she was. It was easily seen.

He walked her out of the building and to the main gate as rapidly as he could. He wanted to get her the hell out of there before she fell apart. He guided her quickly around the potholes in the parking lot and eased her into the car. He was feeling almost as shocked as she. He had known something was wrong, but he had had no idea what Luke had in mind. And he knew what a bitching tough thing it had been to do. Lucas needed her there, her visits, her love, her support. But he knew what it would do to her too. She would have hung on for years, destroying herself, maybe even drinking herself to death while she waited. It couldn't have gone on, and Luke knew it. Kezia had been right way at the beginning. Lucas Johns was a man with incredible guts. Alejandro

363

knew he wouldn't have had the courage to do it. Damn few men would, but damn few men faced what Luke was now facing – survival in a place where his life had been marked. And with who Kezia was, they could have gotten to her first. That had been the worst of Luke's fears, but now that was over. Everything was, for Luke.

'I . . . where are we going?' Kezia looked frighteningly vague as Alejandro started the car.

'Home. We're going home. And everything's going to be fine.' He spoke to her as one would to a very small child, or a very sick one. Right then, she was both.

'I'm going to come back here, you know . . . I'll come back. You know that, don't you? He doesn't really mean it . . . I . . . Alejandro?' There was no fire in her voice, only confusion. Alejandro knew she wouldn't be back. Luke was a man of his word. By that afternoon, her name would be inexorably cancelled from his list. It would leave him no choice. He couldn't have had her reinstated for six months, and by then much would have changed. Six months could change a lot in a life. Six months before, Kezia had met Luke.

She was no longer crying as they drove away. She merely sat very still in the car, and then in the hotel room, where he left her under the careful guard of a maid, while he attended to the interview he could no longer keep his mind on. It was a hell of a day to have to worry about that. He rushed through it, and got back to the Ritz. The maid said she hadn't moved, or even spoken. She had merely sat there, in the same chair she'd been in when he left her, staring at nothing.

With misgivings, he made plane reservations for six o'clock that night and prayed she wouldn't come out of shock until he got her home to her own bed. She was like a child in a trance, and one thing was for sure, he didn't want to be in San Francisco with her when she came out of it. He had to get her back to New York.

She ate nothing on the tray the stewardess put before her, and nodded uncomprehendingly when Alejandro offered her the earphones for music. He settled them on her head, and then watched her remove them dreamily five minutes later. She sang to herself for a little while, and then lapsed back into silence. The stewardesses eyed her strangely, and Alejandro would nod with a smile, hoping no one would make any comments, and praying that no one would recognize her. She looked sufficiently vague and dishevelled by then to be less easily recognized. He could barely handle her as it was, without worrying about the press. They might set her off, and unleash the flood of reality she was holding in abeyance by staying in shock. She looked drugged or drunk, or more than a little crazy. The flight was a nightmare he longed to see end.

Today had been the last straw, and he ached thinking of Lucas. He ached for them both.


'You're home, Kezia. Everything is all right.'

'I'm dirty. I need a bath.' She sat on a chair in her living room, seeming not to understand where she was.

'I'll run a bath for you.'

'Totie will do it.' She smiled at him vaguely.

He bathed her gently, as he had his nieces long ago. She sat staring at the ornate gold dolphin faucets on the white marble wall. It didn't even strike him that it was she he was bathing. He wanted to reach out to her, hold her, but she wasn't even there. She was gone, somewhere, in some distant world hidden from the broken one she had left.

He wrapped her in a towel, she dutifully put on her nightgown, and he led her to bed.

'Now you'll sleep, won't you?'

'Yes. Where's Luke?' The vacant eyes sought his, something in them threatening to break and pour all over the floor.

'He's out.' She wasn't ready to deal with the truth, and neither was he.

'Oh. That's nice.' She smiled vapidly at him, and climbed into bed, clumsily as children do, her feet struggling to find their way into the sheets. He helped her in, and turned off the lights.

'Kezia, do you want Totie?' He knew he'd find her number in Kezia's address book, if he had to. He had been wondering if he should hunt through it for the name of her doctor, but everything seemed under control, for the moment.

'No, thank you. I'll wait for Luke.'

'Okay. Call if you need me. I'll be right here.'

'Thank you, Edward.' It was a shock to realize that she didn't know who he was.

He settled down for a long night's vigil on the couch, waiting for the scream he was sure would come. But it never did. Instead she was up at six, and in the living room in her nightgown and bare feet. She didn't seem to question how she'd gotten home, or who had put her to bed. And he was stunned when he realized how lucid she was. Totally.

'Alejandro, I love you. But I want you to go home.'

'Why?' He didn't trust her alone.

'Because I'm all right now. I woke up at four this morning, and I've been thinking everything over for the last two hours. I understand what happened, and now I have to learn to live with it. And the time to do that is right now. You can't sit here and treat me like an invalid, love, that's not right. You have better things to do with your life.' Her look told him she meant it.

'Not if you need me.'

'I don't . . . not like that . . . look, please. Go away. I need to be by myself.'

'Are you telling me you're throwing me out?' He tried to make it sound light, but it didn't. They were both much too tired for games. She looked worse than he did, and he hadn't slept.

'No. I'm not throwing you out, and you know it. I'm just telling you to go back to what you have to do. And let me do this.'

366

'What are you going to do?' He was frightened.

'Nothing drastic. Don't worry about that.' She sank into one of the velvet chairs and took one of his cigarettes. 'I guess I'm not ballsy enough to commit suicide. I just want to be alone for a while.'

He got up tiredly from the couch, every bone and muscle and fibre and nerve ending aching.

'All right. But I'll call you.'

'No, Alejandro, don't.'

'I've got to. I'll be goddamned if I'm going to sit uptown and wonder if you're dead or alive. If you don't want to talk to me, then tell your answering service how you are and I'll call them.' He turned to face her, with his coat in his hand.

'Why does it matter so much? Because Luke told you to do that?' Her eyes poured into his.

'No. Because I want to. You may not have noticed it yet, but I happen to care what happens to you. You might even say that I love you.'

'I love you too . . . but I want you to leave me alone.'

'If I do, will you call me?'

'Yes, in a while. When I get it together a little. I guess in my heart I knew it was over the day he walked out of the law library at the hearing. That's when it should have been over. But neither of us had the guts to let go. I didn't anyway. And the bitch of it is that I still love him.'

'He loves you too or he wouldn't have done what he did yesterday. I think he did it because he loves you.'

She stood in silence and turned away from him then, so he couldn't see her face. 'Yeah, and all I have to do now is learn to live with it.'

'Well, if you need someone to talk to . . . yell. I'll come running.'

'You always do.' She turned, and a small smile appeared on her lips and then vanished.

He walked to the door with bent shoulders, carrying his valise from their trip, his jacket and coat slung over his back. He turned at the door and knew for only the briefest of seconds how Luke must have felt the day before when he sent her away.

'Take it easy.'

'Yeah. You too.'

He nodded and the door shut gently behind him.


She was drunk day and night for five weeks. Even the cleaning woman stopped coming, and she had sent her secretary away the first week. She was alone with her empty bottles, and plates caked with half-eaten food, wearing the same filthy robe. Only the delivery boy from the liquor store was a regular 'visitor' anymore. He would ring twice and deposit the bag outside her door.

Alejandro didn't call her till the news hit the papers. He had to call then. He had to know how she was. She was drunk when he called, and he told her he'd be right down. He took a cab, terrified she would see the papers before his arrival. But when he got to her door, he saw five weeks of newspapers unread and stacked in the foyer. He was stunned by the condition of what had once been her home. Now it looked like a barnyard . . . bottles . . . filth . . . plates . . . overflowing ashtrays . . . chaos and disorder. And Kezia. She didn't even look like the same girl. She was tear-stained, reeling, and drunk. But she still didn't know.

He sobered her up long enough to tell her. As best he could. But after her fourth cup of coffee, and opening the windows for air, the headlines did it for him, as her eyes scanned the type. She looked up into his face, and he knew that she understood. It couldn't get much worse for her now. It already had.

Luke was dead. Stabbed on the yard, so they said. 'A racial disturbance . . . well-known prison agitator, Lucas Johns. . . .' His sister had claimed the body, and the funeral was being held in Bakersfield the day Kezia was reading the news. It didn't matter. It didn't change anything. Funerals weren't Luke's style. Neither were sisters. He had never even mentioned her to Kezia. The only thing that mattered was that he was gone.

'Do you know when he died, Alejandro?' She still sounded drunk, but he knew she was coherent.

'Does it matter?'

'Yes.'

'No, I don't know exactly. I guess I could find out.'

'I already know. He died in court at the hearing. They killed him. But that day, the day he really died, he died beautiful and proud and strong. He walked into that hearing like a man. What they did to him after that is on their hands.'

'I suppose you're right.' Tears had begun to stream down his face. For what had happened to Luke. For what had happened to her. She was already as dead as Lucas, in her own way. Drunk, dirty, sick, tired, ravaged by memories, and now his death. He remembered that day in the law library, before Lucas walked into the hearing. She was right, he had walked tall and proud, and she had been so sure, so powerful beside him. They had had something he'd never seen before. And now, one was dead, and the other was dying. It made him feel sick. It was all like living a nightmare; his best friend was dead and he was in love with Luke's woman. And there was no way he could tell her now. Not now that Lucas was dead.

'Don't cry, Alejandro.' She smoothed a hand across his cheeks to wipe off the tears, and then ran a hand over his hair. 'Please don't cry.' But he was crying for himself as much as for them, and she couldn't know that. She tilted his face up to hers then, and held him so gently he hardly felt her hands on his shoulders. She looked into his eyes, and then slowly, quietly, she bent over and kissed him, carefully, on the mouth. 'The funny thing is that I love you too. It's really very confusing. In fact, I've loved you for a very long time. Isn't that strange?'

She was still more than a little bit drunk and he didn't know what to say. Maybe she had finally gone crazy from the constant shocks and the grief. Maybe she was mad now. Or perhaps he was. Maybe she hadn't even kissed him . . . maybe he was only dreaming.

'Alejandro, I love you.'

'Kezia?' Her name felt strange on his lips. She was Luke's. And Luke was dead now. But how could Luke be dead? And how could she love them both? It was all so totally crazy. 'Kezia?'

'You heard me. I love you. As in, I'm in love with you.'

He looked at her for what seemed like a very long time, the tears still wet on his cheeks.

'I love you too. I loved you the first day he brought you up to meet me. But I never thought . . . I just . . .'

'I never thought either. It's like all the stuff you read in bad novels. And it's very, very confusing.' She led him to the couch and sat down beside him, leaned her head back and closed her eyes.

'It's just as confusing for me.' He watched her as she sat there.

'Then why don't we leave each other alone for a while?'

'So you can drink yourself to death a little faster?'

His voice was suddenly loud and bitter in the quiet room. She had shown him everything he wanted, but she wanted to destroy it before she would give it to him. What a horrible joke.

'No. So I can think.'

'No drinking?'

'Mind your own business.'

'Then get fucked, lady. Just get fucked!' He was on his feet and shouting. 'I don't need to fall in love with you to watch you fucking die! To watch you commit suicide like some pathetic skid-row alcoholic. If that's what you plan to do with your life, then leave me alone! Oh God, Kezia . . . God damn you!' He pulled her to her feet and shook her until she felt the world shake under her, and she had to protest.

'Stop it! Leave me alone!'

'I love you! Don't you understand that?'

370

'No. I don't understand that. I don't understand anything anymore. I love you too. So fucking what? We get attached to each other and love each other and need each other and then the sky falls in all over again? Who needs it, goddamn you . . . who fucking needs it?'

'I do. I need you.'

'Okay, Alejandro, okay . . . and now will you do me a favour and just leave me alone? Please?' Her voice was trembling and there were tears in her eyes again.

'Okay, baby. It's up to you now.'

The door closed quietly behind him, and five minutes later there was the sound of shattering glass. She had taken the newspaper with the ugly article on the front page and thrown it at the window with such force that it had gone through the glass.

'Fuck you, world! Go to hell!'


## CHAPTER XXXIII


At the end of that week, Alejandro saw the same picture as Edward. Edward saw it with pain, Alejandro with shock. Edward had known. *Women's Wear* carried it too. Kezia Saint Martin boarding a plane for Geneva. 'For a rest from the rigours of the social season.' The papers already seemed to have forgotten her association with Lucas. How quickly people forget.

The papers said she was planning to go skiing, but it didn't say where, and her hat was pulled so low over her face that Alejandro would never have known her if he hadn't seen the name. As he looked at the picture, he marvelled again at the absence of reporters on their last trip to San Francisco and back. In the state she'd been in, that would really have made news.

He sat for a long time in the small office with the paint

peeling off the walls, looking at the picture, at the hat pulled low over the face. At the word, Geneva. And what now? When would he hear from her again? He still remembered the kiss of the last morning he'd seen her, only a few days ago. And now she was gone. He felt heavy, as though he were nailed to the chair, glued to the floor, part of the building and crumbling like the rest of it. Everything was going to pot in his life. His job stank, he hated the city, his best friend was dead, and he was in love with a girl he knew he could never have. Even if Luke had wanted it that way, as Alejandro suspected he might have. ... There was something about Luke's insistent summons to come out with Kezia that last time. Luke knew she'd need help. But it was never meant to be. He knew that, and Kezia must know it too. It was all very crazy, and he had to work out his own life. But he kept staring at the word, hating it. Geneva.

'Someone here to see you, Alejandro.' He looked up to see one of the kids poke his head in the door.

'Yeah? Who?'

'Perini's probation officer, I think.'

'Tell him to get fucked.'

'For real?' The boy looked thrilled.

'No, not for real, asshole. Give me five minutes, and send him in.'

'What'll I do with him for five minutes?'

'I don't know, dammit. Do whatever you want to do. Beat him up, roll him, kick him down the stairs. Give him coffee ... I don't give a shit what you do.' Alejandro threw the newspaper off his desk and into the garbage.

'Okay, man. Okay. Don't get all pissed off.' He had never seen Alejandro like that before. It was scary.

The hotel in Villars-sur-Ollon suited her purposes perfectly, high up in the mountains and in a town that was crawling with schools. There were virtually no tourists there, except a few visiting parents. She stayed in a huge hotel that was mostly uninhabited, and took tea

372

with seven old ladies to the sound of violins and a cello. She went for long walks, drank a lot of hot chocolate, went to bed early, and read. Only Simpson and Edward knew where she was, and she had told them both to leave her alone. She didn't plan to write until further notice, and even Edward had respected her wishes. He sent her weekly papers to keep her abreast of her financial news, and expected no response, which was just as well, because he got none. It was the middle of April before she was ready to leave.

She took the train to Milan, spent a night, and then went on to Florence. She mingled with the early spring tourists, toured the museums, wandered in and out of shops, walked along the Arno, and tried not to think. She did the same in Rome, and by then it was easier. It was May. The sun was warm, the people were lively, the street musicians were funny, and she ran into a few friends. She had dinner with them, and found that the urge to jump up and scream had finally left her. Little by little, she was healing.

In the early weeks of June, she rented a Fiat and drove north to Umbria, and to Spoleto where later in the summer the music festival would be held. And then she drove through the Alps, and eventually into France.

She danced in St. Tropez in July, and gambled in Monte Carlo, boarded the yacht of friends in St. Jean-Cap Ferrat for a weekend, and bought new Gucci luggage in Cannes. She began to write again when she drove up through Provence, and spent three weeks lost in a tiny hotel, where the terrine was superb, better than any pâté she had eaten.

Luke's book reached her there, hesitantly sent to her by Simpson, with the reviews. She opened the package unsuspectingly one morning, bathed in sunshine as she stood barefoot in her nightgown on the little balcony outside her room. She could see hills and fields beyond, and for almost an hour she simply sat cross-legged on the balcony floor with the book in her lap, holding it, running

373

her fingers over the cover, but unable to open it. The jacket design was good, and there was a marvellous photograph of him on the back. It had been taken before she had met him, but she had a copy of the same photo on her desk in New York. He was walking down a street in Chicago, wearing a white turtleneck sweater, his dark hair blown by the wind, his raincoat slung over his shoulder. One eyebrow raised, he was looking sarcastically into the camera with the beginnings of a smile. She had squeezed the photograph out of him the first time she had seen it.

'What the hell do you want that for?'

'You look so sexy in it, Luke.'

'Jesus. You nut. I hope my readers don't think so.'

'Why not?' She looked up, a little surprised, and he had kissed her.

'Because I'm supposed to look brilliant, not sexy, silly lady.'

'Well, you happen to look both. Can I have it?' He had waved an embarrassed hand at her, and gone off to answer the phone. But she had taken the photograph, and framed it in silver. It was a glimpse of the real Luke, and she was glad it was on the book jacket. People should see him as he was . . . people should . . .

She had looked up after what seemed like hours, the book still cradled in her lap, unfelt tears rolling steadily down her face, misting the view. But she had been looking into the past, not at the fields in the distance.

'Well, babe, here we are.' She spoke aloud and smiled through her tears, using the hem of her nightgown to wipe her face. She could almost see Lucas smiling at her. It didn't matter where she went anymore, she carried him with her in a warm, tender way. Not in the agonizing way that she had; now she could smile at him. Now he was with her, forever. In New York, in Switzerland, in France. He was a part of her now. A comfortable part.

She looked far into the fields with a soft shrug and leaned back against the legs of a chair, still holding the book in her hands. A voice seemed to tell her to open it, but she couldn't, and then as she watched the face in the photograph yet again, almost expecting him to move along that long-forgotten street in Chicago, it was as though she could see his face growing stern, his head shaking in teasing annoyance.

'Come on, Mama, open it, dammit!'

She did, gingerly, carefully, not wanting to breathe or to look or to see. She had known, known it when she touched the book, but seeing it would be different. She wondered if she could bear it, but she had to. Now she wanted to see, and she knew he had wanted her to. He had never told her, but now it was as though she had always known. The book was dedicated to her.

Fresh tears ran down her face as she read it, but they were not tears of grief. Tears of tenderness, of gratitude, of laughter, of loving. Those were the treasures he had given her, not sorrow. Luke had never been a man to tolerate sorrow. He had been too alive to taste even a whisper of death. And sorrow is death.

To Kezia, who stands by my side wherever I go. My equal, my solace, my friend. Brave lady, you are the bright light in a place I have long sought to find, and now at last we're both home. May you be proud of this book, for now it is the best I can give you, with thanks and my love.

L.J.

'. . . and now at last we're both home.' It was true, and it was late August by then, and she had one final test. Marbella. And Hilary.

'My God, darling, you look divine! So brown and healthy! Where on earth have you been?'

'Here and there.' She laughed and brushed her hair from her eyes. It was longer now, and the harsh angularity of her face had melted again. There were small lines on either side of her eyes, from the sun, or whatever, but she looked well. Very well.

'How long can you stay? Your cable didn't even give me a hint, naughty child!'

Yes, she was back in that old familiar world. Dear, darling Hilary. But it amused her to be called a naughty child. Hell, why not? Her birthday had come and gone in late June. She was thirty now.

'I'll be here for a few days, Aunt Hil, if you have room.'

'That's all? But darling, how awful, and of course I have room, how absurd.' She was currently having room for at least fourteen others, not to mention the staff. 'Why don't you think about staying longer?'

'I've got to get back.' She accepted an iced tea from the butler. They stood near the tennis courts where the other guests played.

'Get back to where? My Jonathan has improved his serve, hasn't he?'

'Undoubtedly.'

'Of course, how silly of me. You don't know him. Perfectly beautiful man.'

He looked like a carbon copy of Whitney. It made Kezia smile.

'So where is it you're going back to?' Hilary returned her attention to Kezia, over a well-chilled martini.

'New York.'

'At this time of year? Darling, you're mad!'

'Maybe so, but I've been away for almost five months.'

'Then another month can't possibly hurt.'

'I'm going back to do some work.'

'Work? What sort of work? Charity? But no one's in town in the summer for heaven's sake. Besides, you don't work, do you?' For a moment Hilary looked slightly confused. Kezia nodded.

'Yes, I do. Writing.'

'Writing? What on earth for?' She was quite bemused, and Kezia was trying hard not to laugh. Poor Aunt Hil.

376

'I guess I write because I enjoy it. Very much, as a matter of fact.'

'Is this something new?'

'No, not really.'

'Can you write? Decently, I mean.' But this time Kezia couldn't help it; she laughed.

'I don't know. I certainly try to. I used to write the Martin Hallam column. But that wasn't my best work.' Kezia wore a mischievous grin. Hilary gaped.

'You what? Don't be insane! You . . . Good God, Kezia, how could you!'

'It amused me. And when I had enough of it, I retired. And don't look so upset, I never said anything mean about you.'

'No, but you . . . I . . . Kezia, you really amaze me.' She relieved the butler of another martini and stared at her niece. The girl was really quite strange. Always had been, and now this. 'In any case, I think you're a fool to go back in August.' Hilary had not yet recovered. 'And that column doesn't run anymore.' Kezia giggled; it was as though Hilary were trying to trap her into admitting that she hadn't actually written it. But that was wishful thinking.

'I know, but I'm going back to discuss the terms on a book.'

'A book based on gossip?' Hilary blanched.

'Of course not. It's sort of a political theme. It's really too long to go into.'

'I see. Well, I'd be thrilled if you wanted to stay . . . as long as you promise not to write naughty things about all my guests.' She tittered sweetly, as it occurred to her that this might make for some very amusing gossip of her own. 'Did you know my niece used to be Martin Hallam, dear?'

'Don't worry, Aunt Hil, I don't write that kind of thing anymore.'

'What a pity.' Her third martini had softened the blow. Kezia watched her as she accepted her second iced tea. 'Have you seen Edward yet?'

'No. Is he here?'

'You didn't know?'

'No, I didn't.'

'You have been off the beaten track, haven't you? Where did you say you'd been all this time?' Hilary was watching Jonathan's serve again.

'Ethiopia, Tanzania. The jungle. Heaven. Hell. The usual spots.'

'How nice, darling ... how really very nice. See anyone we know?' But she was too engrossed in Jonathan's game to listen or care. 'Come darling, I'll introduce you to Jonathan.' But Edward appeared on the scene before Hilary could sweep her away. He greeted Kezia with warmth, but also with caution.

'I never thought I'd see you here!' It was an odd greeting after so much and so long.

'I never thought you would either.' She laughed and gave him a hug that reminded him of old times.

'How are you, really?'

'How do I look?'

'Just the way I'd want to see you. Tanned, healthy, and relaxed.' And also sober. That was a relief.

'And that's how I am. It's been a long bunch of months.'

'Yes, I know.' He knew that he would never know the full story, but he was certain it had come close to destroying her. Much too close. 'You're staying for a while?'

'Just a few days. Then I have to go back. Simpson is in the midst of making a deal for me, for a book.'

'How perfectly marvellous!'

'That's how I feel.' She smiled happily, and hooked her arm in his, as he prepared to lead her away for a walk.

'Come. Tell me about it. Let's go sit down under the trees over there.' He removed two more iced teas from a silver tray and headed for a gazebo far from the courts. They had a lot to catch up on, and for the first time in years she seemed willing to talk. He had missed her very badly, but the time had done him good as well. He had realized at last what she represented in his life, and what she could never be. He too had made peace with himself and the people he dreamed of, as much as he ever would. Most of all he had accepted what seemed to be his role. Acceptance. Understanding. As life's trains passed him by. The last lonely gentleman standing on the platform.

Kezia was almost sorry to leave Marbella, for the first time in her life. She had come to terms with a thousand ghosts in the months she'd spent alone, not only Luke's ghost, but others. She was even free of the ghost of her mother. At last. And now she had to go home.

It was funny, on the plane home from Spain she remembered something Alejandro had said a long time ago. 'That whole life is a part of you, Kezia. You can't deny it.' Though she didn't want to live it anymore, she no longer needed to exorcise it either. She was free.

It was a pleasant flight, and New York was hot and muggy and beautiful and throbbing when she arrived. Hilary was wrong. It was exciting even in August. Maybe no one who mattered was there, but everyone else was. The city was alive.

There were no photographers to greet her, nothing, no one, only New York. And that was enough. She had so much to do. It was late Friday night. She had to go home and unpack, wash her hair, and first thing the next morning, she would take the subway to Harlem. First thing. She had flown home from Spain for her book, but to see Alejandro too. It was time now. For her anyway. She had planned it for a long time. And she was ready. For him. For herself. He was part of her past, but not the part she had put away. He was the part she had saved for the present.

And the present looked and felt splendid. She was unfettered now, unbound and happy and free. She tingled with the excitement of all that lay ahead ... people, places, things to do, books to write, her old conquered

379

world at her feet, and now new worlds to conquer. Above all, she had conquered herself. She had it all now. What was there to fear? Nothing, and that was the beauty of what she had found. No one owned her anymore, not a life-style, not a man, no one. Kezia owned Kezia, for good.

The days with Luke had been treasured and rare, but a new dawn had come ... a silver and blue morning filled with light. And there was room for Alejandro in her new day, if he was around, and if not, she would ride laughing and proud into noon.

*Every dream demands a sacrifice*

For Crystal Wyatt, growing up on a ranch in Northern
California, Hollywood seems a million miles away. Bold,
passionate and enchantingly beautiful, she knows her destiny
is waiting for you.

But no one said it was going to be easy. Singled out for her
devastating looks and captivating singing voice, Crystal soon
embarks on the dangerous road to stardom. Her dreams are
creeping closer, but then so are those determined to stop her.
And when the darkest of scandals comes out, Crystal must
face the challenge of her life.

In this wonderful novel, Danielle Steel tells the story of
an extraordinary young woman and her determination to
achieve her ambition – whatever the odds.

*Every choice has its price*

Hollywood, 1945. Shipping heir Ward Thayer and screen star Faye Price are reunited after a chance meeting two years earlier. Unable to forget the connection they shared and helpless to resist it, romance quickly sparks.

But for Faye, daring and passionate, the life she's heading for with Ward is a threat to her ambition. How can she decide between Hollywood and motherhood? Is it right to choose fame over family? Faye is on the brink of an impossible choice that will shape her life – and the lives of those she loves – in ways she could scarcely have imagined.

In a novel that is filled with unforgettable scenes and a wonderful cast of characters, Family Album explores one woman's dilemma with sensitivity, compassion and warmth.